Praise for all four of Lauren St John's  adventures of Martine and Jemmy, the white giraffe –

The White Giraffe

'a heartwarming story that has the feel of a classic'
The Bookseller

'St John brings Africa to vivid life in this . . . stirring story.'
Guardian

Dolphin Song

'stirring stuff'   *Daily Telegraph*

'another stunning novel'   *Angels and Urchins*

The Last Leopard

'another magical African thriller'   *Times*

'A thrilling and enchanting story'   *Lovereading*

The Elephant's Tale

'. . . there is a warmth and love for animals that raises this above the herd. It is an enjoyable, action-packed tale.'
Telegraph

Lauren St John

The Last Leopard
and
The Elephant's Tale

Two African Adventures

Illustrated by David Dean

Orion
Children's Books

This omnibus edition first published in Great Britain in 2012
by Orion Children's Books
Originally published as two separate volumes:
The Last Leopard
First published in Great Britain in 2008
by Orion Children's Books
The Elephant's Tale
First published in Great Britain in 2009
by Orion Children's Books
a division of the Orion Publishing Group Ltd
Orion House
5 Upper St Martin's Lane
London WC2H 9EA
An Hachette UK Company

1 3 5 7 9 10 8 6 4 2

A catalogue record for this book is available from the British Library

Printed in Great Britain by Clays Ltd, St Ives plc

ISBN 978 1 4440 0559 2

www.orionbooks.co.uk

· Contents ·

the last leopard

LAUREN St JOHN

For my godson, Matis Matarise Sandile Sithole,
in the hope that he grows up to love Zimbabwe
and its wildlife as much as I do . . .

And in memory of Felix and Michina,
my London leopards
1990 – 2007

Dawn was casting spun-gold threads across a rosy sky over Sawubona Game Reserve as Martine Allen took a last look around to ensure there weren't any witnesses, leaned forward like a jockey on the track, wound her fingers through a tangle of silver mane, and cried, 'Go, Jemmy, go!'

The white giraffe sprang forward so suddenly that she was almost unseated, but she recovered and, wrapping her arms around his neck, quickly adjusted to the familiar rhythm of Jemmy's rocking-horse stride. They swept past the dam and a herd of bubble-blowing hippos, past a flock of startled egrets lifting from the trees like white glitter, and out onto the open savannah plain. An early morning African chorus of doves, crickets and go-away birds provided a soundtrack.

For a long time Martine had only ever ridden Jemmy at night and in secret, but when her grandmother had found out about their nocturnal adventures she'd promptly banned them, on the grounds that the game reserve's deadliest animals were all in search of dinner after dark and there was nothing they'd like more than to feast on a giraffe-riding eleven-year-old. For a while Martine had defied her, but after several close calls and one terrible row with her grandmother, she had come to accept that Gwyn Thomas was right. When lions were on the hunt, the game reserve was best avoided.

Another of Gwyn Thomas's rules was that Martine ride sedately at all times. 'No faster than a trot and, in fact, I'd rather you stuck to a walk,' she'd counselled sternly.

Martine had paid almost no attention. The way she saw it, Jemmy was a wild animal and it was only fair that he should have the freedom to do what came naturally, and if that meant tearing across the savannah at a giraffe's top speed of thirty-five kmph, well, there wasn't a lot she could do about it. It wasn't as if she had reins to stop him. Besides, what was the point of riding a giraffe if the most he was permitted to do was plod along like some arthritic pony from the local stables?

Jemmy clearly agreed. They flew across the grassy plain with the spring breeze singing in Martine's ears. 'Faster, Jemmy!' she yelled. 'Run for your life.' And she laughed out loud at the heart-pounding thrill of it, of racing a wild giraffe.

A streak of grey cut across her vision, accompanied by a furious, nasal squeal: '*Mmwheeeh!*'

Jemmy swerved. In the instant before her body parted company with the white giraffe's, Martine caught a glimpse of a warthog charging from its burrow, yellow tusks thrust forward. Had her arms not been wrapped so tightly around the giraffe's neck, she would have crashed ten feet to the ground. As it was, she just sort of swung under his chest like a human necklace. There she dangled while Jemmy pranced skittishly and the warthog, intent on defending her young, let out enraged squeals from below. Five baby warthogs milled around in bewilderment, spindly tails pointing heavenwards.

The pain in Martine's arms was nearly unbearable, but she dared not let go. She adored warthogs – warts, rough skin, pig ears and all – but their Hollywood movie star eyelashes didn't fool her. In a blink of those lashes, their tusks could reduce her limbs to bloody ribbons.

'Jemmy,' she said through gritted teeth, 'walk on. Good boy.'

Confused, the white giraffe started to lower his neck as he backed away from the warthog.

'No, Jemmy!' shrieked Martine as the warthog nipped at the toe of one of her boots. 'Walk! Walk on!'

Jemmy snatched his head up to evade the warthog's sharp tusks, and Martine was able to use the momentum to hook her legs around his neck. From there, she was able to haul herself onto his back and urge him into a sprint. Soon the warthog family was a grey blur in the distance, although the mother's grunts of triumph took longer to fade.

Martine rode the rest of the way home at a gentle walk, a rueful smile on her lips. That would teach her to show off – even if it was only to an audience of hippos. At the game reserve gate, Jemmy dipped his head and Martine slid down his silvery neck as though she was shooting down a waterslide. That, too, wasn't the safest way of dismounting, but it was fun. She gave the white giraffe a parting hug, and strolled through the mango trees to the thatched house.

In the kitchen, brown sugar-dusted tomatoes were turning to caramel in the frying pan. Martine's nose wrinkled appreciatively. She was starving. Six days a week her grandmother served up boiled eggs and toast, with the occasional bowl of cornflakes as light relief, but on Sundays and special days like this she made up for it by cooking delicious brunches or roasts or allowing Martine to go for a campfire breakfast on the escarpment with Tendai, the Zulu game warden.

Martine took off her boots on the back *stoep* and stepped inside barefoot. ''Morning, grandmother,' she said.

'Hello, Martine,' Gwyn Thomas said, closing the oven and standing upright. She wore a red-striped apron over a denim shirt. 'Wash your hands and come take a seat. Did you have a nice ride? Did Jemmy behave himself today?'

'Jemmy was an angel,' Martine responded loyally,

thinking: When does he ever *not* behave himself? It wasn't his fault if the warthog had woken up on the wrong side of her burrow.

There was a polite knock at the door.

'Ah, Ben,' said Gwyn Thomas with a smile, 'good timing. Breakfast is almost ready. Come and join us.'

'Thank you, ma'am,' said a clear young voice.

Martine turned to see a half-Zulu, half-Indian boy entering the kitchen a little shyly. He wore an army-green vest, heavy brown boots and ragged jeans – the only pair he owned since turning his others into shorts during an island adventure a little over a month earlier. He had glossy black hair and skin the colour of burnt honey and, though very slim – some might even say thin – he was sinewy and strong.

He rinsed his hands at the sink and sat down at the table. 'Have a bit of trouble with a warthog this morning, Martine?' he teased. 'You and Jemmy left skid marks all over the bush. The ground was so torn up it looked like the starting grid of the East Africa Safari car rally.'

'What happened?' demanded Gwyn Thomas. 'Were you going too fast, Martine? You know very well that you're expressly forbidden to gallop Jemmy. I won't have you breaking your neck on my watch. Ben, did the tracks show that she was going very fast?'

Martine glanced quickly at Ben. She knew that he knew she'd be in big trouble if she was caught racing the white giraffe, but she was also aware that he never lied about anything. Nor would she expect him to. She braced herself for a scolding and a temporary ban on riding Jemmy. Just her luck. And on the first day of the school holidays, too.

'I think . . . ' Ben shifted uncomfortably in his chair.

Her grandmother put her hands on her hips. 'You think what? Out with it, Ben.'

' . . . I think the toast is burning,' Ben said brightly.

Gwyn Thomas jumped up and seized the smoking grill pan, blowing on it to put out the flames licking at the four bits of charcoal that had once been bread. Just then the oven timer started beeping to indicate that the mushrooms were done and Martine noticed the tomatoes were starting to smoke. By the time they'd managed to rescue their charred breakfast, make more toast and hastily scramble a few eggs to go with it, her grandmother appeared to have forgotten about Martine's dangerous riding.

Ben distracted her further by relaying a warthog story Tendai had told him that morning, about an apprentice hunter he'd met during his game ranger studies. One afternoon the young hunter decided to entertain the other apprentices and demonstrate his bravery by tormenting a warthog in a game enclosure just for the fun of seeing her riled. He planned to hop over the fence if she came after him.

'Only problem was, the fence was electric!' reported Ben with a grin. 'The hunter was hanging on for twenty minutes, sort of sizzling, before she got bored and went away.'

Martine, whose arms still ached from her own encounter with an exasperated warthog, laughed, but not quite as hard as her grandmother.

'What do the two of you have planned for the holidays?' asked Gwyn Thomas, pouring them each a glass of paw paw juice. 'Apart, Martine, from riding the white giraffe very, very slowly.' She gave her granddaughter a meaningful glance, indicating that she hadn't forgotten what Ben had said but was prepared to let it go just this once.

Martine smiled gratefully. 'Don't worry,' she said, 'I'll be riding so slowly that even tortoises will overtake us.'

When she wasn't doing that she was hoping to brush up on her bushcraft skills and paint watercolours of the animals in Sawubona's sanctuary, a hospital and holding area for injured wildlife and new arrivals to the game reserve.

Ben, meanwhile, had his parents' permission to spend almost the whole holidays at Sawubona, studying under Tendai as an apprentice tracker.

When Martine first met Ben, he'd been almost completely silent, never speaking a word to anyone but her and his parents. Most kids at school had believed he was dumb. Some still did. But at Sawubona he seemed to really enjoy chatting to Tendai, Gwyn Thomas or anyone else who happened to be around.

As she listened to him describe his morning in the reserve, Martine absent-mindedly speared the last few potatoes on her plate and took in the scene in the kitchen. Eight months ago, her mum and dad had been killed in a fire in England on New Year's Eve and she'd been shipped like a parcel off to Africa to live with a strict grandmother she hadn't even known existed. For the first month or two Martine had been convinced she would never be happy again. Yet here she was sitting contentedly at the breakfast table with that same grandmother who, after a rocky start, had become one of her very favourite people, and with Ben, her best friend in the world apart from Jemmy.

Through the open doorway Martine could see zebras splashing around the distant waterhole. She would never stop missing her parents, but it definitely helped that her new home was one of the most lovely game reserves in South Africa's Western Cape and that she could ride through it on her own white giraffe and get close enough to zebras and elephants to touch them. She preferred the weather in Africa too. It was early but already the sun was spilling orange across the kitchen tiles and Shelby, the ginger cat, was stretched out in its warmth.

The telephone trilled loudly, making them jump. Gwyn Thomas checked her watch and frowned. 'It's barely seven o'clock. I wonder who's calling us so early on a Saturday morning.'

She went into the living room to answer it. Evidently the line was a bad one because she had to speak very loudly.

'Sadie!' she cried, her voice carrying clearly. 'What a lovely surprise. How nice to hear from you. How are things at Black Eagle Lodge . . . ? Oh, no. Oh, surely not. I'm very sorry to hear that. Well, if there's anything I can do, don't hesitate to let me know. *Excuse me?* Oh. OHHH . . . !'

Ben and Martine looked at each other, and Ben raised an eyebrow. 'Sounds like trouble,' he murmured.

'Uh, uh, yes, I understand,' Gwyn Thomas was saying. 'No, no, it's not an imposition. Please don't think that for a minute. In fact, the timing couldn't be better. We're on our way. Try not to worry. We'll see you very soon. Take care of yourself in the meanwhile.'

There was the sound of the receiver being replaced, followed by a long silence. When she returned to the kitchen, Gwyn Thomas's face was sober. 'Martine, Ben,' she said, 'I'm afraid you're both going to have to put your plans on hold. Martine, we leave first thing in the morning. We'll be gone for a month. We're going to Zimbabwe.'

Martine stared at her grandmother uncomprehend-ingly. 'Zimbabwe? What? Why? No, I can't leave Jemmy. I just can't. It's the beginning of the holidays.'

'I realize it's a bit of a bolt from the blue and I'm incredibly sorry,' said Gwyn Thomas, putting her hand on Martine's shoulder. 'It hurts me to disappoint you both. I know how you've looked forward to this time. I wouldn't entertain the idea of tearing you away from Jemmy or Sawubona if I could see any way of avoiding it. It's just that Sadie, one of my oldest and dearest friends, has had an accident and she desperately needs our help.'

'Do you mind if I ask what happened?' asked Ben. He

was just as crushed as Martine but was doing a better job of hiding it.

'Not at all,' replied Gwyn Thomas, sitting down and pouring herself another cup of coffee. 'Sadie runs a hotel called Black Eagle Lodge in the Matobo Hills in Matopos, one of the most remote regions of Zimbabwe. Matopos is famous for its extraordinary rock formations – great boulders that balance on top of one another – and also for its history. Many people believe that the lost treasure of Lobengula, the last king of the Ndebele people, is buried there.

'Unfortunately, a week ago Sadie slipped and broke her leg very badly. She has a plaster cast from her ankle to her thigh and is hobbling around on crutches. Zimbabwe is going through a hard time and life is very difficult for people there, what with crop failures and political problems. Last month Sadie had to lay off most of her staff. This accident means she's struggling to cope. Black Eagle used to be a popular riding centre, but now Sadie has only one man to exercise the horses and nobody to do the cooking or cleaning if any guests do show up. I thought that since Martine is a good giraffe rider and I'm a reasonable cook, it might be nice if we eased her workload for a month.' She gave Martine an appealing glance.

Martine pretended not to see it. She sat silently in her chair, arms folded, tears burning the back of her eyes. It seemed as if everyone and everything was continually conspiring to take her away from Jemmy. If she wasn't getting stranded on desert islands or being banned from riding him, then poachers were trying to steal him. And now this. She couldn't recall hearing her grandmother even mention Sadie before, but all of a sudden she was claiming that Sadie was one of her oldest and dearest friends. Why couldn't Sadie find someone nearby to help her out? Zimbabwe was hardly down the road. It was over a thousand miles away.

There was no doubt that the Matobo Hills sounded intriguing, what with exotic rock formations and the Ndebele king's missing treasure, and she'd always longed to ride a horse, but given a choice she'd rather stay at Sawubona with Jemmy.

Ben, who knew how much it meant to Martine to be with her precious white giraffe, said, 'Is there anything I could do? I mean, maybe I could take Martine's place and come to Zimbabwe and do some work around the retreat. I've never ridden a horse before and I'd have to ask my mum and dad, but I'm sure I could learn, or at least feed the horses and muck out their stables or something. Then Martine could stay here and be with Jemmy. Umm, that is, if you'd like me to . . . ' His voice trailed away.

'Ben, that's extremely generous of you, but Martine can't possibly stay here on her own,' Gwyn Thomas told him. 'Tendai's much too busy to take care of her. And I'm not sure that your mum and dad would want you coming with us to Zimbabwe for four weeks – not to such a remote area. But if they do agree, we'd love you to have you with us, wouldn't we, Martine?'

Martine was torn. She didn't want to leave Jemmy, but

nor did she want Ben going off on an adventure without her.

'Martine,' said her grandmother warningly. 'Remember your manners. We'd love Ben to come to Zimbabwe with us, wouldn't we?'

'Ben knows that without me having to say it,' muttered Martine.

Normally Gwyn Thomas would have told her off for being so rude, but under the circumstances she just sighed. 'Martine, the last thing I want to do is make you unhappy or take you away from Jemmy. But I'm really worried about Sadie. I had the feeling that—' She hesitated. 'Maybe it's my imagination.'

'What?' Ben pressed.

'It's probably nothing, but I had the feeling that there was something Sadie wasn't telling me. She's the proudest, most independent woman I know, yet she practically begged me to help her. That's not like her at all. It made me wonder if something else is going on behind the scenes.' She took Martine's hand. 'I just feel she needs us. Do you understand?'

What could Martine say? Her grandmother had done so much for her.

'I'm sorry,' she said, giving Gwyn Thomas a hug. 'It's a bit of a shock, that's all. Of course I understand. I'll miss Jemmy terribly but it'll be great to see another country, especially if we can help Sadie and ride a few horses at the same time.'

'Wonderful,' said her grandmother with evident relief. 'In that case we should start packing immediately. We'll

13

make a holiday of it. It's a long drive so we'll break it up with a night or two at Rainbow Ridge and other attractions along the way. Come with me, Ben. Let's call your mum and dad.'

She gave Martine's hand a squeeze. 'It'll be fun, I promise.'

Martine kept a smile on her face until her grandmother and Ben had left the kitchen. Then she walked out of the house and along the sandy track leading to the animal sanctuary, sat down beside the run housing two orphaned caracal kittens, and burst into tears.

She really did understand why her grandmother wanted to go to Zimbabwe to help a friend in need; she was quite sure that if she had a friend who was hurt or in difficulty, she'd react the same way. She just didn't see why she should have to go to the Matobo Hills as well. It wouldn't be so bad if Ben was allowed to join them, but if she had to be without both of her best friends for four whole weeks it would feel like a life sentence. Surely there was someone she could stay with right here in Storm Crossing. Someone like . . .

Martine stopped feeling miserable immediately. Why hadn't she thought of it sooner? She could stay with Grace, Tendai's aunt. Grace was a *sangoma,* a medicine woman and traditional healer with Zulu and Caribbean origins. Since she'd arrived in Africa, Martine had had a special relationship with her because it was Grace who'd first told her that she had a secret gift which would shape her destiny. 'The gift can be a blessin' or a curse. Make your decisions wisely,' was her advice to Martine only hours after she'd got off the plane from England.

The gift was a mystery even to Martine. She knew it had something to do with healing, and with a Zulu legend which said that the child who could ride a white giraffe would have power over all the animals. However, Martine, who'd recently been stung by a bee, and whose arms were still sore from the incident with the warthog, was quite sceptical about that particular detail.

Twice her future had been eerily mapped out on the wall of a cave. The paintings were hidden deep inside the Secret Valley, the white giraffe's sanctuary. On each occasion they'd made sense only after something had happened to her.

'That's not fair,' Martine had complained to Grace. 'If the San Bushman knew so much about my destiny, they should have made their paintings a lot easier to read. That way, I could avoid any bad stuff happening to me. For instance, if I'd known what was going to happen on the ship in June, I would have refused to set foot on it.'

'Exactly,' Grace retorted. 'If you could see your future, you'd only choose the good stuff, the easy stuff. Then you would never learn and never experience the important things in this world because oftentimes they's tha hard things. If you'd never gone on that boat, where'd those dolphins be now?'

'Ohhh,' said Martine. 'Oh, I see what you mean.'

Martine loved being around Grace, who was wise, funny, and full of fascinating knowledge about African medicine. She liked Grace's eccentric house, which had chickens wandering in and out, and she especially liked her banana pancakes. The only thing about staying with Grace was that Gwyn Thomas would probably return from her travels to find her granddaughter three times heavier than when she left. Then again, she might see that as a positive because she and Grace were always trying to fatten Martine up.

The more Martine considered it, the more of a good idea staying with Grace seemed. Grace was Gwyn Thomas's closest friend in Storm Crossing and she saw no reason for her grandmother to disagree. All that remained was to convince Grace herself.

The plan had hardly finished forming in Martine's mind when a voice with a pronounced Caribbean twang declared, 'I was jus' drinkin' tea with my nephew when I hear this terrible weepin' and wailin'. I says to myself, there ain't no reason for a chile, livin' on Sawubona under God's sweet sun, to be cryin' like the world is gonna end at midday. Let me see what's goin' on. And now I find ya smilin' and wit' mischief in your eyes. What's up wit' you, chile?'

The *sangoma's* sudden appearance at the exact moment she was thinking of her had the effect on Martine's mood of sunshine bursting through storm clouds. 'Grace!' she exclaimed, jumping up to embrace her. 'I was just thinking about you.'

16

Grace sank down onto the bench beside her. Usually she wore traditional dress, but today she was in a vivid pink skirt and top with a purple headscarf and matching purple shoes, an outfit made all the more eye-catching because Grace was a woman who'd indulged in many of her own pancakes. She looked at Martine expectantly.

Martine explained about her grandmother's Zimbabwe trip, ending with a heartfelt, 'Grace, I wanted to ask you a favour. Is there any chance I might be able to stay with you for a month?'

Grace was silent for so long that butterflies started to flutter around Martine's stomach. Surely Grace wasn't going to reject her? Finally the *sangoma* said, 'You can stay wit' me any time, chile, but not *this* time.'

Martine was taken aback and a little hurt, but having come up with the perfect plan she was not about to give up on it. 'I know four weeks is a long time, but I'll be as good as gold,' she promised. 'You'll hardly notice I'm there. I don't even need a bed. I can sleep on your sofa or your grass mat.'

But Grace's next words stopped her in her tracks. 'And what about the message from the forefathers. Ya goin' ta ignore that?'

'What message?' Martine began, and then it came back to her. In June she had been walking along a beach with her grandmother, Ben and his mum and dad, when she'd seen a leopard drawn in the sand. The image was so crisp and detailed, with even the whiskers and spots meticulously drawn, that it could only have been there a matter of minutes. And yet apart from a couple of fishermen unloading their catch in the distance and her friends, who'd gone on ahead, the beach was empty. She'd called Ben to come and see it, but in the split second her back was turned a wave had washed the sand smooth.

Martine could still remember the chill that had come over her when she realized the drawing had vanished, almost as if it had been meant for her eyes only.

The same chill went through her now. 'How could you possibly know about the leopard? I was the only person who saw it.'

'You must go to Zimbabwe,' Grace continued as if Martine hadn't spoken. 'What will be is already written. It is your destiny.'

Martine tried to decide whether the knowledge that none of the morning's events had been random – not the phone call, Sadie's accident, Grace's sudden appearance, not even, in all probability, the incident with the warthog – that it was all connected in some way, was comforting or infinitely creepy.

A gust of wind blew and two feathers floated out of the owl's cage. They twisted in the breeze and came to rest beside the bench, one lying across the other in the shape of the letter X. Oddly enough, they were not spotted and tawny like the owl himself, but jet-black and gleaming. Almost, Martine thought later, like the feathers of an eagle.

At the sight of the feathers Grace became extremely agitated. She seized Martine's arm. 'That boy,' she said urgently. 'The quiet boy, the Buddhist.'

Martine was startled. 'Ben?'

'Yes, yes, that one. You know now he is part of your story. You are bound together. When you journey to Zimbabwe, arl the time you must stay together. Any time you be separated, danger will follow you.'

Martine was used to finding Grace's predictions and warnings difficult to fathom, but this request struck her as both unreasonable and unrealistic. 'It's impossible for us always to be in the same place,' she told Grace. 'Ben likes to spend lots of time on his own, and he's always going off tracking. And anyway, his parents might not even allow him to come to Zimbabwe.'

But Grace was adamant. 'You *must* stay together,' she insisted. 'You must.'

Martine leaned back against the bench and closed her eyes. When she opened them again, Grace was putting the feathers into the leather pouch she wore around her neck.

'What does all this mean, Grace? Will I ever be able to have a normal life? I mean, I'm glad I have my gift, even if I don't exactly know what it's for, and I want to be able to heal as many animals as I can, but it would be nice if I could have just one school holidays where I could relax and read books and ride Jemmy and do the things that other kids do.'

Grace put a warm arm around her shoulders. 'How many kids have you seen ridin' white giraffes? Hmm? We don't always get to choose the paths of our lives, chile, and the path that be chosen for you is not an easy one. Trust in your gift. Your gift will keep you safe.'

The caracals began to fight over their food then, and Martine had to open their run and separate them. It only took a minute but Grace was already a splash of pink in the dusty distance, swishing away down the track without so much as a goodbye. As Martine watched, she lifted her hand and waved without turning her head.

Martine sat down on the bench again and stared unseeingly at the sanctuary animals: the caracals with their fur-tipped ears, the owl, Shaka the little elephant, and his new companion, a zebra foal who'd been rejected by his mother and was being bottle-fed by Tendai. She was thinking about the leopard in the sand. It had seemed an extra large leopard. It had been crouched, as if it was on the verge of pouncing. She could still remember its claws and the way its lips curled back over its teeth in a snarl.

The caracals started pacing about their run again, alerting her to footsteps. She looked up, expecting to see Grace returning, but it was Ben. A huge grin lit up his face.

'I've spoken to my mum and dad,' he said. 'I'm coming with you. I'm coming to Zimbabwe.'

So softly that only the caracal kittens heard her, Martine replied, 'So am I.'

Martine put down the book that she'd been attempting to read for the past hundred kilometres and hauled herself wearily into a sitting position. She was cramped, tired and slightly carsick, and her eardrums throbbed with the endless noisy hum of the Landrover. They had already been on the road for a day and a half and they'd shortly be arriving at Rainbow Ridge, where they were staying the night. Martine couldn't wait. Travelling was fun when there were fields of wildflowers or quaint historic towns to admire, but when there was nothing on view except a long, tapering ribbon of black asphalt, it was the most boring experience on earth.

'Is it far now? How long until we get there?' she kept asking Gwyn Thomas on the first day, until her grandmother threatened to play really loud opera music from there until Matopos if she dared raise the subject again.

They'd spent the first night at an ostrich farm midway between Cape Town and Johannesburg. Most ostrich farms bred the birds for their pocked, leathery skin, popular for belts and handbags, and also for their meat, but this one was a sanctuary for mistreated ostriches or those rescued from the slaughterhouse.

At dusk, Martine and Ben had sat on the rails of a corral and watched them strut around their paddock in clouds of sunset-tinted dust, their wrinkly necks gliding up and down like periscopes. The farmer told Martine that the great birds could be quite bad-tempered at times, and wouldn't hesitate to use their prehistoric toes to kick anything or anybody they disliked. They had an air of being very pleased with themselves, as if they thought everyone else at the farm was beneath them. They didn't seem at all grateful to have been rescued.

Martine's ears popped, and she became aware that the Landrover was climbing sharply. The mountains which had been a mauve outline for so long were all around them. Forested slopes gave way to sheer cliffs and crags and, just beneath them, a knife-edge ridge. Curlicues of smoke rose from it.

As they drew nearer they saw that the smoke was

actually mist caused by spray, and that a perfect rainbow arched over it.

'Rainbow Ridge!' said Ben, hanging out of the window with excitement. 'You can't see it from here, but beyond it is one of the highest waterfalls in Southern Africa. That's where we're going this afternoon, Martine. That's what we're going to climb.'

In the front seat of the Landrover, Martine, who was a fan of neither heights nor strenuous activity – not unless it involved giraffes – gave an involuntary shudder.

The campsite they were staying in was situated in a secluded valley well off the beaten track, so they were taken aback to find a buzzing throng of people around the reception desk. A photographer was snapping away and autograph hunters were circling. Gradually the crowd cleared to reveal two bearded young men in climbing gear. They had the healthy suntanned skin of outdoorsmen. A whispered enquiry revealed that they were Red West and Jeff Grant, famous Canadian mountaineers, who were on a tour of South Africa.

After a lengthy delay, the climbers moved off and their fans dispersed. A flustered receptionist checked Gwyn Thomas and the two children in and gave them keys to the log cabin where they'd be spending the night. She seemed quite overwhelmed by her celebrity guests.

'They're such gentlemen,' she said dreamily, 'and so handsome.'

Gwyn Thomas had difficulty getting her attention again. When she did, the receptionist had bad news. The campsite guides were all booked and there were no more tours to Rainbow Ridge until the following day.

'But it's an easy walk and very well sign-posted,' she said. 'As long as they're sensible, they'll be fine on their own.'

'I might be old-fashioned, but I really wouldn't feel comfortable allowing them to do a three-hour hike through forests and mountains with which I'm not in the least familiar,' was Gwyn Thomas's tart response. 'Unfortunately I've been driving for hours and don't have the energy to accompany them. Martine and Ben, I'm so sorry. Once again, I'm going to have to disappoint you.'

Martine was about to protest, not for her own sake but for Ben's, when the receptionist became all starry-eyed again.

'Excuse me, ma'am.'

They turned to see the taller of the two mountaineers. He introduced himself as Red.

'Forgive me for butting in,' he said to Gwyn Thomas in a Canadian drawl, 'but I couldn't help overhearing your dilemma and I wonder if my climbing partner Jeff and I might be able to offer our services. If Vicky here would be kind enough to vouch for us, we'd be glad to accompany these young people to Rainbow Ridge. We're on our way to the summit of the mountain range above it, so it's on our way. We won't be able to walk back with them, but we'll be able to show them the route.'

Vicky blushed furiously and was not able to give a coherent response, but a journalist who'd interviewed the climbers earlier assured Gwyn Thomas that Red and Jeff were men of impeccable character. He and the campsite manager persuaded her that Martine and Ben would be in safe hands.

Soon Martine and Ben were hiking through a pine forest with two of the world's most accomplished mountaineers, listening open-mouthed as Red and Jeff told stories about their epic climbs of the highest summits on seven continents.

'Which was the hardest?' asked Ben.

'Denali in Alaska,' Red replied without hesitation. 'There is something about hanging off an ice cliff in an Arctic wind that is uniquely terrifying.'

The track to Rainbow Ridge was, as the receptionist had promised, a straightforward and well sign-posted one, but after an hour of trying to keep up with the long strides of the mountaineers, Martine's leg muscles were screaming. She was thankful when they passed a picnic spot and Jeff declared himself starving.

'And I could murder a cup of tea,' Red agreed. Martine suspected that they were only stopping out of consideration for her and Ben, but she was not about to complain.

While Jeff fired up his miniature gas stove, Red dug out a kettle, teabags and sandwiches. Martine sat on a log, glad of a chance to rest and take in the scenery. Ben waited politely but they were within sight of the ridge and Martine noticed that he couldn't take his eyes off it. His eagerness made her smile. Ben always came alive in nature.

'You can go on ahead if you like,' she told him. 'I'll catch you up.'

'Would that be all right?' Ben asked Red and Jeff.

'No problem,' said Red. 'We're almost there anyway. Watch yourself, now.'

Ben bounced to his feet. 'Great, I'll see you in a few minutes.' He jogged off up the steep track.

The climbers were impressed.

'He's very fit, your friend,' commented Red. He switched off the gas stove and poured the tea. Jeff munched on a sandwich and rummaged through his rucksack. He wanted to show Martine a photograph of his children.

Ben grew smaller and smaller. He reached the top of the ridge and stood outlined against the rainbow and the hazy grey sky, mist roiling up all around him. As Martine watched, he leaned over the smoking void as if he was trying to see into the very heart of it.

Ben was the least annoying boy Martine knew, but she suddenly felt very irritated with him. What was he thinking, doing something so risky? His mum and dad would have a fit if they saw him teetering so precariously on the brink of a waterfall. Her heart began to thud in her chest.

'Sugar?' queried Red.

'What?' Martine blurted out. In her anxiety, she'd

forgotten about both tea and climbers. 'Oh, excuse me. No sugar, thanks.'

She took the mug from him, sipped some tea, and looked back at the ridge. Ben was no longer there. She shaded her eyes and scanned the horizon in case the clouds of mist and spray had temporarily obscured him, but he was gone.

Martine flung down the tea and leapt to her feet.

'Ow!' cried Red, as the scalding liquid splashed him. 'What the heck do you think you're doing?'

'He's fallen,' Martine heard herself say in a grown-up voice which didn't belong to her. 'Grab a rope, he's fallen.'

And then she was off up the twisting, rocky trail, running faster than she'd ever run in her life, her breath coming in short, painful gasps. When she reached the top of the ridge, it was immediately obvious what had happened. A jagged section of the overhanging bank was missing, as if a gap-toothed dinosaur had taken a chunk out of it. As Martine approached, a fresh shower of shale crumbled into the void.

'Ben!' she called, hoping against hope that there was a perfectly rational explanation for his disappearance. Red and Jeff were moving swiftly up the slope with their climbing gear. She lay flat on her belly, so that if another section of the bank broke off some part of her might be left on solid ground, and crawled towards the edge. The thunder of the waterfall filled her ears and mist drenched her face.

Steeling herself, she peered over the side. The

cascading rush of water ended over a hundred feet below in a foaming, sucking whirlpool. A ring of spiky rocks surrounded it like a fence of spears. The chances of Ben surviving either were zero.

'Ben!' screamed Martine hysterically. 'BEN!'

'Martine!' Ben's voice was so faint that it was barely audible against the roar. It seemed to come out of the ground beneath her stomach. 'Down here!'

Martine wriggled forward. There was nothing to grip on to and the yawning cavern gave her a strong feeling of vertigo, as though it was pulling her over the edge.

'Here,' Ben called again, and that's when she saw him. He was about thirty feet below, clinging to the withered grey trunk of a bonsai-shaped tree that grew sideways out of the rock. He didn't appear to be injured, but he was soaking wet and very pale. Several of the tree's shallow roots had been ripped from the rock by the force of his fall and the trunk sagged ominously.

'Ben!' cried Martine. 'Ben, hold on. Help is on the way.'

This time Ben didn't reply or move his head, in case the mere act of talking severed the tree's fragile grip.

Martine was inching her way back to safe ground when the climbers ran up.

'Where is he?' Red asked briskly. His eyes widened when Martine pointed over the brink.

The men went smoothly into action. With the ease of professionals accustomed to dealing with life-threatening situations, Jeff constructed a pulley system, using two jutting rocks as anchors, while Red made a harness from the other end of the rope and lowered it down to Ben. As he worked, he talked to Ben in a soothing, almost jokey way, explaining clearly to him what he needed do.

'Ben, I want you to pretend you're a spy. You're surrounded by laser lights which will trigger an alarm if you cross them. The only way for you to escape and get the bad guy is if you put this invisible cloak over your head – only you have to do it very, very slowly, using incredibly tiny movements. Great. You're doing brilliantly. Now slip the rope under your arms. Pull it a little tighter . . . '

Without warning, several more roots ripped free from the rock. Ben lurched forward, almost losing his balance. He lay doubled over on the wet, slimy wood, breathing hard.

Red's tone never altered. 'Oops, don't worry, we've got you. Now I want you to sit up very, very slowly – remember the laser lights, you don't want to set off the alarm. Okay, hold on to the main rope with both hands and keep as still as you can. Ready, Jeff? Good. Here we go.'

Just as Ben's feet lifted clear of the grey trunk, the entire tree detached itself with a cracking noise that sounded like bones breaking. Wood, stone and moss plummeted into the smoking gorge. All four of them watched the tree shatter and nobody said a word. The thought that Ben could have fallen with it and been crushed by the force of water, impaled on the spear-like rocks, or drowned in the whirlpool far below, was too

29

hideous to contemplate.

Red whistled through his teeth as he and Jeff hauled Ben up over the edge and onto solid ground. 'That was a bit too close for comfort,' he said, 'but you'd make one helluva spy!'

Martine was in such a state that she hardly knew how to react to Ben's safe return. 'That could have been you,' she said, throwing her arms around him. 'You could have fallen down there.'

'But I didn't,' Ben told her, gently extricating himself. There was a tremor in his voice, but otherwise he seemed remarkably calm. Aside from a few scratches and bruises, he was unhurt. He offered his hand to the climbers. 'Thank you so much for your help. I don't know what we'd have done without you. I'm sorry for causing you so much trouble and for delaying your climb.'

'No trouble,' Red assured him. 'Good thing we were around.'

Jeff eyed Ben's soaking clothes. 'You need to get those off and get dry as soon as possible. We'll walk to the campsite with you – you know, to make sure you get back in one piece. The mountain's not going anywhere.'

'We're fine,' Ben and Martine responded in unison.

'Thanks for offering,' Martine added hastily, in case they seemed ungrateful. 'My grandmother's waiting for us in one of the log cabins down in the valley. Don't worry, we'll go straight there. She was planning to light a fire, and make Ben some Rooibos tea or soup and get him warm.'

But the climbers insisted on taking them to the gates

of the campsite before saying their goodbyes. 'It isn't that we believe you can't get there quite safely by yourselves,' Jeff said. 'It's just that Ben has had a terrifying experience, and the combination of shock and cold can be as dangerous as any fall.'

Forty minutes later they were once more back at the campsite. 'Thanks for the tea and for rescuing Ben,' Martine said as the climbers turned to go. 'Sorry I burned you, Red.'

He smiled down at her. 'No worries. All's well that ends well,' he said, and Martine marvelled at the way he and Jeff were able to take a near-catastrophe in their stride.

It was only when the climbers were out of sight and Martine and Ben were alone that they began to take in what had happened. What *could* have happened. Ben started shivering quite badly and Martine, who felt responsible because she'd sat drinking tea while Ben went to the ridge on his own, was wracked with guilt.

'It's because we were apart,' she said in anguish. 'I should have stayed with you. Grace warned me. She said that any time we were separated during this journey, danger would follow us.'

'I know Grace is very wise,' said Ben, removing his wet fleece and rubbing his arms to generate some body heat, 'but it was nobody's fault but mine. I stood on the edge of a waterfall. It was a dumb thing to do. If it hadn't been for you, I'd be in bits and pieces at the bottom of Rainbow Ridge right now.'

Martine tried to block the image from her head. 'It

was Red and Jeff who saved your life,' she reminded Ben as they started down the mountain. 'I was so scared I could hardly even speak.'

'No,' Ben said, 'it was you. They had the equipment and the expertise, but if you hadn't acted as quickly as you did I wouldn't have been around *to* save.'

Martine had a sudden flashback of Ben as she'd last seen him before his fall. 'Why *were* you so close to the edge? What were you trying to prove? You seemed to be leaning right over it.'

Ben gave an embarrassed laugh. 'This is going to sound crazy. I thought I saw something, that's all. A picture – a sort of drawing. It was on the rocks, practically hidden behind the curtain of water. I couldn't really see it clearly, but it looked like a spotted wild cat of some kind. A leopard or cheetah or jaguar or something. I went closer to take a better look and that's when the ground gave way beneath me. I guess it was just my imagination.'

Martine's mouth went dry. She tried to think of a suitable response but none came. 'We have to stay together,' was all she could manage. 'Promise me we'll stay together.'

Ben saw that she was serious. 'Okay, okay,' he said, putting a reassuring hand on her arm. 'I promise.'

The remainder of the journey to the Zimbabwean border was uneventful. It wasn't particularly scenic, consisting mainly of long stretches of dry bush and scrubland; the fast, scary highways of outer Johannesburg, and ugly mining towns – *dorps*, Gwyn Thomas called them. Martine and Ben dozed until they reached Messina, where they stopped for a lunch of Hawaiian burgers decorated with juicy rings of pineapple, and chips slathered with spicy tomato sauce, all washed down with chocolate milkshakes.

Back in Storm Crossing, Gwyn Thomas refused to allow Martine to eat fast food, and she was at great pains to make it clear that this was a special one-off holiday treat. Martine had to hide a smile when the meal arrived and her grandmother tucked into her burger and fries with relish while doing her best to pretend that she really wasn't enjoying it at all.

'It's pretty good, considering that it's fast food,' Martine remarked innocently to her grandmother.

'I've had worse,' Gwyn Thomas admitted grudgingly, eyeing a passing ice-cream sundae with what looked a lot like envy.

She'd said very little about the incident at Rainbow Ridge, largely because Martine and Ben had said almost nothing about it themselves. On the way down the mountain, they'd decided that to mention Ben had nearly been killed falling down a waterfall would jeopardize the whole trip, which even Martine was now looking forward to. They'd told the truth but not, as judges say in courts of law, the whole truth. Ben had been very open about how he'd unwisely stood too close to the edge of the bank and tumbled headfirst into the water. He'd just left the word 'fall' off the end of 'water'.

He and Martine had received a mild telling off for taking unnecessary risks, but Gwyn Thomas's main concern had been getting Ben dry and making sure he had hot tea, a hearty dinner, and an early night in the cosy log cabin. Apart from being stiff and sore, he was as good as new today, and the trio were in high spirits when they reached the Zimbabwe border in the early afternoon.

'Are you treasure hunters or leopard hunters?'

demanded the customs official when he heard that they were on their way to Matopos. He studied them suspiciously over the tops of their passports, which he held fanned out like a poker player with a handful of aces. 'Treasure hunters, I think. You want to come to Zimbabwe to get rich?'

'We're doing nothing of the kind,' snapped Gwyn Thomas, trying and failing to keep the annoyance out of her voice. 'We're on our way to take care of a sick friend.'

'Ah, you are Good Samaritans?' He gave a smile worthy of a toothpaste advert. 'In that case, you are most welcome to Zimbabwe.'

It was a three-hour journey to Matopos, which stretched to four when they visited six different filling stations in the hope of finding fuel in Bulawayo, the nearest city. They drove through wide, curiously old-fashioned streets, overhung by jacaranda and flamboyant trees. Everything seemed to be in an advanced state of disrepair. There were potholes in the roads big enough to swallow whole cows. A friendly attendant at one of the garages where they stopped, who was sitting on a wall eating a banana in the absence of any trade, told them that the electricity worked for only four hours a day and it was nothing for the water to go off for days at a stretch.

'How do you manage?' Gwyn Thomas wanted to know.

'We make a plan,' he told her, and laughed.

Martine knew almost nothing about Zimbabwe, except that it bordered South Africa, was shaped like a teapot on the map, and was home to one of the seven natural wonders of the world, the Victoria Falls. Martine hoped the waterfall was a long way from where they were going. She was not in a hurry to see another one.

She'd learned a couple of new things in the few hours since they'd crossed the border. The first was that it cost millions of Zimbabwe dollars to buy three drinks. Martine had watched in disbelief as her grandmother counted out the notes.

The other was that 'Bulawayo' was the Ndebele word for 'place of slaughter'. The petrol attendant told them that the city was named after Lobengula's first big battle when he came to the throne – a battle in which his warriors were victorious. Martine thought it a creepy name for a town.

Their failed petrol search meant that they had to leave Bulawayo with the gauge almost on empty. Gwyn Thomas tried to put a brave face on it. 'I'm sure we'll be fine,' she said. 'The reserve tank usually lasts for ages and we don't have far to go.'

It was early evening when they reached the gates of the Matopos National Park. A park official unfolded himself from a makeshift table as they pulled up. He and three uniformed guards had been playing a game of drafts using bottle tops and a piece of cardboard on which they'd drawn squares with a red pen. Their rifles lay on the ground beside them.

'Good evening,' he said formally. 'It is after six p.m. The park is closed to visitors.'

'But it can't be,' cried Gwyn Thomas. 'We've driven all the way from Cape Town. We need to get to a ranch on the other side.'

'Eeeh, I'm sorry for that,' said the official, sounding genuinely sympathetic. 'You must spend the night in a hotel in Bulawayo and come back tomorrow.'

'We can't possibly do that,' she told him. 'For one thing, we can't afford it and for another we're almost out of petrol.'

'You have no fuel?' He tutted disapprovingly. 'It is not a good idea to come to the Matobo Hills with no fuel. Then you must sleep in your car and wait for morning.'

'But my friend is expecting us,' said Gwyn Thomas despairingly. 'Sadie – Sadie Scott at Black Eagle Lodge.'

Behind her, Martine saw the guards exchange a look, although what the look meant she couldn't tell.

'Sadie Scott?' repeated the official. There was a split second's hesitation before he continued warmly, 'Why didn't you just say so? Allow me to direct you.'

He drew the route on a tourist map, waved them through the open barrier, and the Matobo Hills were finally in front of them.

From the outset, Martine had expected the national park to be a disappointment. She'd been looking forward to hearing more about the Ndebele king's lost treasure, but as far as the rocks were concerned she'd been convinced that everyone was making a fuss about nothing. After all, how interesting could piles of boulders be? She'd pictured one or two particularly impressive rocky hillocks of the type Southern Africans called *kopjes* and pronounced 'kopies', maybe with monuments on the top, or one or two balancing rocks. Instead, there were hundreds, if not thousands, of geological marvels.

There were great stacks of teetering boulders – many leaning at angles that defied gravity, or sitting on perches a bird would have had difficulty balancing on. There were individual rocks as wide and high as mountains, and others shaped like animals or castles or faces. Some were thickly encrusted with jade and silver lichen, or streaked with orange or lime stains, as though they'd rusted in the rain. Others were smooth, grey and bare, with mysterious spaces between them suggesting caves or tunnels or vast, rainwater-filled hollows as big as Olympic swimming pools. Threaded through the rocks or surrounding them, were green tufts of African bush.

It was an awe-inspiring sight, and there was not a soul to witness it but the three of them.

'You'd think there'd be lots of tourists here,' observed Ben.

'You would think that,' agreed Gwyn Thomas, 'but I suppose people are nervous of coming to a place where it's hard to find petrol. I have to tell you that I'm beginning to feel the same way.'

The sun was setting, turning the tops of the rocks copper. Martine had never seen such a wild, lonely place. It made Sawubona seem as tame as a suburban garden.

'Look!' Ben said. A kudu bull and two kudu cows were

watching them with wide, almond-shaped eyes. As the Landrover passed, they took fright and loped away through the bush.

The park ranger's map indicated that they should turn shortly after passing a great baobab tree. Gwyn Thomas steered the vehicle off the main road and bumped along a steadily deteriorating track. The needle on the petrol gauge crept further into the red. All three of them noticed it happen, but nobody said a thing. The towering rocks seemed to close in on them. The potholes and craters worsened until Martine was sure that every tooth would be shaken loose from her head. Her grandmother fought to control the bucking vehicle. Martine felt for her. She was plainly exhausted.

After about a mile the track levelled and became smooth and sandy. They passed a village of five mud huts. Ngoni cattle with wide horns and hides so prettily patterned they might have been decorated by an artist rested in the dust. They chewed cud sleepily as they watched the Landrover go by.

At the edge of the village a crudely written sign indicated that Black Eagle Lodge was one mile ahead, beyond a gate and cattle grid.

Gwyn Thomas exhaled. 'Thank goodness,' she said. 'We'll be fine now. Living in such a remote area, Sadie's bound to have spare fuel.'

Ben hopped out to open the wire gate and they set off again. The grass along the edges of the track was overgrown and the trees crowded close, rapping the roof of the Landrover with their branches. Seedpods cracked and popped beneath the wheels. The air was muggy and still.

Martine began to feel claustrophobic. She was glad when they finally rounded a bend and found themselves in a clearing at the foot of an imposing, elephant-shaped mountain cast from a single slab of granite. Stone cottages with sagging, rain-darkened thatch were dotted around the foot of it. Two black eagles wheeled overhead. There was no other sign of life.

Gazing upon the empty scene, Martine was struck by the silence. There was something spooky about it. It was a silence so intense she could almost touch it and taste it. It swirled around her like a cloak of fog. It wouldn't have surprised Martine to learn that there was nothing at all beyond the mountain; that the landscape stopped right here. It was, she thought with a shiver, as if they'd taken a wrong turn, and found the end of the world.

· 5 ·

Gwyn Thomas was the first to speak. 'Well,' she said
huffily. 'I must say it's not quite the welcome I was
expecting. Especially after a two-thousand-mile drive.'

But almost immediately a worried frown came over
her face and she added, 'Oh, my goodness, what if
something's happened to Sadie? I'd never forgive myself
for not getting here sooner.'

Ben said, 'I think I just saw a curtain move.'

He didn't tell them what he'd really seen, which was
what appeared to be a frightened face at the window of
a house partially concealed by the mountain's long
shadow, just in case he was mistaken and alarmed

41

Martine and her grandmother unnecessarily. Before he could make up his mind what to do next, the door of the house opened and an attractive woman, who appeared years younger than the sixty Gwyn Thomas had told them she was, swung out on crutches. She had on a floral sundress that had seen many summers. It flared over the bright pink plaster cast encasing her left leg and foot. The sandal she was wearing on the other foot had apparently been crafted from a piece of recycled car tyre.

'You can wipe that sour expression off your face for starters,' was her opening remark to Gwyn Thomas. 'I know what you're thinking. *"I've driven all the way from the Western Cape and Sadie hasn't put the welcome mat out."* Well, I'm sorry. Service is not quite what it used to be at Black Eagle, and it's even worse when I'm out the back trying to do the laundry on one leg.'

There was a brief pause, during which Martine expected there to be an explosion of some kind from her grandmother. Instead Gwyn Thomas's nut-brown face creased into a huge smile. 'I see that apart from the cherry-pink plaster-cast nothing much has changed,' she retorted. 'Still as crusty as ever!'

Then she rushed forward and embraced the other woman, taking care to avoid Sadie's injured leg. 'It's wonderful to see you, my dear,' she said. 'It's been far too long. Sadie, I'd like you to meet my granddaughter, Martine, and her best friend, Ben.'

Sadie hugged them both. 'Hello, Martine, and her best friend Ben. I've been counting the hours until you all arrived. When the sun started to set today with still no sign of you, I began to feel quite desperate.'

There was so much emotion in her voice that Martine, recalling her grandmother's words about Sadie being the proudest, most independent woman she knew, wondered if Gwyn Thomas had been correct in her suspicions that there was something more going on at Black Eagle than a broken leg.

'We came as soon as we could,' Gwyn Thomas responded. 'But I felt it only fair that Martine and Ben get to see one or two sights along the way.'

'Of course, of course. And I don't mean to sound selfish. I've just been so looking forward to your visit. Anyway, you're here now and that's all that matters. I'm actually surprised that the national park guards let you through the main gate. I've had a few difficulties with them recently. Having said that, one of my ex-employees recently started working on the gate and if you're lucky enough to come into the park when it's his shift, he's always a sweetheart.'

Her eyes widened as Ben and Martine began unloading bags of rice, buttermilk rusks and cans of guavas, smoked tuna and chopped tomatoes, along with their suitcases, from the boot of the car. 'What's all this?'

Gwyn Thomas smiled. 'I wasn't sure if there were enough groceries in the whole of Matopos to feed these two for a month. They might look undernourished, but given half a chance they'll eat you right out of Black Eagle Lodge!'

'You didn't have to do that,' responded Sadie,

laughing, 'but the more the merrier.' However, Martine noticed that she didn't protest.

As if suddenly reminded of her duties as host, Sadie exclaimed, 'You poor things, you must be worn out. Let me show you to your cottage.'

They ate dinner by candlelight. 'More romantic,' Sadie said.

Martine wondered if the real reason was that the electricity wasn't working, but decided it didn't matter. It was more romantic or, at least, more magical, to do everything by candlelight.

Night had fallen on the retreat with typical African abruptness. At 6:45 p.m. the red sun slid behind Elephant Rock, the mountain that gave Black Eagle its spectacular backdrop, and by 7 p.m. an ink-black darkness of the type only found in places far from city lights had descended. Sadie had shown them to their cottage along paths lit by cat's eyes, which, she explained, were solar-powered, and not dependant on the erratic power supply. There were three bedrooms, a lounge and a bathroom, all very simple, with faded curtains and threadbare rugs, but comfortable enough. The occasional gecko or blue-tailed lizard skittered across walls of glittering stone.

Over butternut squash stew, Sadie talked to them about the Matopos, an area rich in African history, much of it documented in the cave paintings found among the balancing rocks. Martine's ears pricked up at the mention of cave paintings, and for an instant she caught herself wondering about the likelihood of finding further clues to her destiny in Zimbabwe. But that, she told herself, was ridiculous, not to say egotistical. The San artists had had better things to do than go around Africa predicting the future of some white child they'd never heard of.

'Tomorrow morning, you'll meet Ngwenya, my right-hand man,' Sadie said. 'He's the groundskeeper and horse wrangler here at Black Eagle. He's also the only remaining staff member. Ngwenya is from the Ndebele tribe and he's much more of an expert on Matopos than I am, so you should save all your questions for him.'

Gwyn Thomas pursed her lips. 'Ngwenya? That's similar to the Zulu word for leopard – "Ingwe". Is there any connection?'

'There is. *Ingwenya* means leopard in Ndebele. Ngwenya has an ordinary name like you and I, but it's respectful to address him by his clan name. As a member of that particular clan he has a sworn duty to protect and honour all leopards, but that's a hard thing to do in these difficult times. We used to have the highest concentration of leopards in the world right here in the Matopos, but not any more.'

'Leopards?' interrupted Martine. 'Here? In the Matobo Hills?'

'Yes, leopards,' Sadie responded. 'Why? Are you particularly interested in them?'

Martine started chewing then, as if her mouth was full and she couldn't speak, so Sadie continued, 'Leopards are nocturnal which, as I'm sure you know, means they mostly hunt at night. They're the shyest and most elusive of the big cats. There are rangers in the Matopos who have worked here for twenty years without seeing one. For that reason it's very hard to keep a count of them.'

'You said you "used to" have a lot of leopards here?' said Gwyn Thomas. 'What happened to them?'

'Poaching and uncontrolled hunting has wiped them out.' Sadie's tone was bitter. 'And elsewhere some have simply starved to death because the animals they eat have also been poached and killed. They are on the verge of extinction in Zimbabwe. Here in Matopos, we know of only one. Few people have ever seen him but those who have say he is the largest leopard ever recorded. He is so cunning and elusive that the locals are convinced that when every other big cat in the country has been hunted down he'll be the only survivor. They call him Khan. They believe the day is coming when he will be the last leopard.'

'Have you ever seen him?' Ben asked.

Sadie glanced at Ben oddly, as if noticing him for the first time. 'Once,' she said abruptly. 'I saw him once, but it was so long ago I can hardly remember it.'

They were finishing their meal when Gwyn Thomas gave a tut of annoyance. 'Sadie, I forgot to mention that we're clean out of fuel. We did try to find some in Bulawayo but had no luck all. We limped up your driveway on the smell of an oil rag. I assume you keep some petrol on the premises.'

'I'm afraid not,' Sadie said. 'It comes in once a month. My next fuel delivery is not until – ooh, let me see . . . ' She stood up with the aid of her crutches and hopped over to a calendar illustrated with local wildlife. 'August 12th, it looks like.'

'TWO weeks away!' Gwyn Thomas burst out, but she caught herself and added more politely, 'That's not for nearly a fortnight. What if there's an emergency? What if we want to take a drive around the Matobo Hills?'

'That's what the horses are for,' Sadie told her cheerfully, and Martine had the distinct impression she wasn't exactly sorry that they were stuck here at Black Eagle for weeks on end – probably wouldn't be sorry if they were stuck here forever.

'This is a disaster,' cried her grandmother.

'Gwyn, Gwyn, Gwyn,' Sadie scolded reproachfully, as if Gwyn Thomas was a misguided child. 'You're on holiday now. I'm sure you haven't had a proper break in years. I'm aware that I've asked you to help me run the retreat for a month and that there'll inevitably be a few mundane chores each day, but the present lack of visitors means there should be plenty of time to relax. At least it's peaceful here. Matopos is so isolated that it forces you to forget about the modern world for a while. We have no television or email, and the phones are hopelessly unreliable.

'As for emergencies, Zimbabweans have a saying: "Make a plan." It's our national motto. It means that no matter what life throws at you, you keep smiling and figure out a solution.'

'You might have a point, Sadie,' said her friend. 'I'm so used to my routine at Sawubona, where there are always visitors arriving or animals needing attention, that some enforced rest and relaxation might do me the power of good. It won't do Ben and Martine any harm either. They're still recovering from a disastrous school trip they took in June. We're definitely all in need of a holiday. If we have to wait a few weeks for the fuel to arrive, then so be it.'

Martine caught Ben's eye and saw he was just as stunned as she was. It was one thing being at the end of the world by choice. It was a totally different matter being stranded there.

Later, Martine was climbing into bed in her pyjamas when she remembered she'd left her survival kit hanging over the back of her dining room chair. She was so sleepy that she was tempted to leave it till morning, but Tendai had drummed into her the importance of having it with her even when she least expected to use it. 'Keep your survival kit with you for when you need it most, little one,' he always said. 'When you need it to survive.'

Ben and her grandmother had turned off their lights, so Martine tiptoed out of the cottage and along the path to Sadie's house, which also served as the retreat reception, lounge and dining area. Cat's eyes lit the way. The kitchen door was ajar. The survival kit was exactly where Martine had left it. Out of habit, she wrapped the pouch around her waist and secured the Velcro straps. She was hurrying from the building when she heard Sadie's voice raised in anger. Surprised, Martine crept back along the passage and put an ear to the lounge wall.

Sadie was on the phone. 'I don't want your blood money,' she was saying furiously. 'I want you to leave us alone. Nothing you can say will change my mind. *Ever.* Over my dead body will you take him.'

She slammed down the receiver, and there was the clack of wood as she gathered her crutches. Martine darted out into the night. A key turned in the lock and the kitchen windows went dark.

Despite her tiredness, Martine was awake for a long time, replaying in her mind what she'd heard. Who was threatening Sadie and why? 'Over my dead body will you take him,' she'd said. That was a very extreme statement. Who was the 'he' Sadie was protecting? Who did 'they' want to take? Even more disturbing was the comment about blood money. Was Sadie being blackmailed in some way?

She was just drifting off to sleep when the silence was split by what, even through the fuzziness of half-consciousness, she recognized as a leopard's roar. But it was no ordinary roar. It was an expression of rage and absolute defiance, both the protest of a savage, untamed creature and a declaration of war, and it touched the very core of Martine's being.

When she woke up in the morning, she had no idea whether or not she'd dreamt it.

*T*uk-tuk-tuk. *Tat-tat-tat. Tuk-tuk-tuk. Tat-tat-tat.*
'Come in!' Martine shouted for the fourth time,
her voice cross and thick with sleep. She couldn't
believe it was already daybreak and she was very
annoyed with whoever it was who kept knocking but
refusing to enter. It was only when she took the pillow
off her face and sat up that she realized the sound was
coming from the window rather than the door.

She pulled back the curtain. A black and white-
speckled hornbill with a big yellow beak was staring in
through the window. As Martine watched, its beady eyes
slid to her survival kit. She'd opened it to take out her

torch the previous night and it was still lying on the ledge.

'Don't get any ideas,' Martine told the bird, zipping up the pouch and tucking it under her pillow, out of view. She checked her watch and yawned. 'And next time wait until at least seven o'clock before you even think about waking me up.'

'That's Magnus,' Sadie informed her over a breakfast of butternut fritters and scrambled eggs prepared by Gwyn Thomas. 'He loves shiny things and he's an awful thief, so watch your possessions. The locals say that the person who finds Magnus's nest will be able to feed everyone in Matopos for a year there'll be so many rings, rubies and riches in it. But so far he has managed to outwit us all. I have to warn you he gets very attached to visitors. Don't be surprised if he starts following you around.'

Martine studied Sadie from under her fringe, but although her grandmother's friend had dark circles under her eyes and seemed a touch distracted, she made no mention of the telephone row the previous night. If she was being blackmailed or threatened, she certainly didn't show it.

'"Over my dead body will you take him." Are you sure that's what you heard?' Ben asked as they walked down to the stables after breakfast. Magnus the hornbill accompanied them, waddling ponderously alongside.

'I'm not a hundred per cent certain, because I was tired and listening through a wall,' admitted Martine, 'but I'm pretty sure. And anyway she definitely made the comment about blood money.'

They followed the path through a grove of gum trees. The smell of horses, Martine's favourite next to giraffe breath and baking bread, grew stronger. In front of her, Ben halted. The hornbill paused at the same time. On the far side of the stableyard, Sadie was in deep conversation with a man they assumed was Ngwenya. Their heads were close together and their expressions were serious.

'Maybe it was Ngwenya who Sadie was referring to on the phone,' Ben said in a low voice. 'It could be that somebody's trying to tempt him away to a better job and she's doing her best to hold on to him. She did say he was her right-hand man.'

Before Martine could answer, Sadie's companion spotted them. He murmured something to Sadie. She motioned them over with a crutch.

'Martine, Ben, let me introduce you to Ngwenya. Black Eagle would have gone out of business long ago if it weren't for him.'

Ngwenya shook their hands with calloused, sun-warmed palms. 'Gogo is being too kind,' he said. 'She would get along very well without me.'

'*Gogo* means grandmother in Ndebele,' Sadie explained, seeing their puzzled expressions. 'It's a term of endearment and respect used for all older women. And no,' she said fiercely to Ngwenya, 'I couldn't manage without you. I just couldn't.'

Ngwenya chuckled. 'Come and meet your new friends,' he said to Ben and Martine. 'You are good riders, yes?'

Ben shook his head. 'I've never ridden a horse in my life.'

'And I've only ever ridden a giraffe,' Martine said.

The horse wrangler smirked and waited for her to finish the joke. When she didn't, he glanced at Sadie as if to say, 'Is your friend's granddaughter in the habit of making up such ridiculous fantasies?'

Sadie laughed. 'I've never actually witnessed it, but I'm told it's true. On the game reserve where she lives in South Africa, Martine rides a giraffe called Jemmy.'

Ngwenya clapped a hand to his forehead. 'A giraffe!' he exclaimed dramatically. 'You ride a giraffe?' He examined Martine with a great deal of interest. 'With horses,' he said, 'I think you will be a natural.'

As it turned out, he was an excellent judge of potential. For most of her life Martine had been hopeless at every sport she'd ever tried apart from giraffe riding, but she swung into the saddle as if she'd been doing it since the day she was born. Everything came easily to her. Everything *was* natural. After months of learning to stay aboard a ten-foot-high wild giraffe – one who had a disconcerting habit of making unexpected detours to snatch at clumps of juicy acacia leaves, sometimes in mid-gallop – riding a schooled, responsive horse was a breeze.

Mounting and dismounting using stirrups was simplicity itself, and Martine bumped only twice before mastering the rising trot. But the thing that really impressed Sadie and Ngwenya was her affinity with Black Eagle's six horses. So tranquil did they become when she touched them that after ten minutes of watching her ride Jack, a big-boned black horse, Ngwenya declared that it would be her responsibility to exercise Sirocco and Tempest during her stay at the retreat.

Sirocco and Tempest were highly strung Arabs, with arched necks, dished faces and delicate, flaring nostrils, but once Martine had saddled Sirocco under Ngwenya's expert guidance and trotted her round the paddock, the chestnut mare became positively placid.

Ben, meanwhile, was having a terrible time. It's not that the horses disliked him; Ben was so gentle and treated animals with such kindness and respect that the opposite was true. It's just that Cassidy and Mambo, the pot-bellied white ponies Ngwenya had told him it would be his duty to exercise, sensed that he had no idea what he was doing and played up mercilessly.

Hardly had they rounded Elephant Rock than Cassidy shied at some imaginary object and threw Ben off into a bush. And every few strides she'd pause to snatch mouthfuls of grass, or make a dash for home. Eventually, Ngwenya attached a lead rope to her bridle and she was forced to accompany him and Jack. She did it meekly but reluctantly, with lots of yawning and snorting.

One part of Martine felt sorry for Ben, but then again he excelled at so many things – he was a straight A student, Caracal Junior's cross-country running champion, a gifted swimmer, and wonderful at wilderness activities like building shelters and fishing – that it was quite nice to find a chink in his armour. Still, she didn't like to see him struggle so she helped him as much as she could.

There was something about negotiating Matopos's extraordinary terrain on horseback that made it all the more spectacular. They felt connected to it. In daylight, the intense silence was not creepy but simply peaceful, and as Martine adjusted to the short, bouncy strides of Sirocco, so different from Jemmy's long lope, a calm feeling came over her. Sadie had told her that the Matopos was the spiritual home of the Ndebele tribe and she could understand why. The domes and spires of the boulders were like a living force all around them. When they reached a high point, distant *kopjes* unfolded in watery blue and violet layers against the horizon.

Not long after they set off, they came across two girls – one six-year-old and one aged eight, neatly dressed in dark green school uniforms. Martine and Ben couldn't hide their astonishment. There was not a building in sight. The girls were strolling through the thick bush with their exercise books under their arms, as if it was perfectly normal for Zimbabwean children to walk unaccompanied to non-existent classrooms through lonely areas teeming with wildlife and poisonous snakes.

Ngwenya spoke to them in Ndebele and they stared up at Martine and burst into fits of giggles, covering their faces shyly with their books. They went on their way with smiles and waves, pausing periodically to look back over their shoulders and giggle some more.

'I told them that your usual horse is a giraffe,' Ngwenya explained to Martine. He added that not only did the girls walk alone through the bush almost daily, they walked an incredible six kilometres to school and six back during term time.

'Why?' asked Martine, bewildered. Six kilometres was more or less the distance from Sawubona to Caracal Junior, and even that journey seemed to take forever in Gwyn Thomas's car. Martine didn't much like school, which gobbled up time she'd have much preferred to spend riding Jemmy, and she couldn't imagine wanting to go to class so badly she'd risk life and limb to walk twelve kilometres on her own.

'Because their parents are poor and have no car.'

'No, I mean, why do they go all that way by themselves?'

Ngwenya shrugged. 'They are hungry to learn. They want to grow up to be doctors or scientists. They have seen the life of their parents, who are unemployed or tend goats or cattle, and they want something better for themselves.'

Martine immediately felt guilty that she didn't have a better attitude towards school. She made up her mind to be more appreciative in the future and to try harder in lessons.

The bush they were riding through seemed jungle-thick and untouched, almost as if they and the schoolgirls were the first human beings ever to cross it. But according to Ngwenya there'd been human beings in the area for over 40,000 years. Many tribes had come and gone. The Banyubi hill people had been followed by a whole mix of Mashona and other tribesmen, most of whom fled or were conquered when Mzilikazi, the first Ndebele king, came to the Bulawayo and Matopos areas in 1839 with his wives and warriors.

'Mzilikazi called this area "Matobo" because the rocks reminded him of the heads of bald men,' Ngwenya said.

Martine smiled at him as she considered this. She liked Ngwenya, who had an open, pleasant face. There was nothing particularly striking about him. He was of medium height and build and was the sort of person you would pass without noticing on the street. But he had an infectious laugh, like an especially cheerful bird, and was a man she felt she could trust implicitly.

They were winding their way along a narrow path when Ben saw a splash of colour ahead. 'What's that?' he called to Ngwenya.

Ngwenya reacted as if he'd been poked with something sharp. 'Get down! Get down!' he hissed, leaping off Jack and pulling the horse into a thicket of trees. Martine and Ben barely had time to do the same with Sirocco and Cassidy before three men came striding along the path in the opposite direction. The one in front was wearing a trilby hat and a shirt with the sleeves rolled up. The others were in overalls, open to the waist. Their muscular bodies, shining with sweat, could have been carved from wood. One had a heavy sack of maize meal on his head; the others were loaded down with equipment. They were arguing about something and didn't notice the horse tracks.

'Looks like they're trying to find some kind of metal,' Ben said softly to Martine. 'The man in the hat is carrying a metal detector.'

'Are you sure?' Martine watched as the men followed the path around a dinosaur-shaped boulder and disappeared. 'What if they're poachers?'

'They are not poachers, I can promise you that,' Ngwenya said. He sounded almost angry. 'One is my uncle's son. He is my cousin.'

'Why are you avoiding your own cousin?' asked Ben.

'He is not a good man,' Ngwenya replied. 'He and his *shamwaris*, his friends, are *tstotsis* – troublemakers. They do not want to find a job; they want to find the treasure of Lobengula.'

'Does that mean it's true? The story of the king's lost treasure?'

Ngwenya grimaced. 'So you have heard about it. Yes, it is true.'

'Can you tell us something about its history?' Martine pleaded. 'How did the treasure go missing? What exactly is it? Is it precious jewels?'

Ngwenya sat down in the shade and leaned against a tree. He took a packet from his pocket and offered them some dried mango. 'Make yourselves comfortable,' he said. 'I will tell you what I know.'

According to Ngwenya, Mzilikazi and his followers had travelled 500 miles and taken ten long years to reach the hills they called Matobo from their original home in South Africa. It was a journey known as the 'Pathway of Blood', so many battles did they fight along the way. Mzilikazi had been the Zulu king Shaka's bravest and most brilliant lieutenant. When his popularity grew too much for Shaka, the Zulu king wanted to have him murdered. Mzilikazi fled, taking his wives and loyal warriors with him. His fighting skills and those of his men were so legendary that their enemies called them the AmaNdebele, 'People with Long Shields'. They became known as the Ndebele: 'The ones who followed' or even 'Children of the Stars'.

Mzilikazi reigned successfully for nearly two decades in the Matobo Hills and his reputation as one of the greatest African kings of all time spread throughout the continent. But when he died it was found that his eldest son, the heir to his throne, had mysteriously vanished. All efforts to locate him failed. After a debate lasting two years, a council of *indunas*, chiefs, appointed Lobengula, Mzilikazi's son by an inferior wife, as his successor in 1870.

Lobengula's nickname, *Ndlovu*, meant 'Great Elephant' and he grew to embody it, standing well over six feet tall and filling out until he resembled a bull elephant. He was almost as great a warrior as his father and successfully led a rebellion against the white settlers, but some suspected him of having several of his own brothers murdered and distrusted him greatly.

'But what about the treasure?' Martine said impatiently. She had a low boredom threshold with history. 'Where did the treasure come from?'

Ngwenya laughed. 'You want me to "cut to the chase", as the American tourists say?' He ate another piece of mango before continuing.

'The treasure came from raids on other tribes and from gifts from the Colonial hunters, miners, and explorers. The elders say he had three tins filled with diamonds, raw gold from the mines of the Mashona, and many bags of British and Kruger sovereigns. He also had much ivory. I have heard it told that some nights he would order his secretary, a white man from Cape Town called John Jacobs, to cover his body in gold sovereigns from head to foot.

'One day he came rushing from his house and gave orders for his treasure to be taken into the bush to a safe place. Lobengula, Jacobs and four *indunas* went with the treasure on the wagons, followed by the fourteen Matebele who would bury it. They hid it well and sealed the entrance with a stone wall. When they returned that night, Lobengula ordered all who had buried the treasure to be killed in case they had thoughts of stealing it. Many were slain but some escaped . . . '

A baboon's eerie cry, 'Qua-ha, qua-ha-ha!' suddenly split the silence. Ben and Martine, who were absorbed in the story, jumped at least an inch off the ground. Ngwenya rapped a stick loudly against the trunk of the tree and the rest of the troop loped away, the babies riding high on their mothers' backs. The male baboon took his time following, pausing to scratch a flea and eat a few imaginary berries for their amusement. 'I'll go when I'm good and ready,' he seemed to be saying.

'Did any of those who escaped ever say where the treasure is buried?' Ben asked Ngwenya.

'If they did, each person took the secret to the grave. After Lobengula's death, John Jacobs led many expeditions into Southern Rhodesia, as Zimbabwe used to be known, to try to recover it, but each time the expedition was cursed as the witchdoctors, traditional healers and fortune tellers – they are like your *sangomas*, I think – had foretold it would be. Men were struck

61

down with illnesses none had ever seen before; charged by elephants or murdered by rivals; one even had his nose licked by a lion. The same fate befell others who tried to find Lobengula's surviving *indunas*. Jacobs was sentenced to hard labour for entering the country without the proper permit.

'Some people believe that the treasure is definitely in the Matobo Hills. Others say it is in the Batoka Gorges or as far away as Zambia. Over the years hundreds of people have come in search of it. We have seen Englishmen with maps drawn by their great-great-great-grandfathers; descendants of Lobengulu's *indunas*; Zimbabwean officials; Japanese tourists; Russian geology experts; Australian archaeologists. Nobody has found any trace of it.'

His gaze shifted to the path taken by his cousin. 'Many good men have been driven crazy by this quest.'

'Then what makes your cousin and his *shamwaris* so confident they can find it?' asked Martine, surveying the mountainous landscape. Hunting for a needle in a haystack would be nothing compared to searching for the treasure troves of Ndebele royals in this Land of a Thousand Hills.

Ngwenya's reply chilled her to the bone. 'They believe that the leopard they call Khan will lead them to it.'

'What do you mean?' Martine said.

The horse wrangler was clearly uncomfortable talking about it. He kept checking uneasily over his shoulder as if he thought his cousin was about to pop up from behind a rock and smite him to the ground for saying the words out loud. At last he said, 'Can you keep a secret?'

Martine nodded furiously, and Ben gave his word.

Ngwenya looked around once more before continuing in a low voice, 'They have spoken with our local witchdoctor, and he has told them that the last resting place of the king of leopards is the hiding place of the king's treasure.'

Martine swallowed. 'The *last* resting place. You mean . . . ?'

Ngwenya's mouth twisted. 'Exactly. I mean that before the treasure can be found the leopard has to be dead.'

For most of the next week, they rode twice a day, going out on Sirocco, Jack and Cassidy in the morning and Tempest, Mambo and a thoroughbred called Red Mist in the evening. Ben's riding improved and he slowly developed the right muscles, stopped being quite so saddlesore and was able to sit down again at meals.

They always went out with Ngwenya who, they found, had the dry humour that characterized many Zimbabweans. He would tease them about the local tree that was said to chase naughty children in the night, and was very funny on the subject of past guests at Black Eagle Lodge.

'If a bird watcher comes, that's when you know you are in for a bad day,' he said, his Ndebele accent turning *birds* into *beds*. 'These people, they only want to see small beds, big beds and medium beds. Even if you see a lion chasing something, they don't mind. Even if one elephant is killing another, they don't mind. They only want to see beds. You need a lot of patience because they will look in their book, "Oh, it's the Blue-Mantled Crested Flycatcher!"'

Ngwenya was as good a guide as Sadie had boasted. One afternoon he showed them grain bins used by the Bushmen, and biting ants so fierce they were known as the Enemy of Lions. 'Where you find these, you won't find any lions. Even snakes, you won't find them here.'

The shadows were lengthening by then, so they turned the horses in the direction of the retreat and threaded their way through the balancing rocks and bush-filled gullies. The air was filled with the exotic scents of plants and animals and the woodsmoke of unseen villagers in faraway huts preparing their evening meals.

Twice Martine thought she saw a streak of gold in amongst the foliage on the knobbly hills, and she found herself wondering if the leopard was watching them. She had been incredibly distressed by the story of Ngwenya's cousin and had found it hard to understand why the witchdoctor would tell men who obviously had ulterior motives that it was only when the leopard was dead that they'd find their treasure.

'Doesn't the witchdoctor have an obligation to protect

the leopard if he is a member of your clan?' she asked Ngwenya.

But the horse wrangler had explained that, although he and the witchdoctor were both from the Ndebele tribe, the witchdoctor was from a different clan.

'Even so, it seems wrong that he would tell them something that might tempt them to go out and kill the leopard,' Martine said.

'I agree,' was Ngwenya's response. 'But not all witchdoctors do things for the right reasons.'

Riding beside Ben now, Martine scanned the hills for any sign of the treasure seekers, the leopard or even a leopard spirit. She hadn't been able to think about the Matobo Hills in quite the same way since discovering that they were riddled with shrines created by the early Mashona tribesmen, who had worshipped Mwali, the High God. Each shrine had its own guardian and they were looked after to this day.

Ngwenya had many stories about ghostly goings on amid the rocks and hills, which he said were full of spirits. He claimed that Lobengula had regularly visited the Umlimo Cave on Mount Injelele, the Hill of Slippery Sides, to consult a spirit which could 'bark like a dog, crow like a cock or roar like a lion'.

'The pilgrims who visit the shrines often say they hear the voice of Mwali coming from the rocks,' Ngwenya said. 'You might even hear it yourself. But don't worry; the "Voices of the Rocks" also has a scientific explanation. The boulders expand in the sun and shrink at night when it is cool. When they get smaller, they moan or growl like thunder.'

Martine listened hard but could hear nothing but the faint whistle of the wind through the rocks and crags.

Ngwenya explained that each shrine had its own guardian or messenger who was in communication with Mwali or the cave spirit, and that one famous shrine messenger, a seven-year-old girl, had lived underwater at Dzilo shrine for four years 'just like crocodiles do'. The spirit had taught her good manners, how to be humble and kind-hearted, and how to teach others to live in harmony with nature.

Martine could think of quite a few pupils at Caracal Junior who would benefit from the teachings of such a spirit, but she found it hard to credit that an intelligent man like the horse wrangler could actually imagine that a young girl could spend four years underwater like a crocodile.

'But surely you don't believe that?' she pressed Ngwenya. 'Surely you don't believe in the supernatural?'

He looked at her in surprise. 'These things are not supernatural,' he said. 'These are our truths and the truths of our ancestors.'

On their sixth day in the Matopos, Ngwenya and Sadie decided that Martine and Ben were familiar enough with the landscape around the retreat to be trusted to go out alone. Gwyn Thomas was concerned but Sadie assured her that as long as they stayed on Black Eagle land and didn't venture into the national park, they were unlikely to run into anything more deadly than an antelope.

'Provided,' she cautioned them, 'that you don't go near the northern boundary fence. Rex Ratcliffe runs a hunting and safari operation on his ranch, the Lazy J, just the other side of it. They're a trigger-happy lot and I wouldn't want you getting shot by mistake.'

Martine could tell that her grandmother didn't appreciate her friend's humour. It wasn't until later that it struck her that perhaps Sadie hadn't been joking.

It was Tempest's turn to be exercised that day, so Martine rode the grey Arab colt while Ben tried to coax some life into Mambo. It wasn't an easy task. The pony had a fat stomach and a plump rump, and was both greedy and lazy. His nature was sweet enough, but he did everything in his own time and would not be hurried. Martine was sure that a charging elephant couldn't persuade Mambo to do anything more energetic than swish his tail.

'He's the perfect horse for a beginner,' Sadie told poor Ben, as it took the combined efforts of him and Ngwenya to drag the pony away from the feed trough.

Once they were on their way Mambo's behaviour improved, but the fastest he ever went was a trot. On this particular afternoon, that suited Martine and Ben fine, because Ben wanted to demonstrate some of the tracking skills he'd learned from Tendai. Sadie had lent them her binoculars and she asked them to report back if they saw any unusual birds or wildlife.

'Tendai says that anyone can learn the basic principles of tracking,' Ben told Martine as they rode across a plain about an hour away from the lodge. 'But the best trackers understand that it isn't just about reading "sign", which is things like broken twigs or whatever, but about trying to think like the animal or person you're following. It's a mind game. See this . . . ' He leaned down and pointed at some torn leaves lying in the long grass.

'These are crushed but they haven't wilted yet, which means that a large animal passed this way within the last hour or so. That's called 'sign' and it's obvious to an experienced tracker. The hard part comes if whatever you're following crosses an area where it leaves little or no trace, like a river or bare rock. That's when you have to use psychology. Tendai says that people crossing a stretch of water unconsciously walk in the direction they intend to travel, even if they're trying not to.'

Martine listened in admiration. Until a couple of years ago when his sailor father moved the family to Storm Crossing, Ben had grown up in one of Cape Town's roughest inner city areas. Dumisani Khumalo had taken his son fishing, or out on boats whenever he could, but before Martine had invited Ben to Sawubona he'd never had an opportunity to be close to wild animals or out in the bush. And yet to see him now anyone would think that he'd been having wilderness adventures all his life.

Martine supposed that in that way, at least, they were the same – kids from the suburbs, delivered by fate to Sawubona, where they'd fallen totally in love with nature. That's why they connected. That's why they understood each other. That's why Ben was her best friend.

The afternoon sun lit the top of the waving grasses so they shone blond against the blue sky. Ben stood in his stirrups, holding on to Mambo's shaggy white mane for balance. 'Hey, Martine, look over there. The way the shadows fall on the bent grass show us the path the animal has taken.'

Martine shaded her eyes and saw that he was right. A wiggly line of shadow gave away the creature's route across the plain as surely as if it had been advertised with neon lights. A little further on they found a heap of fresh dung. Ben identified it as being from a rhino.

'Rhino?' said Martine, pulling up Tempest. 'What's a rhino doing here? Didn't Sadie tell us that, snakes aside, there's nothing scarier than antelope on Black Eagle land?'

'She did,' agreed Ben, giving up his attempt to stop Mambo guzzling grass. 'A rhino shouldn't be here. That probably means it's either broken through a fence or walked through a fence that's been cut by poachers. We'd better follow it.'

Martine looked at him uncertainly. 'Ben, if we carry on past that *kopje*, we'll reach the northern boundary fence. Remember what Sadie said about us not going near it in case we're accidentally shot.' Ever since her row with Gwyn Thomas about riding Jemmy at night – a row that had gone unresolved for weeks because it happened hours before Martine left Sawubona for a school trip – she'd been trying very hard to do the right thing.

'Oh.' Ben was crestfallen.

Martine's resolve weakened. After a moment's hesitation, she continued, 'Mind you, we'd feel really bad if we went back without doing anything and the rhino was shot by mistake. We know we have to be careful if we're anywhere near the Lazy J, but the rhino doesn't.'

'I agree,' Ben said, 'but how are we going to keep it away from the boundary fence? Rhinos are incredibly lethal. We can't just herd it away as though we're rounding up a cow.'

Martine gathered up Tempest's reins. 'Let's stop when we reach the other side of the *kopje*, check out the situation with binoculars and decide what to do next. My grandmother will kill me if I end up getting shot.'

They both laughed at that. After a brief battle with Mambo, who was so determined to eat his fill of grass that Martine had to reattach his lead rope and tie it to the back of Tempest's saddle, they continued on their way.

As soon as they rounded the *kopje*, they spotted the rhino. It was grazing under a tree. Luckily the wind direction was in their favour and rhino have poor eyesight, so it didn't notice them. It did, however, notice the sharp crack that suddenly split the air. Its horn jerked up and its piggy eyes swivelled as it tried to assess the threat. It didn't hang around for long. With astonishing speed, it tore around the *kopje* and out of view.

The combination of the rifle shot and the rhino's hasty exit was too much for Tempest, who bolted a few strides before being brought up short by Mambo's lead rope. He reared in panic. Martine had to use all her giraffe-riding experience to cling on and soothe him. If Ben's pony hadn't stayed relatively placid throughout, disaster would have quickly followed.

'What was that?' Martine demanded when she'd finally managed to settle the Arab. 'I know it was a gun shot, but who fired it? Were they trying to hit the rhino?'

Ben put the binoculars to his eyes. 'I don't think so,' he said. 'It looks like there's something going on at the Lazy J, but it's hard to make out what at this distance. There are a lot of people gathered around a sort of paddock enclosed by a high fence. Let's go a bit closer.'

They rode until they were practically touching the boundary fence that divided Black Eagle from the Lazy J. Martine felt guilty about going against Sadie's wishes, but she was as determined as Ben not to leave until they knew what had happened at the hunting lodge.

Ben lifted the glasses again. 'There's a man entering the enclosure on his own. He's wearing a hat and a khaki safari suit and he has a really big stomach. It's huge. He looks pregnant. He's holding something in his hand but I can't see what it is. Either a stick or a gun.'

'Let me look,' said Martine, reaching for the binoculars.

Ben held them out of range. 'Hold on a second. A small gate is opening in the wall and . . . Oh, wow. A male lion has come out. Martine, he's so beautiful. He has the most amazing dark mane and he's a tawny colour with big muscles.'

'Ben, please!' Martine begged, but before she could say anything else another shot rang out.

Ben's body went rigid. The colour fled from his face and an expression of absolute horror came over it.

'What is it, Ben?' cried Martine. 'What have you seen? Has something happened to the lion?'

'It's nothing,' he mumbled. 'Martine, let's get away from here. The Lazy J is a wicked place.' He looked as if he was about to cry. 'Come on, Mambo, let's go.'

Martine took advantage of his struggles with the pony to snatch the binoculars, which he'd hooked around the pommel of his saddle.

'No, Martine, don't!' yelled Ben.

But Martine had already wheeled Tempest and was lifting the glasses to her eyes. The lion lay dead on the ground. The hunter had one foot on its chest and one hand on his rifle and he was smiling and posing for photographs. The lion's blood was leaking out onto his boot, but he didn't seem to notice.

Tears started to pour down Martine's face. She put down the glasses, buried her head in Tempest's mane and sobbed uncontrollably. She wept for the proud lion, cut down without a chance so that a fat man could have a lion-skin rug in his home and a bloody photograph on his wall. She wept for the white giraffe whom she missed and who was safe at Sawubona when he, too, could so easily have lost his life to hunters. She wept for all the other animals whose fate it was to die alone and unloved at the hands of cruel, selfish human beings.

And gradually she became aware that Ben – the bravest boy she knew – was crying for exactly the same reasons.

That evening the sun, slipping below the ragged green hills, was the colour of blood, and as they rode home through the lengthening black shadows the rocks moaned just as Ngwenya had described, only it was not the voice of Mwali that Martine heard, but the cries of all the animals who would go helplessly to their graves at the Lazy J unless she and Ben did something to prevent it.

· 9 ·

'Canned Hunting,' Sadie said heavily. 'That's what it's called.'

They'd confronted her soon after returning to Black Eagle, their faces dusty and streaked with tears. She and Martine's grandmother had come rushing to meet them at the stables, ready to scold them for returning so late, but Sadie had taken one look at them and dispatched Gwyn Thomas, protesting loudly, to deal with dinner. Ngwenya wouldn't hear of them feeding or rubbing down their horses. They'd ended up sitting outside the stables with Sadie who'd listened without saying anything to their passionate account of the

75

horror they'd witnessed at the Lazy J.

Now they were gathered around the kitchen table in the flickering candlelight. It was spring in Southern Africa and the temperature still dropped steeply at night so there was a crackling fire burning in the grate. Under any other circumstances, Martine thought, the scene would have been magical.

Gwyn Thomas said, 'What is canned hunting?'

'It's when animals which are dangerous, rare, or hard to track, such as lion, leopard or rhino, are put into small enclosures in order for hunters to safely and easily shoot them,' Sadie explained. 'These hunters are usually rich tourists or powerful men like government ministers who want a guaranteed kill with minimum risk. They want to go home with a skin or a horn or a couple of tusks, and tell stories about how they stalked and shot a deadly wild animal.

'Rex Ratcliffe, who owns the Lazy J, has always claimed that he is running a respectable safari and hunting operation, but Ngwenya and I have suspected for many years that he is up to all sorts of tricks, including canned hunting. What you've seen today proves it. I'm sorry you had to witness that. I hope you can put it behind you and enjoy the rest of your stay at Black Eagle.' She reached for a serving plate. 'Anyone for butternut fritters?'

Martine couldn't believe her ears. Sadie had as good as told them that her next-door neighbour was murdering wildlife in cold blood. She couldn't seriously expect them to continue their holiday without a care.

As for the fritters, well, Martine liked butternut squash as much as anyone, but after almost a week of eating it for breakfast, lunch and dinner, she was heartily tired of it. She found it peculiar that the groceries they'd brought had gone into the locked pantry and never come out again, but suspected that if times were as hard at Black Eagle as they appeared to be, Sadie was probably saving the interesting food for any visitors who might show up. Not that it mattered this evening. Every time her stomach rumbled Martine remembered the lion and felt sick again.

'You must eat something,' urged her grandmother. 'Have some potatoes or even just a slice of bread and peanut butter.'

Martine took a few potatoes to keep Gwyn Thomas happy but did little more than move them round her plate. Across the table, Ben was doing the same.

Sadie seemed determined to ensure there was no more talk of hunting or dead lions. She launched into a dreary rant about the high price of spare parts for cars. Martine started to simmer. She was fed up with Sadie pretending that everything at Black Eagle was completely fine when it obviously wasn't. The fire was making her very hot and that didn't help her mood either.

Ben seemed to guess what she was about to do and gave a warning shake of his head. When she ignored him, he kicked her under the table. Martine took no notice. She waited until Sadie paused for breath and said, 'Why are you being blackmailed?'

Sadie's fork paused on the way to her mouth. Her

fingers lost coordination and she dropped it with a clatter.

'Martine!' her grandmother said angrily. 'Have you taken complete leave of your senses? What on earth are you talking about? Apologize to Sadie at once.'

Sadie was staring at Martine. 'What did you say?'

'It *is* blackmail, isn't it?' Martine demanded, risking her grandmother's wrath. 'Whose blood money don't you want? Who are you trying to hold on to? Is it Ngwenya?'

Gwyn Thomas jumped to her feet. 'This is outrageous. I've heard more than enough. Martine, go to bed at once and we'll talk about this in the morning. I'm so sorry, Sadie. I've no idea what's got into her.'

Sadie stopped her. 'Sit down, Gwyn,' she ordered. 'You too, Martine. You've done nothing wrong. Quite the reverse. Ever since I telephoned you at Sawubona and asked you to come here, I've been wracked with guilt. I felt I was deceiving you all, asking you to come here and not telling you what you might be letting yourselves in for. But I was desperate. When I broke my leg, I had no one else to turn to. No one else I trusted enough to ask, at any rate. Ngwenya has been wonderful, but he has a family to go home to at night. I guess I was afraid.'

Gwyn Thomas seemed unsure whether to be curious or furious. 'But who are you afraid of? Are there bandits around here? Poachers?'

'No,' responded Sadie. 'At least, yes, of course there are, but it's not them that I'm afraid of. I'm not really afraid of anyone. I'm afraid *for* someone . . . Well, not someone as such . . . '

Gwyn Thomas sat back in her chair. 'Now I'm really confused.'

Sadie sighed. 'Let's make a strong coffee,' she said. 'I think I need to explain from the beginning.'

It all started when Sadie's father, Colonel Scott, agreed to rehabilitate a young leopard into the wild on Black Eagle land on behalf of a famous Bulawayo wildlife orphanage, Chipangali. The project was an instant success. The leopard, a male named Khan after the Indian doctor who'd found him as a week-old cub, orphaned by a bushfire, took to the Matobo Hills as if he'd been in the wilderness all his life.

'You told us that you'd only seen him once,' Martine reminded Sadie. 'It must have been more often than that if your father was rehabilitating him.'

Sadie gave a small smile. 'No, I was telling you the truth about that. I saw Khan the day he came to Black Eagle, but the following day I had to leave for South Africa for a hotel management course I was booked on. When I returned Khan had already made his home in the bush and was as elusive as any other leopard.

'At the time of my father's death a little over a year ago, our main feeling regarding the leopard was pride, I suppose. Animals belong in the wild, not behind bars

79

like prisoners, and we were proud that we'd been able to give Khan his freedom. Our problems started when I began to get reports of his immense size from the few people who glimpsed him. Male leopards have a territory of up to forty kilometres square. I'd hear tales of his magnificence from far and wide. Once he was grown, he no longer stayed exclusively on Black Eagle property.

'Four months ago, I was approached by Rex Ratcliffe. He offered me several thousand pounds in foreign currency if I would sell him Khan for use in one of his 'safaris'. I was sure that he really wanted him for canned hunting, but in any case I said that Khan was not mine to sell. He was free and that was the way he was going to stay. I told Ratcliffe that if I ever caught him or any of his hunters near my land, I'd shoot him myself.'

Martine was on the edge of her seat. 'Go on,' she encouraged as Sadie stoked the fire with the tip of one of her crutches.

'Khan was only ever seen in two areas – Black Eagle and the Matobo National Park. Since the wildlife in the national park is protected, Ratcliffe focussed his efforts on Black Eagle. He began to blackmail me. He did it in ways so subtle that I could never prove he was behind it, but it was obvious. Tour operators started calling me to say they'd heard rats had been found in Black Eagle kitchens. Rumours circulated of thieving staff and dirty rooms. Within weeks, my business had all but dried up at the retreat. To add to our problems, five of our cattle died mysteriously, probably from poisoning, and one of our main waterholes was contaminated. Plus the guards on the national park gate gave me trouble when I travelled to and from Bulawayo. I held out for as long as I could, but last month I was forced to lay off most of my staff. Then, of course, I broke my leg slipping on a greasy substance that had been left on my doorstep, and had to call you.'

'Did you contact the police?' asked Gwyn Thomas.

'What could I say? There's absolutely no evidence to connect Ratcliffe or the Lazy J to what's going on.'

'What about the phone call?' Ben suggested. 'There'll be phone records. You could tell the police that he's been threatening you.'

Sadie gave a dry laugh. 'Rex Ratcliffe's much too smart for that. He uses an unlisted number, which means that no number appears on the telephone bill. And he's very careful to be polite and not use threats. He always calls a couple of days after something bad has happened, such as the poisoning of the cattle, and offers me more and more money for Khan. He talks to me as if I'm senile and too simple to know what I'm turning down. He says things like, "Think about it. It's not as if Black Eagle's doing very well these days, is it now, Sadie?"

'"The Rat", as I call him, partly because he bears a remarkable resemblance to a rodent, believes everyone has a price. He doesn't understand what it is to love a person or animal so much that you would lay down your life for them.'

She looked around sheepishly. 'You don't think I'm senile as well, do you?'

'I don't,' Martine told her. 'I can totally understand what it's like to love an animal so much you'd do anything for them. That's how I feel about Jemmy, my white giraffe. He's—'

'Let's have no more talk of laying down lives,' interrupted her grandmother. 'Let's talk about solutions. However, I'm upset with you, Sadie, for not telling me this before we came. I'm responsible for Martine and Ben and it was unfair of you not to inform me what was going on so that I could use my judgement about whether or not it was safe to bring them.'

'I'm sorry,' Sadie mumbled. 'I know I did the wrong thing. But I was sure that if you knew the truth you wouldn't come.'

'Having said that,' Gwyn Thomas went on, 'I can appreciate what an ordeal this must have been for you, and since we are here I think I speak for Martine and Ben when I say that we'll do everything we can to help you keep Black Eagle Lodge and protect Khan. We just have to figure out how.'

Martine and Ben voiced their enthusiastic agreement, and Martine was very proud of her grandmother for caring so much about helping her friend and saving the leopard that she was willing to overlook Sadie's deception. Still, she couldn't help thinking back to Ngwenya's words about the treasure seekers' quest: 'In order to find the treasure, the leopard first has to be dead.'

That meant they were up against two groups of potential leopard assassins: Ngwenya's cousin and his gold-digging *shamwaris*, whom she and Ben had promised Ngwenya they wouldn't speak about, and Rex Ratcliffe and goodness knows how many hunters from the Lazy J.

'Thank you all for your kindness,' Sadie said, her eyes shiny in the firelight. 'You've no idea how much it means to me. But I have to be honest with you. We have a fight on our hands and I want you to be under no illusions about how difficult that fight will be. The Rat and his hunters want the leopard. They want Khan. And they won't stop until they get him.'

· 10 ·

Martine was being buried alive. Moist, cool earth – earth that smelled of worms and rotting leaves – was filling her mouth and eyes and ears, and as fast as she tried to spit it out or push it away from her, more came in. She tried to scream, but no sound came out of her mouth. She tried to run, but her legs wouldn't work.

'Martine. Martine, wake up.'

Martine sat up in bed, gulping for oxygen, relieved when no sand or worms came with it. Her eyes adjusted to the darkness. Ben was standing in front of the window, his small, strong frame backlit by a sky of glittering stars. He was fully dressed.

'Hey, I didn't mean to scare you,' he whispered. 'Were you having a nightmare or something? Are you all right?'

Martine rubbed the sleep from her eyes. 'What time is it?'

'It's a little after four a.m. I know it's awfully early but I can't sleep. I keep thinking about Khan. I feel like we need to find him. How can we protect him when we don't even know where he is?'

Instantly Martine was alert. 'You're right. We have to find him so we can figure out a way to save him. But what are we going to tell Sadie and my grandmother? Somehow I don't think they'll agree to us going in search of one of the world's biggest leopards in pitch darkness, even if we are trying to help him.'

'We'll leave a note telling them we've gone on an early morning ride,' said Ben. 'Which is true. We *are* going on an early morning ride. It's just that it'll be a few hours earlier than usual, and we'll be keeping an eye out for a leopard at the same time.'

Put like that the plan sounded perfectly reasonable, so Martine hopped out of bed and put on her jeans, boots, and a sweatshirt while Ben went to write a note for Sadie and Gwyn Thomas. On the way out of the cottage, they filled their pockets with buttermilk rusks, the only treat that hadn't disappeared into Sadie's locked pantry. As they hadn't touched their dinner the previous night, they were ravenously hungry.

The hornbill was the only one to see them go. He followed them to the stables and watched with his head cocked as they saddled the horses by torchlight.

'Don't you ever get any sleep, Magnus?' Martine asked the bird, jumping to intercept him as he hopped slyly towards her shimmering pink Maglite on the stable floor. 'And I've told you before, keep your claws off my stuff.'

They took the path around Elephant Rock, keeping to the grassy edges so that the horses' hooves were muffled. 'Shhh, Sirocco,' said Martine as the Arab gave a series of loud sneezes and jingled her bit in the process. Ben was riding Cassidy and Martine was leading Jack.

They were at the gates of Ngwenya's village in under ten minutes. The silhouettes of the hut roofs looked like pyramids under the night sky. They tied up the horses and entered through the main gate. The smell of sadza – the maize meal porridge that is the staple food of Zimbabweans – hung in the air, mingled with the smoky smell of old fires. A sleeping dog roused itself and gave a few feeble barks, but Ben stroked it and it quietened.

Ngwenya had pointed out his home when they'd been riding one day, so they had no trouble locating it. They knocked on his door and he stumbled out blinking.

'What are you doing here?' he said in alarm. 'Do Gogo and Mrs Thomas know you are here? Is there trouble at the house?'

Ben assured him that everything was fine and briefly filled him in on the events of the previous afternoon and evening, which he hadn't heard because he'd been tending to the horses.

'So you see, we have to find the leopard,' Martine said

eagerly. 'We can't protect him if we don't know where he is. Only we need your help because we wouldn't even know where to start. Especially in the dark.'

Ngwenya gave a snort of laughter. 'Do you know how difficult it is to find this leopard? I myself have never seen him. There are many, many caves and tunnels and hiding places in these hills. It is impossible. Go back to sleep and at breakfast you can speak to Gogo.'

Martine tried not to let her irritation show. 'But you must have some idea where he is,' she persisted. 'From time to time people must have mentioned to you that they've glimpsed him on this hill or that one. We could start by going to the last place anyone saw him. He might not be there any more, but maybe Ben could track him to his new den.'

'*Hayikona*,' Ngwenya said stubbornly. 'No. Gogo and Mrs Thomas will be too angry with me. First you must speak with them. This is not a cat from your house you are looking for. This is a leopard which can kill you with one paw.'

'This is also a leopard that the hunters can kill with one bullet if we don't stop them,' Martine pointed out.

Ngwenya went back into his hut without another word and slammed the door.

'We're wasting our time,' said Ben. 'He's not going to change his mind.'

Martine put her mouth close to the clay wall of the hut. 'What about your cousin?' she said loudly. 'I thought it was your clan oath to protect the leopard. Does anyone else in the clan know that your cousin and his friends want the leopard dead so they can get their hands on Lobengula's treasure?'

The hut door flew open. 'Please,' implored Ngwenya. 'You must not speak of these things. There are people in this village who are not of our clan.'

'Then will you help us?'

He stared at her in exasperation. 'I don't know where to find him,' he said. 'There are only rumours, stories. Nobody knows for sure.'

Martine's gaze was unflinching. 'You know in your heart where he is.'

Ngwenya dropped his eyes. It was plain that he was wrestling with his conscience. Finally he came to a decision. 'Wait,' he said, 'I will get my shoes and my rifle.'

The sheer rock was rough and warm beneath Martine's fingertips. Thanks to the long hours spent on horseback, time she wasn't able to spend riding the white giraffe during term time, she was much fitter than she had been when she first arrived at Black Eagle. But it was still a stiff climb up a seemingly endless granite mountain.

At the very top was a cave. Unlike the Memory Room in the Secret Valley, this one was open to the air and formed of a rock so pale it was almost white. In the fading blue of the departing night, it was visible from quite a distance. A pillar-shaped boulder stood like a sentinel at its entrance, which was perfectly round. As they approached, they could see the cave was decorated with vivid Bushmen paintings and that there was a narrow tunnel tucked away in the back.

'This is the last place that the leopard was seen,' Ngwenya said, gesturing with the rifle he'd brought in case of an emergency. 'But it is many weeks since I heard this.'

'Martine, Ngwenya and I will go down the tunnel to see if we can find any trace of him,' Ben said. 'It's too dangerous for all three of us to go at once. You keep a look out.'

'No!' Martine cried in panic. 'We can't be separated. Remember Grace's warning.'

'Don't worry,' Ben said. 'We won't be gone long and we won't be far away. If you need us, yell, and we'll come running.'

Ngwenya agreed. 'It's much safer for you here. If the leopard is in his den, we will be exiting as fast as cheetahs. Two will be quicker than three.'

'And we need someone on guard,' Ben added. 'If the leopard is out hunting and comes back when we're inside the cave, it'll be a disaster.'

Martine wasn't at all happy about being left alone, but she didn't want them to think she was a coward either. And it was important that someone kept watch.

After they'd gone, she tried to take her mind off her fears by being a good security guard and keeping a very close eye on the valley below. In the few minutes since their arrival, a blush of orange had crept above the horizon. Dawn was on its way. Martine started to feel better. There was something about the rising of the sun that helped chase away the lingering anxiety caused by her nightmare.

She took off her sweatshirt and tossed it onto a nearby rock, and a cool breeze brushed her skin. All around her the hills of the Matopos unfurled in lumpy folds of green and brown. Boulders like domes and spires and beasts and birds perched, reared or leaned precariously. As far as Martine could tell, the only things moving in the shadowed valley below were the horses tethered at the bottom of the mountain. A lone *dassie*, a favourite food of leopards, sniffed along the base of the cave until it saw it had company and darted away.

As it grew lighter, Martine went over to examine the paintings. She never tired of looking at cave pictures, finding them endlessly fascinating and thrilling, and the sketches here were especially well-preserved. Their dusky pink, grey and ochre colours had survived thousands of years with barely a blemish. There were the usual scenes of hunts, feasts and ceremonies, but she was surprised to find that there were quite a lot of similarities between these pictures and those in the Memory Room cave at Sawubona, almost as if they were the work of the same artist. She supposed that the painting techniques of the San had been handed down through the generations.

One image was set slightly apart. Martine wandered over to take a look at it. It showed a girl standing at the entrance to a cave – the cave Martine was in now, if its round mouth and sentinel-like pillar were anything to go by. And crouched on the pillar, as if it were about to pounce, was a leopard – the leopard she'd seen in the sand.

Martine froze. What if *she* was the girl in the picture? What if the leopard . . . ?

But she knew the answer even before she'd finished the thought.

She smelt him before she saw him. It wasn't an unpleasant smell – if anything, there was something wonderful about it. It was the scent of a wild, free thing. But it was also the smell of a killer.

At Sawubona, Martine had rehearsed this moment a hundred times in case she was ever confronted by a predator when out riding Jemmy. But in her imagination she'd always been able to gallop away on the white giraffe. Now she was alone.

She dragged her eyes upwards. The leopard was on the ledge above her, regal both in stature and in size. His creamy gold coat had the rich sheen of the finest silk, his black spots gleamed, and his yellow eyes blazed like topaz fires. She had always admired leopards in photographs, always yearned to see an adult one in real life. Her glimpse of the rescued leopard cubs at Sawubona had been brief because Tendai had been anxious to return them to their mother. But nothing could have prepared her for the unquenchable spirit of Khan in the flesh. Power and wildness radiated from him.

With one bound, he smashed her to the earth. His great paws thudded against her chest and his claws pierced her skin, and then she was on the ground, winded and in pain. She could feel blood trickling down her armpit.

Khan stood over her, his huge paws on either side of her body. The look in his eyes was one of undiluted fury and hatred. She knew he'd kill her without a care. He gave a savage snarl and his whiskered lips curled back over pink gums. His teeth were so close to her throat that Martine could feel his hot breath on her face.

'Yell and we'll come running,' Ben had promised, but she'd be dead long before he could get to her and Khan would probably die too, because in spite of his clan oath Ngwenya wouldn't hesitate to shoot the leopard to try to save her.

Twice in the past, Martine's gift had allowed her to halt a deadly attack: once when a rottweiller dog had tried to stop her from rescuing Jemmy, and another time when a Great White shark was on the verge of eating an American tourist. But that had required concentration and a supreme effort of will, and now she was so frightened she was incapable of summoning either of those things. She lay on the ground like a blob of jelly. And yet she couldn't hate the leopard for what he was about to do to her. There were very good reasons for his loathing of humans. She understood that he was afraid himself.

But there was something else in his yellow eyes, something besides hatred and fear. There was a sadness and tiredness that seemed bone-deep, as if he was exhausted by the endless struggle to survive. And it was those things that made Martine realize that, even without knowing him, she cared for him. She felt the same pure love for the leopard she'd felt for Jemmy on the night they'd first met.

'Please don't hurt me,' she said to Khan. 'All I want to do is help you.'

The leopard roared. She recognized it as the defiant, rage-filled sound she'd heard on the first night at Black Eagle. At close quarters, it was bloodcurdling.

There was a drumbeat echo of footsteps as Ben and Ngwenya returned at speed. Martine wasn't sure which she feared most – that Khan would maul her before they could reach her, or that they'd reach her in time but shoot him to save her. She was about to close her eyes and pray that the end, whether it was the leopard's or her own, was quick, when some of the wildness seemed to leave Khan. He gave her a last, unfathomable look before melting away into the bush. Martine scrambled to her feet and dusted herself off.

Ben burst out of the tunnel mouth first. 'Martine! Martine! Oh, thank God you're okay. Did you hear that roar? It nearly frightened the life out of us. We should never have left you. I don't know what I was thinking. It just seemed the safest thing to do.'

He suddenly became aware that Martine wasn't saying anything. Then he noticed the red specks on her T-shirt. 'Is that blood?'

It was on the tip of Martine's tongue to tell him about Khan, but then Ngwenya came rushing over and wanted them to leave right away in case Khan was still in the vicinity, and Martine realized that there was no way of putting into words what had just taken place.

How could she say that the leopard which had eluded rangers who'd worked in the Matopos for twenty years had knocked her to the ground and stood over her with the clear intention of killing her, but that something had passed between them – an understanding – and at the last conceivable second he'd changed his mind.

How could she explain that she'd looked into his blazing yellow eyes and seen beyond the hatred to the weary sadness of a creature hunted almost every day of his existence? How could she explain that without even knowing him, she loved him?

'I'm fine,' she replied. 'I slipped on a rock, that's all. I did hear the roar and I was a bit scared, but I knew you were close by. I knew you'd come running if I needed you, and you did.'

11

They rode back through the honeyed light of the breaking morning, munching on rusks. All three of them were lost in thought. Martine was thinking about Khan, and if and when she'd ever see him again. She was determined to do everything in her power to protect him from Rex Ratcliffe's evil hunters.

Ben was thinking about Cassidy, who never seemed to go where she was meant to go, and he was thinking about Martine. He was positive she'd seen the leopard, and not only seen him, but been clawed by him. But far from being upset that she hadn't admitted it, her silence on the subject made him admire her even more.

Ben couldn't stand vain or boastful people. He knew perfectly well that, with the exception of Martine, there was not one kid in Caracal Junior School who could have survived an encounter with the largest wild leopard ever recorded and not gloated about it forever and wanted to see themselves on the evening news.

Martine was the opposite of them. She'd done what she thought was best for Khan. He watched her guide Sirocco skilfully over a narrow stream and up the bank on the other side and grinned to himself. He couldn't have wished for a better best friend.

Ngwenya, meanwhile, was feeling like a failure. Ever since Khan's release into the wild at Black Eagle he'd vowed to do whatever was necessary to keep the leopard out of the hands of hunters and poachers, but it had taken two children who were not even from the Matopos to spur him into action and point out the most obvious thing: how can you save the leopard if you don't even know where he is?

Ngwenya had helped Colonel Scott set Khan free, and it had been clear to him even then that this was no ordinary leopard. Khan's paws had been the size of baseball mitts. Ngwenya was desperately disappointed to have been so close to the leopard again and yet miss him. Like Ben, he was certain that Martine had seen the leopard. It seemed to have scratched her. It was puzzling that she'd not breathed a word about it and was now riding her horse quite contentedly as if being clawed by leopards was an everyday event for her.

There was no doubt that she was a most unusual

child. She looked perfectly ordinary with her cropped brown hair, green eyes and skinny limbs, but he'd noticed that Magnus and the horses had formed very strong attachments to her. Then there was this business of her riding a giraffe. Clearly there was much more to her than met the eye.

It was almost eight a.m. when the trio rounded Elephant Rock, riding three abreast. The first thing they saw was a blue-and-white-striped car in the retreat driveway, visible through the gum trees. Ngwenya suddenly yanked at Martine and Ben's bridles, pulling up their horses with a start.

'The police,' he whispered. He put a finger to his lips and dismounted rapidly, indicating that they should do the same.

'The police?' cried Martine, forgetting to keep her voice down. 'Then what are we waiting for?' She sprang off her horse. 'I'm going to run and see what's going on. My grandmother or Sadie might have had an accident. There could have been a robbery. Anything could have happened.'

'No!' Ngwenya snatched her back roughly. 'In this country, the police can be more dangerous than the criminals. Maybe they are on a routine patrol or maybe they have been called by Gogo and your grandmother, but we must approach with caution.'

They led the horses back the way they came and tied them up beneath an overhang screened by trees. Then they crept round the back of the stables and through the gum trees until they were within spitting distance of the police car. A low stone wall provided them with cover. Nothing happened for a few minutes and then Sadie and Gwyn Thomas emerged from the house with two policemen. Martine gasped. Her grandmother was in handcuffs and Sadie was remonstrating with a young constable who was gripping her arm as she swung along on crutches.

'I'm not going to deny I told Mr Rat that I'd shoot him and his hunters if they set foot on my land . . . ' she was saying unrepentantly.

'Mr Rat*cliffe*,' corrected the constable. 'His name is Mr Ratcliffe.'

Sadie frowned. 'Whatever. I'd tell him the same thing again. But that's a very different thing from actually doing it – shooting him, that is. Mr Rat is still alive, isn't he?'

'Sadie,' interjected Gwyn Thomas, appalled, 'I think the less said the better, don't you? Let's cooperate with these nice policeman and go down to the station and I'm sure we'll have it all sorted out in no time.'

'Why you want to kill Mr Rat— er, Mr Ratcliffe?' demanded the other policeman. 'Are you jealous that his business is doing well and Black Eagle Lodge is in some difficulty?'

'Don't be ridiculous,' snapped Sadie. 'How can I be jealous of a man whose business is murdering animals? And besides, if Black Eagle is in difficulty it's because Mr Rat has driven away all my customers. It's him you should be arresting, not me, and certainly not my friend who has done absolutely nothing.'

'Sadie,' cried Gwyn Thomas, 'not another word. Do you want them to lock us up and throw away the key? Officer, can you read us our rights?'

The young constable looked bemused to be asked to do his job. Behind the wall, Ngwenya and the children were struggling to take in this bizarre turn of events. 'You have the right to remain silent,' the constable parroted dutifully. 'Anything you say can and will be held against you . . . '

'Wait,' said the other policeman. 'Where is the man who usually works with you? Ngwenya, is it? Also, Mr Ratcliffe mentioned some children.'

Fear flitted across Gwyn Thomas's face.

'How did he . . . ?' Sadie began. 'Never mind. Yes, you are quite correct, Mrs Thomas's granddaughter and a boy, Ben, were here, but you know how children are these days – in constant need of entertainment. They were bored in the bush with nothing to do. They missed television or video games or something. I had Ngwenya take them to Bulawayo to stay with some friends of mine for three or four days. He had some business in the city. He was going to spend time there and bring them back towards the end of the week.'

'Kids, they are very expensive,' agreed the young constable moodily. 'All the time my son is wanting new shoes, new clothes, new CDs, new books for school. And he is always eating. I tell him . . . '

'Shut up, Shepherd,' said the surly policeman. 'You talk too much. Let's take these women down to the station.'

The officers were marching their unlikely prisoners to

the car when Magnus flew down from the trees and landed on the wall. He hopped along the chestnut bricks until he was close to Martine, and then cocked his head and opened his beak as if he was about to start chatting to her.

From her crouching position, Martine tried to wave him away before he drew attention to them. Ngwenya even prodded him with a stick. But the hornbill just hopped out of range.

'What is that funny bird doing?' enquired the policeman, locking Gwyn Thomas in the back of the car and striding in their direction.

Through a hole in the wall, Martine saw it dawn on Sadie why Magnus was behaving so oddly. 'I wouldn't go too near if I were you,' she cautioned the policeman. 'You've heard about the deadly bird flu which kills human beings within twenty-four hours? Well, it's been proven that hornbills are particularly likely to get it. That hornbill has been sneezing for days.'

Magnus chose that very second to swoop off the wall and make a lunge for the keys that dangled, gleaming, from the policeman's belt.

The policeman screamed like a girl. 'Get away, sick bird,' he squawked, flapping his arms. 'Get away!' He dived into the car and turned on the ignition.

Sadie took advantage of the distraction to say loudly, 'I'm really glad that the children aren't here, because if they were they'd be worried about us and there's really no reason to be. This is a ridiculous misunderstanding. We'll be back by lunchtime, I'm sure. But whatever happens, it's nice to know that they'll be safe with Ngwenya. He'll take care of them.'

'Why are you shouting when I am right here?' barked the constable. He bundled her into the back seat, tossing her crutches in after her. 'Get a move on. You are making us late.'

The police car departed in a crunch of gravel. The engine faded and the blanketing silence descended once more.

Martine felt ill. Usually it was her grandmother who worried about her. Now it was the other way round.

'What do we do now?' Ben said.

Ngwenya's face was grim. 'We make a plan.'

12

'Don't you bring trouble to our door.'

The speaker was Ngwenya's uncle's wife, Mercy. She stood with her arms folded like a bodyguard, glowering at the horse wrangler. A baby was strapped to her back with a towel. Her husband, a wiry man a third of her size with the mournful expression of a bloodhound, trembled slightly at her side. His eyes never left the ground, although from time to time he stooped to pet two mongrels.

Mercy jerked her chin towards Martine and Ben, whom she hadn't even greeted. 'My baby is not well. She has been crying all day. We have many problems and now you ask us to hide the children of a grandmother wanted by the police. Ha! You are very irresponsible, Ngwenya.'

Martine thought it might be the wrong moment to inform her that a) Gwyn Thomas was not wanted by the police but had been wrongfully arrested; and b) Ben was not her half-brother.

Mercy shook her head in disgust. 'You are very irresponsible, Ngwenya,' she said again. 'Do you think we want trouble coming to our house? Do you think we need the police at our door?'

Ngwenya threw an anguished glance at Martine and Ben. 'Mercy, please,' he begged. 'These are two innocent children. Gogo and Martine's grandmother are also innocent. They need our help. I cannot keep them in my own village because it is too near to the retreat. You would not want somebody to turn away baby Emelia if she is ever in need of sanctuary when she is older. It is not their fault this has happened. It is the fault of Mr Ratcliffe.'

Mercy said sharply, 'Mr Ratcliffe? What has Mr Rat been doing now?'

'He is the reason that Black Eagle Lodge is going out of business,' Ngwenya told her. 'He is the reason that Gogo has had to lay off most of her staff. I have not spoken of this to anyone because I promised her I would not, but he has made her life hell by starting rumours about thieving employees and dirty rooms. He has poisoned our cattle and threatened Gogo. We can't prove it, but we know he is behind these things. It is blackmail.'

Mercy was briefly dumbstruck. 'But why? What reason would he have to make his neighbour suffer like this?'

'He wants the leopard. Gogo would not allow him to buy Khan so that he or his hunters could kill him, and he is not a man who understands the word no. She warned him she would shoot him if he came on our land, and he sent the police to arrest her. They have taken Martine's grandmother for no reason.'

Mercy addressed Martine and Ben for the first time. 'This man Rat cost my husband his job,' she said. 'Odilo, my husband, was a proud man, but Mr Ratcliffe has friends in the government and together they shut down the mine where Odilo worked because it was close to the edge of Mr Ratcliffe's land. Now Odilo has a lot of sadness and life is not easy for us. There is little money. But an enemy of Mr Ratcliffe is a friend to us. You will stay here, of course. Please, sit down for a cup of tea.'

Martine was worried sick about her grandmother, but she found the experience of being in an African village fascinating. The huts had thatched roofs like inverted ice-cream cones, and their clay walls were prettily decorated. They were insulated with cow dung to keep them cool during the day and warm at night. Inside, mattresses with woven quilts were placed on platforms of bricks, raised to keep the sleeper safe from the dwarf spirit Tokoloshe, who, Mercy told them, kidnapped his victims and took them down to his watery den. Everything had the faint smell of woodsmoke.

Chickens pecked around the outdoor cooking area, where two women were pounding maize into the meal used to make sadza porridge. The village was set on the edge of a large, flat plain, across which could be seen the low grey buildings of a school. Behind Martine and Ben's temporary home, a red-brown hut with zigzag patterns, was a circle of low *kopjes*, shaggy with shrubs and trees. The hills formed a natural paddock with only one exit. Mambo, Sirocco and Red Mist were in there grazing with the cattle and sheep. Ngwenya was planning to return to Black Eagle for the night so that he could keep an eye on the retreat and take care of the other horses.

Apart from the rhythmic thud of the *mielie* crushers, the village was quiet, so quiet that any approaching police car would be heard for miles.

'Don't be frightened for Sadie and Mrs Thomas,' Ngwenya counselled Ben and Martine. 'They've done nothing wrong and will be home very soon. Not even Mr Ratcliffe can make the police lock away innocent people for more than one or two days. They are just going to question them and release them – maybe even by this afternoon.'

The thing that bothered Martine was what would happen if her grandmother and Sadie didn't return to Black Eagle in a matter of days. She and Ben could hardly ride their horses through the streets of Bulawayo, like characters out of a cowboy film, and demand that the women were freed. An unfamiliar feeling of powerlessness had come over her as Gwyn Thomas was driven away.

Ever since she'd returned from the island, she and her grandmother had grown closer and closer. For the first six months after her parents died, a little part of Martine had kept expecting to wake up and find that the fire had been a hideous nightmare and they weren't really dead after all. She'd kept thinking that at any second her mum would walk through the door, or her dad would grab her around the waist and tickle her until she cried with laughter. But at a certain point, a little over a month ago, she'd realized that it was never going to happen. She was never going to see her parents again. It was then that her grandmother, Jemmy and Ben had become the centre of her world. She depended on them utterly. And now two of those loved ones were far away and she didn't know when, or if, they'd all be reunited.

Ben read her thoughts. He was very concerned about how long it would be before he saw his own parents again, and more than a little worried about what he and Martine had got themselves into in pursuing the leopard, but he was determined to be strong for Martine's sake. He said, 'There's no point in dwelling on what we can't do. Let's figure out what we can do.'

'I don't know what that is,' Martine burst out. 'I don't know where to begin.'

'Why don't we start with the Lazy J?' Ben suggested.

13

That evening, the aroma of chicken sizzling over the coals and the nutty smell of bubbling sadza filled the air. Mouths watering, Martine and Ben warmed themselves beside the fire as the villagers buzzed around them, cooking, chopping, preparing. Martine could imagine that on most nights a relaxed, sociable atmosphere of community and friendship would prevail in the village, but tonight there was tension in the faces of the men, women and even children. Mercy's baby had a fever and was now desperately ill. Odilo had sent for the witchdoctor.

When the baby finally fell asleep, Mercy joined them

for the meal, although Martine noticed that she barely touched her food.

'How is Emelia?' enquired Ngwenya.

Mercy's expression told him all he needed to know. 'I would feel much better if I knew we didn't have to depend on the witchdoctor,' she said. 'He is the best we have, but he has a weakness for . . . '

She trailed off in mid-sentence. 'Let us hope that he has had a good day.'

Martine and Ben followed the lead of Ngwenya who, like everyone else, ate with his hands, rolling the sadza into snowy balls which he used to scoop up chicken pieces and a spicy relish of spinach and tomato. He and Odilo were interested in Sawubona and asked lots of questions. Odilo wanted to know if the game reserve had what rangers called the Big Five: lion, leopard, rhino, elephant and buffalo.

'It does,' Martine said proudly. 'We don't have any cheetahs though. We do have three leopards – a mother and two cubs. They were given to Sawubona by a wildlife park that went out of business. I've seen the cubs but never the mother. She's very elusive.'

'Here in the Matopos, we have the Small Five,' Ngwenya told her with a grin.

'The *Small* Five?'

He counted them off on his fingers. 'The Leopard Tortoise, the Rhino Beetle, the Ant Lion, the Elephant Shrew and the Buffalo Weaver!'

Everyone laughed and for a moment the gloom over the village was lifted.

Before Ngwenya could continue, the dogs bounded up barking. Martine glanced nervously at Ben.

'Who's there?' Odilo called out.

Out of the night strode a tall young man dressed very smartly in a shirt, tie and trilby. He had a handsome face, blighted by a perpetual sneer, and smelled quite strongly of cologne.

Martine stared at him in shock. It was Ngwenya's cousin.

The cousin who wanted the leopard dead.

'Good evening, good evening,' he said pleasantly, though it was obvious that no one in the circle was pleased to see him. 'I am in time for supper? That is great news. Thank you, Mercy. It's very nice of you to make it for me.'

He unfolded a plastic sheet from his pocket, sat cross-legged on it and took off his hat. 'Pass me a bowl, Ngwenya.'

Ngwenya made no move to hand it to him, but he took one anyway and helped himself to a large portion of everything. He was sucking the marrow out of a chicken bone when his dark eyes alighted on the young strangers.

He flashed Martine and Ben a sinister smile. Thrusting out his hand so they had no choice but to take it, he said. 'My name is Griffin. How do you do?'

'What are you doing here, Griffin?' Ngwenya demanded. 'You are not welcome.'

Griffin did not seem in the least offended by this comment. He bit the top off another chicken drumstick, drained it of marrow and said placidly, 'Ah, my cousin, you will be singing a different song when I come home with Lobengula's treasure. I will be welcome then, I am sure. Any day now I will be returning with sacks full of diamonds and gold sovereigns and then all of you will want to be my friend.'

'Griffin, my son, you are talking nonsense,' Odilo said in his quiet way, and Martine started at the revelation that shy, mournful Odilo was father to this sharp-dressing vagabond.

Mercy's face was expressionless. She heaved herself to her feet and went to her hut to be with her child. Odilo soon followed.

The atmosphere around the fire was strained. For a while there was no sound but the crackling of the smouldering wood. Then, to Martine's astonishment, Ben asked, 'What will you do with the treasure if you find it, Griffin?'

Griffin seemed pleased to be asked. He said grandly, 'I will buy a Mercedes Benz and a house with many bathrooms and a flat-screen television in Bulawayo. I will fly to England first class and buy some suits for myself. Some cigarettes. Some whisky.'

Ngwenya said abruptly, 'Lobengula's treasure belongs to the tribe; to the Ndebele people. If you find it, you will have to give it to the chiefs. The elders will come together and will have to make a decision whether or not to keep it.'

Griffin gave a scathing laugh. 'Are you mad, Ngwenya? Do you think that if I find gold and diamonds I will

110

share it with those doddering old men? They know nothing. Chief Nyoni will probably put it back in the ground. Or maybe he will use it to buy false teeth. No, if I find the treasure I will keep it for me and my friends. If you want to share it, you must look for it yourself.'

'I don't want to find the treasure,' Ngwenya told him. 'All over Africa, men have gone crazy with greed trying to follow this false promise. We do not want this to happen in our tribe. If the treasure is never found, it may be for the best.'

The conversation was getting heated and Martine was afraid that a fight would break out, but it was interrupted by a swirl of black, white and yellow. Before Martine could register what was happening, the hornbill had swooped out of the night and landed on her knee, using the creases in her jeans as brakes.

'Magnus!' she cried, inexplicably cheered by the reappearance of the odd, serious bird, her last connection with her grandmother and Sadie. 'How did you find us?'

'We think his nest is in the place we call Rock Rabbit Hill in our language,' said Ngwenya. 'It is very close to here so perhaps he spotted you when he was on his way home to roost for the evening. Rock Rabbit Hill is riddled with holes and tunnels. If you fall into one, you might never come out. Some guests at the retreat who have lost their jewellery have tried to locate this nest, but it is very unsafe to climb up this hill and no one has ever managed. I myself think that when the nest is found it will be full of bottle tops and other rubbish.'

Martine rubbed the top of the hornbill's head and his eyelashes fluttered up and down in ecstasy.

Griffin wiped chicken grease from his mouth and scrutinized her as if she were a specimen under a microscope. 'I have just come from visiting the witchdoctor, who will be coming here shortly. He told me that there were some children staying in my uncle's village tonight, and that he has been hearing some stories that one of these children, a white girl, rides a giraffe back home in South Africa. He threw the bones and they helped him to remember the Zulu legend about the child who rides the white giraffe having power over all the animals.'

He nodded at Magnus. 'You are obviously a friend to the wild birds. Does this mean you are the girl in the ancestor's story? Is your giraffe in South Africa white?'

Martine didn't respond. She didn't want him, of all people, knowing anything about her or Jemmy. She hoped that if she ignored him he'd get the message and leave her alone, but Ngwenya innocently put her on the spot.

'A *white* giraffe?' he exclaimed. 'An albino one? Is this true, Martine? *Now* I understand. Now it becomes clear. When Gogo said you rode a giraffe, I wasn't too sure whether to believe her. Then I saw how the horses loved you and what a good rider you are, and I thought that maybe some people had helped you to train a giraffe from when it was very young. Nobody told me it was a white one. Is this correct? Are you the child in the Zulu legend?'

Forced to respond, Martine said: 'Trust me, I don't have power over any animals. Sometimes I help them a little, that's all.'

'Which way do you help them?' Griffin wanted to know.

Martine had no intention of answering him. 'Would you like me to wash the dishes?' she asked Mercy's sister.

'Maybe we can help each other, Martine,' Griffin persisted. 'There is an animal I would like to have power over. If you assist me, maybe I can let you have a little piece of treasure. A gold sovereign, perhaps, or a diamond.'

That was the final straw for Ngwenya. He knew full well that the animal his cousin wanted power over was Khan. 'That is enough, Griffin,' he shouted. 'I told you that you are not welcome here and now it is time for you to leave.'

Martine expected Griffin to protest, but he jumped up in one lithe, easy movement, took off his hat and bowed. 'Goodbye, friends,' he said. 'Next time you see me I shall be a rich man.'

Turning on his heel, he flashed another sinister smile. Martine had a bad feeling it was intended for her.

Not surprisingly, she and Ben found it nearly impossible to sleep. They were still awake, discussing the events of the day and how best to tackle the problem of getting into the Lazy J, an hour after saying goodnight to Ngwenya. The horse wrangler had gone to check on the retreat, some twenty minutes' ride away. He was planning to spend the night there and return at the crack of dawn. Martine had been afraid he'd try to stop them; that he'd tell them they were insane to imagine they could sneak into the hunter's ranch and attempt to find evidence that the Rat was blackmailing Sadie and behind the arrests at Black Eagle. But all he said was, 'Martine and Ben, I think you are both *penga*. This is the word we have in Zimbabwe for people who are mad. But if you are *penga*, then so am I. We will leave before sunrise.'

Martine and Ben were making another attempt to close their eyes when they heard a commotion outside.

Ben bounded up and pushed back the hessian cloth that covered the doorway. 'Martine, there are a lot of people milling around the fire and waving their hands in the air as if they're angry or upset. Either the police are on their way or baby Emelia is really ill. I think we should see what's going on.'

They put on their sweatshirts and went out into the cold night air. As they neared the fire, they saw the witchdoctor. He had his back to them and was sitting opposite Mercy and Odilo, whose faces were tense with anxiety. The villagers were gathered in a circle behind them, buzzing with anticipation. Baby Emelia lay between Mercy and Odilo, wrapped in a sheepskin rug.

Nobody noticed Ben and Martine approaching through the darkness – nobody, that is, except the witchdoctor. After holding up his hand for silence, he slowly and very deliberately turned to face the young outsiders. There was something very ancient and tribal about his necklace of horns, belt of ostrich feathers and leopard-skin kilt. It was as if the modern world had never touched him. It was impossible to say how old he was. He could have been ninety or thirty.

Martine found herself looking at his leopard-skin kilt and thinking about something Ngwenya had told her. He'd explained that the kilts were handed down from one generation to the next. The hide of leopards was specially chosen because the leopard was regarded by the Ndebele as the politest and most respectful of all the animals, and the witchdoctors wished to show the same politeness and respect to the ancestral spirits. Martine's own opinion was that it might have been more polite and respectful not to rob the leopard of its skin, but she'd known better than to say that.

The witchdoctor fixed her with a fierce glare, as if he'd known her in a past life and she'd done him a great wrong. 'There is no work for you here,' he said.

The villagers murmured in alarm, and one or two motioned her and Ben away. The witchdoctor held up his hand for silence again. He turned his back on Martine, took a swig from a brown bottle at his side, removed his ceremonial pouch, scattered some bones on the ground and began to chant.

Martine and Ben retreated to the shadows, feeling like unwanted guests intruding on a sacred ritual. Which, in effect, they were. But after half an hour of chanting they were so cold they dared to creep back to the fireside.

Nobody chased them away. They were too absorbed in another spectacle. In between chants, the witchdoctor had continued to take long swallows from his brown bottle, and two other empty bottles of what Ben suspected was 'some powerful homebrewed moonshine' lay on the earth beside him. His eyes were red and streaming. He was swaying over his bones and his chanting sounded slurred.

'It's her ssshhtumach,' he mumbled at last. 'Sh-sh-she has shtumach flu. She needs—' and he reeled off a plant name Martine recognized. His glazed eyes singled out Martine in the crowd. He lifted a forefinger and waggled it at her, as if to say, 'I'm warning you.' Then he keeled over and began snoring loudly.

Mercy recovered first. 'That drunken idiot!' she shouted. 'My baby is dying and he can't control his thirst for this poison for even one night.'

She aimed several kicks at the sprawling figure before a couple of villagers restrained her. Tears began to stream down her face. Odilo put his arms around her and looked as though he might weep too. In the sheepskin rug, the baby whimpered feebly.

'I might be able to help,' Martine offered in a small voice.

She spoke so softly that nobody heard her above the babble of voices. Martine was too shy to repeat what she'd said, but Ben went over to the sad couple. 'Mercy and Odilo, Martine might be able to help,' he told them.

This time Odilo and some of the villagers turned, although most seemed displeased at the interruption.

'You have a power with babies?' Odilo asked doubtfully.

Martine shook her head. 'No, I don't. But in my survival kit I have medicine made from the plant the witchdoctor mentioned. My friend Grace, a South African *sangoma*, gave it to me.'

Odilo was unsure, but between sobs Mercy urged her to fetch it quickly. Martine raced to get it from the hut and unzipped it in the firelight. There were gasps as she removed her pink Maglite, Swiss Army knife, silver whistle, compass, magnifying glass, tube of superglue, and three small brown bottles: one for headaches and pain, one to treat Bilharzia, a disease found in Zimbabwean rivers, and one for stomach ailments.

Mercy read the label on the stomach one, removed the cork from the top of it and sniffed. Evidently it met with her approval.

'Odilo and I will take Emelia to our hut and talk about whether we should take a chance and give it to her,' she told Martine. 'It must be our decision.'

Martine sank down beside Ben to wait, warming her hands on the fire. One of the villagers handed her a mug of tea and its fragrant sweetness temporarily revived her. But not for long. She checked her watch and realized that she and Ben had been up for twenty hours. So many things had happened. It felt like the longest day on earth. It was hard to believe that nineteen hours ago she'd come face to face with the largest leopard ever recorded.

By the time Odilo returned, she could no longer see straight she was so tired, and Ben was so sleepy he was nodding like one of those nodding dogs in cars.

'Mercy says to thank you very much,' Odilo told Martine. But her heart sank when he added ominously, 'Whatever happens . . .'

She opened her mouth to say that she wasn't a doctor or even a *sangoma* and maybe it had been a bad idea to hand over Grace's stomach *muti* without a medical practitioner's diagnosis, but Odilo guessed what was troubling her and said, 'Go to sleep. Have faith in your *sangoma* friend's medicine. There is nothing more we can do. We must wait for the *muti* to do its work.'

As the moon crept higher in a sky that was more white than blue-black it had so many stars in it, the whole village slumbered. The only creature still awake was Magnus. Frustrated that Martine had disappeared into a hut and seemed not to be coming out again, the hornbill was strolling about in search of entertainment. He found nothing to interest him until he reached the cooking area, where the contents of Martine's survival pouch still winked in the dying embers of the fire.

Unnoticed, the hornbill hopped nearer.

14

Martine tossed and turned for the remainder of the night on the hard, unfamiliar bed, agonizing over her grandmother and whether or not she'd done the right thing giving Grace's *muti* to the sick baby. She fell asleep just before dawn and was woken minutes later by Ben. 'Emelia is much better and is drinking her breakfast,' he said. 'Ngwenya is back and has heard the whole story. He says that Odilo is smiling from one ear to the other for the first time since he lost his job.'

As glad as Martine was to receive this news, it was agony to be wrenched from her dreams after a mere catnap. She was as keen as anyone to get to the Lazy J and search for answers, but she longed for some proper sleep. The epic drive to Zimbabwe, the strain of keeping her encounter with Khan secret, Gwyn Thomas's arrest and the witchdoctor's frightening reaction to her, had all been too much.

She could just imagine what the conversations would be like when she and Ben returned to Caracal Junior. Luke and Lucy would be going on about surfing and sunbathing in the Mediterranean, Jake would be talking non-stop about rugby camp, and Claudius would be full of tall tales about hiking in the Drakensberg Mountains with his dad.

Finally they'd get round to asking what she and Ben had done on their vacation and Martine would pipe up: 'Well, let me see. First, Ben was nearly smashed to bits falling down a waterfall, then we saw a lion being shot in cold blood, and next day I was nearly mauled by a leopard. Oh, and my grandmother was taken away to jail by two corrupt policemen, and Ben and I had to hide in a remote village, and while we were there a baby developed a raging fever and I had to help save it. Apart from that, we had a very relaxing time.'

Ngwenya interrupted her thoughts by putting a mug of tea and a bowl of *mielie*-meal porridge in front of her.

'Eat quickly,' he said. 'We must go to the Lazy J before the sun gets up.'

Ben joined her. He'd endured a 'bird bath' using a bucket of ice-cold water, and he was shivering in the crisp morning air. 'How are you feeling?' he asked, rubbing the goosebumps on his arms. 'You got even less sleep than I did.'

'I'm scared,' Martine admitted. 'I'm scared for us but mainly I'm frightened for Khan, my grandmother, and Sadie. What if we can't help them? We're up against corrupt policemen, blackmailing hunters and all this wilderness. There seems to be a different set of rules in Zimbabwe. The law doesn't seem to mean anything here.'

She swallowed a few spoonfuls of porridge. 'How 'bout you? How do you feel about today?'

'I don't think Rex Ratcliffe should be allowed to get away with making so many people and animals suffer,' Ben said. 'Somebody has to try to stop him and it may as well be us. I know it seems impossible, but I think we're a pretty good team when it comes to doing the impossible. Let's visualize the outcome we want and try to make it happen. We want your grandmother and Sadie to come home safely. That's No.1. But we also want to save Khan and find him a place where he can live in freedom, away from any hunters. Try it, Martine. Try to picture it.'

Martine closed her eyes and conjured up an image of Sawubona. She visualized herself and the white giraffe standing beside Gwyn Thomas watching the sun come up over the lake. Jemmy was resting his head on her shoulder. Her grandmother was pointing at the hippos and saying something that made Martine laugh.

Next she tried to picture Khan in a place of safety. In Martine's opinion, Sawubona was the best game sanctuary in the world, so that's where she saw him. He was lying on a boulder high up on the mountain that overlooked the lake, his forelegs stretched out like a Sphinx, watching her, Gwyn Thomas and the white giraffe. In Martine's vision, he got up and began to make his way down the slope, dislodging a rock as he did so.

Then the picture went fuzzy. Martine squinted at the image in her head, trying to conjure it up again, but it was gone.

She went back to the hut to collect her survival kit and only remembered when she got there that she'd left it by the fireside the previous night. She was on her way out again when she noticed a baby tortoise heading towards her. Martine gave a cry of delight. 'You're so sweet,' she said. 'Where did you come from?'

She picked it up and saw the tortoise had something strapped to its back. It was too dark inside the hut to see it, so she carried it over to the light. Ngwenya had hung a lantern from a hook on the wall. She lifted the tortoise to the flickering glow and had to bite back a scream. Strapped to its back was a perfectly crafted miniature coffin.

Ben came up, carrying her survival kit. He stared at the tortoise in bewilderment. 'Is this someone's idea of a sick joke? Where did you find it?'

'Someone put it in our hut,' Martine said, shivering. She was so sickened she wanted to hurl the tortoise into the bushes, but she knew very well it wasn't the tortoise's fault. She untied the coffin, crushed it under her boot, and set the tortoise carefully on its way. 'It's a warning.

No prizes for guessing who sent it.'

'The witchdoctor?'

'The witchdoctor. By giving the *muti* to Mercy and Odilo, he probably feels I've humiliated him.'

'He humiliated himself,' Ben reminded her. 'It's not your fault he was drunk.'

'All the same, we need to be on our guard.'

She blew out the lamp and fastened her survival kit around her waist. Through the half dark came the clip-clop of horses' hooves. Sirocco's leather reins were thrust into her hands.

'Come,' said Ngwenya. 'We must hurry.'

They reached the Lazy J at six a.m., tethering the horses and walking the last kilometre. It was already light and Ben was concerned that they were too late to do any meaningful searching, but Ngwenya had timed it so they arrived while the hunters were out shooting. He estimated that they had about an hour until the men came back, laden with the bloody carcasses of wildlife they'd killed, for a meaty fry-up of crocodile steak and buffalo sausage.

'We must split up in case we are discovered,' he said. 'It is easier for two to rescue one than for one to rescue two.'

Martine was about to object, but Ben got in before her.

'Sorry, Ngwenya,' he said. 'I made that mistake at the

leopard cave and I'm not going to do it again. Martine and I can't be separated. What we're about to attempt is very risky. If we can't do it together, we can't do it at all.'

'I agree,' Martine said. 'I'm not going anywhere without Ben.'

Ngwenya was amused by their protectiveness towards one another. 'As you wish. I will go to the lodge where the tourists stay and try to get into the office, where there might be some records.'

'Great,' Martine said. 'We'll go and check out the animal enclosure.'

Ngwenya bridled. 'You will stay away from the lions and cheetahs? It is bad enough that you have persuaded me to bring you here. Please do not get into any trouble with the animals. Just because Magnus and the horses like you, it does not mean lions and cheetahs will be your friends.'

Martine smiled angelically. 'Don't worry, Ngwenya. We'll look but we won't touch.'

Getting into the Lazy J was simplicity itself. The guard at the gatehouse was accustomed to people arriving by vehicle, not on foot. He never even lifted his eyes from his newspaper as they sneaked under the barrier and sprinted across the parking area that lay between the razor-wire-topped perimeter fence and the gates of the hunting lodge.

Ngwenya turned to Martine. 'I hope that your grandmother and Gogo are not angry with me for bringing you here.'

'They won't be,' she told him. 'Especially if we can find

evidence showing that Mr Ratcliffe is trying to drive Sadie out of business and sell Khan's skin for thousands of US dollars.'

'Be very careful,' Ngwenya said. 'The Rat is a wicked man. You've seen what he is capable of. If he catches you, I don't know what he might do.'

Crouching low, he followed the wall around to the tourist lodge. Ben and Martine wasted no time. They slipped beneath the turnstile into the wildlife enclosure. Their plan was to stay out of sight if possible, but act casually if they were caught and brazen it out.

As soon as they entered the concrete and steel enclosure, they realized they were in a hunting zoo. The majority of the cages were filled with lions and cheetahs, but there were also three black rhino in a paddock, and a walled-off pond where half a dozen crocodiles could be seen basking in the sun.

The male lions charged at the wire mesh of their cages, snarling with rage. The cheetahs paced up and down their runs relentlessly, as though their prison had driven them demented.

The animals were well kept and their cages clean, but their eyes were frantic with fear. Martine couldn't stop thinking about the shot lion, his life leaking out onto the hunter's boot while the big-bellied man posed for photographs. She knew that the other animals knew what was going to happen to them. Day after day, they heard the dying roars of their companions and had to wait, trembling, for the clink of keys that would mean they too were being summoned before the executioner.

'Martine,' Ben said. 'Someone's coming.'

They flew down the corridor between the runs, and up the steps of a storage room beside the crocodile pond, darting inside in the nick of time. A man carrying a bucket pushed his way through the turnstile and made his way along the rows of animals, whistling as he sloshed water into their drinking containers. When his bucket was empty he went out the way he came in.

As soon as he was gone, they began their search in earnest. Like everything else at the Lazy J, the storage room was clean and tidy. Half of it was a basic office. There was a desk and chair, a filing cabinet, and a couple of boxes overflowing with glossy brochures describing the Lazy J as the 'ultimate safari experience'. The other half was piled high with sacks of a well-known brand of dog food.

'It's a cheap way of feeding lions and cheetahs,' Martine explained to Ben. 'Lots of wildlife parks do it, but it isn't the best thing for the animals.'

But it was the electrical panel on the back wall that interested them most. It featured two rows of red lights numbered up to thirty. One row was labelled: 'Gate Open'. The other read: 'Gate Shut'.

Ben looked at Martine. 'Are you thinking what I'm thinking?'

Martine gave a nervous laugh. 'It's very tempting, but we can't set the lions free . . . Can we?'

Ben went over to the desk and sat in the chair. 'It's a nice idea. Unfortunately they might end up eating Rex Ratcliffe or one of his hunters and that wouldn't be a good thing.'

'Even though they deserve it,' said Martine.

'Even though they deserve it.'

Ben opened the journal on the desk and started flicking through it. 'This is sickening. It seems to be a record of daily hunts and kills. On a single day last week, they shot five kudu, one lion, two sable antelope and two elephants.'

'Is there any mention of Khan?'

Ben flicked through once again. 'Not that I can see.'

'Try checking the dates still to come. Maybe it's scheduled,' said Martine, taking a quick peek out of the door. She saw no one apart from the keeper who was pouring water into the rhinos' trough.

Ben finished his search. 'No, nothing . . . Hold on a minute. The entry for tomorrow is different to all the rest. It's written in capital letters and it says: OPERATION WILDCAT – 5 a.m. Elephant Rock.'

'Elephant Rock!' cried Martine. 'That's on Black Eagle land. How dare they trespass on Sadie's property. That proves that Rex Ratcliffe had her and my grandmother arrested to get them out of the way. And Operation Wild Cat has to mean they're going after Khan.'

Ben tore the page out of the journal and put it in his pocket. 'I'm taking this as evidence. It has the Lazy J logo at the top and it might hold up in court.'

Footsteps rang on the concrete path outside. Ben barely had time to dart around the desk and pretend to be studying a poster of an elephant before a man with a bushy blond moustache strode in.

He seemed stunned to see them – so stunned that it

took him a second or two to react. Then he growled, 'Who are you and what do you think you're doing in here?'

'Good morning, sir,' Ben said smoothly. 'I apologize if we're not supposed to be in here. Our parents are up at the lodge and we were curious to see how a real hunting operation worked.'

'Were you now,' the man said sarcastically. 'I suppose that's okay then. And how might I assist you?'

'We were just wondering if you had a brochure,' Ben said.

'A brochure? Yes, of course you can have a brochure.' He handed Ben one from the box. 'What did you say your parents' names were?'

'Jones,' Martine said. 'Mr and Mrs Jones.'

'My parents' names are Moyo,' added Ben. 'Mr and Mrs Moyo.'

'Moyo and Jones?' he repeated slowly, as if he was trying to place their faces. 'That's very interesting. The reason it's so interesting is because I happen to be the duty manager and I can categorically confirm that nobody by either of those names is staying at the lodge.'

'We're not staying,' Martine explained. 'We've just popped in for meal and a safari.'

He chuckled. 'Good try, but we have a no-children policy here and it's very strictly enforced. Kids tend to get a bit weepy over all the dead animals.'

He picked up the telephone. 'Security? Yes, we have two intruders in the lion and cheetah compound.'

Martine glanced at Ben and moved her chin

fractionally towards the electrical board.

'I think that's a very good idea,' Ben said out loud.

The man put down the receiver. 'You think what is a very good idea? Calling security?'

He never got to finish his sentence. Before he could move a muscle, Ben had flown like quicksilver around the desk, hit the row of switches labelled 'Gate Open', and was out of the door with Martine behind him.

Ben had a split second to say, 'Martine, let him come after me, then lock the door so he can't get back in to lock the cages. Climb over the wall – I'll meet you on the other side.'

Martine almost collided with the duty manager as he clattered down the steps, but he made only a half-hearted attempt to grab her before racing after Ben, the real object of his wrath. As Ben neared the first of the cages, two security guards appeared at the turnstile. The manager gestured for them to catch Ben. It had belatedly struck him that his own priority should be preventing the lions and cheetahs from escaping. He tore back to the storeroom, but it was too late. Martine had locked the door and was sitting on top of the wall with the key.

'Give that to me,' shouted the manager, dancing with fury below her. 'Have you any idea what you've done?'

'You want it?' Martine said, holding the key out of his reach. 'Go and get it.'

She threw it into the crocodile pen where, by a complete fluke, it hit a rock and ricocheted into the open mouth of a basking reptile. His jaws snapped shut and he gulped. Martine took advantage of the manager's apoplexy to jump down the other side of the wall and make a run for the car park.

Her biggest fear was that she wouldn't be able to find Ben, but he came flying over the turnstile like a hurdler and was just as relieved to see her.

'Where are the guards?' Martine asked in panic.

Ben grinned. 'I believe they were detained by one or two lions.'

A moving cloud of dust on the horizon wiped the smile off his face. 'The hunters,' he said. 'They're on their way back.'

He took Martine's hand and they ran down the driveway and past the guardhouse. This time the guard did see them, but his attention was diverted when two cheetahs streaked by, followed by a lumbering rhino. The cheetahs slipped under the barrier; the rhino crashed straight through it. They were so preoccupied with the sight of the open savannah and a chance at freedom that they ignored Martine and Ben. As Martine and Ben headed after them, they could hear the guard yelling into his radio for back-up.

Ben was a champion long distance runner and he sprinted easily along the road towards the thick bush that would give them cover. Martine, on the other hand, was one of Caracal Junior's slowest athletes. Halfway back to the horses, her legs started to feel like lead and she developed a stitch. A couple of camouflage-painted four-wheel drives zoomed into view. They were coming from the opposite direction.

Martine paused, trying to catch her breath. 'You go on

without me,' she said to Ben. 'Find Ngwenya and get word to Sadie and Gwyn Thomas about the hunt at Black Eagle tomorrow. I'll be fine. Even Rex Ratcliffe must draw the line at putting children in jail.'

'Don't be crazy,' said Ben. 'There's absolutely no way I'm leaving you. Remember what Grace told you.'

They started to run again, but there were shouts from behind and one of the safari vehicles left the road and roared after them through the bush. Martine's stitch became unbearable and she pulled up, gasping.

'I can't go on,' she panted as they entered a grove of trees. 'Please, Ben, I'm begging you, save yourself. For Khan's sake.'

'No,' said Ben, gripping her hand more tightly. 'We'll face them together.'

The safari vehicle ploughed through the long yellow grass and screeched to a halt beneath an old mopani tree. Five men in khaki clothes spilled off the back and surrounded them. None of the men spoke. They just stared at the vehicle expectantly.

The passenger door opened slowly and out came a pair of alligator-skin cowboy boots, followed by their owner: a gaunt figure with unnaturally white skin, sporting a safari suit and slicked-down black hair. He had the weirdest face Martine had ever seen. Every feature was sharp and thrust forward so that they came together in a point, at the tip of which was a bloodless mouth and two yellow buck teeth. He was like the product of a rodent-human genetic experiment that had gone horribly wrong.

Leaning on a cane, he walked stiffly over to Ben and Martine and glared down at them from a great height. 'Are these them?' he enquired, his voice high-pitched with outrage. 'Are these the children who have jeopardized my entire hunting operation?'

'Mr Rat, I presume,' Martine said.

· 15 ·

'Ratcliffe,' squeaked the rodent man. 'The name is Ratcliffe.'

That was as far as he got because from above their heads came a roar so terrifying that Mr Rat's cane dropped from his fingers and one of the guides fainted on the spot.

Then Khan dropped from the sky.

Martine caught a rapid-fire glimpse of unforgettable images, the most striking of which was the golden body of the leopard completely covering Mr Rat, as if the hunter had suddenly acquired the leopard-skin coat he was after. Then she and Ben were running for their lives.

They swerved through the trees, along a narrow path and up to the rear gate of Black Eagle, where the horses were waiting.

'Where is Ngwenya?' Martine fretted.

'I am here,' the horse wrangler replied, running up behind them with a large plastic canister in his hand. He, too, was breathing hard.

He put his hands on their shoulders and started laughing. 'I saw everything,' he said. 'I was waiting in the trees for you and I watched the jeep chase after you. I heard Mr Ratcliffe and his guides threatening you. I was waiting for my chance to do something when I noticed the leopard sitting in the mopani tree. I saw him getting ready to strike. Oh, Martine, he is the most beautiful animal I have ever seen. His colours! His coat glows like it is on fire and his spots are like black diamonds.'

Martine was too upset to be interested in the merits of Khan's coat. 'Did you see what happened to him?' she said. 'I'm petrified they might try to shoot him.'

Ngwenya grinned. 'Don't worry, my friend, there was no shooting. One of the guides went to get his rifle and Khan opened up his chest with a swipe of his paw. That man will be spending many months in hospital, I think. The others carried him and Mr Ratcliffe back to the car. Mr Ratcliffe was bleeding and whimpering like a puppy, but I was close enough to hear him say, "Operation Wildcat must go ahead as planned." I don't know what that means.'

'We do,' Ben said, handing Ngwenya the page from the journal. 'The hunt for Khan starts at five tomorrow morning. Somehow we have to stop it.'

Ngwenya scanned the entry. 'Elephant Rock? They are meeting at Elephant Rock? Who are they to trespass on Gogo's land?'

'That's what we said,' Martine told him. 'The good thing about it is it proves that the Rat had Sadie and my grandmother arrested to get them out of the way. All we need to do now is get the information to the authorities.'

Ngwenya held up his plastic container. It sloshed with brown liquid. 'That's what this is for. I found two things at the Lazy J. I found an Ndebele waiter who had some very interesting things to say about the poison he was paid to put in a water tank for cattle at Black Eagle. He admits he put a little in the tank but felt too guilty to add the rest. His father and his father before him were cattlemen, and he felt that by hurting cows he was dishonouring his ancestors' memory.

'He hid the bottle in a baobab tree on Black Eagle land. He promises to show the police where it is if I can guarantee to find him another job.'

'You said you found two things,' Ben said. 'Is the other one petrol?'

'It is. I am going to ride to the retreat at Black Eagle, fill up one of the vehicles, and go to Bulawayo to give this information to the District Attorney. I have heard he is an honest man. With any luck, your grandmother and Gogo will be home by this evening.'

'We'll come with you,' Martine said.

Ngwenya shook his head. 'In case there is trouble with the police, it is better for you to stay with Mercy and

Odilo. Before I go to Bulawayo, I will accompany you to the village.'

'We'll be fine on our own,' Martine said. 'I think you should go to Bulawayo right away. The sooner you can persuade the DA to release my grandmother and Sadie, the better.'

Ngwenya wasn't convinced. 'You will be safe by yourselves?'

Ben smiled at him. 'Safe as houses.'

After Ngwenya had galloped away on Red Mist, they began the long trek to the village through the rocks and hills of Black Eagle. Martine would have liked to gallop as fast as the terrain allowed, but Ben's riding was not up to that yet and Mambo refused to cooperate.

'We should have brought Cassidy,' Martine grumbled as Mambo plodded tiredly along, giving an Oscar-worthy performance of a poor, abused pony who'd only ever known hardship and toil, when the truth was that he was fat, spoilt and spent the greater portion of his time eating and sleeping.

'It's not the horse, it's me,' Ben said charitably. 'I don't think I'm cut out to be a rider. Next time I'm bringing a bicycle.'

'You're too nice,' Martine told him. 'They know they can get away with murder with you, that's the problem.'

'You're an angel to them and it works for you,' Ben

pointed out. 'I think the difference is that you can communicate with them. They understand you. Even the leopard understands you. That's why he came to your rescue.'

'He wasn't rescuing me,' protested Martine. 'He doesn't even know me. He probably spotted Mr Rat and thought he was looking at the largest rodent he'd ever seen and fancied a meal.'

Ben regarded her intently. 'Are you sure? I mean, are you sure that Khan doesn't know you?'

'I'm sorry,' said Martine, ashamed that she'd hidden it from her best friend. 'I was waiting for the right time to tell you. Ben, he could have killed me, but he didn't. He stood over me and I felt as though I looked into his soul. It was so magical and frightening I didn't know how to put it into words.'

Ben smiled at her. 'You didn't have to. I understood.'

'Ben?'

'Yes.'

'We have to save him.'

'We will. I promise.'

'Ben?'

He laughed. 'Yes, Martine.'

'Thank you for staying with me when the hunters came after us. You could easily have got away. You're a fantastic runner.'

'You would have done the same for me.'

She smiled at him, 'Yes, I would.'

A strange expression crossed Ben's face. 'Martine?'

There was something in his voice that made her

halt Sirocco. 'Ben, what is it? You look as if you've remembered something scary.'

'It was Khan I saw that day, wasn't it?' he said. 'The day I fell down the waterfall, I mean. The drawing on the rocks was Sadie's leopard, I just know it was. But who could have put it there – behind the curtain of water? I was nearly killed simply leaning over the edge to look at it. Do you think it was some kind of prediction? Do you think Grace was right and our destinies are connected in some way?'

'I'm not sure,' Martine answered, although she actually was sure. She was quite certain she and Ben were connected, and that he saw the sketch when he was meant to see it; that he saw it for a reason. As to who put it there, well, it could have been done a century before by the same people who'd predicted Khan would pounce on her.

Before she could say any more to Ben, Sirocco shied violently. If riding Jemmy hadn't taught Martine to have lightning reaction times she would have had a nasty fall. As it was she ended up with her legs on either side of Sirocco's ears and had to climb off the mare and remount.

The grass rustled and Ngwenya's cousin and his *shamwaris* stepped onto the path. Griffin was still dressed like a gangster, in a trilby and waistcoat, although all were very grimy.

'So it's true then?' he said. 'The child who rides the white giraffe does have power over all the animals. Horses, birds, even leopards.' He laughed. 'News travels quickly on the bush telegraph.'

'What do you want?' Ben demanded, moving Mambo as close to Sirocco as he could.

Griffin reached up and grabbed the bridles of both horses, and Martine caught a whiff of cologne. 'I want your friend to help me with a little problem I have.'

Martine was livid. She knew that the tiniest pressure of her heel would send the Arab mare hurtling into the hills, leaving Griffin and his greedy, treasure-seeking buddies spitting dirt, but that would mean abandoning Ben and Mambo to their mercy and never in a million years would she do that.

'I know what you want,' she said scornfully. 'You want to use me to control the leopard so that you can find him and kill him. You think that Khan will lead you to Lobengula's treasure.'

Griffin smiled his wolfish smile. 'So you've heard about our plans. Maybe you are correct; maybe you are not. I told you that if you assist us with the leopard, we might give you some gold or maybe a diamond.'

'I wouldn't assist you if my life depended on it.'

'It might,' he said matter-of-factly.

139

16

An hour after Operation Wildcat had officially started, Martine was balanced on a crate in a boarded up storeroom of what had once been a shop, peering through a vent at their captors. Two of them were asleep on the old shop counter, one wrapped in a tatty blanket, the other on an old mattress. Griffin had not been up long himself. He was out on the veranda, poking half-heartedly at the ashes of the previous night's fire and clutching at his head as if he was trying to make sure it belonged to him.

Martine hoped that he had an extremely painful hangover or, better still, a migraine requiring a lobotomy. She was furious with him. She and Ben had been held captive by him and his fiendish friends for almost twenty-four hours, and every one of those hours had been misery. They'd been kidnapped at about nine o'clock in the morning and denied food or water until six in the evening because Martine refused to give Griffin any information on her gift.

'It is up to you if you want to starve yourself and your friend,' he said. 'It is easy for you to talk.'

'We are not criminals,' one of his friends told her. 'Don't worry, we are not going to hurt you. We are only looking for treasure that is lying in the ground, wasted, when it is the right of any Ndebele man with initiative to enjoy its beautiful golden fruit if he locates it.'

In the end, she and Ben were so thirsty and hungry that Martine made up a story about how she had the power to read tea leaves if they were brewed with aloe juice and lucky beans. She explained that the liquid was very poisonous and could not be drunk, but that she would strain it away using a special method. Griffin immediately rushed off to gather all three items, and Martine pored over the mug and pretended to be shocked to read in the leaves that Mr Ratcliffe was organizing a big hunt for the leopard which would leave Elephant Rock at five a.m. next morning.

This information earned her and Ben as much water as they could drink and a dinner of sadza and tripe and other cow innards, which they couldn't eat. The meat was so revolting that the smell alone made them nauseous, although they did force down a little sadza.

Martine had told Griffin about the hunt for a reason. She'd gambled that he would want to get to the leopard before Ratcliffe's men did, and that she and Ben might still have a chance to escape and save Khan. It didn't occur to her that the treasure seekers would be so eager to get to Khan first that she and Ben would be dragged up and down every hill in the Matopos until one o'clock in the morning in a bid to unearth him. By that time, Martine, who felt as if she hadn't slept in weeks, was nearly sobbing with tiredness.

Since then, she and Ben had been locked in the dusty, windowless storeroom with nothing but a bottle of water, a wooden crate and a couple of sacks. The sacks were Griffin's idea of bedding. Outside in the ruined store, the treasure seekers had drunk Zambezi beer until the small hours.

Martine had not slept a wink. One of the many things that had kept her awake was the frustrating fact that her survival kit was still tied to Sirocco's saddle. She'd taken to hanging it there when she was riding, reasoning that she could impale herself on her Swiss Army knife if she fell off and landed on it. She hadn't counted on Griffin and Co showing up.

Now she was a wreck. Her hair was standing on end and she would have given anything for a shower. Squinting through the vent, she was pleased to see that Griffin looked even worse. Ben, on the other hand, was sitting cross-legged on the floor with his palms on his thighs and his eyes closed. He was the picture of tranquillity.

'I don't understand how you can sit there so peacefully when the Rat's hunters are out searching for Khan,' Martine said accusingly, climbing down from her unsteady perch. 'He might be lying bleeding somewhere. Don't you care what happens to him?'

Ben opened his eyes. 'I think you already know the answer to that.'

He sprang gracefully to his feet and started to inspect every inch of their windowless cell – walls, floor and ceiling.

'Now what are you doing?'

Ben didn't reply. He put his nose close to a rusty water pipe and stared at it so hard, for so long, he went cross-eyed.

Martine became concerned that the stresses of the last week had taken more of a toll on him than she'd realized. 'Ben, come and sit down,' she said. 'I'm sorry about that comment about Khan. I know you care about him as much as I do.'

Ben continued to stare into the pipe. 'Martine, what did Ngwenya tell us about the Enemy of Lions?'

'What are you talking about?'

'I'm serious. Can you remember what he said?'

She sighed. 'Sure. He said, "Where you find these ants, you won't find any lions. Even snakes, you won't find them here."'

He grinned. 'That's what I thought. Lie down on the floor. I have an idea.'

17

The walls of the old shop were a dirty beige, but Ben guessed that they'd once been painted with white limewash. He broke off a corner of the crate and used it to scrape off a teaspoonful of chalky powder, which he daubed carefully onto Martine's face. Soon she was vampire white.

'The same colour as Mr Rat,' Ben teased, earning himself a hard slap for his cheek.

After checking through the vent that Griffin's companions were still asleep, he knocked and called 'Help!' just loud enough to attract their leader's attention.

'What do want?' Griffin growled through the door. 'Do you think this is a hotel where you can order breakfast?'

'Griffin, this is an emergency,' Ben said. 'Martine is ill.'

'I don't believe you,' came the response. 'It's a trick so you can get away. Don't worry; we're not going to hurt you. We will let you go when we find the leopard.'

'Griffin, what if something happens to her? Do you really want that on your conscience?'

There was a long pause and then a key scraped in the lock and the rusty metal door screeched open a crack. Griffin peered suspiciously into the storeroom. His eyes were bloodshot and he smelled of beer. When he caught sight of Martine lying white and prone on the concrete, he was aghast.

'Heh!' he exclaimed, stepping into the room and locking the door behind him. 'What has happened here? What is wrong with her?'

'She's hypoglycaemic,' Ben said gravely. 'Her blood sugar has gone down. She urgently needs some form of liquid sugar, like a sweet fizzy drink or even just some sugar in water. If she has that, she will be fine. Otherwise . . . '

'Otherwise what will happen?'

'I'm not exactly sure,' Ben said. 'But it'll probably be bad.'

On cue, Martine writhed on the floor and made a choking noise.

'Mwali, don't desert us now,' Griffin cried. He unlocked the door. 'We have a bottle of cream soda but

145

we have no fridge so it is warm. Would that be okay?'

Ben gave him a winning smile. 'Warm cream soda would be perfect.'

Half an hour later, he and Martine were cantering towards the granite mountain where Martine had first encountered Khan. A leadrope tied to her saddle forced Mambo to keep up with Sirocco.

Martine could not get over the genius of Ben's escape plan, or his audacity in pulling in off. He'd not lost his cool for a second. 'But what made you think of it?' she said, slowing the horses to give them a breather. 'What made you think of the Enemy of Lions?'

'Easy,' he said. 'An ant crawled over my foot when I was sitting on the floor and it made me think that if there were ordinary ants in our cell, there might also be the biting kind. I thought how brilliant it would be if the Enemies of Lions could be turned into the Enemies of Leopard Hunters.'

Martine giggled at the memory. 'Boy, did they ever.'

After Griffin had brought the cream soda in a plastic cup, 'Just in case you get any wrong ideas', Ben had sent him away, explaining that Martine needed to be kept very quiet, but that he'd let him know how she was doing very shortly. He'd poured a trail of the green fizzy drink from the waterpipe to the door, then sprinkled the remainder over the sacks they'd slept on, leaving a corner of each dry.

Lured by the sugar, a thick black column of the ants was soon marching out through the pipe, down the wall and along the floor to the threshold. The sacks became shimmering black rectangles of massed ant armies. Holding the dry corners, Ben pushed them carefully behind the wooden crate.

When he judged there were enough of them, he summoned Griffin again. Martine, who'd wiped the paint dust off her face and pinched her cheeks so she looked flushed, pretended to be revived and ready to at least discuss helping to find the leopard if it would mean he would let them go sooner. Her job was to keep Griffin standing on the threshold long enough for the Enemies of Lions to make their way up his trouser leg.

Their plan came close to failing. Once Griffin was satisfied that Martine was once again in possession of her powers, he wanted to leave right away. Martine had to fake a sudden relapse to keep him in the room. Ben used the distraction to flick the dregs of the cream soda onto Griffin's shoe in the hope that it would encourage the ants to make the climb up his leg.

Seconds later, Griffin let out a tormented scream. He unlocked the storeroom door and went tearing out into the overcast morning. He was leaping, twisting and screeching like a madman. His friends sat up, bleary-eyed. As soon as they saw the storeroom door open, the keys swinging in the lock, they came barrelling towards it, but Martine and Ben were ready with the sacks. A single swish sent showers of biting ants all over the men. They ripped off their shirts, shouting and cursing, and went tearing into the bush after Griffin. None of them were in any condition to prevent their prisoners' getaway.

Now Martine and Ben were racing to try to reach Khan, not knowing if the hunters had got there first. A pair of Black Eagles and a few vultures was circling the granite mountain where Martine had initially encountered him and she feared the worst, but Ben insisted that birds of prey often hovered in the vicinity of hunts, knowing there might be easy pickings.

They were trotting again when Odilo suddenly came rushing out of the bush, his mournful face transformed by a smile. Sirocco shied again, but this time Martine was ready for her and barely lost her seat.

'Please, my friends, you must go to Black Eagle Lodge straight away,' he said, reaching up to give them each an African handshake. 'Straight away. Ngwenya came to our village with your grandmother and Sadie not even one hour past. They are searching for you.'

'My grandmother and Sadie are at the retreat?' Martine cried. 'That's fantastic. Are they all right? Have the charges been dropped?'

'Yes,' said Odilo, 'but they are very frightened because we had to tell them we had not seen you both since yesterday. Ngwenya is too much upset. He is very cross with himself for not accompanying you to the village. He is searching for you in the hills. Where have you been?'

As thrilled as she was to hear that her grandmother was at the retreat and unharmed, Martine was aware that every second was precious if she and Ben were to get to

Khan in time. She gave a sketchy account of their night at the hands of Griffin and his friends, leaving out the part about the Enemies of Lions. The details would keep for another day.

Odilo's expression resumed its customary mournfulness. 'I'm sorry for this,' he said. 'My son, even as a small boy he was very, very smart. For many years he dreamed of going to university to be a lawyer. But after school he met these *tsotsis* and they turned his head with stories of the life he will have if he finds this treasure. Now all he can talk about is gold, gold, gold. I tell him, "Griffin, no good can come of this. It will end with you crying in jail."'

He looked up at Martine. 'I'm sorry for what he did to you, especially after you gave us the *muti* that made our daughter well again.'

Gunshots rang out in the distance. Sirocco danced skittishly and pawed at the ground. There was a knot of panic in Martine's throat as she tried to control the Arab.

Ben urged Mambo up beside her. 'We need to go,' he said.

'Yes,' agreed Odilo, misunderstanding, 'you must get back to Gogo and your grandmother at Black Eagle.'

'Sorry, Odilo,' said Martine. 'We can't until we've found Khan. We have to try to save him from Mr Rat's hunters.'

Odilo couldn't believe what he was hearing. 'This is madness,' he protested. 'Mr Ratcliffe and his hunters, these are very dangerous men. This is something for the police. Please, children, you must get home to Gogo and your granny. Come, let me go with you.'

Martine's chin was set with determination. 'Tell my grandmother that I love her and can't wait to see her. Tell her that I hope she understands why we can't come back just yet. Right now we have a promise to keep.'

· 18 ·

It was the witchdoctor who told them they were too late.

They came cantering out of the bush in a headlong rush and were confronted with a sight so surreal that it was too much even for Mambo. He slammed on brakes and Ben sailed over his head, fortunately landing agilely on his feet. Sirocco reared and threatened to bolt, and Martine had to dismount in order to calm her. Then she and Ben stood transfixed by the bizarre, almost mystical scene before them.

Beneath a low, charcoal sky was a ring of ten vultures. With their hunched shoulders, grey crests and shifty, all-knowing eyes, they resembled judges – spiteful, bad-tempered judges, going by the way they were hissing, cawing and pecking at each other over something unseen. In the centre of the circle, wearing his necklace of horns, belt of ostrich feathers and leopard-skin kilt, was the witchdoctor.

Martine jolted herself out of her trance and moved forward. Ben was close behind her. She stopped so suddenly that Ben ran into her. At the witchdoctor's feet was a sticky pool of blood, buzzing with flies.

'You have come too late,' he said. 'The leopard has been shot with the Rat Man's bullet.' He put a hand close to his heart to demonstrate where the lethal bullet had struck. An odour of alcohol drifted in Martine and Ben's direction.

'No!' cried Martine in anguish. 'He can't be dead. He just can't. I promised him I would save him.'

'I don't believe it,' said Ben. 'It's too quiet. If the leopard were dead, the hunters would be celebrating. There would be drag marks from where they loaded his body onto their jeep. And the vultures would not be here. They'd be circling the area where his carcass was, possibly even the jeep.'

The witchdoctor waved his arms and the vultures lifted screaming into the air, a sinister cloud of beating, dark wings. They settled in the tops of the peeling plain trees nearby, watching and waiting.

'I did not say he was dead,' he told Ben a little irritably. 'But he is dying. He has run for his life with the hunters behind him. Soon those who want Lobengula's treasure will be chasing him too.'

'Can you help us?' Martine begged. 'Can you throw the bones and tell us how we might get to him before they do?'

The witchdoctor gave a harsh chuckle. 'You shame me in front of my tribe; in front of people who believe that I am the best healer in Zimbabwe. You make me look like a fool, and now you expect me to assist you. You are dreaming, child. Go back to your *sangoma* friend and ask her. See if she can tell you where the leopard is.'

'Firstly, I didn't shame you,' Martine said angrily. 'You brought shame on yourself. Before you came, Mercy told us that you were the most talented traditional healer in Zimbabwe. You could have at least stayed sober until after you'd treated her sick child. You made the choice to drink and behave like a fool.

'As for my friend, Grace, if she was here, she *would* be able to tell me where the leopard is. But she's a few thousand miles away and you're right here. I don't know what Griffin bribed you with to make you tell him that the leopard needed to be dead before he could find the treasure, although I can guess. It doesn't matter. What's done is done. You have a chance to make things right. Are you going to take it?'

For a moment, the only sound was the eerie cries of the disgruntled vultures. Martine began to take in the enormity of what she'd done. She'd read the riot act to one of the most powerful figures in the Matopos and now there could be hell to pay.

She glanced at Ben and he was staring at her in

153

amazement. The witchdoctor, who at the beginning of her speech had produced a brown bottle from the depths of his kilt and was in the midst of taking a swig, flung it away from him. It hit a rock and shattered. A clear liquid gushed out.

'There are many curses I could put on you for saying these things,' he said quietly. 'You received my warning this morning, I am sure. But you have spoken the truth in the way that only an outsider could. It is painful for me to hear and it is shameful, but I cannot deny it. This thing, this *poison*, has a hold over me and I have found no herb, no plant, which can cure me. It is like a python around my neck, strangling me. Men such as Griffin have been feeding that python, bringing me these brown bottles so that I might help them with their wicked quest. I have been too weak to resist.'

'Is there anyone you would trust to help you?' Ben asked. 'Anyone you could talk to.'

The witchdoctor didn't seem to hear him. He removed his ceremonial pouch, stepped away from the buzzing patch of red and faced Martine. 'You humiliated me in front of my tribe and I will not soon forget it,' he said. 'But I will also remember something else. If it were not for you and your *sangoma*'s *muti* the baby might have died.'

'I would never have known Grace's medicine would help Emelia if you hadn't said the name of the plant.' Martine said graciously. Her rage had subsided and, after his courage in admitting that his addiction was squeezing the life from him, she felt an urge to comfort him.

The witchdoctor shook his head. 'I will throw the bones and tell you what you need to know. Perhaps there is still time for you to save your friend.'

He squatted and began chanting to himself, though whether it was in Ndebele or some ancient African language they couldn't tell. His rough hands, like the parched skin of an elephant, scattered the bones onto the dry earth. Martine tried her hardest to visualize Khan safe and well and happy, and once again she saw him on a mountainside at Sawubona, golden and whole.

The witchdoctor looked up from his bones. 'The one who reads the sign best will find the leopard first.'

'Oh,' said Ben.

That's not particularly helpful, thought Martine.

But the witchdoctor hadn't finished. He addressed them both, but his eyes were on Martine. 'You are bound together but you will be torn apart. When that happens, look to the House of Bees.'

'That's not a lot to go on, especially if we have to interpret the sign before the hunters do,' said Martine, urging Sirocco forward. She was finding it hard not to panic at the thought of Khan's life ebbing away. 'They have a head start.'

'It's not a lot to go on,' agreed Ben. He was leaning down from his saddle, scanning the ground for tracks or spots of blood as they went. 'But he did tell us something that could prove vital. He said we'd be torn apart. Now that we know that, maybe we can prevent it.'

Martine had a flashback to her conversation with Grace before she left Sawubona, the one where she'd said that if the San had only made her destiny clearer in their paintings she could have avoided all the bad stuff.

'We can try,' she said to Ben, 'but I don't think it really works that way. Grace says that if a person could see their future, they'd "only choose the good stuff, the easy stuff". They'd never learn from their mistakes and never experience the important things in life because they're usually the hardest things. But I do think it's a bit weird that both Grace and the witchdoctor talked about us being bound together. What do you think the witchdoctor meant when he said "Look to the House of Bees"?'

'I don't know,' Ben said absently. They had reached a stretch of bare rock leading down to a river, a tracker's biggest challenge. 'Maybe we're meant to look for a beehive, or maybe it's the name of a local house or even a hill?'

He got off Mambo. It took several minutes of casting around before a trace of sand in a crevice of the rock revealed a partial boot-print. A little way on he found a smear of blood.

'They're right behind him,' he said. 'I wish Tendai was here. He has such an amazing eye for this. It's going to take me years to learn even half of what he knows about tracking.'

Martine was on tenterhooks. She was worried about what would happen if they didn't find the leopard, but she was even more afraid of what would happen if they did. When she'd had to rescue Jemmy, she'd done so knowing that he was a gentle, beautiful creature who

157

would never harm her. She and Ben hadn't thought through the rescue of Khan in any way. If he were wounded he would be lashing out at everyone and everything. He'd be more likely to bite her head off than lie around waiting for her to summon up her gift.

Ben was at the river's edge. 'Martine, it looks like Khan and the hunters have crossed here. We should probably go on foot.'

Martine opened her mouth to say that the best thing they could do was race back to Black Eagle and get Sadie and her grandmother to call the police. But that would take hours. No, she and Ben would have to press on and hope for the best.

'All right,' she said, putting a hand on her survival pouch to check that it was fastened securely. 'Let's give the horses a drink of water and tie them up in the shade.'

It was easy for Ben to track the men across the river, because their boots had left bits of mud drying on the flat rocks on the other side. But where the grass began, there was a problem. There were two faint leopard paw prints heading southwest, one smudged and slightly twisted, but then, inexplicably, they vanished. It was as if Khan had been plucked into the heavens. The hunters had obviously spent a considerable time searching the area for some trace of him, before setting off in the direction that the leopard had last been taking.

Ben lingered by the riverbank.

'Let's go, Ben,' Martine said impatiently. 'We're going to have to run for a while or at least jog if we're going to overtake the hunters.'

He stood without moving. 'Something's wrong. The locals believe that after even every leopard in Zimbabwe is gone, Khan will survive; that he'll be the last leopard. They believe it because he's so cunning. Remember what I told you about Tendai's theory that people crossing rivers unconsciously walking in the direction they intend to travel, even if they're trying not to?'

'That's people,' Martine said. 'Surely a leopard's not capable of thinking like that?'

'Maybe not. But we already know that Khan is no ordinary leopard. His tracks show him heading southwest as he crosses the river and then when they appear again he's going due south. What if he doubled back? What if he had the wit to jump onto the rock from the path, which would explain the way his claws seemed to have dug into the ground, and then he waded along the river for a while.'

Martine was frantic, but she knew that all the rushing in the world wouldn't help if they misread the sign and ended up in the wrong place. 'Okay,' she said. 'It's worth a try.'

Ten minutes later, Ben gave a triumphant shout. He'd found a series of upturned pebbles on the riverbank, about fifty yards along from where they'd started, their undersides black and moist from the wet clay. 'That shows they've recently been turned,' he explained to Martine.

Next he spotted a ball of bloodstained cobwebs that had been wiped from a bush. From then on, they moved very quickly. After leaving the river, the leopard had started to bleed profusely and tracking him, at least to Ben's sharp eyes, was simply a matter of following the trail of blood. Ben jogged swiftly through the bush with Martine struggling to keep up. She could only just make out his blue T-shirt and jeans through the trees when she heard him shout, 'Martine, I think he's up here. Isn't this Rock Rabbit Hill – the one Ngwenya told us about?'

A hand was clapped over her mouth. There was a faint smell of cologne mingled with tripe. Griffin! He pulled her off the path and into a ditch, making almost no sound.

On the path ahead, Ben tensed when Martine didn't answer. He spun round. 'Martine? Martine!'

He guessed immediately that she'd been snatched or worse. He sprinted back down the path and began studying the ground where he'd last seen her. So absorbed was he in his task that he didn't see the hunters until he almost walked into them.

'What an unexpected pleasure,' drawled the duty manager from the Lazy J sourly, his bushy blond moustache twitching. He was with one of the guides who'd surrounded Ben and Martine in the forest.

Ben could still have made a break for it, but he didn't want to go anywhere until he knew where Martine was or if the hunters themselves had taken her.

'Where's your girlfriend?' the duty manager demanded in the next breath, answering one of Ben's questions at least. 'I have a score to settle with her.'

'I think she has a few to settle with you,' Ben replied coolly. 'Unfortunately, she's not here at the moment. She's at Black Eagle Lodge with her grandmother, and the police are on their way to arrest you for trespassing.'

The duty manager laughed. 'The police here are in the pay of Mr Ratcliffe whom you've grievously offended. If I were you I wouldn't count on them to come riding in like knights on white chargers. They know we're here. Now I'm going to ask you for the last time. Where's your girlfriend? What were you yelling just now – Mary?'

'If you're talking about my friend, her name is Susan,' Ben said. 'And like I told you, she's back at the retreat. I was calling for Mrs Scott's dog, Magnus. Maggy, I call him.'

In the ditch nearby, Martine listened in horror. If Griffin hadn't been holding her in such a vicelike grip, she would have burst from the ditch and confronted the hunters, regardless of the outcome.

'You're a terrible liar,' the duty manager told Ben, 'and if you continue to lie you're going to make me lose my temper.'

Ben folded his arms. 'Well, you're just going to have to lose it, then. If you think I'm lying, why don't you try to find Susan yourself? I mean, can you see her anywhere?'

'No,' admitted the hunter. 'But then I don't see your dog around either.'

'That's because he ran away when he saw the leopard,' Ben told him.

'The leopard!' cried the guide. 'Where is the leopard?'

'The leopard you shot?' Ben said. 'Do you really think I'm going to tell you where he's gone so you can finish him off? Anyway, they're expecting me back at Black Eagle. I need to go.'

The guide lifted his rifle menacingly. 'You're not going anywhere. You're going to show us where the leopard is hiding.'

'And why in the world would I want to do that?' said Ben.

'Ernest, put down the gun and stop acting like a gangster,' the duty manager ordered gruffly. 'Look, kid, you might not be aware of it but there's a bounty on the leopard's head. A thousand dollars dead or alive. It's yours if you can lead us to him.'

Ben grinned. 'In that case, follow me.'

Griffin waited until the only sound was the cooing of a lone dove before taking his hand from Martine's mouth and pushing her none too gently out of the ditch. He'd taken off his white shirt and hat and was wearing his soiled black waistcoat and trousers. His face, neck and bare arms were covered in swollen ant bites. He looked like the victim of some ghastly disease.

'You are lucky to have such a good friend,' he said. 'Loyal friends who will stand by you no matter what, those are hard to come by these days.'

'Yeah, well, maybe if you'd gone to law school like your father says you wanted to, instead of hanging about with lowlifes looking for gold and diamonds which doesn't belong to you, you might have met those kind of friends,' Martine responded coldly.

'Papa remembered my dream?' Griffin said. A wistful expression flickered across his face, but then he shook himself and scowled. 'You are too young to know anything about life. It is not always easy.'

He gave her a shove. 'I was very prepared to be nice to you and your friend, but you tricked me and caused me to be attacked by the Enemy of Lions. Have you felt their bites? It is like being pierced by needles made red-hot in fire. So now you have two choices. You are going to help me, or you are going to pay. The leopard has been shot and the witchdoctor says it is dying. Perhaps it is dead already. You will use your gift to locate Khan. Before the sun sets, the prophecy will be fulfilled. In the last resting place of the king of leopards I will find the king's treasure.'

'The witchdoctor told you that?' Martine felt a sense of disappointment. She'd really believed that he might change.

'No,' replied Griffin. 'I tried to give the stubborn old drunk some wine in payment for a prediction, but he smashed it against a rock and became very abusive. He said that the leopard was dying and I was wasting my time. Luckily I found your footprints down by the river and followed you here.'

He jerked her arm. 'Come, let's go. Let's find the leopard.'

Martine took a couple of steps along the path taken by

Ben and the hunters, but Griffin wrenched her back so brutally that she winced in pain.

'No more tricks,' he shouted. 'I heard your friend telling you that the leopard is on Rock Rabbit Hill. Start walking.'

The climb to the top of the fortress of rocks was agony for Martine. She was tired, hungry and thirsty, and with every arduous step she expected to come across the bloody body of Khan and to have to deal with Griffin tossing it aside to scrabble for the king's treasure.

She tried to think of an escape plan but her brain was like cotton wool. She didn't even have the energy to sneak a hand into her survival kit – not that there was anything in it that could help her at this moment. And besides, Griffin was right on her heels. The witchdoctor's words kept running through her head. 'You are bound together but you will be torn apart. When that happens, look to the House of Bees.'

'*What* House of Bees?' Martine thought frustratedly.

A police siren wailed in the distance. It was so unexpected that Griffin, in mid-stride between two rocks, lost his footing and slipped.

Martine seized the opportunity to make a run for it. Somehow she had to get to the top of the hill and signal the distant police car. It was her only hope. Up she went, forcing one exhausted leg in front of the other. Griffin came scrambling after her. Martine felt like she sometimes did in dreams, when she was being pursued by some unknown assailant and her legs refused to work.

In seconds, Griffin would grab her and this time there would be no Khan, Ben or Ngwenya to save her. The sweat ran into her eyes, stinging them and blurring her vision. Through a red haze, she saw a swollen dark mass suspended from a tree. Black specks circled it.

The House of Bees!

Martine scooped up a rock as she ran and threw it with all her might. The rock hit the bees' nest square on. It vibrated crazily – the black cloud of bees vibrating with it, hung momentarily suspended, and then plunged to earth.

The swarm swerved towards her with a hum so loud it resonated in her chest like a bass drum. Martine threw herself on the ground and lay motionless. There was a rush of whirring air as the bees swept over her, followed by a strangled yell as they descended upon Griffin. He turned and fled down the mountainside.

Martine got to her feet, swaying and stumbled on. Her sole intention was to make it to the top of the hill, where she could more easily be seen. She was almost there when she stepped on a piece of honeycomb. It stuck to her shoe. She paused to detach it and that's when it happened.

That's when the ground gave way beneath her feet.

Her stomach was left behind, and she was falling, falling, falling, an avalanche of earth falling with her. Each time she thought she'd reached the bottom, the bottom would give way and she'd fall again.

When she did hit the ground it was with a nasty crunch, and yet still the avalanche kept coming. Moist, cool earth – earth that smelled of worms and rotting leaves – was filling her mouth, eyes and ears, and as fast as she tried to spit it out or push it away, more came in. She was choking on it. She couldn't breathe.

Seconds before the last chink of daylight was erased she saw Khan. He was trying to get to her through the debris, although whether he wanted to save her or attack her, she didn't know. She just knew she was about to be buried alive.

Quite suddenly, everything was black and still. The roof stopped falling and she could breathe again. Gingerly, she tested her limbs. They were sore, but it didn't feel as if anything was broken. Not yet at least. But who knew what Khan had in mind. Maybe he'd just chew her up whole. She strained her ears. Was he readying himself to pounce? She unzipped her survival kit and groped inside for her torch.

It was gone.

Disbelief and a panic so extreme she felt as if she'd been stabbed in the stomach, hit Martine like a tidal wave. This couldn't be happening. Through every adventure and every near-death disaster she'd experienced since arriving in Africa, she'd been kept going by the knowledge that there were tools in her survival kit that could save her. But it wasn't only about what was in the pouch. It was that everything in it had been given to her by someone she cared for – by the

Morrisons back in England, by Grace, Tendai, Gwyn Thomas and even by Caracal Junior's most infuriating boy, Claudius. Now it was almost empty.

Martine couldn't understand it. The survival kit had been with her nearly every minute, apart from a few hours the previous night when she'd forgotten it by the fire after the crisis with baby Emelia. It was hard to believe that her pink torch, Swiss Army knife and other items could have held any interest for the weary villagers. Then who? The witchdoctor? She doubted it. The dogs? A roaming night animal?

A picture of fluttering eyelashes and a long yellow beak popped into Martine's head. 'Magnus!' she gasped.

The irony of it was too cruel. She'd escaped the human treasure seekers, only to be robbed by a treasure seeking bird, and now she was alone in the blackness with the most dangerous animal on earth: a wounded leopard.

· 21 ·

Khan gave a menacing growl that was somehow magnified by the dead air and the blinding dark. Martine tried to curl herself into a small ball. If she could have seen his eyes she could have attempted to use her gift to stop him from attacking her, but without light she could do nothing.

Without changing position, she opened the pouch again and rummaged through it in case it contained some life-saving device she'd somehow missed. But it was empty apart from Grace's headache potion and a tube of superglue. The hornbill had done a pretty thorough job of nicking the shiny things. Oddly, it was

169

still quite heavy, which was why Martine hadn't noticed the missing items sooner. She unzipped an interior pocket she rarely used and her fingers touched something hard and smooth. Something waxy. Candles! And, behind them, slightly crushed, was the box of matches. She and Ben had taken them, along with one or two other supplies, as they left the house and she'd put them into her survival pouch without thinking.

She couldn't hear Khan, but sensed he was very near. It would have been comforting to think that he could see as little as she did, but she knew leopards were nocturnal and had perfect night vision. In all probability, he was watching her every move.

Striking a match, she held it to the candlewick. Khan snarled at the sizzle and the flare of yellow light. As she'd suspected, he was very close to her, but he wasn't poised to pounce. He was in a smooth hollow on the rock floor of a long cavern. His ribcage was rising and falling very rapidly and his breathing was distressed. She soon saw why. A pool of treacly blood had collected around his chest, staining his golden fur scarlet. A gaping wound was the source of it.

Martine's eyes filled with tears. She forgot to be afraid, forgot that he was a killer, forgot everything except that she'd promised to protect him and failed.

'Khan,' she whispered, 'I'm sorry.'

Khan's eyes were glazed with pain. He rose with effort and wandered unsteadily over to a shadowed area. Martine lifted the candle so that the wobbly circle of light illuminated him. He was lapping at a tiny spring.

Judging from the watermarks on the smooth rocks that surrounded it, it had once been the source of a large stream – perhaps even an underground river – but it had dried up over the years and was little more than a trickle.

The leopard drank for a long time, and then he returned to the hollow and lay down again. Blood leaked steadily onto the floor beneath his chest. He growled softly to himself and licked hopelessly at his scarlet paws.

Martine was in despair. It was agony to see such a proud, magnificent animal reduced to a pitiful invalid. She was sure that if he carried on losing blood at the present rate he would die within the hour.

Since he was too preoccupied with his own suffering to pose a threat, Martine climbed stiffly to her feet and began to take stock of their surroundings. It didn't take long to establish that their situation was desperate. The cavern they were in seemed to be the end of a tunnel hewn by the water and now blocked by an immense boulder. Martine tried holding the candle to the hole where the spring flowed out but couldn't see what was on the other side. Whether the boulder was part of the landslide or had been there for centuries was difficult to tell.

She checked the cavern roof but that didn't look hopeful either. The hole through which she'd fallen was also blocked, and was much too high for her to reach even if it wasn't. It's not as if there was a chair or a ladder she could use to stand on. Last she examined the walls. They were solid rock. Or at least she thought they were. There was something subtly different about the wall behind the leopard. She stared at it for a long time but couldn't work out what.

Realistically her, and Khan's, only chance of survival was to be saved by someone on the outside. Problem was, nobody knew they were there. She could try shouting, but it was hard to believe that anyone would hear her.

Martine wanted to cry. Some of the ordeals she'd faced over the past eight months had been so horrific she'd been quite sure that if she lived through them she'd never experience anything worse. And yet here she was, buried alive with a wounded leopard. 'You couldn't make it up,' she said out loud and very nearly managed a smile.

She eyed the bleeding leopard, sniffed loudly, and pulled herself together. Tendai was always telling her that the more hopeless things seemed in a survival situation, the more you had to focus on doing what you could do, minute by minute. And what she needed to do now was help the leopard.

Her priority was to stop him bleeding. But how? She was in a solid rock cavern with a virtually empty survival kit. And yet Tendai and Grace insisted that even the most barren places had something to offer in terms of healing herbs or tools that could save a life.

'When you have looked with your own eyes and you can't see anything to help you, that's when you must look with the eyes of a Bushman or an animal,' Tendai would say. 'The San lived in the deserts of the Kalahari where you or I would see nothing but sand. But they found every medicine they needed and all the food they could eat.'

Martine tried looking around the cave with San eyes. The only natural resource there was water. She didn't know how clean it was, but animals have very good instincts about such things and the fact that Khan had drunk so much of it was a positive sign. Water on its own was not going to be much use, but if the spring had ever been exposed to sunlight there might be moss. And Grace had taught her that moss was almost as effective as gauze dressing when it came to wounds.

She carried the candle over to the thin stream, keeping a wary eye on Khan. Worryingly, he didn't even lift his head. Martine knew that his condition was getting critical. She sighed with relief when she saw the luxuriant bed of green growing up on the far side of the water. Using a sharp triangle of broken rock, she cut two square mats of nature's best field dressing.

It was her first breakthrough.

All she had to do now was find some form of antiseptic or antibiotic. Would Grace's headache potion be any use?

She went over to examine her survival kit again and noticed that the bottom of her right shoe kept sticking to the floor. That reminded her that she'd stepped on some honeycomb shortly before her fall. Honey! Honey was an excellent natural antibiotic and wound healer. What if the chunk of honeycomb had tumbled with her? That would make all the difference.

She rushed over to the pile of earth and stones and scrabbled at it like a terrier after a bone. Thanks to its stickiness, she found the honeycomb almost immediately. She rinsed it clean and ate a few chunks to give her energy. It had a rich toffee taste, which boosted her spirits. They needed boosting. The hard part was still to come.

Khan's head rested on the worn hollow of rock with a familiarity that made Martine wonder if he came here often; if this was his secret lair. She'd assumed that he'd tumbled through the cavern ceiling like she had, but if this was his secret den he must have been here already. And if that was true, a landslide must have sealed the tunnel *after* he was inside.

Sensing he was the object of her attention, Khan gave a warning snarl so vicious Martine's heart almost leapt from her chest. Her only consolation was that he'd had two previous opportunities to hurt her and hadn't. On the second occasion, he'd actually saved her from Mr Rat and his thugs.

Martine decided that the only solution was to pretend that the leopard was just an oversized version of Shelby and Warrior, her grandmother's cats. She picked up the moss, honey and her almost empty survival kit, marched purposefully over to him, and sat down beside him as if she dealt with injured leopards every day of the week.

In the flickering candlelight, the expression on Khan's face was priceless. Had his condition not been so serious, Martine would have dissolved into giggles. He looked too shocked to object. He lay on his side and, for once, was quite docile.

Before he had time to change his mind, Martine pressed the moss to the wound on his chest, earning a savage growl for her bravery but nothing worse. Her other hand covered his heart. She closed her eyes. Nearly two months had passed since she'd last drawn on her gift and she was not entirely confident it would work, but she focussed on Khan's silken fur beneath her palms and the steady *doof, doof, doof* beat of his heart. Her hands grew hotter. Flashes of light and memory, like incoming pictures on a faulty television, began to crash around her head.

She saw the faces of the ancients, the San people, and somehow they were kinder and wiser than she could ever have imagined, and they were chanting with her, encouraging her, and it seemed to Martine that they were speaking in the language that the witchdoctor had used and that she could understand it. A magical energy came from them and passed through her as if she were a lightning conductor.

At first the leopard writhed beneath her touch as if her hands were so hot they were singeing him, but gradually his muscles relaxed and a peace came over him. She opened her eyes and lifted away the moss. The bleeding had stopped. Using her hankerchief as a wet cloth, she rinsed shrapnel from the wound and wiped the area around it. Then she dribbled honey onto the exposed flesh.

Throughout this process Khan lay still, although he trembled slightly. Once the blood had been cleaned away Martine was pleased to see the bullet hole wasn't as wide or deep as she'd feared. It had bled a lot, but the wound itself was clean. That meant she could use superglue to close it. A long time ago she'd employed soldier termites to stitch up a fallen kudu, but Grace had wisely pointed out they weren't always going to be handy and that the glue would be a worthwhile addition to her survival kit.

'I would have thought that you'd prefer to use something more natural than hardware-store glue to treat wounds,' Martine had said.

'T'aint about what's natural, honey,' Grace had replied. 'It's about what *works*.'

The superglue also meant that no termites were decapitated in the process of stitching, which was definitely good. And it was more efficient. Martine squeezed a minute amount along one edge of the wound and pressed the two sides together. It sealed perfectly.

By now she felt confident enough in Khan to pour Grace's painkilling potion into the side of his mouth. He licked his lips and wrinkled up his nose, baring his fearsome teeth. It was obvious he loathed the foul taste, but he seemed to understand it was for his own good.

With the immediate crisis over, Martine realized how shattered she was. As long as she'd been focussed on Khan, she hadn't had time to think about herself. Now she couldn't stop shaking. She washed her hands and face in the spring. The thing she kept thinking about was what would happen if nobody found them. What if this cold cavern was to become their tomb?

As far as she could tell, she'd done everything she could for the moment. She had light and food (well, a few tablespoons' worth of honey) and they both had water. Water could keep them alive for weeks, although if nobody found them that might not necessarily be a good thing. They'd simply starve to death over a longer period. What's worse, they'd starve to death in the dark. There were only two candles in the survival kit and the first one was half gone.

She wondered how Ben was doing. He'd protected her from the hunters at great risk to himself, but she had a feeling he would have outsmarted them or, at the very least, outrun them. With any luck the police siren she'd heard belonged to a squad car full of good police, rather than corrupt police, who'd rescue Ben from the clutches of the Rat's men and then start combing the hills for her and Khan.

She thought, too, about her grandmother, who she hoped was not too distressed about her disappearance; about Jemmy, who she missed with every fibre of her being; Grace, who would be proud of how she'd used the knowledge she'd been give to heal the leopard; Tendai, whose bushcraft lessons had helped her think her way through the situation methodically when a lot of kids she knew would have been hysterical with despair; and, of course, her mum and dad, who might be gone but were always with her and watching over her, every minute of every day.

Her watch showed that it was early evening, but time was meaningless in the cavern. Martine propped herself up against the cold rock wall and tried to doze. She was as scared to blow out the candle and face the suffocating darkness as she was to keep it burning and see it melt away to nothing. She would keep it lit until she felt sleepier. It gave the illusion of warmth. The temperature in the cave was dropping by the minute.

Martine looked longingly at the leopard's golden form. She wondered if he was as scared and lonely as she was. She tried to remind herself that leopards were the most unpredictable and fierce of the big cats and that he was unlikely to be feeling any such thing, but she had very little to lose.

She went over to him and lay down in the hollow. It was strangely soft, almost cushioned. Khan half-opened one eye but did nothing to suggest he minded. Heart pounding, Martine blew out the candle and snuggled against his silky back, carefully avoiding his wound. When he didn't react, she put an arm over him and rested her palm on one of his great paws, feeling the sharpness of his claws and the heat of his rough, fleshy pads.

She was just dozing off when he began to purr – big, tractor-type purrs that vibrated through them both. A slow grin spread across Martine's face.

It was a strange kind of heaven, sleeping with a wild leopard, but it was heaven nonetheless.

· 22 ·

Tuk-tuk-tuk. Tat-tat-tat. Tuk-tuk-tuk. Tat-tat-tat.
'Magnus, leave me alone,' grumbled Martine. 'It's too early. I've told you before not to wake me at the crack of dawn.'

She stretched stiffly and her arm touched something soft and silky. It let out a noise that was somewhere between a growl and a purr. Martine sat bolt upright in the darkness. The terror of the previous day came back to her. She was hundreds of feet underground with the world's biggest leopard and they were in a cave that could soon become their tomb.

She groped about for the candle and matches and the

cavern filled with light. Khan sat up too and his yellow eyes swung on her like headlamps. The hatred she'd once seen in them had been replaced with a look that definitely wasn't love, but wasn't far from it either. She leaned forward without fear and examined his chest wound. There was hardly any swelling and the tissue around it was pink and healthy. Martine felt quite pleased with her handiwork. 'Not bad for an amateur,' she boasted to Khan, and ran her hand over his amazing spotted coat.

The leopard gave a blood-curdling snarl and surged to his feet. Martine froze. Was she about to pay the price for crossing a line with him? Was he going to turn on her? Then she heard it again – a faint knocking.

Khan moved on silent paws towards the centre of the cavern and crouched there, listening. The noise seemed to be coming from above. He looked round at Martine for reassurance.

'Maybe it's our friends,' Martine told him. 'Maybe they've found us. Maybe we're going to be saved.'

She was astonished to find that she experienced a slight twinge of sorrow at the thought. Of *course* she wanted to be rescued. Of *course* she wanted to see Ben and her grandmother and everyone else. But she also knew that the magic of this time with Khan, when it was just the two of them against the world and they were utterly dependant on one another, would never come again. As soon as anyone else entered the cavern, the specialness of these moments would be banished with the morning light.

Another more disturbing thought entered her head. What if the distant hammering wasn't her friends at all? What if it was Griffin and his crew wanting revenge, or Rex Ratcliffe's hunters, ready with their rifles? Those possibilities kept her from crying out for help. And yet anything must be better than starving to death in a black hole.

She got up from the hollow, thinking to herself that it had been surprisingly warm and comfortable for a rock bed. Too warm and comfortable. A ghost of an idea flitted across her mind, but it was gone before she could get a grip on it. The hammering outside had started again but it was not so loud. The rescue party was moving away.

Martine lifted the candle and was struck again by how the back wall of the cavern seemed slightly different to the rest. She rapped it with her knuckles to test it.

The elusive thought floated into her head. It had to do with a comment Ngwenya had made when he was telling them about Lobengula's treasure. He said that the burial party had 'hidden it well and sealed the entrance with a stone wall'.

Martine ran a hand over the wall, and that's when she knew. It was man-made! That's what was 'wrong' with it. Whoever had built it had done it superbly, going to enormous lengths to replicate exactly the colour and grain of the rock. Only someone who'd spent as much time in the cavern as she had would have noticed it was any different to the other walls.

The hairs stood up on the back of Martine's neck. She stared at the hollow. *The last resting place of the King of*

Leopards is the hiding place of the King's Treasure . . .

It wasn't the last resting place of the leopard, but it very nearly had been.

Khan was snarling at the boulder, his tail swishing furiously. He paced the cave on legs wobbly from blood loss. Martine thought she heard voices, but she was so preoccupied she dismissed it as being her imagination.

She bent down and studied the smooth impression in the cavern floor. It had a worn appearance which she'd put down to it having been used for months or even years as a sleeping area by Khan. But now she saw that it wasn't rock at all; it was ancient leather. She used the sharp piece of rock to prise up a corner. Underneath was a platform of wood, which was easy enough to lift off. And beneath that was a vault hewn from the rock. It was filled with dusty sacks and three rusty tins that might once have been silver. One of the sacks had a small rip in it, out of which protruded a single gold sovereign. It winked in the candlelight.

'Martine!' Ben's voice was muffled. 'Martine, are you in there? Oh, please be alive. MARTINE!'

As if in a dream, Martine replaced the wooden platform and the leather cover, went over to the pile of debris and used her sweatshirt to carry several loads to the hollow. She patted it down and put her sweatshirt on top of it. Then she walked slowly to Khan's side. She squatted down and put her arm around him.

'Ben! Ben, I'm here!' she shouted, and her voice echoed back at her, 'Ben-en-en-en! Ben-en-en-en, I'm here-ere-ere-ere!'

Martine would always remember that day as one of the happiest and saddest ever. Happy because she and Khan were saved, and Ben, Sadie and her grandmother were in one piece, although all were a bit shaken. Happy too because there were lots of hugs and tears of joy, and because after the boulder had been pulled away from the tunnel entrance, she, her friends, and practically everyone from Mercy and Odilo's village had travelled to Black Eagle Lodge on the back of a tractor and trailer and enjoyed a celebration barbecue in the sunshine.

There was plenty to celebrate. A wave of arrests, for

starters. The District Attorney had been appalled to discover from Ngwenya that the involvement of several police officers in the pay of Rex Ratcliffe had led to the wrongful incarceration of two elderly women, one with a broken leg. He'd had his eye on the Lazy J for quite some time, and the evidence provided by the horse wrangler and the waiter finally gave him the ammunition he needed to get a search warrant. Not, however, before Sadie and Gwyn Thomas had spent a night in the cells with a host of petty thieves and one murderer.

'I haven't laughed so much in years,' declared Sadie, who seemed, bizarrely, to have relished the experience.

The District Attorney had taken a rather more dim view of his officers' conduct, and after a day of enquiries had banged them up in the same cells. The police car Martine had heard when she was fleeing Griffin belonged to constables sent from Bulawayo by the DA. They'd been on their way to arrest the hunters for trespassing and attempting to kill a protected animal without a licence. After they'd caught the duty manager chasing Ben with a stick, the policemen had added 'attempted assault' to the charge sheet.

On their way back to the retreat, they'd discovered a comatose figure by the roadside. It was Griffin, suffering an allergic reaction to the bee stings. He was so swollen that one of the constables described him as looking as if he'd been blown up with a bicycle pump. He'd been rushed to hospital and was sleeping off the medication. One of the first questions the police asked Martine was whether she and Ben wanted to press charges against the treasure seeker when he came to his senses. His *shamwaris* had fled the area and would have to be dealt with later.

After talking it over, Ben and Martine agreed not to press charges. The ants and bees had punished Griffin enough and they felt he'd probably learnt his lesson.

'Deep down, he's not a bad person,' Martine told Odilo. 'As you said, he's just fallen in with the wrong crowd and lost his way. If he gets a second chance, maybe he'll think about going back to school and ending up on the right side of the law.'

Rex Ratcliffe had been arrested for illegal hunting, foreign currency violations and other offences too numerous to list, and was likely to be in jail for quite some time. The Lazy J had been closed down with immediate effect, and all the animals were going to be re-homed in new sanctuaries.

'Good Rat-ence,' Sadie quipped when she was told about the Lazy J owner's grim future behind bars. She was full of smiles. On her release, she had checked her post office box in Bulawayo and found a heap of bookings from an American travel agent, plus a $1,000 cheque from an anonymous benefactor. It all meant that she could rehire her former Black Eagle staff, with one new addition: Odilo was to replace Sadie as chef.

'I don't have any imagination as a cook,' she admitted. 'The only recipes I know all seem to contain butternut squash.' But she was also beaming for another reason. 'I saw the leopard again,' she said over and over. 'I saw

Khan and he was worth every second of every day I spent fighting for him.'

Late afternoon, Martine and Ben climbed Elephant Rock and sat on the hill's summit watching the sun go down over the ancient landscape of the Matopos. They could see almost as far as the Hill of Benevolent Spirits and World's View. Magnus, the hornbill, had flown up with them and was perched on Martine's knee.

'Tell me again how you found me,' Martine said to Ben, unpacking the slices of chocolate cake she'd brought with her.

He stretched out his brown legs on the warm granite rock and ate a mouthful of cake before replying. 'Well, after the cops showed up and arrested the hunters, Ngwenya and I started searching for you. He's a pretty good tracker himself and between us we tracked you to the top of Rabbit Warren Hill. There your footprints just stopped. We could see that the ground near the tree had recently collapsed, as if there'd been a landslide or an old mine shaft had fallen in, and we were scared to death that you'd been buried alive, or were wandering around the catacomb of tunnels with concussion or even lying somewhere with a broken limb.'

He stopped. 'I was frightened I might never see you again.'

Martine grinned. 'You're not going to get rid of me that easily, you know.'

'Promise? Anyway, it took a long time to get a rescue effort together because it's impossible to dig up a whole hill and nobody could agree on where or how to start. If we'd got it wrong, we could have made things much worse for you. We needed equipment, a paramedic and a wildlife vet to tranquilize Khan if necessary. Plus your grandmother and Sadie wanted to be there, and most of the villagers insisted on helping.'

'It sounds as if it was one of those "too many cooks" situations,' Martine said sympathetically.

'It sort of was. Tribal custom meant that Chief Nyoni, who is the highest-ranking chief in the Matobo Hills, also had to be present. By coincidence, it turned out that his grandson was a famous wildlife vet. That was good news, but both of them were coming from different places and they took ages to arrive. It was very hard to be patient, but I just kept hoping that you'd figured out what the witchdoctor meant when he said, "Look to the House of Bees".'

Martine shuddered at the memory of the collective hum of the swarming bees. 'I did,' she said.

'We started digging at first light but we were getting nowhere fast,' Ben went on. 'Sadie and Mercy were waiting at the bottom because Sadie couldn't climb with her crutches and Mercy is ... well, Mercy is the wrong shape to clamber up mountains, and they kept shouting conflicting instructions. It was a bit annoying. But if it hadn't been for them and Magnus, we might never have found you.'

Martine stroked the hornbill's head and he swooned with delight. 'You're a bad bird for stealing my survival stuff, but I might have to forgive you,' she said. She took off her silver dolphin necklace and gave it to him. In a trice he'd scooped it into his yellow beak. 'Now we're connected, too,' she told him.

To Ben she said, 'So it was Mercy who noticed Magnus was behaving oddly?'

'Yes. She remarked to Sadie that it was weird how the hornbill kept flapping around this one shrub on the side of the hill. Sadie put two and two together and realized that Magnus might be trying to get to you. We pulled back the shrub to discover the old water tunnel, and the rest . . .'

'The rest is history,' finished Martine.

She knew the rest of the story off by heart. Ropes had been put around the boulder and the tunnel roof had been propped up with two big planks of wood in case it was unstable. Nobody, including Martine, knew how the leopard would react when the tunnel was cleared, so a decision was made that no more than four people would enter. At Martine's insistence, they were Ben, Ngwenya, Chief Nyoni, a frail, birdlike man, and the wildlife vet, Chief Nyoni's grandson. He'd travelled overnight from Hwange Game Reserve.

The vet was not able to approach Khan and had to examine him from the other side of the cavern, but he saw enough to be impressed that Martine had managed to stem the bleeding, and disinfect and seal the wound with only moss, honey and superglue to hand.

'All those years at veterinary school and I could have just stayed in the Matopos picking up tips from an eleven-year-old,' he joked.

After that, things got serious. Chief Nyoni sat Martine and Ben down and told them that late the previous night the leopard clan had gathered together to discuss Khan's future if he was found alive. Their number one priority was preserving Khan and his descendants for the benefit and enjoyment of future generations in the Matopos, and they agreed that if he had to be sent away to a place of safety for a few years until peace returned to Zimbabwe, then so be it. The following morning, they'd talked it over with Sadie and Gwyn Thomas, and the clan had unanimously agreed that if Khan survived he should go to live at Sawubona.

'Sawubona!' gasped Martine. 'That's awesome. But how will we get him there?'

Ngwenya laughed. 'We have a network,' he said. 'Since Mzilikazi's time, the Ndebele people have had many enemies, so we have learned to have friends in many places. Chief Nyoni's grandson is the best wildlife veterinarian in Zimbabwe. He is authorized to sign the necessary papers. He will sedate Khan now and they will leave within the hour for the border. The fuel delivery truck came today and we have already arranged the transport. At the border we also have friends among the customs officials.

'Chief Nyoni's grandson will stay with the leopard until they reach Sawubona. Mrs Thomas said that your game warden, Tendai – did you know that Tendai is an

Ndebele word for thank you? – will take care of him in your wildlife sanctuary until he is well enough to be released into the wild.'

Martine could hardly believe what she was hearing. The magnificent creature now growling in the circle of her arms was going to be living at Sawubona. Even if she rarely glimpsed him, she'd always know he was there. Watching her.

Watching over her.

'But how long will he be able to stay with us?' she'd asked excitedly.

'Perhaps a couple of years, perhaps for ever,' the chief replied. 'We give you our word that we will never send for him or for his sons and daughters until they can once again live without fear in the Matobo Hills.'

The vet had tapped his watch then. 'Time is running short if we are to make the border before nightfall,' he said.

Tears had poured down Martine's face as she realized that, after everything they'd been through together, she and Khan were about to be parted. To the shock and awe of the onlookers, she put her nose to that of the leopard in a sort of Eskimo kiss.

'I'll always love you, Khan,' she whispered, and was rewarded with a final purr.

Minutes later, he'd been sedated and was fast asleep, and Chief Nyoni's grandson and men with a stretcher bore him away. His long journey south had begun.

Chief Nyoni broke the awkward silence that followed. 'I'm glad to have seen with my own eyes that we have appointed the right guardian for the leopard,' he said.

At a word from Martine, Ben left the cavern and she was alone with the chief and Ngwenya.

'I have something for you,' Ngwenya told her. He dug in his pocket and handed her a pink Maglite torch, a Swiss Army knife and one or two other shiny things from her survival kit.

Martine was thrilled. 'Where did you find these?'

'In the hornbill's nest. At the top of the hill, a bees' nest had been knocked down. Magnus's house was behind it. It was full of money and jewellery, like Aladdin's cave.'

'Enough to feed the whole of the Matopos for a year?' Martine teased.

Ngwenya laughed. 'For a year at least.'

'I also found something,' Martine said.

Chief Nyoni sat up straight.

'You found what?' Ngwenya said carefully.

Martine handed him the candle. 'I've left my sweatshirt back there in the shadows,' she said. 'I'll leave it up to you to decide what to do with it.'

She almost ran from the chilly cavern after that, rushing along the tunnel and emerging, blinking, into blazing white sunshine and the waiting arms of her grandmother.

'To think that I was worried about you having a little canter on the white giraffe,' Gwyn Thomas said, hugging her. 'Instead I bring you to the Matopos, where you're chased by hunters, kidnapped by treasure seekers and buried alive with a leopard. The next time I suggest dragging you across the countryside for a so-called holiday, say to me, "Grandmother, I'd much rather stay home and read books and ride Jemmy."'

'Umm, I did try,' Martine reminded her with a grin.

'I know,' said Gwyn Thomas. 'But next time I'll listen.'

They were waiting by the tractor and trailer when Ngwenya and Chief Nyoni appeared at the tunnel entrance. Ngwenya was holding Martine's sweatshirt but nothing else. They were halfway down the hill when there was a muffled explosion. Martine guessed that they'd removed the planks holding up the tunnel roof and triggered a landslide. A dust cloud blasted out of the space where the tunnel had been, and then the whole hillside seemed to buckle and change shape. It was as if the cavern and its contents had never been.

Ngwenya and Chief Nyoni never looked back. When they reached the tractor, Ngwenya handed Martine her sweatshirt.

'Was that the only thing you found?' she couldn't resist asking him.

'The only thing worth keeping,' he said. 'We have love, freedom and enough to eat in the Matobo Hills. That's all we could possibly need.'

The evening star was sparkling over Elephant Rock by the time Martine and Ben made their way down to the retreat. With the coming of night, the intense silence of the Matopos which had so unnerved Martine on their arrival was settling over the hills and valleys, and she thought how much she'd miss it when she was gone. It was quite the most beautiful sound she'd ever known.

The change in Sadie's fortunes and the decision to send the leopard to Sawubona meant that she, Ben and Gwyn Thomas were leaving Zimbabwe earlier than planned. She'd have time to spend reading and riding Jemmy after all. She was ecstatic about that but her heart ached at the thought of leaving the Matobo Hills. She was also wondering whether she'd ever see the leopard again.

'Of course you will,' said Ben. 'Especially if he's going to be living at Sawubona.'

'Yes, but it won't be the same,' Martine told him. 'I won't ever get to fall asleep cuddled up next to him again.'

They were on their way to say goodbye to the six horses when they bumped into Ngwenya, who'd just finished feeding them.

'I wanted to wish you both a safe trip,' he said. 'I am going to the far village with Mercy and Odilo and I won't be back before you leave in the morning. Thank you again for what you did for Khan. And please convey our gratitude to your *sangoma* for providing the medicine that helped Emelia.'

'Come with us,' Martine pleaded. 'Tendai's always saying he could do with an extra pair of hands at Sawubona. Travel back with us. You'd love it.'

Ngwenya laughed. 'I'm sure I would, but no matter

how difficult things get in Zimbabwe, no matter how much we have to struggle, I will never leave the Matopos. My ancestors have walked in these hills.'

'I understand,' Martine said. She shook his hand in the African way, gripping his hand, then his thumb, and then his hand again. 'Goodbye, Ngwenya.'

He smiled. 'No, not goodbye. The Ndebele have a proverb, "Those who once saw each other will see each other again."'

EPILOGUE

The leopard lay with his forelegs stretched out before him, his spotted coat gleaming like liquid gold in the early morning sunlight. In the valley below, the dark shapes of buffalo and striped hides of zebra moved in slow motion across the plain surrounding the lake. Ordinarily the sight of so much food on the go would have made him think of dinner, but today he was only interested in the girl and her rather odd companions, an old woman and a white giraffe. The three of them were watching the sunrise over the lake, and the white giraffe was resting his head on the girl's shoulder.

For reasons that Khan found confusing and nice all at

once, his heart felt soft and full whenever the girl was around. Once, without realizing it, she'd been so close to him in his new den in the Secret Valley that she'd brushed his fur. She'd reacted as if she'd been scalded, she hadn't seen him in the dark. She'd had a bright light with her, but she had chosen not to shine it his way.

He'd followed her into the cave with the pictures after that, and watched from the shadows as she'd met with an exuberant African woman of colourful dress and considerable proportions. After they'd embraced, they'd sat gazing at the pictures and talking. Neither of them looked around, but Khan sensed they knew he was there.

On that occasion as on several others, the leopard could have killed the girl with one bound. She'd trespassed into his territory. But the only urge he ever felt was a burning desire to protect her. She had, after all, saved his life. On the long night in the airless cavern, when he'd suffered ten kinds of agony and felt the strength ebbing from his limbs with every breath, the magic from her hands had been a balm. She'd done something to the wound on his chest (at one stage he was quite sure he smelt honey, which he loathed) and had sort of tricked him into swallowing the most revolting liquid he'd ever tasted.

But afterwards the bleeding had stopped, the pain had gone away, and the hole in his chest had vanished as if by a miracle.

Then something most peculiar had happened. She'd dared to lie beside him and snuggle up to him as if he was her pet cat. She'd even put a hand on his paw. And much to his own bewilderment he hadn't just tolerated her presence because he was too weak to do anything about it, he'd cherished every moment, because the energy that flowed from her was pure love.

It was a strange kind of heaven, sleeping with a small human, but it was heaven nonetheless.

Now they were connected and would be for all their lives. Whether she turned to look at him or not, he knew that she was aware of him. A smile would play around her lips whenever she was close to him and he sensed that she was proud of her part in bringing him to this place of safety.

Since he'd come to Sawubona, the fear that Khan endured all his life had almost gone. There was no reason to be afraid here. It was a wildlife paradise. Still he would always be wary. The girl apart, he'd learned the hard way that humans were not to be trusted. The old woman and the Zulu man who ran the game reserve appeared to be good people and on the side of the animals, but he would always be suspicious of outsiders.

Recently, though, he'd spotted one of his own kind – a female leopard with two cubs. In the coming days he planned to make her acquaintance. He was tired of being alone.

Khan stood up, stretched and prepared to make his way to his hidden sanctuary for his daytime snooze. As he did so, he dislodged a rock. That rock dislodged another rock, which in turn exposed two elephant tusks that had lain undisturbed for more than a thousand years. They tumbled crookedly down the mountain and came to rest with their tips touching, like the head of an arrow.

The leopard saw them land. He paused to sniff them as he moved fluidly down the slope towards his den. They were pointing northeast, beyond the boundary fence of Sawubona, to a place of hot, dry winds, red rippled dunes, and skies like billowing blue canopies.

They were pointing to the land where it all began.

AUTHOR'S NOTE

The inspiration for the last leopard of this book comes from a real leopard, also named Khan who, for the past four years, has resided at Bally Vaughan Bird and Game Sanctuary in Harare, Zimbabwe. Like the fictional Khan, he is, at nearly seventy-five kilograms, one of the largest leopards ever recorded. Khan was orphaned when his mum and dad died of anthrax poisoning, and he is taken care of by Sarah Carter and other dedicated volunteers at Bally Vaughan, who battle against near insurmountable odds to keep Khan and the other precious animals at the sanctuary safe and out of the hands of hunters.

Khan is one of the lucky animals in Zimbabwe. In 2005, when I first came up with the idea for *The Last Leopard*, it was as a reaction against reports I kept hearing about the rise of 'canned' hunting in Zimbabwe, the wicked and widespread practice of putting lions, leopards and other dangerous and hard-to-hunt animals in small enclosures so that 'hunters' are guaranteed a 'kill' or a trophy to hang on their wall. I imagined a worst-case scenario: that the day might dawn when there might only be one last leopard in Zimbabwe. Now, just two years on, the unthinkable is in danger of becoming a reality.

When I set off with my father on a road trip to the Matobo Hills in March 2007 to research this book, I have to admit that I was a little concerned I might have made a mistake deciding to send Martine, Ben and Gwyn Thomas to such a scary place in *The Last Leopard*. On the drive from Harare to Bulawayo, we were stopped at numerous roadblocks by police brandishing machine guns, demanding to know if we were carrying smuggled diamonds – 'I wish!' was my dad's response – or any other contraband. Like Gwyn Thomas, we struggled to find petrol, and the whole of Zimbabwe was stricken by chronic water and electricity shortages.

Entering the Matobo National Park was like entering a totally different country. Martine's first impressions were my first impressions. I had the same sense she does that I'd reached the end of the world. The silence is awesome. The immense, balancing rocks and granite mountains, streaked with jade lichen and chestnut water-stains, are both humbling and breathtaking.

Reviewers of *The White Giraffe* and *Dolphin Song* have described them as magical realism, meaning that they have elements of fantasy and the supernatural in them but also lots of real life and fact. Doubtless the same is true of *The Last Leopard*. But for many people in Africa, and perhaps particularly in the Matobo Hills, cave spirits and the prophesies and healing powers of witchdoctors and *sangomas* are not the stuff of fantasy, but part of every day life – as real as you or I.

For many residents of the Matopos, the cave spirits and guardians of the shrines I've described in *The Last*

Leopard, including the one about the girl who lived under water with crocodiles for seven years, are incontrovertible truths, not fiction. And in Zambia, the sending out of miniature tortoises with coffins or toy ambulances on their backs as a warning or curse is a favourite method of witchdoctors.

What struck me most about the Matobo Hills is that, in spite of the fact that Zimbabwe is in crisis, the gentle, likeable people of this special area seemed almost untouched by the problems in the rest of the country. Life continued much as it did a hundred years before. Peace reigned. Every day, we came across laughing girls, some as young as five, walking six kilometers through the bush to school as if nothing could be more enjoyable or normal.

Yet even for this remote, lovely region, time is running out. The Matobo Hills has always had one of the highest concentrations of leopards in the world, but illegal hunters have moved in and recently one was caught trying to smuggle leopard skins into America. Cheetahs, lions and hippos, animals we thought would be around for ever, are moving onto the endangered list, and the leopard, one of world's most elusive and beautiful creatures, is in danger of being wiped out. Unless we act soon, we'll wake up to discover that there *is* only one last leopard.

Lauren St John
London, 2007

the elephant's tale

LAUREN St JOHN

For my niece, Alexandra Summer, who,
being my sister's daughter, is guaranteed
to grow up wanting to save elephants!

· 1 ·

The first time Martine saw the car, she was high up on the escarpment at Sawubona Wildlife Reserve tucking into a campfire breakfast. She didn't take much notice of it then because Tendai, the Zulu game warden, distracted her by saying something to make her laugh, and because she was too busy savouring the smoky-sweet taste of her bacon and fried banana roll, and also because the car – a black saloon with blacked-out windows – turned around before it reached the distant house and drove away, so she just thought it was someone lost.

It wasn't until the following day, when the black car

came again while she was tending to the sanctuary animals, that she remembered the strange, slow circuit it had made, as if it was in a funeral procession. This time she had no choice but to pay attention to it, because it glided up to the runs housing Sawubona's injured and orphaned animals as if it had a right to be there. The rear door opened and a tall, bald man wearing an expensive navy suit and a watch that could have been hand-crafted from a gold ingot stepped out. He looked around as if he owned the place.

'Can I help you?' she asked, trying not to show how annoyed she was that he and his big car had frightened the sick animals. She was prepared to bet that he wouldn't dream of driving into a human hospital and disturbing the patients, but a lot of people didn't feel that animals deserved the same consideration.

'Oh, I think I've seen all I need to see,' he said. But he continued to stand there, a pleased smile playing around his lips. He reached into his pocket for a lighter and a fat cigar, and began puffing away as if he had all the time in the world.

'We're not open for safaris on a Sunday,' Martine told him. 'You'll have to make an appointment and come back during the week.'

'I'm not here for a safari,' said the man. 'I'm here to see Gwyn Thomas. And who might you be?'

Martine smothered a sigh. She had three very hungry caracals to feed and an antelope wound to dress and she wasn't in the mood for small talk. Added to which, her grandmother had given her all the usual lectures about not speaking to strangers, although she hadn't said anything about what to do if a stranger who'd come to Sawubona on official business started plying her with questions. 'I'm Martine Allen,' she said reluctantly. 'If you want to see my grandmother, she's at the house.'

'Allen?' he repeated. 'How long have you lived here, young Martine? You don't sound South African. Where are you from?'

Martine was getting desperate. She wished Tendai or Ben, her best friend in the world apart from Jemmy, her white giraffe, would show up and rescue her, but Tendai had gone into Storm Crossing to buy supplies for the reserve, and Ben was at the Waterfront in Cape Town seeing off his mum and dad. They were leaving on a Mediterranean cruise. She wanted to tell the bald man that her name and where she came from was none of his business, but she was afraid to be rude to him in case he was an important customer.

'A year,' she replied. 'I've been at Sawubona for nearly a year.' She could have added, *Ever since my mum and dad died in a fire at our home in Hampshire, England, last New Year's Eve,* but she didn't because she was not in the habit of sharing her private information with nosy strangers. Instead she asked: 'Is my grandmother expecting you? I can show you to the house.'

'A year is a good long time,' remarked the man. 'Long enough to become attached to a place.'

Then he said something that sent chills through Martine. He said: 'Shame.'

Just like that. Just one word: 'Shame.'

He said it in a way that made Martine want to rush home and take a shower she was so creeped out, even though he had in fact been perfectly polite and kept his distance throughout. His only crime had been polluting Sawubona's wildlife hospital with his cigar.

Before Martine could come up with a response, he continued briskly: 'Right then, I think it's time I had a word with your grandmother. Don't trouble yourself, I know the way.'

He climbed back into his shiny black car and was chauffeured away, leaving the sickly smell of cigar smoke and that one weighted word hanging in the air.

'Shame.'

· 2 ·

After he'd gone, Martine considered taking the shortcut to the house to warn her grandmother that a sinister man was on his way, but she hadn't thought to ask his name and Gwyn Thomas sometimes got impatient with what she called Martine's 'gut' feelings. And anyway what reason would she give for her suspicions? He was a well-dressed man in a smart car, and he hadn't done anything worse than ask who she was and remark that she didn't seem to be from around here. Martine decided to give him the benefit of the doubt. It wouldn't be the first time her instincts had been wrong.

The caracals were practically chewing the wire of their run they were so hungry, and they crouched down, ready to pounce on their food, as Martine went into their enclosure. They had arrived at Sawubona as spitting kittens with long, fur-tipped ears, so weak and small that they'd slept on Martine's bed for the first few weeks of their existence. Now they were as muscular as young mountain lions. When she tossed their meat into the air, they leapt as if they were jet-propelled, springing eight or ten feet to claw at it and then swallowing it whole with fearsome growls. Soon they would be ready to return to the wild. Martine knew she'd miss them terribly.

She tended to the rest of the animals with Ferris, the baby monkey, clinging to her shoulder. They all had to be fed and watered, and the dik dik, a dainty, miniature antelope with short pointy horns, needed his wound dressed. He stared up at Martine with big trusting eyes as she applied a special potion given to her by Grace, Tendai's aunt. Grace was a *sangoma*, a traditional healer of part Zulu, part Caribbean extraction. She was also the only person who knew the truth about Martine's secret gift – a gift to do with healing animals not even Martine fully understood. For that reason and many others, they had a special relationship. Now it was the school holidays Martine was looking forward to seeing more of her.

Martine returned a protesting Ferris to his cage and headed off down the track to say good morning to Jemmy. The game reserve gate was close to the house. As she let herself into the garden through a side entrance, she saw the black car still sitting in the driveway like a hearse. The chauffeur was leaning against the bonnet, smoking. He lifted a hand when he saw Martine crossing the yard. She waved back without enthusiasm.

Jemmy was waiting for her at the gate, just as he did every morning. He stood outlined against a kingfisher-blue sky, his white, silver and cinnamon-etched coat shimmering in the sunshine. Martine's spirits always soared when she saw him. It was ten months since she'd tamed him and learned to ride him but neither had lost their thrill for her. He greeted her with a low, musical fluttering sound and lowered his head. When she scratched him behind his ears and planted a kiss on his silky silver nose, his long curling eyelashes drooped in blissful contentment.

'Three more weeks of holidays, Jemmy,' she said. 'Can you believe that? Three brilliant weeks of no homework, no maths, no history, no Mrs Volkner ranting at me for staring out of the window, no detention; no school, period. And the best part about it is that Ben's coming to stay. It's going to be heaven on a stick. We're going to explore every inch of Sawubona in blazing sunshine and paddle in the lake and maybe even go camping.'

Jemmy gave her an affectionate shove with his nose. Martine was tempted to go for a quick ride on him, but she resisted because Ben would soon be back from Cape Town and she wanted to hear about his morning. She also wanted to help him get settled in to the guest room, where he'd be staying during the Christmas break while his Indian mum and African dad were away on their cruise. They'd wanted him to go with them, but Ben was studying under Tendai to be an apprentice tracker and had asked if he could stay behind to brush up on his bushcraft skills.

He and Martine were determined to have a peaceful, fun vacation at Sawubona after spending their last one trying to save a leopard from some evil hunters and a desperate gang of treasure seekers in the wilds of Zimbabwe.

Martine was locking the game park gate when the long black car suddenly vroomed into life. It reversed down the driveway at speed, almost knocking over a flowerpot. To Martine's surprise, her grandmother, who considered politeness to be the number one virtue and insisted in accompanying visitors out to their cars and waving until they'd gone, was nowhere to be seen. An uneasy feeling stirred in her.

She was hurrying through the mango trees towards the house when Tendai's jeep came flying into the yard. Ben was in the passenger seat. He grinned when he saw Martine, his teeth very white against the burnt-honey colour of his face.

'I hitched a ride from the main road with Tendai,' he explained when the jeep bounced to a halt. He hoisted his rucksack over one shoulder and jumped down from the battered vehicle. He was wearing a khaki vest, baggy camouflage trousers and hiking boots. 'The people who gave me a lift seemed reluctant to come all the way to the house in case they were eaten by a lion.'

Normally Martine would have cracked a joke, but she

was still taking in that the house was oddly silent. At eight o'clock Gwyn Thomas was usually drinking tea and eating gooseberry jam on toast at the kitchen table while listening to the news and weather on the radio. She'd also been planning to bake some scones to welcome Ben.

'Where is your grandmother, little one?' the game warden asked. 'I've been calling her on both the landline and her cellphone to check with her about a delivery. There's no answer.'

Martine stared at him. 'Tendai, something's wrong. This creepy man came to see her and now something's wrong, I just know it is.'

'*What* creepy man?' asked Ben, dropping his rucksack on the lawn.

Tendai frowned. 'Are you talking of the man in the black car? He almost ran us off the road.'

He started towards the house, with Martine and Ben following. Martine was kicking herself for not insisting that she go with the man to the house. If anything had happened to her grandmother . . .

Warrior, Gwyn Thomas's black and white cat, was sitting on the front step in the sunshine, his tail swishing furiously. His fur was standing on end. Tendai stepped around him and into the living room. 'Mrs Thomas?' he called. 'Mrs Thomas, are you all right?'

'Grandmother!' yelled Martine.

'No need to shout.' Gwyn Thomas's subdued voice echoed faintly along the passage. 'I'm in my study.'

Martine flew along the corridor and knocked at the

study door out of habit. Her grandmother was sitting hunched at her desk, her face the same colour as the sheaf of papers she was holding. When she looked up, Martine was shocked to see that her blue eyes were rimmed with red, as if she'd been crying.

'Come in, Martine, Tendai,' she said. 'You, too, Ben. You're part of the family.'

'That weird, creepy man has done something to upset you, hasn't he? I knew he was bad news as soon as I saw him.'

'Martine, how many times do I have to tell you not to judge people on the basis of your gut feelings?' Gwyn Thomas scolded. Her hands tightened on the documents. 'However, in this case I fear you may be right.'

She paused and gazed lingeringly out of the window, as if trying to imprint the view of springbok and zebra grazing around the waterhole on her mind. 'I wish I didn't have to say what I'm about to say to you all.'

'Whatever it is, I'm sure it will be okay, Mrs Thomas,' Tendai reassured her.

Martine wasn't in the least bit sure things were going to be okay. 'Grandmother, you're frightening us. What happened? Who *was* he?'

'His name is Reuben James,' Gwyn Thomas answered at last, turning to face them. 'He was a business associate of my late husband. I have a vague recollection of meeting him once and distrusting him on sight, although from what I remember the deal he and Henry did together went quite smoothly. Mr James spends most of his time in

Namibia and overseas and claims to have discovered only recently that Henry was killed by poachers two and a half years ago. He has just arrived with this.'

She held up one of the documents. Across the middle of it was written: *Last Will and Testament of Henry Paul Thomas*. In the top right-hand corner was a wax stamp, wobbly at the corners, like a splash of blood. Peering closer, Martine made out the logo of Cutter and Bow Solicitors, Hampshire, England.

Tendai was confused. 'But what is he doing with such a private document?'

'Good question. And the first one I asked him. It turns out that, three years ago, when Sawubona was in financial difficulty, Henry borrowed a large amount of money from Mr James. He apparently agreed to change his will to say that if the money was not paid back by 12 December this year – today, in other words – the game reserve and everything on it would automatically belong to Reuben James.'

'My God,' said Tendai. He sank into the spare chair.

Martine stood frozen, the words searing a path from her brain to her heart. *The game reserve and everything on it . . . The game reserve and everything on it.*

Ben said, 'Does that mean that the original will, making you the owner of Sawubona if Mr Thomas passed away, is now worthless?'

Gwyn Thomas nodded. 'Yes, because that will was written a decade or more before the one produced by Mr James. But that's not the worst part . . . '

Martine gasped. 'There's worse?'

'I'm afraid so. We've been served with an eviction order. We have thirteen days to leave Sawubona, give notice to all the staff, and say goodbye to all the animals. In thirteen days Sawubona will no longer be ours.'

· 3 ·

Whenever Martine thought about the fire that killed her parents – which wasn't very often because it was a no-go place in her head – one moment stood out for her. It wasn't the moment when she'd woken in a fogged-up terror on the night of her eleventh birthday to realize her home was ablaze and her mum and dad were on the other side of a burning door. It wasn't even when her room had turned into a furnace and her pyjamas began melting off her back, and she'd had to improvise a rope from her bed sheets and shimmy down two storeys before crashing into the snow far below.

No, it was after all of that. After she'd come rushing

round the side of the house to find a crowd gathered on the front lawn. There'd been horrified gasps as people who thought she'd perished in the flames turned to see her running towards the smoldering wreckage, screaming for her parents. One of the neighbours, Mr Morrison, had managed to catch her, and his wife had held her while she struggled and sobbed.

Martine could still remember when it hit her that her mum and dad, with whom she'd shared a laughter-filled birthday dinner of chocolate and almond pancakes just a few hours earlier, were gone forever.

That's the moment when her life had officially ended. That's when everything she'd ever loved was lost.

Now it was happening again.

The bulldozers were at Sawubona by 9 a.m. next morning. They came up the road like a line of yellow caterpillars, ready to chomp everything in their path. They parked right outside the animal sanctuary and their clunking, roaring engines terrified the sick and orphaned creatures a thousand times more than Reuben James's car had done.

Gwyn Thomas went out to stop them with an expression so ferocious that Martine was amazed their operators didn't turn tail and flee. She stood in front of the first bulldozer with her hands on her hips, like a protestor facing down an army tank.

'And what exactly do you think you're doing, coming onto my property and frightening already traumatized animals?' she demanded.

The lead operator clambered off his machine, smirking. 'Just following orders, ma'am.'

'You'll be following orders right into jail if you don't leave immediately. If you're not off my land in three minutes, I'm calling the police.'

'Go right ahead.' The man took a piece of paper from his pocket and unfolded it. 'This is a court order giving us permission to start work on this site. We understand that you won't be vacating the reserve for another two weeks, but in the meantime we need to start laying the groundwork for the Safari Park.'

'I don't care whether you're laying the groundwork for Windsor Castle,' Gwyn Thomas ranted. 'You're not moving one grain of sand—' She stopped. 'I'm sorry. I think I misheard you. You're doing *what*?'

The man handed her the document. Gwyn Thomas put on her glasses. Martine, watching from a safe distance, saw her shoulders stiffen.

Her grandmother's voice became dangerously quiet. 'The White Giraffe Safari Park? That's what you're intending to build here?'

The man's grin began to fade. 'I guess so. That's what it says.'

'Well,' said Gwyn Thomas. 'Let me save you a great deal of trouble. There will be no White Giraffe Safari Park here. There will be no Pink Elephant, Black Rhino or any other themed safari park you care to mention.

Over my dead body will Mr James inherit Sawubona.'

'Now hold on a minute,' objected the bulldozer operator. 'There's no need for that kind of talk. I'm only doing my job.'

Gwyn Thomas handed him the document with exaggerated politeness. 'Of course you are. How unreasonable of me. You're only following orders. In that case you won't mind if my game warden follows orders to leave this gate open so that the lions can take their morning stroll around your bulldozers while I drive into Storm Crossing to see my lawyer? Hopefully they've already eaten their breakfast. They do love a bit of fresh meat in the morning . . .'

But Martine was no longer listening. The sick, sad feeling which had enveloped her ever since she'd learned of Sawubona's fate had been replaced by one of pure rage. The showpiece of Mr James's grand plan to turn the game reserve into a glorified zoo was to be Jemmy. Not only was her soul-mate to be taken from her, he was going to become the star of the Reuben James Show.

Trailing after Gwyn Thomas as she stalked back to the house, Martine silently echoed her grandmother's words: 'Over my dead body, Mr James.'

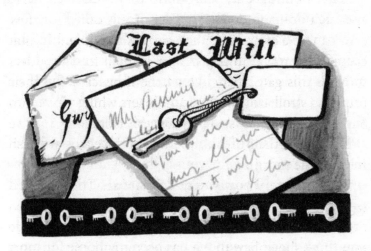

4

Three hours later, Gwyn Thomas was back from Storm Crossing with good news and bad news.

'Tell us the nice news first,' said Martine, as she and Ben followed her grandmother into the study. She gestured to her friend to take the spare chair while she perched on top of a filing cabinet.

Gwyn Thomas held up a legal letter. 'For what it's worth, that would be this – an injunction to prevent Mr James and his crew of heavies from laying a single brick until the day we officially leave Sawubona: Christmas Eve. The bad news is that we can't stop them from coming to the game reserve as often as they want to in the meantime. They're entitled to bring along as many architects, designers and wildlife experts as they feel necessary in order to plan for their takeover of the reserve.'

'That's outrageous,' said Martine, who didn't tend to use such dramatic words, but felt it was called for now. 'We can't possibly have that hateful man planning his stupid zoo and bringing people to poke and prod our animals while we're still living here. If he lays a finger on Jemmy, I might be tempted to do something violent. At the very least I'll have to let down his tyres.'

'Martine!' Gwyn Thomas was horrified. 'I will not have you talking like a young thug; I don't care how upset you are. I know you're devastated at the prospect of losing Jemmy, but really that's no excuse.'

She stood up and walked over to the window. 'How do you think *I* feel? Sawubona has been my home for more than half my life, and it was your mum's home before it was yours. It was your grandfather's dream before I met him and then it became our shared vision. And now I have to face up to the fact that the man I loved may have deceived me by signing away that dream to Mr James.'

She turned around. 'But, you know, I'm not willing to believe that. Your grandfather wasn't perfect, but he was an honourable man. If he did sign away Sawubona, he'd have done it with the best of intentions – perhaps to protect me from knowing how bad our financial situation was. Either that, or he was tricked into changing his will.

'Unfortunately, none of that matters now. However noble his intentions, his actions are probably going to cost me my home and my livelihood. And that hurts. It really hurts. Barring a miracle, Martine, in two weeks' time you and I and the cats are going to have to pack up everything we own and move into a rented apartment.'

Martine tried to picture her grandmother, who loved nature more than life itself, in a poky city flat far from the wilderness of Sawubona. She was upset with herself for being so selfish. Devastated at the thought of losing her home and almost everything she loved twice in one year, she'd forgotten that it must be a thousand times harder for her grandmother.

'We can't just give up,' she said. 'There must be something we can do. Surely a judge would understand that a lot of the animals in the game reserve are like Jemmy. They're orphans or they've had a really horrible life and they need us to protect and love them.'

Her grandmother grimaced. 'Unfortunately, when it comes to property, judges tend to see things in black and white. I had hoped that the signature on the will produced by Mr James would turn out to be a forgery, but my lawyer called in a handwriting expert and he assured us it's genuine.'

Tendai knocked at the door. Gwyn Thomas ushered the game warden in with a sad smile before continuing: 'No, I'm afraid there's nothing we can do.'

Martine looked at Ben. He was wearing the expression he always got when the two of them were in a crisis. She could see him trying to figure out a solution.

He said: 'What if there was another will – one written more recently than the one held by Mr James – leaving Sawubona to you? Wouldn't that change everything?'

Gwyn Thomas nodded. 'It would. But if there was a more recent will, Henry would have told me about it or I would have found it when I was going through his papers after . . . after he passed away.'

There was an awkward silence. Nobody wanted to point out the obvious, that if Henry hadn't told her about the will held by Mr James, he might not have told her about other things.

Martine thought about the grandfather she'd never known. He'd been killed trying to save the white giraffe's mother and father from poachers, leaving her grandmother heartbroken and without her companion of forty-two years. She said again: 'We can't just give up. We have to fight.'

'I agree,' said her grandmother. 'But I'm at a loss to think exactly *how* we fight.'

'Would you like me to break the news about Sawubona to the game reserve staff?' offered the game warden.

'Thank you, Tendai. I couldn't face it myself, but it would be most helpful if you would.'

'In the weeks before Mr Thomas passed away, did he do or say anything unusual?' asked Ben. 'Did he ever seem worried or agitated?'

'Quite the reverse,' Gwyn Thomas told him. 'He was happier than I'd ever seen him. He was very excited about the future of the game reserve and had all sorts of projects on the go. Weeks before he died, he even made a sudden trip to England for a meeting.'

She brought her hand down hard on the desk. 'That's it, isn't it? Something happened on that trip. I know he was planning to see your mum and dad, Martine, but I wish I could remember what business he had there.'

'When exactly did he go?' asked Martine. 'Maybe you could check the date on the will produced by Mr James and see if the two things coincided.'

'I know it was during our winter,' said her grandmother, 'but I'd have to look in his old passport to see the exact date. I think I still have it.'

She opened the bottom drawer on the right side of her desk and went through a folder. The passport was not where she'd thought it would be so she closed the drawer again. Only it wouldn't shut properly. She wrestled with it in annoyance before wrenching it open again and feeling down the back. 'Something's stuck.'

She lifted out a heap of crumpled and torn bits of paper and a stiff blue envelope, a little mangled around the edges. On the front, in bold blue ink, was the word 'Gwyn'.

Martine was on the verge of asking if she'd like to read it in private when her grandmother seized the letter opener. She read the enclosed note and passed it to each of them in turn.

My darling,
    I hope there is never any need for you to use this key. If you do it will mean I got too close to the truth.

*You always thought me so brave. I don't feel that way
today. I hope you can find it in your heart to forgive
me.*
All my love always,
Henry

For several long minutes nobody said anything. Nobody
knew *what* to say. It was as if Henry Thomas had spoken
from the grave. At last Martine plucked up the courage
to ask: 'What is the key for?'

Her grandmother removed it from the envelope and
examined the business card tied to it with a piece of
string. 'It would appear that it's for a safety deposit box
in a bank vault in England.'

She slumped in her chair. 'Oh, what can it all mean?
What is it that I have to forgive?'

'Maybe you're right,' Ben suggested. 'Maybe
something *did* happen on Mr Thomas's trip to England.'

'Perhaps. But his secret, if he had one, has gone with
him to the grave.'

'Not necessarily,' put in Martine. 'If you went to
England, the answer might be in the safety deposit box.
You could do some investigating and find out what my
grandfather was doing there and who he was meeting
with.'

Her grandmother was aghast. 'I can't travel halfway
across the world and leave you alone in the house,
especially when Sawubona is crawling with strangers.
And I'm certainly not leaving Tendai alone to face the
music on the reserve. Who knows what nefarious plans

Mr James has up his sleeve.'

'Martine won't be alone,' Ben told her. 'I'll be here to protect her.'

In spite of her distress, Gwyn Thomas managed a smile. 'And who's going to protect you, Ben Khumalo?'

'Why don't we call Grace and ask her if she'll come and stay for a week or two,' suggested Martine. 'Then Ben and I won't be alone and Tendai will have some grown-up support. One look from Grace and Reuben James will probably run for his life.'

'Grace is away in Kwazulu-Natal visiting relatives,' her grandmother reminded her.

'Yes, but she is back in a couple of days,' Tendai pointed out. 'I can have Tobias, our new guard, watch the house at night until then.'

'I can't believe we're even considering this,' said Gwyn Thomas. 'What if it's a wild goose chase? What if I fly thousands of miles and spend a small fortune – at a time when we can least afford it – only to discover there's nothing to discover? That the note was just something Henry wrote when he was feeling guilty about borrowing money from Mr James.'

'Then at least you'll know,' Martine told her. 'You'll know that there was nothing to find and you'll know that you did everything possible to save Sawubona.'

But even as she spoke, a feeling of doom crept into her bones, joining the anger and dread already lurking there. 'Maybe it's not such a great idea,' she backtracked. 'It's too far away and we'll miss you.'

'No, I think you were right the first time, Martine,'

Gwyn Thomas said. 'I should travel to England, otherwise I'll spend the rest of my life wondering if it would have made a difference if I'd only gone. I should go if it means saving Sawubona.'

5

The morning after Gwyn Thomas had flown away, Sampson, an elderly game guard who patrolled the reserve on foot, radioed at 6 a.m. to say that he had found a buffalo needing urgent treatment for a suspected viral disease. Without medicine, it would die.

Martine heard the crackling of Tendai's responses and went down to the kitchen to find out what was going on. Ben had already showered and was sitting at the table drinking coffee and eating anchovy toast. In contrast to Martine, who was not a morning person and was bleary-eyed and in her pyjamas, her hair sticking up on end, he looked cool, alert, and ready to face anything the day could throw at him.

'There's a sick buffalo near the northern boundary,' he told Martine. 'Will you come with us? We could do with your help.'

Adrenalin began to course through Martine's veins. Nothing woke her up faster than an animal needing help. She took a few swallows of Ben's coffee and stole his last bit of toast, ignoring his protests. 'Give me a minute,' she said. She raced upstairs for her survival kit, which she never went anywhere without, threw on a pair of jeans and a blue sweatshirt and sped outside.

As it turned out, her haste was unnecessary. Tendai and Ben were not hanging around waiting for her, they were peering under the bonnet of the jeep and arguing about sparkplugs and fuel injectors.

'This old lady has been running since I came to work for your grandfather twenty years ago and has been patched up many times, but in between she has always been so reliable,' Tendai told her. 'She was working well last night. I can't think why she is refusing to cooperate this morning.'

They were testing the battery when Reuben James came roaring into the yard in an open-topped Land Rover so new it sparkled.

'Perfect timing,' muttered Ben.

Reuben James stepped down from his vehicle. He was crisply dressed in a white shirt and tailored khaki trousers, his bald head shining. He looked every inch the successful Safari Park owner. 'Trouble in paradise?' he asked, strolling over to them.

He offered a hand to Tendai. 'I'm Reuben James. And you must be Sawubona's famous game warden? I heard about you during my business dealings with Henry Thomas a few years ago, but I think you were away on a course at the time. You were a tracker then if I'm not mistaken.'

Without waiting for a reply, he turned very deliberately and smiled down at Martine. 'We meet again.'

Martine wished she had a rotten egg at hand with which to wipe the grin from his arrogant, self-satisfied face. 'Unfortunately,' she said.

Reuben James laughed. '*Unfortunately?* Come now, Martine, I'm sure we're going to be the best of friends.'

The Zulu's jaw tightened, but he'd been taken aback by Martine's rudeness and made an extra effort to be polite. 'Yes, sir, I am Sawubona's game warden. Unhappily, my jeep won't start. I will need to call the garage when they open at 8 a.m. It wouldn't be a problem except that we are rushing to save a sick buffalo.'

'A sick buffalo?' James waved an arm in the direction of his gold Land Rover. 'Please,' he said. 'Take my vehicle.'

They all stared at him in astonishment. Martine wondered what the catch was.

'Uh, thank you for your kind offer, Mr James,' Tendai managed, 'but there is no need for that. I have friends I can telephone in an emergency.'

But Reuben James wouldn't hear of it. 'I insist. It would be my pleasure. My driver will be happy to escort you. Lurk, take these good people into the game reserve

233

to find this ill creature and spend as much time there as they need. I have some paperwork to attend to that will keep me busy until you return.'

He nodded towards the jeep. 'In the meantime, with your permission, I'll have one of my mechanics take a look at your engine.'

Before they could raise a single objection, he had ushered them into the new-leather-smelling interior of the Land Rover, personally shutting the doors behind each of them as if he were the chauffeur, and not Lurk.

As they rolled out of the yard, Martine, who was in the back seat with Ben, risked a glance behind them. Reuben James was standing in the driveway waving, just like Gwyn Thomas usually did.

It's as if he's already won, fumed Martine. It's as if he's already moved into our home. It's as if, two days after dropping this bombshell on us, he's already Sawubona's owner.

Then a little voice added: *And Jemmy's.*

The minute they were out of sight of the house, the chauffeur's ingratiating smile slipped from his face, like the moon sliding behind a cloud. He drove in sullen silence. When Tendai asked him a question about the Land Rover, he pretended he didn't understand.

They swept across Sawubona's grassy green-gold plains, and on past the lake and the high escarpment. As they drew nearer to the mountain that hid the Secret Valley, Martine felt a pang. It was months since she'd been to the white giraffe's special sanctuary. Inside the valley was a cave known only to Martine and Grace and, of course, the San Bushmen ancestors who'd recorded their lives on its walls in mystical paintings.

For reasons Martine did not even vaguely understand, they seemed to have predicted parts of her destiny there too. She could never decide whether it was a good thing or a bad thing that she had not been able to figure out how to interpret the fortune-telling San paintings in the cave they called the Memory Room until it was too late. Until she'd already fallen overboard into shark-filled water, or been trapped in a cave with a wounded leopard.

'Only time and experience will give you the eyes to see them,' Grace was fond of saying.

Once, when Martine had complained that it wasn't fair – that what was the point of having your destiny written on a cave wall if you couldn't use it to avoid misfortune befalling you, Grace had told her that that was precisely the point. If a person could see their future, they'd only choose the great times. 'Then you would never learn and never experience the important things in this world because oftentimes they's tha hard things.'

Most days Martine agreed with her. Many of her most painful experiences had led directly or indirectly to some of the most special times of her life. But even Grace would admit that losing Jemmy and every other animal Martine loved at Sawubona was not one of life's necessary experiences. Nothing good could possibly come of it.

Martine stole a glance at the twisted tree that disguised the entrance to the white giraffe's sanctuary as they went by. One night soon she planned to sneak out to the Memory Room to see if the San Bushmen had had anything to say about Reuben James stealing Sawubona. In less than a month she'd be twelve years old. Surely by now she had enough time and experience to read her own future on the cave walls?

The Land Rover slowed. Sampson stepped from the trees.

'Park over there, please, Lurk,' instructed Tendai, indicating a place on the edge of the scarred clearing. The chauffeur responded with a grunt.

'For your own safety you should remain in the vehicle,' the game warden cautioned him. 'We have enough problems with your boss without him suing us because some animal has given you a scratch.'

Lurk gave no indication of having heard. He opened his door and jumped down. Propping himself against the side of the Land Rover, he lit a cigarette.

Tendai's eyes met Martine's. He shrugged, climbed out of the vehicle with his box of emergency veterinary supplies and began speaking in Zulu to Sampson, a bony, wizened man who Martine was convinced was at least a hundred years old. He paused to say, 'Be careful,' to Martine and Ben as they walked slowly into the grove of trees.

'We will,' Martine assured him. Buffalo were among

the most deadly of Africa's Big Five, which also included the lion, leopard, elephant and rhino. Tourists were sometimes fooled into thinking that, because they looked like handsome dark cows with curly horns, all the fuss about how ferociously they could charge had been exaggerated. Not many of those tourists lived to tell the tale.

This buffalo, however, was no danger to anyone. He was a young bachelor who'd probably been evicted from the main herd for fighting, but there was no fight left in him now. He was lying on his side, his streaming eyes wild and terrified, wracked with fever. As they watched he gave a great gasp, as if his life was slipping from him.

Martine's eyes filled with tears. She couldn't bear to see any animal suffer.

'Hurry, Tendai,' she called, but Tendai and Sampson were involved in some sort of row with the chauffeur. He was refusing to put out his cigarette. All of a sudden he threw it from him. There was a shower of sparks and a dry bush on the edge of the clearing began to smoulder. Sampson pulled off his shirt and thrashed at the bush. Tendai sprinted to get water out of the Land Rover, yelling at Lurk over his shoulder.

Martine eased back the buffalo's lip. The young bull's gums were almost white, a sure sign that death was approaching.

'Martine,' urged Ben, 'you have to do something.' He, like Tendai and Gwyn Thomas, knew she had a gift with animals and wasn't really sure what that meant, but unlike them he was also aware that she had a survival kit full of special medicines and could go into a trance that would help her understand how to use them. 'If it helps, I won't watch.'

He was going to turn away but Martine stopped him. 'Wait,' she said, 'I need you to put your hands over his heart.'

She took a small bottle from her pouch. When she removed the lid, a revolting smell like frog slime, mildew and sweaty socks tainted the air, making Ben cough.

'What *is* that stuff?' he asked, screwing up his nose. 'I wanted you to help the buffalo, not gas it.'

Martine paid no attention to him. She poured the green liquid into the buffalo's mouth and it revived sufficiently to sneeze, splutter and look more dejected than ever. Laying gentle hands on the bull's head, Martine stroked his wet nose, his rough, sharp horns and the thick, hard bone and muscle around his jaw and neck. She closed her eyes.

Time passed. Martine could not have said if it was two seconds or two hours. Her hands heated up. So fiery did they become that she almost expected them to start smoking. She heard the voices of the ancients, buzzing in her head, guiding her. The rhythm of their drums pounded in her chest. She saw great herds of giraffe and men in loin cloths holding spears and . . .

'Martine, look out!'

The buffalo was surging to his feet and swinging his horns. Martine stared at him dazedly. Tendai was rushing over from the jeep with his rifle, and Ben was stepping in front of her protectively, at great risk to himself.

But in the end neither the rifle nor Ben's bravery were necessary. The buffalo shook his head a couple of times to clear it, snorted, and trotted away through the trees.

Tendai came running up and hugged them both in relief. 'I told you to be careful. Buffalo are so unpredictable. This one even had Sampson fooled into thinking he was dying and Sampson has about a century of experience. Next time, stay with me.'

'We will,' said Martine, 'but I don't think he had any intention of hurting us.'

She avoided looking directly at Ben, but she could see out of the corner of her eye that he was very shaken. She was about to say something to take his mind off what he'd just seen when the chauffeur wandered up.

'Lurk, I told you to stay in the Land Rover for your own protection,' Tendai said irritably.

The chauffeur glared at him. 'I not take orders from you.'

Tendai rolled his eyes. 'It's not an order. It's for your own safety. Although I'm beginning to think it is the animals who need protecting from you. You almost started a bushfire.'

Lurk didn't answer. He was staring over Tendai's shoulder with a peculiar, stricken expression. 'Elephant!' he whispered hoarsely. 'Mad elephant!'

'It's not an elephant,' Tendai said, beginning to lose his temper with the man. 'It's a buffalo. And it's not mad at all. Possibly it's a little unwell.'

'Tendai,' Ben said in a low voice. 'He's right.'

A female elephant, as vast as a baobab tree, was standing in the shadows of the forest, flapping her ears menacingly. She let out a deafening trumpet. It was clear she was about to charge.

Lurk grabbed Tendai's rifle.

'Are you mad?' shouted Tendai, trying to snatch it back. 'Do you want to get us killed? That is not a gun for elephants. The bullet will be like a bee sting for her and it will make her very, very angry.'

Lurk cocked the rifle and took aim.

Tendai grabbed his wrist and crushed it so hard that Lurk winced and dropped the gun. 'Don't even think about it, or I will shoot you myself. Let's all move very slowly towards the Land Rover. If she starts to charge, we must run, but be careful to run in zigzags in order to confuse her. Ready? Let's go.'

They had only gone a few steps when Lurk panicked. He sprinted for the Land Rover. Martine, who'd only ever seen elephants lumbering around the waterhole or trotting lazily and a little unsteadily, was stunned to see the elephant shoot from the trees like a racehorse from the stalls and gallop after the chauffeur. It gained on him rapidly. It seemed certain he would be trampled to death before he ever reached the vehicle. He'd totally forgotten about running in zigzags.

Tendai had his arms around Ben and Martine, and the three of them watched in horror. 'Take off your jacket, Lurk,' yelled the game warden. 'Take off your jacket and throw it on the ground.'

The elephant bore down on the chauffeur, her great

feet tearing up the earth. In seconds, Lurk would be a bloody pulp.

'Your jacket,' screamed Tendai. 'Take off your jacket!'

Somehow the words penetrated the chauffeur's petrified brain. He peeled off his jacket as he ran and flung it to the ground. The elephant halted in confusion. She looked from Lurk to the crumpled red pile on the ground. For an instant it seemed as if she would continue her pursuit, but then Sampson started up the engine of the Land Rover and she decided to attack the jacket instead. It was easier. Dust roiled up as she pounded it into the ground, trampling it, tossing it, crushing it.

Lurk reached the vehicle and threw himself in, sobbing. Sampson took off almost before he was seated, racing to pick up Tendai, Martine and Ben. They scrambled in and slammed the doors. As Sampson accelerated away from the crazed elephant, swerving onto the track and gunning the engine for home, Martine heard her trumpet with rage.

6

Nobody spoke on the way back to the house. Lurk was too busy snivelling and the others were in shock. They knew they were lucky to be alive.

Martine knew that too, but it's not what she was thinking about. She was remembering the elephant's eyes. During her time at Sawubona she'd been quite close to several adult elephants and very close to a young orphan called Shaka, and the thing that had struck her was how wise and kind their brown eyes were. But the gaze of the elephant who'd attacked Lurk had been anything but. Her eyes had blazed with an unquenchable hatred. There had only been one thought in her head

242

and that was to trample and tear to pieces the chauffeur the way she'd trampled and torn his jacket.

Lurk pulled himself together as they neared the house, and by the time Sampson drew up outside the gate and handed him the keys to the Land Rover, he was his surly self again. He shot Tendai a poisonous look as he climbed into the driver's seat, but he didn't say anything. It was obvious he held the game warden responsible for his ordeal.

Tendai waited until he had driven away before he said: 'I think we all need a cup of tea.'

Ten minutes later they were sitting around the kitchen table drinking steaming Rooibos (red bush) tea, eating milk tart and feeling a lot better.

'I don't understand it,' Tendai said. 'I've seen that elephant almost every day since she came here three years ago, and she is the shyest and most timid of all our animals. Elephants are herd animals. Their family units are very important to them, but Angel – that's what I call her because she has always been the gentlest of giants – is always alone and quick to move away. She is scared of people. But today she behaved like a bull elephant on the rampage. I'm afraid to think what would have happened if Lurk hadn't thrown his jacket on the ground.'

'That was *Angel*?' said Martine, shocked. In the chaos of the moment, she hadn't paused to think which elephant was doing the charging.

There were thirteen elephants at Sawubona. Some had come in a shipment from a Zambian game reserve that had become overpopulated, several were orphans from culls and some had been bought by her grandparents to ensure that herds were the right balance of males and females. Martine didn't know all of their histories and she couldn't really tell one elephant from another, except for two of them: Shaka, the young elephant she'd fed from a milk pail for several months, and Angel. Angel was not a regular African elephant; she was a desert elephant from Namibia, the country that bordered South Africa.

The reason she was so special to Martine was that, according to local tribesmen, Angel was the elephant who saved the white giraffe when his parents were killed hours after he was born. Somehow Angel had helped Jemmy to escape and had led him to the special sanctuary in the Secret Valley. Her own calf had been stillborn days before, so not only had she had a special affection for the grief-stricken and bewildered young giraffe, she was also able to feed him – a sight that Martine thought must have been a very extraordinary one. The two of them had been a big comfort to each other. In a way, Angel was Jemmy's adopted mother.

Riding Jemmy, Martine had been able to get within touching distance of Angel on several occasions. Like the game warden, she'd found the elephant almost painfully shy. She was always alone. She either wasn't welcome or didn't want to join the other elephants. Her only friend was Jemmy and once he was grown she had distanced herself from even him, perhaps so that no one would guess their history. Now this seemingly angelic creature had turned on them for no reason.

'This is why I am always telling you never to take chances with wild animals,' Tendai was saying. 'They can change like the wind. You must never let your guard down.'

'Animals are a mystery,' agreed Sampson. 'I would swear on the life of my nine children that that buffalo was dying of a viral disease. I was sure it was breathing its last breath when I radioed you this morning. And then it jumps up and tears away like a young calf!'

Tendai laughed. 'Your eyes are not what they used to be, old man. I think you have spent so much time on your own in the bush that your imagination is playing tricks.'

He pushed back his chair and put on his hat with its zebra-skin band. 'I must be going. Mr James's men might have fixed my jeep.' He cast a sly look at Sampson. 'Some of us have work to do.'

'You call what you do work?' Sampson retorted. 'You're on permanent safari.' The two of them went out into the yard joshing each other and laughing.

When they'd gone, Ben regarded his friend intently and asked: 'What exactly happened in the reserve with the buffalo, Martine? I mean, how did you heal it like that?'

She met his eyes with a level gaze. 'It was Grace's medicine, not me. That *muti* works miracles.'

And Ben accepted that because he understood that some things are better left unsaid.

'I don't know about you but I was scared to death when the elephant charged,' Martine remarked, grateful to him for not prying. 'Why would Angel turn on us like that?'

'Maybe she saw or scented something that made her angry.'

'You might be right. Tendai says it's true that elephants never forget. There've been studies showing that elephants can identify people from different tribes by the clothes they wear or their smell. But what could she have seen or smelled?'

'Or who?' Ben said.

Martine stared at him. 'What do you mean?'

'Well, maybe she was angry at one of us.'

'But why? We've only ever been loving to her.' As she said it, Martine was reminded again of the hatred in Angel's eyes as she mashed Lurk's jacket into the ground.

Out in the yard, the game warden's jeep roared to life. Martine sprang up and rushed to the door. 'Hey, Tendai,' she called. 'Where did Angel come from? I know she's a desert elephant, but how did she end up at Sawubona?'

Tendai put the jeep into gear. He seemed surprised. 'I thought you knew,' he said. 'She was given to your grandfather by Reuben James.'

7

'How 'bout offering an old woman a ride?'
It was 3 a.m. and Martine nearly leapt out of her
skin. As anyone would if an extravagantly large medicine
woman with a mixed-up Afro-Caribbean accent
suddenly loomed out of the darkness at them.

Martine had not intended to be in the game reserve at
such an hour. Her plan had been to go to bed at 9 p.m.,
sleep for two hours and then go to the Secret Valley at the
fairly civilized time of eleven. But she'd overslept. It had
taken a considerable effort of will to haul herself out of
bed when she did wake, and she'd felt a prick of
conscience when she eventually let herself into the game

reserve. Not about oversleeping, but about disobeying her grandmother. Under normal circumstances she was banned from riding Jemmy after nightfall. But these, Martine told herself, were not normal circumstances.

'Grace!' she cried when she'd recovered from her fright. Jemmy had bolted out of range when the *sangoma* popped up from behind a bush, but he edged closer. The Zulu woman held out her arms and Martine ran into them for a hug.

'I'm so happy to see you. How was Kwazulu-Natal? Has Tendai told you what's been going on around here? It's a total nightmare. Sawubona is going to be taken over by this businessman who claims my granddad never repaid his debt, and we all have to leave on Christmas Eve and Jemmy . . . '

'Relax, chile, there'll be time enough for all that later,' Grace interrupted. 'Right now we mus' be off to the Secret Valley.'

She put a hand on one massive hip and gazed up at Jemmy's sloping white back. 'Now how is old Grace supposed to get up there?'

Martine was rendered temporarily speechless. The idea of Grace, a woman who had eaten many of her own desserts, climbing aboard Jemmy, was alarming to say the least. It could do irreparable damage to the white giraffe's back. And yet she could hardly wound her friend by saying so.

Fortunately, or unfortunately, the decision was taken out of her hands. Jemmy, who was normally petrified of anyone other than Martine, made his musical fluttering sound and lay down on the ground. At which point, Grace stepped regally onto his back, settled herself as if she was relaxing into a comfortable armchair and held a hand out to Martine. 'Well, chile, are ya comin'?'

Martine couldn't refuse to join her without being rude about Grace's size, so she slipped onto the giraffe's withers, grabbed a handful of mane and said a silent apology to Jemmy and the giraffe gods.

Jemmy staggered to his feet. Grace clutched at Martine and started gabbling fervently in Zulu. She was either swearing or praying, Martine wasn't quite sure which. At length, and walking very slowly, they were on their way.

Martine's usual method of entering the Secret Valley was to grit her teeth, hold her breath and cling as hard as she could to Jemmy's mane and back as he ran full tilt at the twisted tree and veil of thorny creepers that hid the narrow slot between the rocks. With Grace weighing him down, that was not an option, so the humans crawled through the undergrowth in an undignified fashion while the white giraffe followed more gracefully.

'The sooner ya grow up and get your driver's licence, honey, the better,' Grace said as she picked leaves, moss and bits of thorn out of her headdress. 'That giraffe ridin' business is for the birds. I'll be walkin' like a rodeo cowboy for days. As for comin' into the Valley through a thorn bush, it's a wonder you ain't tore all ta pieces.'

'I didn't know there *was* another way.' Martine switched on her torch and shone it around the valley, an orchid-scented space between two leaning shelves of mountain. Above them, glittering with stars, was a rectangle of blue-black sky. 'How do you usually get in here?'

Grace smiled enigmatically. 'I have my way, chile, and you have yours.'

No matter how often she visited it, the Memory Cave never lost its magic for Martine. Its charged air, as dense as that of a frankincense-scented cathedral, filled her lungs with history and carried her back to a time when San Bushmen painted their lives on its granite walls. Images of wild animals and men with spears or lions' heads chased each other in fiery shades across the cave.

She and Grace sat down on a low, flat rock that formed a natural bench. Martine was aware of Khan, the leopard she'd helped save in Zimbabwe, stealing up behind them, though she heard no sound. She could picture him lying on the rock behind them like a Sphinx, his golden coat with its rosettes of onyx-black shining in the torchlight. She knew he'd be watching her with an expression that was somewhere between love and confusion. Confusion – because what he felt for her went against every one of his predatory instincts.

Martine, on the other hand, simply loved him.

Tears filled her eyes. Soon all of this would be taken from her. There was some satisfaction in knowing that Reuben James was unlikely ever to find this place, but that was offset by the agony of knowing she would have to say goodbye to Khan and Jemmy. Worse still, she would lose her links with the ancestors who'd written her story on the cave walls.

Grace handed her a tissue. 'Tell me everythin', from the beginnin'. Leave nothin' out.'

So Martine did. She told the woman she'd come to think of as a mentor, guide, friend and earth-mother about her unsettling first encounter with Reuben James, about Henry Thomas's debt and the changed will, about Angel's attack on the chauffeur, about the discovery of her grandfather's letter with its plea for forgiveness, and about her grandmother flying away to England.

'So you see, Grace, I don't have the time to wait for experience to teach me how to read the paintings. I need an answer now. *Tonight*. We have ten days left to save Sawubona. In ten days, everything we love will be lost.'

Grace took her time replying. The silence stretched out until Martine, whose nerves were at breaking point, wanted to scream with impatience. Finally the *sangoma* heaved herself off the rock bench. She went over to what looked like a splotch on the wall and stared at it for several long minutes. Martine went to Grace's side and they studied it together.

'Surely you can't read any significance into that?' Martine said. 'They probably just spilled some paint there or made a mistake.'

Grace shook her head. 'The forefathers did everything for a reason.'

She moved off across the cave, her large, buttery palms roaming across the rock, searching for other clues.

Halfway across they halted. Etched into the granite was something that looked a bit like a compass.

At once, she became agitated. 'Come, chile,' she said, 'we mus' go.'

'Go where?' Martine asked, but Grace's only answer was to reach over and switch off Martine's torch. Darkness descended like a shutter.

Much as Martine adored Khan, she was wary of being in a labyrinth with the world's largest leopard when she couldn't see her hand in front of her face. But the *sangoma* had no such fears. She took Martine's hand and led her through a warren of tunnels which twisted like snakes beneath the mountain – tunnels Martine had always been much too afraid to explore on her own.

How Grace found her way in the blackness Martine had no idea, but the *sangoma* walked as if she knew these caves like she knew her own home.

The air became soupy and oppressive. Martine was beginning to feel claustrophobic and short of breath when a skyful of stars suddenly opened up before her and sweet night air bathed her face.

They were on the mountainside above the Secret Valley. Martine was astonished to see that Khan had come with them, following at their heels like a faithful dog. His yellow gaze focussed on Grace as she picked her way across the slope in the moonlight. She stopped and switched on the torch.

'Now do you see?' she asked.

Martine went over to her. At the foot of a large boulder, lying in a slight depression, were two great elephant's tusks. They were encrusted with dirt, as if some force had uprooted them from their usual resting place beneath the earth. Their tips were touching. They were pointing northwest.

'I see, Grace, but I don't understand. Where have they come from? How did they get here?'

The *sangoma* motioned for her to sit. Khan came and settled beside Martine and it seemed the most natural thing in the world for her to put her arm around him. It was the first time she'd touched him since she'd saved him in Zimbabwe and it was as magical as it had been then. Warmth radiated from his golden fur. He sheathed his claws and let out a deep, contented purr.

Grace took a leather pouch from around her neck. She scattered its contents – an assortment of tiny bones, porcupine quills, a hoopoe bird feather and fresh herbs – around the tusks, and lit a match. Her eyes closed. A spiral of incense filled the air with the scent of African violets and musk. She began to mumble loudly. Martine couldn't understand a word. It sounded as if Grace was having an argument with someone – perhaps the ancestral spirits. She was pleading with them. She crossed her arms over her chest and rocked back and forth, clearly in distress.

Martine was unnerved. She clung to Khan, unsure whether to try to wake Grace from her trance, or if that would be interfering in some sacred ritual. Khan began to growl.

Grace's eyes flicked open. She looked straight at Martine and said: 'The four leaves will lead you to the circle. The circle will lead you to the elephants. The elephants will lead you to the truth.'

'*What* truth?' Martine asked, and was swamped by a feeling of déjà vu. On her first morning in South Africa, she'd asked Grace that exact question. She'd been asking it ever since without ever learning the answer.

'What truth?' Martine asked again because Grace was watching her with an unreadable expression.

'*Your* truth,' Grace answered. She brushed the hair from Martine's face. 'When a thorn is in your heart you must pluck it out, no matter how far ya have ta go ta find the cure that will remove it.'

She refused to say any more, only hugging Martine and urging her again and again to be strong. Martine rode back to the house, deep in thought. She'd offered Grace a lift on Jemmy but the *sangoma* had turned it down, muttering something vague about having a couple of other tasks to attend to. Martine dreaded to think what tasks Grace could possibly be attending to at four in the morning in a pitch-dark game reserve, and she didn't ask any questions. Like Ben, she'd learned that some things were better left unsaid.

She was riding slowly through the game reserve, mulling over Grace's prediction, when she noticed a flare of white light on the horizon. She glanced at her watch. It was only four-thirty and still dark, but every light in the far-off house was ablaze. Either Tendai or Ben had discovered she was gone and panicked, or a drama was unfolding. Holding tight to Jemmy's mane, she urged him into a flat-out gallop.

Ben was waiting for her at the game park gate. 'Go in the front door,' he said quickly. 'I'll keep Tendai and the guard distracted in the kitchen while you change into your pyjamas. Tendai doesn't know yet that you're missing. I told him that once you're asleep it would practically take a bomb to wake you.'

'Thanks,' said Martine, 'but if he doesn't know I'm missing, why is the house lit up like a Christmas tree?'

Ben pulled the gate shut and locked it behind her. 'We've been burgled.'

8

Martine stood in the middle of Gwyn Thomas's not-very-organized but mostly fairly tidy study and stared around in disbelief. Every drawer, box and file was open and their contents spilled, torn and scattered around the room. It looked as if the paper shredder had gone berserk and chewed up Gwyn Thomas's filing.

'As soon as I realized what had happened, I ran to look for Tobias,' Ben was saying. 'When I couldn't find him, or you, I went to Tendai's house and raised the alarm.'

'This is my fault, isn't it?' said Martine. 'I left the back door open when I went out riding Jemmy. It didn't enter my head that someone might break in, especially since

Tobias was watching the house. I was creeping through the mango trees, thinking I'd done a really good job of evading him, when he popped up in front of me. I put my finger to my lips and he grinned.'

She sank down onto the swivel chair. 'Oh, Ben, what am I going to say to Tendai? I'll have to admit that I went out riding Jemmy and left the door unlocked, and he'll tell my grandmother. She's going to be livid that I've disobeyed her when she's on the other side of the world trying to save Sawubona. She'll be so disappointed in me. She'll never trust me again.'

There was a knock at the door. Tendai came in wearing a T-shirt and crumpled work trousers. He was very relieved to see Martine.

'Thank goodness you're safe, little one. When Ben told me an intruder had broken into the house, I imagined the worst – a lunatic with a machete roaming round outside your bedrooms.'

'This is all my fault,' Ben told him. 'I heard a noise but I thought it was nothing and I rolled over and went back to sleep. It was only when I heard the gate screech that I got up and investigated. If I'd listened to my instincts sooner, none of this would have happened.' He didn't add that the real reason he'd gone back to sleep was that Martine had told him she was planning to go for a late night ride on the white giraffe and he'd assumed it was her.

'Don't take any notice of Ben,' said Martine. 'I'm the one to blame because I went out to see Jemmy and forgot to lock the back door.'

The game warden ran a weary hand over his eyes. 'It's nobody's fault and no one is to blame. If the back door hadn't been open, the burglar would have broken a window or picked the lock. He was determined to get in and nothing would have stopped him.'

'But where was Tobias?' Martine wanted to know. 'Did he see anyone? Did he try to stop them?'

'Tobias was knocked unconscious. He made himself a cup of tea at around three a.m., went to check on a suspicious noise near the main gate, and that's the last thing he remembers. He has a splitting headache and a lump on his head, but he should recover in a day or two. Sampson is going to take him to the hospital to be checked over by a doctor. I must stay here and wait for the police.'

'*Knocked unconscious?* Whoever broke in must have wanted something very badly. What do you think they were after?'

'It's impossible to tell. I'm familiar with the game reserve accounts but not, of course, with your grandmother's private papers. This person left behind the petty cash so it seems they were not after money.'

'I've had a look around and nothing else seems to have been touched,' said Ben. 'So he or she was after something specific.'

'I can't imagine who might be interested in getting his hands on my grandmother's secret papers,' Martine said sarcastically.

The game warden gave her a reproving glance. 'You suspect Mr James? Please, little one, you cannot be serious. I know you are bitter about him inheriting Sawubona, as I am at the prospect of losing my job, but he is a highly respected businessman and a millionaire many times over. Respectable millionaires don't break into people's homes and ransack their studies. And why would he want to do such a thing to a house he is about to move into?'

Martine was just about to say that there was nothing respectable about millionaire businessmen who trick people into signing away their dreams, their homes, and the lives of vulnerable animals, when there was a cacophony of screaming engines and wailing sirens outside.

They all ran out into the yard. A lone police car with flashing lights was flying down the long gravel road that led from Sawubona's main entrance to the house, closely followed by an aeroplane that appeared to be using the road as a runway. The police car hooted at the gate just as the light aircraft shuddered to a halt in a mushroom cloud of dust. Behind the game reserve fence, a herd of springbok were springing for their lives.

Tendai shook his head. 'I will admit one thing,' he said. 'Ever since Mr James showed up, Sawubona has become a three-ring circus.'

9

That afternoon, Martine was mopping the kitchen floor and generally trying to rid the house of the dirty bootprints, fingerprint dust and milk tart crumbs left by the police, who'd been 'worse than useless', as her grandmother would have put it, when she spotted the white giraffe at the game park gate. He seemed to be backing away. She went out onto the back *stoep* to see what was bothering him. At the far end of the garden, Reuben James was reaching up and trying to feed him through the fence.

Martine was livid. She sprinted through the mango trees and prepared to confront her nemesis.

Before she could get a word out, he said, 'Ah, Martine. Nice to see you. Your giraffe – Jeremiah, is it? – and I were just getting acquainted. I hear there's a legend around here that says the child who rides a white giraffe has power over all animals. That would be you, I suppose. Lurk was telling me the other day that a buffalo which appeared to be quite dead jumped to its feet like a spring lamb when you touched it.'

'I'm surprised Lurk had time to see anything,' retorted Martine. 'He was too busy trying to start a wildfire with his cigarette, being rude to Tendai and frightening our elephants.'

Reuben James chuckled. 'I rather think that it was the elephant who frightened him. In my experience, elephants are much hardier than people would like to believe. Look at the one I gave to your grandfather. She was skin and bone and could hardly put one foot in front of the other when she arrived here, and now I'm told she's as right as rain. Nothing wrong with her at all.'

Martine wondered if he had made the connection that the elephant he'd given Sawubona was the same one who'd charged his chauffeur. She decided not to say anything in case he hadn't. He might decide to punish Angel when he took over the reserve.

Realizing he could do the same to Jemmy if she upset him, she said more politely: 'Would you mind leaving my giraffe alone and not feeding him? He's nervous of strangers and he only eats acacia leaves.'

Reuben James craned his neck to squint at Jemmy, who was hovering near the fence to be close to Martine.

'Oh, I'm sure he could be tempted with a treat or two.' He held up a sprig of honeysuckle flowers.

The white giraffe leaned towards him, his mouth watering at the sight of such a delectable dish, but his terror of the man was too strong and he pulled back without taking any.

Martine wanted to scratch Reuben James's eyes out. Controlling herself with difficulty, she let herself into the game reserve, shutting and locking the gate behind her just to prove that she still had rights at Sawubona and he didn't. Jemmy put his head down and nuzzled her.

From the other side of the fence, Rebuen James said smoothly. 'I hear you had a break-in last night.'

'And I suppose you had nothing to do with it?' snapped Martine, forgetting her resolution to be polite.

He smiled. 'Come now, Martine, you and I seem to have got off on the wrong foot. It's hardly surprising that you've taken against me, given how much you love Sawubona, but breaking and entering is really not my style.'

'Oh, and taking away people's dreams and wildlife sanctuaries is?'

Reuben James tossed the honeysuckle on the ground and wiped his hands on a monogrammed handkerchief. 'Martine, you're too young to understand about business, but ask yourself this. If your grandfather had cared, *really* cared about Sawubona, would he have overstretched himself financially and put his family's future in jeopardy? I think not. I'm not the bad guy here.'

She had to hand it to him – he was good. For a

moment, he almost had *her* questioning what Henry Thomas had done. But then he went too far.

He leaned against the fence and said: 'I tell you what, Martine, I'm prepared to make a deal with you. Choose an animal, any animal, on the reserve, and it's yours. You can visit it for free whenever you want to. Any animal, that is, except the white giraffe. Did I tell you we're planning to change Sawubona's name to The White Giraffe Safari Park in his honour?'

At the mention of the Safari Park, a cold calm came over Martine. She saw that she and Reuben James were like chess players. He had made his move and now she had to make hers. An image of Grace navigating her way bravely through the catacombs of the Secret Valley entered her mind. She said: 'You know you really shouldn't underestimate us. There are people at Sawubona who have powers you couldn't possibly understand.'

Her green eyes met his blue ones in challenge. 'Somehow we're going to find a way to stop you.'

Something dark and almost savage flitted across Reuben James's face, but it was gone before Martine could take it in. His customary polished smile replaced it.

'Is that a fact?' he said. 'Well, let me give you a word of advice, young lady. I'm a patient man and a generous one, but I'm only patient and generous to a point. Don't make the mistake of crossing me.'

263

The phone was ringing when Martine walked back into the house. She picked up the receiver in the kitchen. Outside, the wind was heavy with the iron scent of rain, and the back door creaked on its hinges. Battleship-grey clouds scudded over the game reserve.

'Martine, thank goodness I've reached you,' cried Gwyn Thomas. 'I've been calling and calling but there's been no reply. I've been worried sick. What's going on there? Is everything all right?'

'Everything's fine,' lied Martine. There was no point telling her grandmother about Lurk being charged by the elephant or the burglary or anything else. She'd only freak out and do something drastic like get on the next plane home without having discovered anything at all in England. Sawubona would be more in jeopardy than ever. 'Sorry you've had trouble getting hold of us. Grace doesn't like to answer the phone and Ben and I have been out on the reserve a lot, helping Tendai.'

'Well, thank goodness for that. I was imagining the worst. Has Mr James been back?'

'Back and forth, but we can handle him,' Martine replied, and changed the subject. 'How's England? Is it freezing?'

'And grey,' confirmed her grandmother. 'And very wet. I'm staying at a country inn straight out of a werewolf movie, with low beams and hostile locals and its very own Hound of the Baskervilles. The room is so small I have to climb into bed as I come through the door. But that's not what I called to talk to you about.'

'The key!' Martine said, remembering. 'What was in

the safety deposit box? Did you find a different will?'

'Not exactly. To be honest, it's all a bit mysterious and it's left me questioning my sanity. I'm wracked with guilt about abandoning you, Ben and Tendai to the mercy of that awful man in order to fly thousands of miles on what appears to be a wild goose chase. The safety deposit box contained nothing much of anything really. Certainly nothing that's going to help us save Sawubona. Just an envelope.'

'An envelope? Is there a letter in it?'

'No, that's the peculiar part. There were only two items in it: a map of Damaraland in Namibia; and another key. The type that might fit a suitcase lock.'

'What suitcase?'

'Your guess is as good as mine. The other thing that's strange is that the envelope is one that belonged to Veronica.'

'My mum?'

'I was surprised too,' said Gwyn Thomas. 'It has your old Hampshire address on the back in her handwriting. I can't think what it's doing in Henry's safety deposit box.'

'Maybe she had something she needed to keep safe?' Into Martine's mind, unbidden, came the thought: *Or maybe she had something to hide.*

'An African tourist map and a key with no address label on it? No, I think it's more likely that whatever she or Henry put in the box has long since been removed and that the map is just a stray memento from some trip or other. The key might be worth looking in to but without an address I don't really know where to start.'

They talked about things closer to home after that. Gwyn Thomas missed Sawubona and everyone on it and wanted an update on almost every animal on the reserve. That roused Martine's suspicions immediately. If there was one thing her grandmother couldn't abide it was wasted money, especially when it came to the telephone, and she was sure the call from England was costing a fortune. And yet every time she tried to say goodbye, her grandmother would find a new way to keep her on the line.

After five or six minutes of this, Martine said: 'Is there something on your mind, Grandmother?'

'No, of course not. Well, naturally I'm very concerned about the future, but apart from that I'm fine. I should go. I'm sure my phone card is about to run out. They're a con, these cards, an absolute con.'

Martine carried the phone over to the kitchen window. Through it she could see the length of the garden and all the way down to the waterhole on the other side of the game fence, over which a black sky hung low. Six pot-bellied zebras were trotting for cover. Martine said: 'Are you afraid of what you might find if you start investigating?'

The voice on the other end of the line was indignant. 'Afraid? Don't be ridiculous.' There was a pause and then Gwyn Thomas said: 'Oh, who am I kidding? Yes, Martine, to be honest, I am scared. I'm scared that the man I loved, the man whose life I shared for forty-two years, might not have been the man I thought he was.'

There was a rush of wind through the mango trees. Fat drops began to fall, drumming the thatch. The roses bowed their heads as the rain fell faster and faster.

'My heart tells me that he was a good, kind man who would never have done anything to hurt me, but at the back of my mind is the nagging doubt that you can never truly know another person . . . ' The rest of the sentence was drowned out by the rain, which was now coming down in sheets.

Martine cupped her hand over one ear, straining to hear. The line crackled and hissed. She hit the button that switched it onto speakerphone.

Her grandmother's disembodied voice burst into the kitchen, echoing round the appliances. 'Secrets destroy, Martine. Never keep one. Henry's secret mission, however noble, might mean the end of Sawubona and everything I've ever worked for and love. I have no wish to depress you, but you're going to have to face the fact that it could also mean the end of the white giraffe.'

10

Dinner that night was a subdued affair. Grace cooked
and the food was as delicious as ever, but nobody
had any appetite. Ben sat wracking his brains for a
solution to the situation at Sawubona. For years he'd
been an outcast, shunned and bullied at school, but
Martine, her grandmother, Tendai and Grace had
changed his life. They'd not only welcomed him into
their world and accepted him for who he was, with no
reservations, they'd helped him to follow his dream of
working in nature and with wildlife. Now they needed
his help and he was frustrated that he'd so far been
unable to think of any way he might provide it.

Martine pushed her food around her plate, feeling blue. It was difficult to enjoy even a meal such as this – fresh bream caught by Sampson in the game reserve lake, accompanied by roasted cherry tomatoes, sweet potato mash and African spinach, with a lemon meringue pie to follow. Every meal at Sawubona now had a 'Last Supper' feel to it.

The phone call had left her deeply concerned about her grandmother. She was accustomed to Gwyn Thomas's feisty confidence, the kind that had allowed her to face down the bulldozer operator without blinking. It distressed her to hear her grandmother sounding so vulnerable and afraid.

Grace watched her without saying anything, but after the meal she took Martine aside and presented her with a small parcel wrapped in brown paper.

'What's this for?' Martine asked in surprise.

Grace smiled. 'I been thinkin' that ya mus' be runnin' low on Grace's special *muti*. Last night, after ya rode away on your giraffe, I went to find some special herbs and some plants for you.'

Martine hardly knew how to respond. The thoughtfulness of the *sangoma* touched her to the core.

Added to which, Grace was right. The traditional remedies Martine kept in her survival kit were almost finished. She'd used the last drop of the medicine Grace laughingly called 'Love Potion Number Nine', after a song she'd heard, on the buffalo. Martine wasn't sure (and didn't care to know) what the tiny brown bottles of *muti* contained, but Grace always wrote a detailed list of symptoms they were meant to treat on their labels. And, boy, were they effective.

She went to open the brown paper parcel, but Grace stopped her. 'Not now,' she said. 'There'll be time enough for that tomorra. Put it away in your survival kit.'

After the events of the day, sleep was not an option for Martine, particularly since the caracals were playing on her bed. Tendai had decided they'd be more effective than any human at guarding the house, and Martine and Ben agreed.

Unfortunately, it was a sweltering night and the caracals made Martine even hotter. She tossed and turned, her heart aching at the thought of life without Jemmy, who, she was sure, would not understand that she'd been forced to leave him to the mercy of Reuben James and the tourist hordes who would descend on the new White Giraffe Safari Park. He'd feel abandoned and betrayed.

At 2.30 a.m. she could stand it no longer. She got up, took a quiet shower so as not to wake Ben and Grace, dressed, and went down to her grandmother's study, followed by the caracals. Tendai had tried to tidy up some of the papers, but the room still looked like a tornado had blown through it. Martine picked though the mess until she found what she was looking for: the logbook for Sawubona's wildlife. Her grandmother and grandfather had always kept meticulous records of the history of each animal.

She found Angel easily enough, though the elephant hadn't had a name back then. Her grandfather had written her entry in bold blue handwriting.

Female desert elephant, approx 10 yrs old, 22 months pregnant, donated by Reuben James who rescued her from a zoo in Namibia, extreme case of neglect, v thin, covered in rope burns and untreated sores, grave concerns for health of her unborn calf.

It was a tragic story, and one that brought tears to Martine's eyes. She wondered if she'd misjudged Reuben James. Perhaps his takeover of Sawubona was just that – business. Fair compensation for the non-payment of a debt. Perhaps he genuinely did care for animals and would continue to rescue them when he was running his own Safari Park. Then she remembered that he was planning to exploit the white giraffe and was angry at him all over again. She was glad he'd saved Angel from the cruel zoo in Namibia, but nothing would make her like him.

She glanced again at her grandfather's notes on Angel and a line naming the elephant's place of birth caught her eye: Damaraland, Namibia.

For a moment Martine couldn't think where she'd heard the name before, but then she remembered her grandmother's call. There'd been nothing in the safety deposit box, Gwyn Thomas had told her, except a map of Damaraland. It was an odd coincidence. And Grace always said that there was no such thing as a coincidence.

Martine went over to the bookcase and took down a guidebook on travel in Africa. She flicked through it to the Namibia section. Damaraland was in the north of the country. It was, the book explained, the home of the rare and elusive desert-adapted elephant. These were taller than regular African elephants, with long legs capable of carrying them 70km a day. Ordinary elephants drink 100-200 litres of water a day, but desert elephants could survive even if they only consumed this amount every three or four days.

Martine returned the book to the shelf and switched off the lamp. Restless, she went out into the garden to see if she could find Jemmy, taking the caracals with her for protection. She didn't fancy being hit over the head by any burglars. The white giraffe was not at the waterhole. Martine was debating whether to return to the house for the silent whistle she used to call him when a different glimmer of white caught her eye: Reuben James's plane.

At dinner, Ben had mentioned that he'd overheard the pilot saying he had orders to have the aircraft ready at five a.m. He and Reuben James were returning to Namibia, James's home. They had no plans to return until Christmas Eve when they officially took over Sawubona. It was the first good news Martine had heard in a week.

Switching on her torch, she went over to the plane. It was a Beechcraft B58. There were six seats and a section for cargo at the back. She walked around to the aircraft's nose. Its name was on its side in red letters: Firebird. Beneath it, so small that you'd only notice it if you were standing right beside it, was . . .

Martine got such a surprise that she dropped the torch. It rolled under the wheels and it took a minute for her to find it again. She shone it at the nose of the plane. Beneath the Firebird banner was a four-leafed clover.

'The four leaves will lead you to the circle,' Grace had told her.

Martine sat down on the rock near the gate. The caracals milled around her, wanting attention. Reuben James was flying to Namibia, a country which just happened to be northwest of Sawubona, the direction the elephant tusks had been pointing. The map in the safety deposit box had been of Damaraland and Damaraland just happened to be the birthplace of Angel.

A plan started to take shape in Martine's head. What if she were to hitch a ride with Mr James and take a look at whatever it was he was up to on his travels? Maybe she could find a bit of dirt on him – some proof that he was a corrupt businessman who'd tricked her grandfather into giving away the game reserve? At the same time, she could try to follow the clues in Grace's prophecy.

Other, more sensible thoughts crowded into her mind. Thoughts such as: Are you *nuts*? You could be killed. You could be sent to jail or a youth offenders' institute or wherever it is they send eleven-year-olds who stowaway on planes to foreign countries. Oh, and if Reuben James doesn't shoot you, your grandmother will when she discovers what you've done.

But it was no use. If Martine listened to the rational part of her brain, it would mean sitting idly by while James turned Sawubona into a petting zoo for tourists who fancied a ride on a white giraffe. It would mean allowing her grandmother's home to be snatched away; Ben's dream of being a tracker to go up in smoke; and

273

Tendai, Sampson and all the other Sawubona staff to be out on the street with no jobs.

Worse still, it would mean finding a sign that Grace had told her would lead her to the 'truth', whatever that meant, and ignoring it. For all of those reasons, the brave and crazy part of her was willing to throw caution to the wind.

Martine decided to submit herself to one final test. Realistically, the only way she'd be able to stowaway on the plane would be to do it tonight, under cover of darkness. And she could only do that if the door had been left unlocked. She tried the door.

It was unlocked.

Martine exhaled in a rush of breath. So that was it decided. She had to do this thing now, whether she wanted to or not. She checked the time again. It was two-fifty. She needed to be on board by four a.m. at the latest.

Ignoring the objections that piled into her mind, she returned to the house. After packing her survival kit, windcheater, a spare T-shirt, extra socks and underwear and her toothbrush into a small rucksack, she went down to the kitchen and filled a lunchbox with two cheese and apricot chutney sandwiches and a bottle of water. She left a note on the kitchen table.

Dear Grace,
    I've gone to pluck out the thorn. Please take care
of Jemmy and the sanctuary animals and do what
you can so that my grandmother doesn't worry.
I love you all.
Martine xxx

As she left the house, shutting the caracals in behind her, she cast a wistful glance at Ben's bedroom window. She didn't know how she'd manage without her best friend, but it wasn't fair to involve him in such an irresponsible scheme.

Clicking the door shut behind her, she sprinted for the gate. There she paused and listened. Apart from the night creatures, there wasn't a sound. Heart pounding, she climbed into the plane and lay down behind the boxes in the hold, a tarpaulin covering her. She couldn't believe how easy it had been.

She was settling down for a nap, using her rucksack for a pillow when she heard a noise. She tensed. It was highly unlikely that Reuben James was making preparations to leave at three forty-five a.m, which meant that someone – with her luck it would be Lurk – had spotted her getting onto the plane. And that was a disaster.

The door hissed open. Martine shrank into her dark corner, trying not to breathe. Terror paralyzed her. The seconds ticked by. Her chest began to burn with lack of oxygen.

Just when she thought she'd either have to breathe or explode, the tarpaulin lifted. Ben grinned down at her. He was dressed and carrying the small khaki pack he took with him when he was tracking. Martine was still spluttering for words when he crawled in beside her.

'You didn't think I was going to let you go on your own, did you?' he said.

11

Martine had cramp. It had started in her foot and spread up her calf and now she had to bite down on her sweatshirt to stop from crying out. She was also freezing, starving and thirsty, and somehow her cold, hunger and dry mouth were made that much worse by the knowledge that her windcheater, sandwiches and the bottle of water were within touching distance, only she couldn't get to them. Not without attracting the attention of the pilot or Reuben James. Not without risking discovery.

She huddled nearer to Ben and managed to straighten her leg enough to ease the pain. They'd been flying for close on three hours. At four-thirty a gust of cold air had alerted them to the opening of the plane door and the lights had flicked on. It had seemed impossible she and Ben wouldn't be caught, but the pilot merely slung a couple of suitcases on top of them and started up the engines. Minutes later, they heard Reuben James's shouted greeting. Another box was piled into the cargo area and then they were bumping down the makeshift runway and taking off into the unknown.

And what happened next?

That was the question which had occupied Martine's mind for the best part of the journey. As usual, she hadn't thought that far ahead. Now she'd had time to reflect on her actions, regret had been added to the list of emotions she'd experienced over the past few days. She and Ben were about to enter a foreign country without passports. Without anyone knowing where they were. Without a plan. And without money. She had a handful of loose change with her but it was hardly enough for a hamburger. How on earth would they ever get back to Sawubona?

All she knew about Namibia were the facts she'd gleaned from the guidebook. That it was one of the most sparsely populated countries on earth, with only 1.8 million people occupying 800,000 square kilometers. That it was home to some of the last nomadic, herding tribes in Africa, the most ancient of which were the San Bushmen. That sixty per cent of Namibia was made up of the deserts of the Kalahari and the eighty-million-year-old Namib, and that December was one of the hottest months of the year there, with temperatures climbing into the forties.

Martine began to feel more panicky by the minute. She'd dragged her best friend into this. She'd left Grace to deal with Gwyn Thomas, although, since Grace had all but given her permission to travel as far as she needed to, Martine didn't feel quite so bad about that. Her main concern was her grandmother. With any luck Gwyn Thomas wouldn't phone for a few days, by which time Martine and Ben would be safely back at Sawubona.

She hoped.

Martine became aware that the aircraft was descending. Her ears popped. She nudged Ben awake, marvelling that he was able to sleep at such a time. His eyes opened and he stared around in confusion before recalling where he was. He smiled at Martine and, as always, that made her feel better. At least she wasn't alone. At least she and Ben were together.

The ground rose unexpectedly to meet them, slamming into the plane's underbelly. They bounced and shuddered to a halt. The engines shut down and all was quiet.

'A textbook landing, even if I say so myself,' remarked the pilot. 'Not far to go now. We'll refuel and clear customs and be on our way. Bet you'll be relieved when this is all over.'

'Right now, I'm most relieved about being away from Sawubona,' responded Reuben James. 'It was bad enough when that old battle-axe, Gwyn Thomas, was around, but her granddaughter is much more disconcerting. She has these green eyes that look right into your soul, like X-rays. She threatened me yesterday, basically said that there were people on the game reserve who had powers I couldn't possibly understand, and that they'd stop me.'

He chuckled. 'The idea that this skinny little kid or one of the game reserve staff could stick pins in a voodoo doll or stir up a magic potion to prevent me from fulfilling a plan that's been years in the making is a joke, but she said it in a way that almost had me believing it.'

'What are you going to do about her?' asked the pilot, but before the other man could answer a customs official was at the window. The next few minutes were taken up with administration and refuelling.

After that the plane took off again and flew for another forty-five minutes. By then, Martine was so desperate for the bathroom she was prepared to give herself up in order to go. Fortunately the plane began its descent as she was trying to communicate this to Ben. They touched down shortly afterwards.

'I'm glad this is our last journey with this type of cargo,' said the pilot when the engines had shut down. 'I don't think my nerves could stand another one. If that customs official had searched the plane, my life would not have been worth living.'

'Think of your Swiss bank account,' Reuben James reminded him.

'It's not going to be much use to me if I'm behind bars.'

'You should have thought about that sooner. In any case, we're not breaking the law; merely bending it. We're performing a national service.'

'Do you think the . . . will see it that way?' Martine missed the word or name because a vehicle drove up outside.

'Sure they will,' said Reuben James. 'Where else are they going to get access to three square meals and fresh water every day?'

He and the pilot greeted the driver of the vehicle and the pair of them clambered out of the plane. An engine revved and faded into the distance.

Martine and Ben climbed stiffly to their feet. They opened the door cautiously and stepped out into a wall of heat.

As far as they could see there was nothing but desert. Not a desert with rippled gold sand, but one with sky-scraping red dunes. It rose around them in mountainous peaks of burnished umber, sculpted by the wind into knife-edged cliffs, ravines and valleys, and thrown into sharp relief by the morning sun. It was a scene of immense beauty but it was a desolate one.

Martine felt faint. She put a hand on the wing of the plane. Ben met her gaze and she could tell he was thinking the same thing. They were alone in the desert, thousands of miles from home, with two cheese sandwiches and a bottle of water.

12

'Now what?' said Martine. It was a relief to say the words out loud after lying on the shuddering floor of the plane for several hours thinking them.

Ben ran his fingers through his black hair. 'Good question. What's the first rule of survival in any situation?'

'Don't panic.'

'So let's not panic. Before we move, let's go over the plane inch by inch and see if there is anything on it that might be of use to us. First, though, we should eat something.'

They shared the sandwiches and half the bottle of

water, reasoning that the cheese would melt and go bad in the heat and then it would be no use to anyone. After that, they returned to the plane and examined its contents meticulously.

There wasn't much *to* find, particularly since they couldn't remove anything that would be missed. They did take two small cartons of juice from a cool box, and some glucose and water-purification tablets and a blanket from the First Aid box, but they drew the line at going through the suitcases.

'Innocent until proven guilty,' Ben said. Martine was of the opinion that Reuben James was guilty until proven innocent, but she agreed that going through his belongings should be a last resort.

They did investigate the boxes in the hold. Most were tightly sealed, but the name of the manufacturer on the exterior and the smell coming from one with a torn corner made Ben fairly certain they were mining supplies.

'Mining supplies?' said Martine. 'Is that how Reuben James is making his millions, then? From diamonds or platinum?'

'I'm not sure. I asked Tendai about it and he thought James was in the business of developing luxury tourist lodges. But he didn't really know.'

He shoved the boxes back into position and the two of them hopped out of the plane and closed the door. Martine caught sight of the four-leafed clover on the nose of the aircraft again and remembered Grace's prophesy.

The four leaves will lead you to the circle. What circle?

'Could you make any sense of the conversation on the plane?' she asked Ben. 'What do you think Reuben James meant when he said that they were not breaking the law, just bending it? And what was all that talk about Swiss bank accounts and jail?'

'It was when Mr James made out that someone, somewhere should be grateful that they were getting three square meals and water every day that I really started worrying. It almost sounded as if he was referring to slave labour. It's all very mysterious but I think we can be certain of one thing.'

'What's that?'

'This is about something much bigger than Sawubona.'

They had no way of knowing when the pilot and/or Reuben James would return to collect the cargo, but they guessed that at the very least the men would be off eating breakfast somewhere. And it was vital that they try to get their bearings before it got any hotter. They were uncomfortably conscious of how little liquid they had.

Within minutes of starting to climb one of the dunes, Martine would have killed for something sweet, fizzy and ice-cold. She and Ben were barefoot, having taken off their boots, tied the laces together, and slung them around their necks, and their toes sank deep into the red sand. On and on they slogged, muscles burning. Halfway up, they shared the remainder of the water. Neither of them said anything, but both of them knew that once the apple juice was gone they'd be in trouble.

'I bet you we get to the top and find there's a lovely hotel with shady palms and a sparkling blue swimming pool on the other side,' Ben said hopefully.

'I bet you we get to the top and there's an air-conditioned shopping centre offering free chocolate chip ice-cream and all the lemonade we can drink!' said Martine.

That cheered them up and they resumed their struggle to the top of the dune. Ben, who was a lot fitter than Martine, made it there first, with a lot less panting. She joined him a minute later, but took her time getting her breath back before looking around. Ben's expression had already told her what she was likely to see and she was in no hurry to have it confirmed.

From horizon to blue horizon stretched layer upon layer of red dunes, tossed and scooped like some gigantic desert dessert. There was no sign of life. Had it not been for a tar road that tapered away in the haze, and the plane, toy-sized on the distant runway, they could have been on Mars.

'If it helps, we're in Sossusvlei,' said Ben. 'I recognize these red dunes from photographs. We're at least six hours by car from the nearest big town.'

'Great,' said Martine, shielding her eyes from the glaring sun. 'Let's hope we don't have to do it on foot.'

She sat down on the dune. 'Ben, I'm so sorry. As usual,

this is my fault. I was in such a state at the possibility of losing Jemmy and Khan and Sawubona, I wasn't thinking clearly. I was sick of feeling helpless. I wanted to do something. It didn't occur to me that Reuben James would be doing business in the middle of the Namib desert. I thought we'd be in a proper place with cars and roads and houses, where I could do some investigating. But this is a disaster. And the worst part is, I've dragged you into it.'

Ben flopped down beside her and opened one of the little cartons of apple juice. He offered it to her before taking a sip himself. 'You didn't drag me in to it. I came because I wanted to, remember? Anyway, you need to take your own advice.'

'What advice is that?'

'What you said to your grandmother. We can't give up. Let's do what we came here to do. Let's get to the bottom of what Reuben James is up to and find enough evidence to prevent him from taking over Sawubona.'

Martine looked at him. 'There's something else.'

Briefly, she told him about Grace's prophesy, about the northwest-facing tusks and finding the four-leafed clover on the nose of the plane. She also relayed her grandmother's conversation about the Damaraland map in the safety deposit box, and told him of the strange coincidence of Angel being from that exact place. 'Grace always says that there's no such thing as a coincidence. So it's a bit odd to find two sets of coincidences in less than 24 hours.'

'Mmm,' murmured Ben. 'And there might be a third.

What if the reason Angel attacked Lurk was that she knew him from Damaraland and that he did something to anger her back then? I think we owe it to Angel, your grandmother and everyone else at Sawubona to investigate this a bit further. We need to find a way to Damaraland.'

For the first time in days Martine felt hope stir in her veins. 'Okay,' she said. 'Let's do what we've come here to do. We've been in worse situations than this. Let's hide near the plane until they return for the cargo and then see if we can sneak into their vehicle.'

They soon found that the easiest way down the steep dunes was to slip-slide on their bums as if they were tobogganing. Descending was a whole lot more fun than going up. They were almost at the bottom when they spotted a swirl of dust on the road. The safari vehicle was returning.

They were completely exposed on the slope and hundreds of yards from the nearest cover, so they skidded to a halt where they were and buried themselves in the powdery red earth until only their heads were showing. Below them, the safari vehicle halted beside the aircraft. The pilot and Reuben James unloaded several long wooden crates, hoisted them onto the plane, and climbed in after the cargo. Five minutes later, they still hadn't emerged. The propellers on the plane started whirring.

'They're leaving!' cried Martine, half sitting up. 'Ben, they're leaving us! I assumed that this was their final destination and we'd have ages to return to the plane. I thought Reuben James either lived near here or had business around here, and that the plane wouldn't be going anywhere for days.'

'So did I,' said Ben grimly. 'I guess we assumed wrong.'

The drone of the engine grew louder as the pilot prepared for take-off. The driver of the safari vehicle waved and sped away.

Martine and Ben watched as the white aircraft taxied down the runway and shot into the blue. Moments later, the sky was empty. It was as if the plane and the men on it had been a figment of their imagination.

A silence in which the only sounds were the whisper of sand and their own short, frightened breathing seemed to swoop down and chill them, in spite of the heat of the day.

'Now what?' said Ben.

· 13 ·

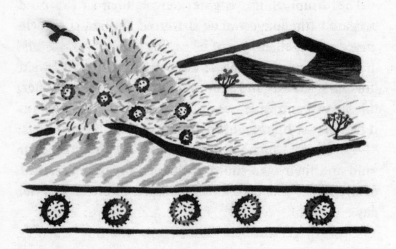

'STOP,' said Martine.

In everyday life she was quick to anger and quick to cry and she definitely felt like doing both now, but when faced with a survival crisis she'd learned the importance of listening to her head and not her heart.

Ben stared at her in surprise. 'Stop what?'

'S.T.O.P. It's an anagram for Stop, Think, Observe, Plan. I read about it somewhere. It's a way of staying focussed and not having a meltdown when you're in a really desperate situation.'

'Which we are,' Ben said with feeling. 'A *really* desperate situation.'

Martine stood up and shook red sand from her clothes and cropped brown hair. 'In a way, this might be a blessing.'

'How's that?'

'Well, supposing we had been on board that plane. Odds are, the longer we were around Reuben James, the more chance there was of us getting caught. All it would have taken was for one of us to sneeze. But now we're free agents. We're in Namibia and on his trail, but we get to say how and when we do things.'

Ben burst out laughing. 'Boy, have you changed over the past year. But you're totally right. We're a zillion miles from anywhere and boiling alive in the desert sun with one tiny carton of apple juice and no transport. We have to think positively if we're going to get out alive. Okay, let's get on Mr James' trail. But first we need shelter, water and food – in that order.'

'I agree. Ben?'

'Yeah.'

'Deep down, I'm terrified, you know. I don't think I've ever been so scared in my life. But I'm also very determined. I'm going to save Sawubona and all our precious animals if it's the last thing I ever do.'

Ben looked from her to the endless cliffs of burning red sand and back again, his dark eyes serious. 'Let's hope it's not,' he said.

The most critical course of action was for them to escape from the sun. Since there was no shelter of any kind for miles and they could not risk getting dehydrated searching for one in the fierce heat, they returned to the airstrip and rigged up a canopy using the blanket and the branches of a dried, stunted tree. They stayed there until mid-afternoon, dozing and daydreaming about food and icy drinks. The apple juice had gone by lunchtime. With the last of it, they used a survival trick, keeping it in their mouths for as long as they could so that their tongues and lips didn't dry out.

Late afternoon, they ate a glucose tablet each and set off into the energy-sapping heat. They had hoped the airstrip might be in regular use and they'd soon be rescued, but they never saw a soul. Both of them knew that in a lot of survival situations it was best to stay where you were until you were rescued rather than move and make your situation worse, but, since nobody was aware they were in need of rescuing, it was up to them to seek help.

They followed the road in the direction the safari vehicle had taken that morning. It was a lot less strenuous than climbing the dunes, and there was always the chance that a busload of tourists or a park warden with a vat of water on board would drive by. That was their hope, at any rate.

It didn't happen.

As the hours ticked past and the sun slipped lower in the sky, Martine's mouth became so dry that her tongue kept sticking to the roof of it, and her lips cracked and bled a little. She'd put on her windcheater and pulled up the hood to protect her from sunburn, but all it did was make her hotter. Her limbs weakened. She put one foot in front of the other and tried not to think of the stories she'd read about people dying in the desert. The longest the body could go without water was three days. In this heat, a person could be dead in twenty-four hours.

Her biggest concern was that they might be walking in the wrong direction. The safari vehicle might not have been heading for a tourist lodge at all. If Ben was right about the contents of the boxes, it could have been taking Reuben James to a mine or perhaps a secret storage unit. There might be armed guards there. She and Ben might be walking into a trap.

A lizard with a snout like a shovel streaked across a nearby dune with a swimming motion. Apart from beetles and a distant eagle, it was the only sign of life they'd seen all day.

'We're not going to die,' Martine said out loud with a lot more confidence than she felt. 'Grace would have mentioned it if we were.'

'She might have left that part out, so as not to alarm you,' Ben teased. 'Don't fortune-tellers abide by some sort of code where they don't tell people if they see something ghastly?'

Martine suddenly felt exceedingly hot and irritable. 'That's really not helpful, Ben,' she said crossly. 'Anyway, Grace is not a fortune-teller. She's a *sangoma* who can commune with the spirits and read the bones. It's not like she's some charlatan with a sequined vest and a crystal ball.'

Ben stopped. 'Hey, I know that. Grace is completely amazing. I'm sorry, it was a stupid thing to say. I was trying to keep things light, that's all.'

Martine squeezed his hand. 'Sorry I snapped at you. I'm just hungry and tired and I keep blaming myself for the mess we're in.'

Ben grinned. 'That doesn't sound like positive thinking to me. Come on, we can do it. Quick march, quick march, quick march . . .'

Sunset brought a breeze so cool and soothing it was like being wrapped in silk. Martine and Ben used the last of their strength to climb the highest dune in the area, where they hoped they'd be out of reach of predators, snakes and scorpions during the long night ahead. They were also hoping to catch a glimpse of a tourist lodge or some indication of water.

Before they climbed, they removed their boots again. The warm red sand slipped through Martine's toes. Close to the top, they paused for breath. The sunset did not have the exotic hues of those Martine regularly saw at Sawubona, but the colours of the desert made up for it. Bathed in the pure light of evening, the great rippled dunes turned every shade of brick-red, burnt orange and chestnut brown.

It was a sight so lovely, so lonely and so ancient that Martine momentarily forgot their plight and felt lucky to be witnessing it. According to the guidebook, the Namib Desert was an estimated eighty million years old. In terms of evolution, she was about as insignificant as an amoeba. She lingered on the slope even after Ben began to climb again, only emerging from her reverie when he let out an agonized yell.

Martine did the last few yards in double time. Ben was lying on the summit of the dune holding his foot, his face contorted with pain. Near by was the cause of his distress – a thorn bush with vicious, curving thorns.

'Typical,' he said through gritted teeth. 'We walk for hours without seeing a single tree or blade of grass and the first bit of vegetation we come to is a thorn bush.'

He let go of his foot and Martine saw five bleeding punctures on the sole. Before he could object, she'd unzipped her survival kit and was cleaning the tiny wounds with an antiseptic wipe. She followed it up with a dot or two of Grace's wound-healing potion, and wrapped his foot in a gauze bandage to keep it sand-free while the *muti* did its work.

It was only when she'd finished and Ben was sitting up again and smiling, that she noticed two things. The first was that there was a valley on the other side of the dune, spread with blond grass and a few trees. The other was that the thorn bush had yellow-green melons on it.

'Is that a mirage?' she said croakily.

'Is what a mirage?' Ben was examining Martine's handiwork, impressed at how professionally she'd patched him up. The potion she'd applied had reduced the pain to almost nothing.

Martine was examining the thorn bush. She tapped the forbidding cluster of thorns with her Swiss Army knife and several melons tumbled to the ground. She sliced one open. Inside it looked like a cucumber. She scooped out some of the yellow fruit and popped it in her mouth, grimacing slightly at its sour, burning taste. Next, she removed the shell from a couple of the seeds and ate the soft pellet inside.

'Martine, has the sun fried your brain?' demanded Ben. 'Have you any idea how dangerous it is to eat unidentified plants? What if the fruit is poisonous? What if you get sick out here when we're miles from a doctor?'

Martine popped another few seeds into her mouth. 'These are yummy. They're almost like almonds.'

She cut open another melon and handed it to him. 'This is a Nara bush. I'd recognize it anywhere. Grace is always going on about them. She says the San Bushmen love the Nara because it's the plant with a hundred uses. The oil from the seeds moisturizes the skin and protects it from sunburn; the root cures stomach pains, nausea, chest pains and kidney problems, and the flesh can be rubbed on wounds to help heal them or eaten to rehydrate you.'

Ben took a bit of convincing, but he was so starving and thirsty that he couldn't hold out for long, especially since Martine had dramatically revived since eating the first melon and was already tucking into the seeds of the second. Soon he was guzzling the seeds with equal enthusiasm.

At a certain point, they looked at each other, juice running down their chins, clothes and bodies filthy, hair sticking up on end from a night on the floor of the plane and a day in the baking desert, and burst out laughing.

It was almost dark by then, so they built a small fire with the dry twigs and foliage beneath the thorn bush and spread the thin blanket from the pilot's First Aid box on top of the high narrow ridge of the dune. They covered themselves with the space blanket from Martine's survival kit, which could withstand temperatures of minus 60 degrees. Or so it claimed on the wrapper.

The Evening Star heralded the coming of the night. Before long it was as if a box of diamonds had been spilled across the heavens, so numerous and glittering were the constellations. A crescent moon rose into the deep blue sky.

Ben and Martine lay with their heads resting on their packs, cosy beneath the space blanket, and gazed up at the Milky Way and Orion and the Southern Cross. From time to time, they heard the sounds of night creatures. It made them feel less alone.

'You know something, Ben?' Martine said sleepily. 'I believe we're going to make it. I haven't a clue how, but I think we are.'

Ben yawned. 'You know something, Martine? I believe you're right.'

They fell into the dreamless sleep of the young and the truly exhausted, innocent and, for the time being, uncaring, of what was to come.

They were woken by the rosy glow of dawn breaking over the red dunes. Ben sat up and declared the view to be the most breathtaking he'd ever seen. Martine, her voice thick with sleep, stayed where she was and moaned and groaned about the hardness of their sand bed and how freezing it was and how much she needed a shower and more sleep, as well as a breakfast of eggs, bacon, coffee and orange juice.

'Coming right up, your ladyship. Just let me dial room service.' Ben stood and pulled the blanket off her. 'Get up, lazy bones. I think you're going to want to see this.' When she didn't stir, he aimed a gentle kick at her ribs.

Martine bolted upright and glared at him. 'Boy, are you going to pay for that when we get back to civilization. Just you wait.'

She shielded her eyes from the burning orange sun. 'What's so special that I have to get out of bed at five a.m.?'

And then she saw them. In the valley below, scattered across the pale grass, were hundreds of Oryx antelope. They had extra-long horns, as straight and sharp as spears, and their coats and faces were patterned in fawn and black in such a way that they looked uniformed and regal, as if they formed part of some warrior queen's elite guard. Martine had only ever seen them in photos, but she'd always considered them to be among the world's most beautiful animals.

Tiredness forgotten, Martine jumped to her feet. 'Ben, we have to go nearer. They're exquisite. A herd that size would need gallons of water to survive. Maybe we can see where they're getting it from.'

Her change of heart made Ben smile, but he thought the better of teasing her. They packed up their things and slid down the dune. When they reached the valley they worked their way slowly towards the herd. Half an hour later, they were behind a tree and not far from a bare patch of earth where two young bulls were mock fighting. They tossed their magnificent heads and rushed at each other with their sword-like horns, turning aside at the last minute.

Martine couldn't bear the thought that they might harm each other. Ben had to restrain her from going to stop them.

'You shouldn't interfere with nature.'

'Of course I'm going to interfere with nature if it means saving an Oryx from ending up stabbed and bleeding,' Martine whispered. 'Ouch, did you see that?'

The bulls clashed horns. The mock fighting was turning into real fighting.

Martine stepped from behind the tree. 'Bad bulls!' she cried. 'Be nice to each other. What's the point of fighting?'

The bulls halted in their tracks. Their tails tossed as they pondered the apparition that had dared to intrude into their game. Then they galloped for the cover of the dunes, the herd stampeding after them.

'HEY!'

A young San Bushman rose seemingly from behind a tuft of grass. He was bare-chested and wearing khaki cargo shorts, and had a bow and sleeve of arrows slung over his shoulder and a professional-looking camera in his hand.

'I don't believe it,' he said. 'Thirty-four thousand square kilometers of desert out here and you have to ruin my shot.'

For much of the year she'd spent in Africa, Martine had been preoccupied with the San Bushmen. Accounts differed as to whether it was a Bushman legend or a Zulu legend or even just an African one which said that the child who rides a white giraffe will have power over all the animals. Regardless, it was the Bushmen, she felt sure, who held the key to her destiny.

Time and time again, their paintings had forecast the challenges she would have to face and overcome.

And yet in all these months it had never entered Martine's head that she might meet a San Bushman in the flesh. Certainly not one taking photographs with a long-lens camera. She'd always imagined them to be living in some remote region of the Kalahari Desert in Botswana or in the far north of Namibia, too nomadic and wedded to the traditions of their ancestors to be touched by the modern world.

But this boy, who looked to be about fifteen, was not enigmatic or far removed from the modern world. He was right here and quite angry.

'Do you know how long I've been lying here, waiting for that shot? I've had to put up with cold, with cramp, with ants nibbling my toes and a scorpion crawling over my leg. At one point a horned adder even came to inspect me. I survive all that, only to have two idiot tourist kids come by and start shrieking at the Oryx as if they're pet donkeys.'

'Look, I'm really, really sorry,' said Martine. 'How was I supposed to know I was interfering with your picture? I was only trying to stop the Oryx from goring each other. Anyway, you were camouflaged behind a blade of grass.'

To her astonishment, the boy let out a shriek of delighted laughter. He clutched at his stomach and laughed some more.

Martine began to get annoyed. 'What's so funny?'

'Camouflaged behind a blade of grass! I wish the elders of our tribe could hear you say that. They think I'm about the most useless hunter and tracker in San history. Which I probably am. Not that I care. All I ever wanted to be was a photographer, so I never bothered to learn any of that stuff. But then after my father . . . well anyway now I wish I had, but it's too late.'

'It's never too late,' Ben assured him. 'I'm an apprentice tracker. I could show you some stuff if you like.'

This brought on another fit of laughter. '*You?* What do you track – the Yeti when it makes midnight visits to your school playing fields?'

He looked them up and down and Martine was conscious of what a sight they must be. 'You're quite funny for tourist kids. And quite scruffy. Don't they have showers at your hotel? Where are all the other people on your tour anyway? I didn't hear an engine.'

'We have a slight problem,' confided Ben.

'A tiny one,' Martine added supportively.

'Yesterday morning, we flew in on a private plane from the Western Cape in South Africa. We were with some . . . friends. They stopped at an airfield a few miles from here and Martine and I went to climb the dunes. They didn't realize we weren't on board and flew away without us.'

The boy raised his eyebrows. 'Your "friends" didn't notice you were missing, even though there were only a handful of you on this plane?'

'That's right,' Martine said brightly. 'They probably got carried away taking pictures of the scenery. Like you!'

'Let me get this straight. You fly all the way from South Africa, stop at an airfield in the middle of the Namib Desert and decide to go off exploring on your own. Despite the dangers, nobody objects. While you're gone, your 'friends' abandon you in forty degree heat, with no food or water, and continue with their holiday as if nothing has happened?'

'It sounds worse than it is,' said Martine.

'Oh, I think it's already pretty bad. With friends like that, who needs enemies?'

The boy looked at his watch. 'All right, I'll take you to the police station in Swakopmond. It's about a six-hour drive from here, but lucky for you it's on my way. Good thing for you that you ruined my shot, hey?'

'We'd really appreciate a ride, but you don't need to go to the trouble of taking us to the police station,' Ben put in quickly. 'If you drop us in Swakopmond, we'll be fine. We'll make a few phone calls and have this sorted out in no time.'

'Really?' said the boy. 'I don't suppose there's anything you're not telling me, is there? You're not runaways or fugitives from the law, are you?'

Martine gave him her sweetest smile. 'We're just ordinary kids having the worst vacation of our life.'

'Right. If you say so.' He took some keys from his pocket. 'Let's go before it gets much hotter. My vehicle is parked behind those trees. Don't look so worried. I know I look about fifteen because I'm so small, but I've just turned eighteen and I do have my driver's license. I'm Gift, by the way.'

'Gift,' said Martine. 'What a beautiful name.'

A shadow passed across the boy's face. 'It was my father's choice. I don't feel as if I've been much of a gift to him so far. Everything that's happened to him is entirely my fault. But that's another story. A long story. What are your names? Ben and Martine? All right, Ben and Martine, let's hit the road.'

· 15 ·

Once he'd recovered from the disappointment of missing out on his photo of the fighting Oryx, Gift was very friendly and chatty. Martine found it difficult to hide how in awe she was at being in the presence of a real San tribesman, even though he didn't fit her picture of a Bushman at all. Especially when he turned up the rap music on the sound system of his four-wheel drive.

It took a while for her to recover from her initial shyness, but after that she couldn't resist questioning him about the history of his tribe. He seemed surprised at her interest, but was more than willing to answer her. He told her how the San had been in southern Africa longer than any other indigenous people, and that their cave paintings dated back thousands of years.

For centuries they'd been skilled hunter-gatherers, living a nomadic life in harmony with nature. Then came the invaders. In the 1800s, white Afrikaaners moving in from South Africa and migrating Bantu tribes, who regarded the Bushmen as cattle thieves and lowlifes, brought so much pressure and conflict into the lives of the San that they were forced off their traditional lands and into the deserts of Botswana and Namibia. Their fragile, contented community began to crumble.

Many other things, such as the colonization of Namibia by Germany in the late 19th century, several wars and the long struggle for independence, had contributed to destroying their way of life.

'Now we're scattered to the four winds and there are many social problems in our communities,' Gift told Martine. 'That's one of the reasons I went away to school. My father wanted me to have a better life than he and his father did. Instead that was the start of all the trouble.'

He paused to slow his vehicle. It bucked and skidded as they descended into a rocky gorge. Martine hung out of the window, enjoying the coppery early morning sunlight on her skin. The scenery had changed from red dunes to vast dry plains and hills ringed with terraces.

The colours of the landscape were extraordinary. Sometimes the soil was so white it glowed beneath the blue sky. Sometimes it was a warm brown and dotted with yellow flowers. Sometimes it was black and striped with mineral shades like purple, blue and even green. They saw bird's nests as big as African huts with multiple entrances and yellow birds darting in and out. Gift explained that they were the home of the community weaverbird and could weigh as much as a ton. Some were so heavy they brought down trees or branches.

'Why was going to school the start of all the trouble?' Ben asked Gift. 'Didn't you want to go?'

Gift steered the four-wheel drive carefully along the winding, rocky trail. 'I very much wanted to go. My dream is to become a famous newspaper photographer. Because of that, I wanted to get the best education I could.

'The problems came when I went to high school in Windhoek. I had lots of cool friends and it made me see my family and old friends differently. When I'd return to our village in the holidays, everything looked so run-down and shabby. People, including my father, seemed ignorant; set in the past. They weren't part of the modern world at all. I had big fights with my father. One night we rowed after he told me he was unhappy with my attitude and was going to pull me out of school. I accused him of destroying my dream. I ran off into the desert. He came looking for me.'

He stopped. Martine thought she saw a tear roll down his cheek, but he swerved to avoid a bounding springbok and when she looked again it was gone.

'Oh, forget it,' Gift said roughly. 'What's the point in me telling you this when I'm never going to see you again? And anyway you're just two weird kids who've probably robbed a bank or something and are on the run.'

'If we were on the run, we'd have chosen somewhere other than a scorching desert wilderness,' Martine told him. 'Look, we've still got a long way to travel. We might as well make conversation. What happened after you ran away into the desert? Did your father find you?'

Gift's strong brown hands gripped the wheel. 'That's the terrible part. I came home the next morning, when I was hungry, to learn that my father had gone out searching for me. I felt sure he'd be back in a few hours. So did everyone else. But he never returned.'

There was the briefest of pauses. 'Not only did he not come back that day, he never came back at all. That was a year ago.'

Martine stared at him in horror. 'You mean, he just vanished without a trace?'

Gift focused on the road. 'Without a trace. We sent our best trackers out to search for him and they didn't find so much as a footprint.'

Martine's heart ached for him. It was bad enough when you *did* know what had happened to your parents. It had to be a thousand times worse having no idea.

'What did the police say?' Ben asked.

'They think he was eaten by some wild animal. They don't suspect foul play. My father was one of the most loved men in our tribe. He was an elephant whisperer.'

'I've heard of horse whisperers,' Ben said, 'men and women who have a special gift for communicating with wild or traumatized horses. But what is an elephant whisperer? Surely you'd be trampled to death if you tried to whisper in the ear of a wild African elephant?'

Gift reached into his pocket and took out his wallet. He tossed it to Martine. 'Show Ben the photo inside.'

Martine slipped the photo out of its sleeve and she and Ben studied it. It showed a San Bushman like the ones she'd seen in books. He was standing between two elephants. The female elephant had her trunk curled around his waist, and he had one hand resting on her trunk and one on the tusk of a massive bull elephant. His face was radiant with happiness.

'Those are wild elephants.'

Martine studied the picture again. 'You mean, they're wild elephants that have been tamed?'

'No, they're totally wild. They'd gore you or I without blinking.'

'But how is that possible?' Martine returned the photo to its sleeve and handed the wallet back to Gift.

He put it in his pocket. 'When my father was four years old, the San camp was raided by desert elephants. There was a drought and they were looking for food. During the raid, he was snatched by one of the elephants. My grandparents assumed he'd been dragged away and killed, but three months later he was found alive and well and living quite happily with a herd of elephants. They rescued him with great difficulty, and were shocked to find he was reluctant to come home.

'Ever since, he has been able to communicate with elephants. Whether they know him or not they seem to accept him as one of their own. Or, at least, they did before he disappeared. People think I'm out of my mind, but I believe that the elephants would not have allowed anything to happen to him. I'm positive that I will find him one day and he'll be living with elephants. I miss him so much.'

'If it's any consolation, I know how you feel,' Martine told him.

'No offence,' Gift answered shortly, 'but a kid like you couldn't possibly understand how I feel.'

The car went quiet after that. They were passing a line of low, golden dunes which looked airbrushed and unreal, like a backdrop in a film set. Soon after that, they reached the little town of Swakopmond. Suddenly the sparkling sea was before them. Palm trees lined the beach.

The Germans had built Swakopmond during their occupation of Namibia, so the architecture was German and the buildings spotlessly clean and prettily painted. The roads had names like Hendrik Witbool Street and Luderitz Street. Martine also spotted the Bismark Medical Centre.

She nudged Ben. Leaning forward, he said: 'Thanks for the ride, Gift. You've saved our lives. I don't know what we'd have done if you hadn't come along. We owe you. But we can manage on our own from now on. If you drop us somewhere around here, we'll find a phone and call our friends.'

'Sure,' responded Gift, but instead of pulling over he stamped hard on the accelerator. He swerved around another car, made a dangerous turn at the lights and screeched to a halt in front of the police station.

Ben grabbed at the door handle, but it was locked.

'Sorry about that, but I couldn't afford to take any chances,' Gift told him. 'You seem like nice kids, but it's obvious you've told me a pack of lies about your so-called friends and their plane and their holiday. You've got thirty seconds to tell me the truth or I'm turning you in to the police.'

· 16 ·

A couple of lean, mean-looking policemen, their hands resting casually on their gun-belts, strolled past the four-wheel drive. One of them turned as he passed and cast a suspicious eye over the vehicle and its passengers.

Martine's blood pressure went through the roof as she imagined her grandmother receiving a phone call in England to say that her granddaughter and Ben were in jail in Swakopmond, charged with stowing away on a private plane and entering Namibia illegally and without passports.

'You're right, Gift,' she said. 'We haven't been honest

with you. We had a fight with our families and we ran away. We've learned our lesson, though, and we just want to call them, say sorry and go home.'

Gift opened the glove compartment and took out a cellphone. 'What's the number? I'll dial it for you.'

Martine swallowed. 'I don't know it.'

'You don't know your own phone number? He looked over at Ben. 'How 'bout you?'

'There's nobody at my house. My parents are away on a cruise.'

'Right, your thirty seconds are up. I'm calling the police and they can deal with you.' He went to get out of the vehicle.

'Wait!' cried Martine. 'I'm sorry. We'll tell you the real story.'

Gift ignored her. He locked the doors from the outside and strode towards the police station. The windows were electric so they had no way of getting out.

'If I'd known I'd be spending my vacation in a Namibian jail, I might not have been so hasty about turning down the Mediterranean cruise,' said Ben.

Martine banged hard on the window. 'Gift,' she yelled through the glass. 'How would you feel if someone threatened to take away your home and everything and everyone you loved? Wouldn't you lie too? Wouldn't you do anything in your power to stop the people who wanted to do that?'

Two hours later, after a much-needed shower at Gift's aunt's house, the three of them were sitting in a restaurant called The Tug. It was an atmospheric place constructed from a tugboat which had been shipwrecked along the coastline – a stretch of ocean so treacherous that early explorers had named it the Skeleton Coast. Watching the Atlantic rollers charge up to the jetty outside and splatter the restaurant windows with grey foam, Martine was not in the least surprised.

'I want the whole truth and nothing but,' said Gift, as they tucked into prawns dripping with lemon and garlic, giant asparagus spears, and the biggest plate of fish and chips Martine and Ben had ever seen. 'If you lie to me again, you'll be spending the next month washing dishes to pay for this meal.'

So they told him the whole story. Well, almost the whole story. Martine explained about the fire that had killed her parents, and about moving to Africa. She decided against telling him about Grace's prediction. It seemed pointless when she had no idea what it meant.

Gift heard her out, his face filled with compassion. 'I'm sorry for saying that a kid like you could never understand what I've been through. Obviously you do.'

Ben took up the story. He told Gift about the sinister businessman who'd shown up out of the blue one day, claiming that Henry Thomas had signed over Sawubona to him as surety for a debt and giving them less than a fortnight to leave the reserve. He and Martine were, he said, so determined to save Sawubona that coming to Namibia to investigate the man who wanted to take everything from them had seemed their only option.

'Do you know where he has his business?' asked Gift.

'No,' admitted Martine. 'We think he might own some tourist lodges, but we're not really sure. A few years ago, he gave my grandfather a desert elephant from Damaraland. She was very badly injured, and we have a sanctuary that helps heal wild animals that have been wounded or mistreated. He said she came from a zoo that had shut down.'

Gift frowned. 'That's odd. I myself am from Damaraland. That's where my father disappeared. We don't have zoos in Namibia and if one had opened or closed down in our area I'd definitely know about it, because my father has records about practically every elephant in the desert.

'The other thing that puzzles me is why this man would send an injured elephant out of the country. We have plenty of wildlife hospitals and sanctuaries of our own. It makes no sense at all.'

He paused to shovel in a mouthful of fish. 'He sounds like a thoroughly evil character. What's his name? Maybe I've heard of him.'

'His name is James,' Ben told him. 'Reuben James.'

Gift choked. His fish went down the wrong way, and he had such a severe coughing fit that he needed almost a whole bottle of water to recover. It was some time before he could speak again.

'That's impossible,' he croaked, eyes streaming.

Martine was bewildered. 'Why is it impossible?'

Gift took another swallow of water. 'Because the man

you're describing sounds like a nasty, heartless piece of work. I've known Reuben James since I was a boy and he is the opposite of that. He's a conservationist. He's poured a fortune of his own money into protecting the desert elephants. When my father disappeared, it was Reuben James who organized all the patrols that went out searching for him. He's the man who paid for my education and he helped me get a job as a freelance photographer for a local magazine.

'Reuben James is the best man I know.'

17

It was Angel who saved the day.

Sitting on Swakopmond beach early next morning, drinking coffee and tucking into a slab of Black Forest gateau from Anton's famous German bakery, Martine thought there was something ironic about the fact that the elephant, who'd been intent on hurting them at Sawubona, had indirectly ended up helping them in Namibia. But then maybe Ben was right. Maybe she'd only ever intended to harm Lurk. And that raised a lot of questions.

The way it happened was this. Gift had taken the news about Reuben James badly to say the least. He'd been ready to cart them back to the police station just for criticizing the man. Even when Martine pointed out that he himself had described Reuben as a 'thoroughly evil character' before he knew who they were talking about, he was still reluctant to accept that his mentor could be flawed.

But then Ben recounted the conversation they'd overheard on the plane, and Martine followed it up by telling Gift about Angel's attack on the chauffeur.

When he heard about Lurk, the stubborn scowl left the San boy's face. He sat up straight. 'Are you telling me that this desert elephant – the elephant given to your grandfather by Reuben James – singled out Lurk and charged him?'

'Apparently,' said Martine. 'And when Lurk escaped by throwing down his jacket, she mashed it into the earth as if she hated it.'

Gift nodded. 'I know how she feels. Lurk is sly. Cunning. Whenever Reuben James is around, he's all smiles and politeness and yes sir, no sirs. The minute Reuben is out of sight, he's an arrogant brute. He'll kick a dog as soon as look as it, and he's forever making spiteful comments about the San people and hinting that we're all cattle thieves and drunkards. No one understands why Reuben has him around.

'What's interesting is that your elephant, Angel, seems to have remembered him years after she left Namibia. That almost certainly means he's done something cruel to her in the past. For that reason alone, I'm prepared to help you. As for what you overheard on the plane, I'm sure there's an innocent explanation. I can't believe Reuben is mixed up in anything illegal.'

Martine and Ben, who were by then so exhausted that their eyes were closing at the dinner table, were too grateful to him for feeding them and agreeing to assist them to argue. They were also thankful to him for providing them with shelter. Gift's aunt hadn't minded in the least allowing two young strangers to sleep on her floor for a night, especially since they were leaving before breakfast. She'd even done their laundry.

Sitting on the beach, Martine popped the last chocolatey morsel of cake into her mouth and checked the time. It was 6 a.m. After depositing them at Anton's café with instructions to pick up supplies and meet him near the Tug restaurant, Gift had gone to get fuel and water. They had another long drive ahead of them.

An early morning sea fog hovered over Swakopmond and the ocean looked grey and wintry. The palm trees creaked and sighed. Martine huddled closer to Ben for warmth. They shared the last of her coffee.

'Have you noticed,' she asked him, 'how everything keeps coming back to Angel? It's almost as if the key to understanding what Reuben James is up to and why he's trying to get his hands on Sawubona is the elephant. If we can get to the bottom of her story, of why he gave her to my grandfather in the first place, we might uncover his secret.'

Ben handed her back the coffee cup. 'That's funny, I just had exactly the same thought. The thread that runs through everything is the elephant's tale.'

Gift materialized behind them. He had a disconcerting habit of appearing out of nowhere. 'What elephant's tail?'

'They're cute,' said Martine, 'elephant's tails.'

Gift jiggled his keys. 'I suppose they are. Come on, we need to hit the road. I can't wait to get home to Damaraland.'

The drive north was not nearly as interesting as the one to Swakopmond, but it had a bleak appeal none the less. For the first hour they followed the Skeleton Coast, still shrouded in sea fog. Martine found her mood lifted as soon as they turned inland and left behind the gloomy cloud.

There followed three hours of flat, rocky desert, interrupted only by the occasional gaily decorated house, or neat roadside stall selling chunks of shimmering pink quartz and leopard stone. They stopped at one, and Martine was sure she could feel a kind of warm energy coming off a piece of pink quartz when she lifted it.

Gift gave the rock seller a crate of water. The man was from the Herero tribe and had buttery brown skin enhanced by many bracelets and other trinkets. He summoned his wife from their thatched house and Martine's mouth dropped open when the woman emerged, followed by three small children. She was magnificently dressed in a colourful dress styled in the manner of a Victorian missionary. A bright yellow banana-shaped hat sat lengthways across her head.

She explained to Martine and Ben that Herero women had worn the dresses for centuries and that they were a symbol of great pride.

Martine felt very self-conscious in her ragged jeans and old T-shirt. She cast a look around the barren landscape, simmering under the harsh desert sun, and couldn't imagine where the Herero mother found the energy, or the water, to look that good.

'We have only ourselves to blame if our country is desert,' the rock seller told her, reading her thoughts. He nodded at Gift. 'If he is from the San tribe, he can probably tell you why.'

'There is a Bushman legend about the lack of water in Namibia,' Gift explained to Ben and Martine. 'It's said that many moons ago, our ancestors were very poor. They complained bitterly about how hard their lives were. They thought of little else. They prayed and wished that they could be rich. They were sure that if they could only be wealthy, their lives would be perfect. So God granted their wish. He crystallized all the rivers and lakes in Namibia and turned them into diamonds.'

'Now we have many diamonds and other precious minerals like platinum,' said the rock seller. 'Namibia is one of the richest countries in Africa. But we have nothing to drink.'

He thanked them again for the water and they continued on their way. A range of violet mountains appeared on the horizon. The desert gave way to grassland and then they climbed the mountains and dropped over the other side. Martine could not get over how the road ahead just seemed to stretch on forever, into infinity. Above them, the sky bubbled with clouds that changed by the second, like some dizzying kaleidoscope.

Early in the afternoon, Gift pointed at a distant hill of massive boulders, a bit like those Martine and Ben had come across in the Matopos in Zimbabwe, and said proudly: 'There's my house.'

The two friends exchanged glances. Even after they'd unloaded the supplies from the vehicle and followed Gift up the steep path between the rocks, they still couldn't see any sign of habitation. Then they rounded a boulder and there, perched on the edge of the hill and overlooking a lovely, tranquil valley were three thatched domes. Beneath the domes were two bedroom tents with showers at the rear, and one living room tent with a splash pool cut into the deck in front of it.

Gift grinned at their expressions. 'This land has been in our family for generations and my father always talked of building a house here. When I started working at the magazine, I saved every cent I made and put it towards creating this place. Reuben James was kind enough to arrange for some of his hotel workers to help me thatch the domes and put up the tents. There have been many challenges, such as drilling a borehole to get water, but it has been worth it. This is my father's favourite valley, because it is the gathering place of many desert elephants. When he returns, I want him to have a special place to come home to.'

Gazing around the tents, which were simply but lovingly furnished in African cotton and wood, Martine felt tears spring to her eyes. Gift's father had gone missing in one of the most treacherous desert environments on the planet, and yet his son had never given up hope they would be reunited. He still talked of his dad in the present tense, as if he might round the corner at any time.

That evening, she sat with Ben and Gift on a high, flat boulder, watching the setting sun sink behind the mountains. As the rocks glowed orange, the clouds became lacy wisps of pink, and the contours of the valley became a carpet of jade-coloured velvet, she thought again of the San boy's courage. It inspired her to keep faith that, against all odds, she'd see Jemmy and her grandmother again.

When Gift moved away to stoke the barbecue, sending sparks flying, Ben said simply: 'From tomorrow, it'll be five days.'

Martine knew exactly what he meant. There were five days until Christmas Eve, the deadline for saving Sawubona and the date Gwyn Thomas was due to return from London. Five days for them to investigate Reuben James's business dealings and get to the bottom of the mystery surrounding Angel; five days to unravel Grace's prophecy; and five days for them to figure out how to travel thousands of miles back to Storm Crossing without money, transport or passports.

They turned at the same moment to look at Gift. The San boy had his back to them and was loading pieces of chicken onto the sizzling grill. Martine's stomach did an uncomfortable flip, as if she were in a lift that was descending too quickly. They had less than a week to achieve a minor miracle and they were utterly dependent on a stranger – one who owed his home and his job to the man they were investigating.

18

Gift's home was so peaceful and magical that, as she lay in bed next morning watching the sun outline the hills with gold and drinking the campfire-brewed coffee Ben had brought her, Martine fantasized about one day owning a tented camp overlooking an African valley herself. The dream lasted only until she nearly developed hypothermia trying to have an outdoor shower using a bucket of icy water. After that, she vowed to stay in her grandmother's comfortable thatched house at Sawubona, with its hot running water, for the rest of her days.

That's not going to happen unless you can outwit

Reuben James, piped up a voice in her head, but she refused to listen to it. It was too beautiful a morning to dwell on the disaster looming back in South Africa.

Breakfast (two fried eggs on toast) out of the way, they went in search of the desert elephants. Gift had warned them not to get their hopes up. Despite the creatures' immense size they were frequently difficult to find, because their daily searches for food and water meant they travelled enormous distances.

'That's one of the reasons it's so hard to keep an accurate count of their numbers,' said Gift, braking to allow a herd of springbok to cross the road. 'Before my father disappeared he'd become concerned about the way elephants kept vanishing, supposedly without any cause. These were not sick or old elephants. They were from herds he'd followed for years, so there wasn't any doubt about what was happening. Young, healthy animals would just go missing from the herd. One day he'd see them, the next they'd be gone.'

Kind of like the elephant whisperer himself, thought Martine. She wound down her window and stared out at the blur of flaxen grasses and twisting red road and far-off violet mountains. The African landscape was so enchanting it was hard to believe that tragedy, in the form of poisonous snakes, plants, scorpions, savage beasts and even the merciless sun, stalked it.

'My father alerted the authorities,' Gift went on, his eyes skimming the trees for any sign of elephants, 'but nobody took him seriously apart from Reuben James, who increased the poaching patrols. People kept telling

Pa that these elephants must have died of starvation or thirst and that the other members of the herd were burying them in an elephants' graveyard.'

'The elephants have a cemetery?' Ben said in amazement.

Gift snorted. 'No, that's just a tourist myth, but they do hold elephant funerals. Sometimes they'll lift up the body of a companion, a bit like a funeral cortege, and they bury their dead by covering them with mud or leaves and branches. Anyway, in the end it was decided that global warming was killing the elephants.'

'Global warming?' Martine was puzzled. 'You mean how the earth's surface is heating up because we're polluting the planet so much with our cars, aeroplanes and factories? What's that got to do with disappearing elephants?'

'Scientists and politicians always seem to be arguing about whether or not global warming exists,' Ben said.

'You can't take any notice of politicians because they're just trying to get elected,' Gift told him. 'It's true that some scientists claim it doesn't exist, but most agree that the warming of the earth's surface is going to lead to sea level rises, the melting of the polar icecaps, and an increase in disease and extreme weather.'

'And if there's an increase in extreme weather, the drought periods in Namibia will be worse than ever and the desert elephants will be pushed to the brink of extinction?' guessed Martine.

'Exactly. We're already witnessing that now. Except that my father didn't feel it was lack of food and water that was causing these elephants to go missing. To him, it seemed too targeted. It was always the prime specimens from every herd that went missing. And yet there was no evidence of poaching.'

'It's almost as if you have a Bermuda Triangle here in Damaraland,' remarked Ben.

'What's a Bermuda Triangle?' asked Martine.

'*The* Bermuda Triangle is this area of the Florida Straits, near the Bahamas and the Caribbean, where loads of aircraft and ships have gone missing and have never been seen or heard from again. It's almost as if they've been swallowed by the ocean. Over the years, hundreds of experts on things like weather and paranormal activity have tried to discover what became of them, but a lot of the vanishings are completely unexplained.'

'I don't know about that,' said Gift, 'but I'm convinced the two things are linked. You know, my father going missing and the disappearing elephants. The funny thing is no elephants have been lost since the day my father vanished.'

Ben interrupted: 'Gift, back up and check out that tree. I'm sure I saw some fresh elephant sign.'

Gift carried on driving. As much as he liked Ben and Martine, he continued to view them as tourist kids who knew nothing about the desert. 'Leave the tracking to me, city boy,' he said jokingly. 'The elephants never come this far south.'

Martine smiled to herself. In the few months Ben had been studying under Tendai as an apprentice tracker, he'd shown such a talent for reading sign, the tracker's word for the traces an animal leaves of its passing, that the game warden said he had the potential to become one of the best he'd ever seen.

Two hours later, her smile had gone and her patience had evaporated. It was clear that Gift was as poor at tracking as he'd joked he was when he met them. They hadn't seen so much as a tail-hair of an elephant.

Gift read her expression and scowled. 'If you and Ben think you can do better, *you* find the elephants.'

Ben said nothing. He sat staring straight ahead while Gift grudgingly drove back to the tree where he'd first spotted the peeled bark and split branches that so often marked the passage of elephants. When they reached it, Ben hopped out and inspected the elephant tracks at close range. Martine pored over them with him. She could never get over the fact that a beast weighing up to seven tons could leave such a faint impression on the earth. They seemed to move as lightly as dancers.

'That way,' Ben said with quiet authority, pointing across a dry riverbed.

Gift did as he was instructed, although his face said: 'Yeah, right.' But his disbelief turned to awe as Ben moved rapidly from sign to sign. By the time they crested a rise to find the desert elephants browsing in the trees before them, Martine could see that he'd gained a new respect for her friend. Not that he admitted it. He said: 'I was planning to check this place next anyway.'

The bull elephant separated himself from the herd gathered in the shade of a thicket of trees and advanced up the dusty trail, his ears flapping warningly. The females, the matriarchs, gathered their youngsters in close.

And now it was Gift's chance to shine, because if there was one thing the San boy did know about it was elephant behaviour. His father had taught him everything he knew.

'A herd of elephants is like a mobile crèche and home for the elderly,' he told them with a laugh, as he parked a respectful distance away and turned the engine off. 'It's a real community with everyone looking out for each other. They know every fellow member by what we call a name and they can use a sort of elephant sonar to find friends who are as far as ten kilometres away.'

'Tendai says that their pregnancy lasts two years,' Ben said.

Martine gazed out of the window at the huge beasts. 'That's got to be mighty uncomfortable, especially when you think how big the elephant baby would be.'

Gift smiled. 'Yes, but elephants get a lot more support than most humans do. An elephant baby is born into a protective circle, with a midwife standing by, and all share in the caring of it, including the feeding. Dolphins do the same thing. A dolphin midwife will even assist the newborn to the surface of the water for its first breath.'

Martine and Ben were quiet for a moment. Both were remembering the days they'd spent swimming with dolphins in the islands of Mozambique on another adventure.

Watching the ponderous progress of an old matriarch,

Ben said: 'If an elephant tried swimming, it would sink to the bottom of the lake.'

'Actually,' Gift told him, 'apart from whales and dolphins, elephants are the best swimmers in the whole mammal kingdom. They've been known to swim up to 300 miles between islands – just for fun.'

At Sawubona, Martine had always regarded elephants as lumbering, prehistoric-looking creatures that were wondrous but unfathomable. Their activities appeared to be confined to eating trees and splashing around the waterhole. Gift showed her that even their tiniest action had significance.

'See that youngster over there. He's using that stick as a fly switch. Elephants have complex brains and an incredible ability to reason, and they're masters at using tools to make tasks easier. They use chewed-up bark to plug holes in riverbeds so that the water doesn't evaporate and they can return to drink later. They uproot trees and push them onto electric fences. There've been stories of them pretending to be chained after they've broken their shackles so they can escape from their captors or take revenge on people who've been cruel to them.'

Martine thought again of Angel and wondered who, or what, had traumatized her in the past.

'Funny,' said Ben, 'whenever I see an animal that's cute and cuddly and small, like a Labrador puppy, or big and gentle, like dolphins or Martine's giraffe, Jemmy, all I want to do it protect it and make sure nothing ever hurts it. But elephants look like they can take care of themselves. They're so big and their hides are so thick that it's never occurred to me they might be able to reason like we do or have similar emotions.'

'Hunters like to believe that when animals are killed they don't know what's happening to them, but elephants feel things every bit as strongly as we feel them,' Gift assured him. 'They have all the same emotions: love, hate, rage, pride, happiness, jealousy and despair. Baby elephants who've witnessed their parents being culled wake up screaming with nightmares.'

Martine, who'd endured many nightmares after her own parents died, regarded the elephants with new eyes. She'd taken those at Sawubona for granted. Although she saw these sensitive, intelligent beasts almost every day, she knew next to nothing about them. Well, that was going to change. She was going to do what she could to make their lives better, and the elephant she was going to start with was Angel.

They were driving back across the plain, their senses full of the majesty of the elephants, when Gift spotted a Velvetchia plant. It was, he said, the oldest in the world and they absolutely had to see it. Some were known to live for thousands of years.

Martine, who was conscious of time slipping away from them like sand through a timer, was too distracted to take much interest in the plant, which was quite ugly.

The calls of a pair of Sandgrouse birds attracted her attention and she wandered over to them. That's when she noticed the circle of red earth. At its widest point it was probably the length Jemmy would be if he lay down, and it was perfectly round and bare. Not a blade of grass grew on it.

She touched it gingerly. The ground was firm and the soil was warm and crumbly. When she sifted it through her fingers, nothing happened. There was no blinding flash of light. No life-changing revelation.

'Gift,' she called. 'Do you know anything about this circle?'

He came over. 'Sure I do. That's a fairy circle.'

'A *fairy* circle? You believe in fairies in Namibia?'

Gift laughed. 'I don't think anyone believes they're created by actual fairies. Then again, nobody knows where they come from. They appear out of nowhere, a bit like crop circles do in places like Britain and America. Some people think they're caused by termites or radioactive granite; others say a forest of Euphorbia trees grew here many years ago and poisoned the ground when they died.'

'What do you believe?' Ben asked.

'I think they were made by little green aliens,' Gift teased. 'They're extra-terrestrial landing pads!'

'You keep saying "they"', Martine interrupted. 'Is there another circle around here?'

Gift clutched at his forehead, as if that was the dumbest tourist question he'd heard. Motioning them to follow, he clambered up a rocky hillock. When they reached the top, sweating from the short climb, he waved an arm in the direction of the grassy plain on the other side. Martine peered over the edge and gulped. As far as the eye could see were dozens and dozens of circles.

The circle will lead you to the elephants, Grace had told her.

'Which circle?' Martine thought in despair.

19

The next step in their investigation was Reuben James's tourist lodge. Gift was friends with one of the guides there and he thought it possible the man might know something about Angel's past. He was less willing to cooperate when it came to the lodge owner himself. 'You're wasting your time doing detective work on Reuben James,' he told them. 'There's nothing to find. But, hey, it's your vacation.'

Martine said nothing on the drive over. She'd not yet recovered from the fairy circle blow. Once again she was haunted by the notion that she and Ben might be in the wrong place at the wrong time. That by coming to

Namibia in the vain hope of stumbling upon some last-ditch way of saving Sawubona and the animals, they might have ruined any chance Gwyn Thomas had of doing just that.

She shuddered to think what would happen if her grandmother arrived back at the game reserve unexpectedly to learn that not only had her granddaughter and Ben been missing for days, but that the police had not been called. She'd go berserk. She'd feel obliged to get a message to Ben's mum and dad on their Mediterranean cruise and all hell would break loose. Grace, who'd promised to take care of Martine and Ben, would be in the biggest trouble of her life. So would Tendai, who was sceptical about Grace's prophesies and would have been livid to discover that the *sangoma* had encouraged Martine to go off on some hare-brained adventure 'to pluck out the thorn' that was hurting her.

Then there was the problem of the prophecy itself. Grace's predictions were often obscure, but this latest one was either deceptively simple or just plain wrong. The circle hadn't led Martine to the elephants. The elephants had, if anything, led her to the circle.

On top of all that, she was worried sick about Jemmy and Khan. Sawubona was crawling with Reuben James's hired workers. What if one took a shine to the white giraffe and rare leopard and decided to steal them?

Gift's voice broke into her thoughts. 'Welcome to Hoodia Haven.'

Martine leaned out the window. They were pulling into a circular gravel driveway lined with beds of cacti and purple and scarlet desert flowers, shaped to spell the name of the lodge.

'That's a strange name for a hotel,' Ben remarked.

'I think it's quite a good one,' Gift said, parking beneath a Shepherd's Tree. They all climbed out. 'Those plump cacti are hoodia plants. The iKung Bushmen call them "*xhoba*". For thousands of years the San have used them as appetite suppressants and thirst quenchers. A piece the size of a cucumber used to keep the old hunters going for a week.'

'That would be handy right now,' remarked Martine. 'It seems at least a century since we ate breakfast.'

Gift took a knife from his pocket and cut them each a piece of cactus, using a rag to protect his hands from the thorns. 'When you've eaten that, why don't you go and wait in the guest lounge? There's an exhibition of my elephant photos in there. I'll go and ask my friend about your elephant.'

Ben waited until he was out of earshot. 'What's our plan?' he asked, screwing up his nose at the bitterness of the cactus leaf, then straightening it again as he realized that it left a refreshing sweet taste on his tongue. 'What exactly are we searching for?'

'We don't know,' admitted Martine, wiping her hands on a tea-tree wipe Gift had provided. 'Some proof that Mr James is involved in diamond smuggling or mistreats animals or is employing slave labour or something. Proof of corruption. Why don't we split up and see if we can find anything interesting?'

'Sounds good. Martine . . . '

'Yes?'

'Watch your back.'

Martine did not have much experience of five star hotels, but there was no doubt that Hoodia Haven was the last word in luxury. The swimming pool looked as if it had been created from dissolved aquamarines. Over-tanned guests were draped around it in elegant poses, ice tinkling in their drinks. One had binoculars and was watching zebra drink from a distant waterhole. Waiters glided around with platters of fruit, shellfish and salad, or whisked away empty cocktail glasses with umbrellas sticking out of them.

The Hoodia plant had taken the edge off Martine's hunger but the food looked so delicious it was hard not to want it. When she passed an unattended bowl of exotic fruit and nuts, she sneaked a handful of salted almonds into her mouth. A waiter noticed and smiled. A few minutes later he came over and kindly presented her with a plate of chopped pineapple.

Martine kept expecting to be outed as an imposter and evicted, but nobody took any notice of her. She sat nibbling the pineapple, which tasted and smelled like nectar. When she'd finished it, she thanked the waiter and set off along a corridor marked 'Spa' and 'Gift Shop'.

With every step, her hopes of finding a clue which might save Sawubona evaporated. Everything about the lodge appeared eco-friendly and above board. The staff had warm smiles and were going about their work contentedly. The guests were in a state of bliss. There could hardly have been a place in Namibia that looked less like a den of corruption.

She rounded a corner and there was Reuben James. He was strolling towards her, but he was focussed on his companion, who was speaking.

Martine wanted to move but her limbs felt heavy and useless and her brain functioned at half speed, as if its batteries were almost flat. At the last conceivable moment, she bounded sideways into the gift shop.

From a small office at the back of the store, a disembodied voice called: 'I'll be with you as soon as I can, honey. I'm just finishing up an order. If you want to try anything on, the changing room is free. I'm Theresa. Give me a yell if you need help.'

'Thanks, Theresa, I will,' said Martine.

She snatched a couple of T-shirts off a shelf and shot into the changing room just as Reuben James came into view. Soon afterwards, she heard his voice raised in cheerful greeting outside in the car park. She stood on the cubicle stool and peered through a slit in the ventilator. Reuben had his hand on Gift's shoulder and was congratulating him on his exhibition of photographs. Gift was smiling.

When Gift moved away, Reuben's companion, who was in shadow and could only partially be seen from Martine's angle, said: 'You genuinely care for that boy, don't you? How can you look him in the eye?'

'Easily,' Reuben James responded shortly. 'First, because what he doesn't know isn't going to hurt him. Second, because very soon I'm going to put everything right. And lastly, because I'm thinking about the bigger picture. What I'm doing is for the good of everyone in Namibia.'

'Oh, sure,' drawled his companion. 'You're all heart.'

'Look around you,' Reuben James said heatedly. 'Can you not see that global warming is a devastating threat to the already impossibly hard lives of the desert tribes and animals here?'

Martine was startled to hear global warming mentioned twice in one morning. She strained her ears, trying not to miss a word.

Reuben James went on: 'Can't you see that the Ark Project is going to transform the lives of thousands, including that of the boy?'

'I can see how it's going to transform your bank balance.'

'And yours.'

'To be sure,' said the stranger. He moved slightly, revealing the back of his head and his broad shoulders. His hair had the shiny blue-blackness of a crow's wing. 'But then I'm not pretending I'm going to save the planet.'

He cocked his glossy black head and studied the other man. 'What I want to know is, are you prepared for the catastrophic effect that this is going to have? Are you prepared for *war*?'

Rebuen James rounded on him angrily. 'What are you

talking about, Callum? There's not going to be a war.'

'Are you sure about that? Can you say that for certain? And anyway, I thought you told me you were prepared to do whatever it took. I wouldn't like to think that you were going soft on me at the eleventh hour. I might have to take drastic measures. I might have to, say, call in that loan.'

Reuben James looked at him with contempt. 'I meant what I said. I *will* do whatever it takes. But when this is over, I don't ever want to lay eyes on you again.' And with that he climbed into a sleek silver car and sped away in a plume of dust.

The stranger watched him go. 'Don't worry,' he said so softly that Martine barely caught the words. 'You won't.'

As if some instinct told him he was being observed, he whipped around and stared straight at the vent.

Martine leapt clumsily off the stool, knocking it over in her haste.

'Is everything okay in there?' called Theresa.

To buy herself time, Martine called: 'These T-shirts are lovely but I need a smaller size.'

A cocoa-brown hand with red-painted nails slipped around the curtain and took them from her. 'I should say so, honey. These are men's extra large. They'd look like dresses on you. I'll nip out to the storeroom and see if we've got them in kids' sizes.'

The gift shop fell silent. Martine's head was spinning. *Are you prepared for war?* That was the sentence that kept going through her mind over and over. She had to talk to

Ben. If she was quick, she could get out to the car park before Theresa returned. She pulled back the curtain.

Standing at the shop counter, half turned away from her but looking every bit as surly as he had when she last saw him at Sawubona, was Lurk.

20

The brass rails screeched as Martine wrenched shut the curtain. Had he noticed her or hadn't he? She thought he might have, but she couldn't be sure.

The seconds stretched into minutes. The gift shop stayed silent. Martine stood pressed up against the back wall of the cubicle, praying for Theresa's return. She seemed to have been gone forever. Then she heard footsteps – not the saleswoman's clicking heels, but the heavy, deliberate tread of a man's shoe. They came round the counter and stopped outside the changing room.

Martine's heart almost stopped with them. She could hear Lurk breathing. He slid back the curtain.

Martine screamed.

A henna-haired Damara woman she took to be Theresa came rushing in, followed by Gift. Martine caught a glimpse of Ben close on their heels but he spotted the chauffeur in the nick of time and took rapid evasive action.

'Lurk, have you lost your mind? What do you mean by terrorizing my customers?' the saleswoman demanded.

'Yes, Lurk, have you lost your mind?' parroted Gift, unable to resist the opportunity to make fun of the man he loathed.

The chauffeur glowered at him. 'I know this girl,' he told Theresa, pointing rudely at Martine. 'She from South Africa. Very bad witch. She make buffalo rise from the dead and the elephant to chase me.'

Theresa went red with annoyance. 'What rubbish are you talking, Lurk? As if a young girl could resurrect buffaloes and order elephants to charge you. Have you been drinking?'

'I *know* her,' Lurk insisted. 'She ride white giraffe.'

'Don't be ridiculous, Lurk,' said Gift. 'This is Anna, the sister of a friend of mine from Windhoek. She's staying at the lodge with her family.'

Lurk's bulging eyes seemed to bulge even more. His chin rose defiantly. 'Not Anna. She Maxine. No, no, *Mar*tine. She from South Africa; from Mr James's new Safari Park.'

'Lurk, you've just heard Gift say that this girl is a friend of his from Windhoek,' snapped Theresa, beginning to lose her temper. 'She is also a guest of Mr James at this hotel and the notion that she's some kind of animal magician, riding giraffes and ordering lions and elephants about, is absolutely preposterous. Now if you want to remain in Mr James's employment another day, my strong suggestion is that you apologize to this young lady, pull yourself together, and get back to work.'

'Sorry for mistake,' growled Lurk, not looking in the least bit contrite. As he slouched from the gift shop, Martine heard him mumble: 'Very bad witch, I no forget this.'

'Please accept my sincerest apologies, Anna,' Theresa said, embarrassed. 'I can't think what's got into him. He can be a bit odd at times but today he seems quite deranged.'

'No problem at all,' Martine assured her, anxious to get away in case Reuben James came to investigate the disturbance. 'It's an easy mistake to make. He obviously has a grudge against this girl, Maxine.'

'*Martine*,' Gift corrected helpfully.

'Let me make it up to you, honey,' Theresa offered. 'Is there anything you'd like? Can I give you a Hoodia Haven T-shirt?'

'Really it's not necessary,' said Martine, feeling like a fraud. The last thing she wanted was a T-shirt advertising her arch-enemy's hotel.

But Theresa was adamant she take something, so Martine reluctantly accepted a piece of rose quartz the saleswoman was using as a paperweight. It wasn't for sale, she told Martine. It was just some rock she'd picked up by the roadside.

Martine suspected that it was worth far more than Theresa made out, but she couldn't refuse without seeming ungrateful. It could be a present for her grandmother if she ever saw her again. *When*, Martine told herself firmly. *When* she saw her grandmother again.

Thanking Theresa profusely, she and Gift left the shop. As soon as they were in the corridor, Gift said in a low voice: 'That was a close call. I think we'd better go before you get yourself into any more trouble. You round up Ben. I need to check with reception to see if the camera lens I've ordered has arrived.'

He strode away across the courtyard. Ben stepped out from behind a potted palm tree.

'Ben, did you see what happened?' cried Martine. 'Lurk recognized me. He came after me like a psycho.'

'Never mind about that now,' said Ben. 'I've got something to show you and I don't want Gift to know about it just yet.'

Ordinarily Martine would have been hurt by his lack of concern, but she could see at once he was on to something. His face was alight with it.

Keeping an eye out for Lurk, who was sure to be as cross as a snake after the gift shop humiliation, he led Martine to the guest lounge where Gift's elephant exhibition had been hung. Three women were sitting in the corner tucking into tea and sponge cake, but they were deep in conversation and barely glanced up.

The photos were of a herd of elephants. They were taken over the course of a single day, starting with the first ray of dawn and ending with the ascent of the evening star. Gift had arranged them in a panorama around the room. The rich and varied life of the herd, and the spirit of individual elephants, shone from them.

'Ben, they're wonderful, but are you sure we have time for this?'

Ben gestured towards three photographs taken shortly before sunset and said: 'This won't take long. What do you notice about these pictures?'

Martine found it difficult to concentrate after the scene in the gift shop. 'Umm, I don't know. I guess they're well composed.'

'Do you see anything unusual about the elephants?'

'They look like a normal herd of elephants to me. Ben, we should go.'

Ben spoke patiently. 'Look closely. There are sixteen elephants in the first and second picture and fifteen in the third.'

'So what?' Martine checked the door, half expecting Lurk to burst through it. 'The pictures were taken five or ten minutes apart. Maybe one of the elephants sloped off to devour a tree.'

'Could be. Only the missing elephant is a young bull. He's walking slightly apart from the others in the first and second picture. He's in the background. That's why you don't notice him if you only glance at the photos. In the third picture, he's not there anymore and the other elephants seem to be milling around as if they're fretting or distressed.'

He paused. 'Now look again at the second picture and see what's in his path.'

Martine squinted at the photo. 'A fairy circle!'

'I think,' said Ben, 'we've just found our Bermuda Triangle.'

21

'The Ark Project?' repeated Gift. 'Those were Reuben James's words?'

'I think so,' said Martine. After questioning Gift and learning that the elephant photographs had been taken on the plain near the Stone Age rock engravings in Twyfelfontein, she'd asked if they could visit them.

'I was listening through a vent,' she went on, 'but I'm fairly sure that's what he called it. He talked about global warming and how what he was doing was for the good of everyone in Namibia.'

'What did I tell you?' said Gift. 'You're both so ready to believe he's a fraudster because you're upset he's bought your game reserve, but what you overheard proves that he's a generous, decent man. The Ark Project sounds like some sort of conservation scheme, or maybe it's a code name for the new hotel he's building.'

'Sounds like a Doomsday project to me,' murmured Ben.

Martine was getting heartily sick of Gift defending his mentor. 'It doesn't prove anything. For starters, he hasn't bought Sawubona, he's tricked my grandfather into signing it away . . . '

'You don't know that.'

' . . . and besides, the man who was with him, the one with blue-black hair like crow's feathers . . . '

'I've never seen him before.'

'Well, he accused your Mr James of pretending to save the planet only because he wanted to make himself richer.'

Gift slowed the vehicle and turned down a gravel track leading to a ring of rocky mountains. 'That doesn't prove anything either. Reuben's a businessman. Of course, he has to work out if a project makes financial sense.'

Martine could have easily burst his bubble by telling him how Reuben James had told Callum that what Gift didn't know 'can't hurt him', and that he planned to 'put things right.' She could have told him that the men were planning to start a 'war'. But she couldn't bring herself to do that – not yet anyway. Not until they had investigated further. She liked the San boy enormously. He'd almost certainly saved their lives. She didn't want to cause him pain when she might have misheard or misunderstood what Reuben James was saying.

She took a gulp of clean desert air and resolved not to be cross any more. 'You're right,' she said, 'it doesn't prove anything.'

Gift's cellphone beeped. He checked the message. 'Typical. The camera lens has just been delivered to the hotel. I'll need to go back for it. I'll drop you at the Welcome Centre café and you can have lunch and tour the Stone Age engravings while I'm gone.'

He pulled up outside a low, stone building set against a rocky mountain. It was mid-afternoon and the oven blast of desert heat that engulfed Martine as she stepped out of the vehicle threatened to roast her alive.

'Wait,' called Martine as Gift prepared to drive away. 'Did you have a chance to speak to your guide friend? Did he know anything about Angel's past?'

'Unfortunately not. He's never heard of any zoo in Damaraland, much less one that went out of business. But he did say something that might interest you. Not long after he started in the job three or four years ago, he disturbed Reuben in the midst of a blazing row with Lurk about his mistreatment of an animal, although which animal they were referring to he had no idea. The reason it stuck in his mind is that Lurk cornered him later and told him that it would be "big mistake" for him to ever repeat what he'd overheard; that his job could be in jeopardy.'

Gift glanced at his watch. 'I really do have to go. We'll talk later.'

'When?' Martine shouted as he reversed. 'When will you be back?'

But Gift didn't seem to hear her. 'See you soon,' he mouthed, and then he was gone and the blanketing heat was closing in on them once again.

Ben sprinkled salt and pepper on his toasted cheese and tomato sandwich, prepared by a smiling cook in the Welcome Centre café and purchased with money donated by Gift, took a bite, and started a list on the back of a Damaraland postcard. 'We have a million questions but these are the most important,' he said. 'Number One: Is Reuben James the rightful inheritor of Sawubona or is he a con artist?'

'A con artist,' Martine answered at once.

'We have to be objective, like real detectives,' Ben reminded her. 'He's not my favourite person either, but Gift thinks highly of him and we should take that into account.'

Martine stirred her 'peace' drink, a refreshing blend of Rooibos tea, orange and lemon juice, and cinnamon, so vigorously that the tourist couple at the next table looked over. As far as she was concerned, if Reuben James was involved in something so explosive it could lead to a war, he was as wicked as she'd thought he was all along. After Gift had gone, she'd filled Ben in on the details of the scene she'd witnessed at Hoodia Haven.

'It sounds as if this man Callum is blackmailing Reuben James,' Ben had said. 'It's as though he wants to start a fight against Reuben's wishes. But surely they weren't talking about a real war? Maybe it's just an expression and they were using strong language because they were angry.'

Martine hadn't been convinced. 'Hopefully. I'd hate my grandmother to turn on the news in England to find that war has broken out in Namibia and we've both been blown to smithereens.'

Now she said: 'Maybe the second question on your list should be: If Reuben James and Callum do start a war, who are they going to be attacking?'

Ben scribbled it down. 'We also need to find out what the Ark Project is and what it has to do with global warming.'

'Question Number Four: Who broke into the house at Sawubona and what were they looking for?' put in Martine. 'Oh, and we still have to find out the truth about the elephant's tale, although I'd be willing to bet that the conversation Gift's friend overheard was about Angel.'

'Last one,' said Ben. 'Are the fairy circles causing the elephants to vanish through: A) Radiation sickness. B) Starvation (global warming). C) Aliens! D) The ground is swallowing them (e.g. Bermuda Triangle)?'

He pushed the postcard over to Martine. 'All we ever get is more questions. After a week of trying we don't have a single answer.'

Martine read the list while sipping at her drink. 'It's as

if someone's thrown a million jigsaw pieces in the air and we're expected to put them together without knowing what the picture looks like.'

'And we've got four days to do it in.'

'Four days,' Martine said despondently. Sometimes the sheer scale of the mission they'd taken on overwhelmed her.

Ben finished his toasted sandwich and went through the list one more time. 'There's a pattern here and we're just not seeing it.' He checked his watch. 'I'm surprised Gift's not back yet, but there's no point in us sitting around moping. Let's do a tour of the rock engravings. Maybe they'll inspire us.'

Martine's spirits rose as soon as they set off up the path that led to the work of the Stone Age artists. The rocks that weren't engraved were, in a way, even more fascinating than those that were. They were riven with swirls, loops and hollows, as if they'd been sculpted by ocean waves and wild gales.

'That is exactly what has happened,' said Edison, their guide. He was a lean, angular man, neatly turned out in a khaki ranger's uniform, who could as easily have been thirty as sixty. Years of guiding had not dulled his passion for his job. He looked at Martine, who was fanning herself with the postcard. 'You are hot today, yes?'

'Yes,' she responded fervently.

Edison grinned. 'Would you believe that hundreds of millions of years ago this entire area was covered in ice? It is incredible, is it not? Later, when the polar ice caps melted and the sea level rose . . . '

'Isn't that what's happening now with global warming?' said Ben. 'The polar ice caps are melting and the seas are rising?'

'Exactly,' agreed Edison, pleased to be guiding such a bright boy. 'Only at that time it was a good thing. The climate became warmer and many species of flora and fauna thrived in the new lakes, rivers and swamps. We think that in the Jurassic period, about 180-200 million years ago, when dinosaurs roamed the Twyfelfontein Valley, this area was a swampy lake.'

Martine, who was eleven and three-quarters, found it impossible to get her head around the idea that the Etjo sandstone boulders she was standing among were hundreds of millions of years old, as old as the dinosaurs which had lumbered around them. It made her feel as insignificant as a grain of sand. Whether or not she and Ben managed to save Sawubona, the boulders would still be here – would, in all likelihood, be here for another 130 million years.

Further along the path were split boulders, which had provided the Stone Age artists with canvases of perfect sandstone. It was on these that they'd engraved striking images of elephant, rhinoceros, lion, ostrich and antelope, though Martine was pleased to note that their favourite animal seemed to be the giraffe. Edison explained that, to the ancient artists, giraffe were a symbol of rain. Often they were accompanied by a rainbow and clouds.

The sight of so many giraffe brought on another bout of homesickness. Martine missed Jemmy so much it was like a constant, nagging ache in her heart. Every hour in Namibia had been dogged by the fear that she might never see him again; that by pursuing this quest, she might very well be squandering her last precious days with her beloved white giraffe.

She wondered what Jemmy was doing now and if he was thinking of her. Was he missing her? She hoped that Angel would encourage him to hide in his old sanctuary, far from the prying eyes of the strangers working at Sawubona until she returned, and that Khan was deep inside the warren of tunnels himself. She and her grandmother had pledged to keep the leopard safe from harm on their game reserve. How could they protect him if they no longer lived there?

These thoughts went round and round in Martine's head.

The engravings also made her nostalgic for the Memory Cave at Sawubona. There, however, the paintings were made from Bushman tinctures like oxgall and iron. The Damaraland images had been painstakingly chipped out of the rock and were up to 20,000 years old.

It was while Martine and Ben were examining them that they noticed a series of circles carved into the sandstone. 'Edison,' Martine called. 'Are these fairy circles? Did the Stone Age artists have a theory about how the circles came to be there?'

The guide came over. 'Those are not fairy circles. They are engravings of Moon Valley – an extinct volcano crater which the locals believe is haunted.' He pointed. 'Look, you can see it from here.'

Across the valley, interrupting the crooked line of purple mountains, was a charred hill shaped like a funnel.

'A local businessman, Reuben James, is building a nature oasis there and there are many who believe he is most unwise. They think the spirits will be displeased.'

Martine was startled. 'Did you say *Reuben James* is building a nature oasis there?'

Edison looked at her sharply. 'You know him?'

'We don't like him,' Martine responded, unwilling to go into how or why she and Ben were acquainted with Mr James.

He nodded sympathetically. 'I myself am not sure how I feel about this man. He has done many good things for people and animals in this area, but this new project, there is something wrong with it. It is causing much unhappiness with the locals.'

'I thought Mr James was very popular around here,' said Ben.

'He was, and for many people he still is. But the building of this hotel has created much controversy. In order to create his oasis, he will require many gallons of the fresh-water spring the Damara people call *Ui-Ais*. It means a "water place where the stones stand clustered together". For thousands of years, the people and animals of this area have depended on this spring for survival. Now it is under threat.

'And that is not the only thing. Unemployment is high in Damaraland and yet there are no local workers at Moon Valley. They are from far away places like Windhoek or Etosha, or foreigners from Zambia or Botswana.'

'I can see why that would cause resentment,' said Ben. 'When is the oasis due to open?'

'Soon, but if you want me to be honest I don't think it will happen. There are rumours that Mr James has big, big debts which are getting worse by the day, but in my opinion this is not the only reason.'

Martine squinted across the valley. A dust-caked truck was beetling across the dusty plain towards Moon Valley. It disappeared into the haze. 'Then why?'

Edison picked up a smooth stone and turned it over and over in his palm. He lowered his voice. 'Maybe it's a strong word, but I'm sure there is something evil about this project. There are stories that if you complain about the building work or how near it is to the stream or ask too many questions about Moon Valley, bad things will happen to you. We had this man living in Damaraland, an elephant whisperer. A year ago he went missing and not even one footprint of his has been found.'

Martine saw Ben's eyes widen at the mention of Gift's father.

'The last place Joseph was seen was at the gates of Moon Valley.'

22

By sunset, Gift still had not returned. The Welcome Centre shut and Martine and Ben found a perch on a hillock a short distance away, from where they could see the road and car park but would not attract the attention of any well-meaning departing staff who might insist on calling their parents.

'It's very unfair of him to leave us here for hours on end,' moaned Martine, wriggling into her sweatshirt. As if a switch had been turned off, the chill of the desert night was moving in. 'What on earth can he be up to? Do you think he's eating a three-course dinner at the hotel? When he shows up, I'm really going to tell him off.'

'*If* he shows up,' said Ben.

Martine stared at him. It was a possibility that hadn't occurred to her. 'But he *has* to come back. He promised to help. Surely he wouldn't abandon us here?'

'Who knows. It's not as if he owes us anything. We're going after a man he obviously likes and respects. Why should he help us? We're also trouble, in the sense that we've entered Namibia illegally and my parents and your grandmother don't know where we are. Maybe he's decided to get out while the going is good. It's not like we could find him again.'

'But we know where he lives.'

'Do we? Could you locate that place again? We should have asked for his phone number, but it didn't occur to me we'd need it.'

Another thought came into Martine's head. 'Ben, what if something's happened to him? What if he went back to the hotel and that ghastly Lurk was lurking and pounced on him. He'll be dying to get revenge for the gift shop incident. He's sly, that man. I wouldn't trust him as far as I could throw him. Why does Reuben James employ him?'

'That's what I mean,' said Ben. 'All we ever get is more questions. It's about time we found an answer.'

It's hard to say which of them first came up with the plan to search Moon Valley, but in the end it didn't matter. As far as they were concerned, they'd gambled with their own fate and that of Sawubona by coming to Namibia; by throwing in their lot with Gift; by pursuing Reuben James. If they didn't finish what they'd started, it would all have been for nothing.

For hour upon hour they'd watched for the headlights of Gift's vehicle to illuminate the Welcome Centre car park, but nothing split the star-showered darkness. They wrapped themselves in the space blanket for warmth and took turns dozing, getting up when Ben's watch alarm went off at three a.m., stiff, sore, cold and worried. They'd nibbled a bit of Hoodia cactus to stave off hunger pangs and thirst, but they couldn't help but feel agitated about their friend.

There were two likely explanations for Gift's continuing absence, neither of them good. Either he'd betrayed them by deliberately dumping them at the Welcome Centre in the belief that staff there would rescue them or call the police. Or something terrible had befallen him. Martine pictured him bleeding by the roadside after overturning his four-wheel drive on the slippery gravel road.

'I'd feel a lot better if there was some way we could leave a message for Gift,' said Ben. 'You know, in case he comes looking for us.'

Martine gazed at the flat, dark valley and ring of black mountains. The moon was on the rise and the stars winked and shimmered. 'I have an idea. We can leave him a message!' she said, remembering something Gift had said about the way desert people communicated in the absence of phones and computers. 'Help me gather up the lightest stones you can find.'

Minutes later they'd left their first desert telegraph – a white giraffe made of stones, its long neck pointing in the direction they intended to travel. They planned to leave one every couple of hundred yards.

They headed out across the plain, their torch lighting a yellow path across the scrub, shale and rocks.

As they walked, Ben said: 'We don't have to do this, you know. We could turn around now and go back to the Welcome Centre. Yes, we'll be in loads of trouble and the police will be called and Gwyn Thomas will hit the roof and my mum and dad will refuse to allow me out of their sight ever again, but it'll be worth it because we'll be safe. We'll be *alive*.'

Martine glanced sideways at him. 'Do *you* want to turn back?'

'Only if you do.'

'Well, I don't. If there's a chance – even a microscopic one – that by going to Moon Valley and finding out what Reuben James is up to we could save Sawubona and Jemmy and Khan, then that's what I have to do . . . Hey, did you see that?'

The crater had lit up, as if the volcano had come to life. At the same time they heard a muffled rumble, like distant thunder. Then it went dark and quiet again.

'Great,' said Martine. 'Like we haven't been through enough. Now we have the prospect of being incinerated by a smouldering volcano to look forward to.'

Ben grinned. 'Hardly. That was a man-made explosion

which was probably caused by the dynamite we saw on the plane. Wouldn't you rather be blown sky high than boiled alive in bubbling orange lava?'

'Those are my options?' said Martine. 'Gee, let me think. Oh, there is another one. I could beat you up.'

She made a fist and chased after him and the two of them ran through the desert laughing, and briefly forgot about their troubles.

They'd reached a cluster of fairy circles when Ben said: 'I'm sure this is the spot where the elephant disappeared in Gift's photograph. I recognize that line of boulders, because they look like a smile with a missing tooth.'

Martine was doubtful. 'Ben, there are hundreds of fairy circles. Even supposing you're right, what does it mean?'

'Well, nothing unless you think about how coincidental it is that Gift's father and at least one elephant disappeared very close to Moon Valley.'

'Ben, that's crazy. I can't stand Reuben James, but you're accusing him of kidnapping Joseph which is a very serious crime.'

She turned to look at the volcanic crater. The burnt slopes loomed before them like the dark side of the moon. There was a phosphorescent glow emanating from it, as if it was lit from within in the manner of a football stadium. 'What he doesn't know isn't going to hurt him,' Reuben James had said about Gift. Later, his crow-haired companion had virtually blackmailed him into doing whatever it took to ensure the Ark

Project was a success. Men like that would surely stop at nothing.

Martine switched off her torch. 'I guess we'd better proceed with extreme caution.'

23

The sky was lightening as they scaled the gritty rim of the crater and wriggled on their bellies towards the edge. By that time they were so filthy they looked as if they'd spent a week in a coalmine. They had considered attempting to get in through the main gate, but it was three times their height, made of solid iron and set into the crater wall. It was also patrolled by two security guards with dogs.

As they inched forward, their eyes, which had grown accustomed to the dark, burned with the brightness of the glare below. Martine shielded hers and peered over the brink. At first all she could see were fizzing white spotlights bent, like preying mantis, over the valley. When her eyes finally adjusted, she gasped. Of all the things she'd expected to find, this was not one of them. She had expected construction site chaos and men toiling away with cranes, concrete mixers and scaffolding. In her wilder thoughts, she'd even envisioned a training facility for soldiers preparing for Callum's 'war'. And when Edison had spoken of Reuben James's plan to create an oasis, she'd pictured three tired palm trees leaning over a concrete pool enlivened with a few fake pink flamingos.

She hadn't imagined a tropical jungle festooned with flowering vines and crisscrossed with wooden walkways. Or a crystal blue fountain. Or clouds of brilliant colour floating over beds of African wildflowers which, when Ben got out his little binoculars, they could see were butterflies as bright as jewels. She definitely hadn't foreseen a futuristic hotel made from wood and glass and suspended in the treetops. Or a maze of the type one might find at a castle in England, with an okapi – a beautiful little creature with zebra-striped hind legs, a close cousin of the giraffe – tripping through it.

She'd never imagined they'd stumble on paradise in the most unlikely place in Africa.

'What do you reckon goes on in there?' asked Ben.

Martine followed his gaze. At the far end of the valley, barely visible through the trees, was a dome of opaque white. It resembled a giant golf ball.

'It looks a lot like the Eden Project, this place my mum and dad used to take me to in Cornwall. Sounds similar to the Ark Project, doesn't it? The domes there are massive greenhouses that house rainforests and waterfalls and all kinds of things. That might be what they're doing here.'

A splash of red appeared in the fading night sky. As if on cue, a sublime chorus of birdsong floated up to them. A gardener in overalls appeared and began tending to the wildflowers.

'Wow,' said Martine. 'Wow, wow, wow!'

'I'm confused,' she said to Ben as they scrambled back down the slope. 'Every time I think Reuben James is Mr Hyde, he turns into Dr Jekyll.'

Ben put out a hand to steady her as she slipped on a loose rock. 'Meaning what exactly?'

'Well, every time I decide that he's a kidnapper, or a con man, or a burglar, or an elephant poacher, he does something unexpected. Like the time he lent us his new Land Rover so we could help the sick buffalo. And now this. Ben, isn't Moon Valley one of the most idyllic places you've ever seen? But I didn't see any elephants. I'm losing hope that, with days to go, we'll find anything on Reuben James so bad it'll stop him taking over Sawubona.'

'What he's done with Moon Valley is incredible,' said Ben, 'but there are too many things that don't add up. If he has this place as well as Hoodia Haven and others, why is he so obsessed with taking over Sawubona? Sawubona is special to us, but there are a thousand game reserves just like it. Yet he's fixated on ours. Don't worry, we'll get something on Reuben James yet. But we're going to need to find a way into Moon Valley.'

'Why don't we take a closer look at the delivery area?' suggested Martine. Earlier, they'd seen a red-lettered sign directing drivers to the drop zone. They were to contact the site office on arrival, using the telephone provided.

'Yes, let's look at the drop zone,' said Ben. 'There might be cargo waiting to be transferred to Moon Valley and we could hide in a box and get in that way. That always works in movies.'

They ran along the curve of the crater until they were at the opposite end of the valley to the main gate, level, Martine estimated, with the white dome. The drop zone was a ramshackle warehouse standing in a circular area of cleared gravel, ground up by thick tyre tracks.

'If it's a storage unit, why isn't it guarded?' whispered Martine.

'It could be that guards aren't necessary,' Ben told her. 'If the trucks are unloaded and their cargo moved to Moon Valley minutes later, the goods are under observation the whole time.'

To be on the safe side, they waited a while longer before approaching the warehouse, but saw no one. As Ben had predicted, it was empty. The concrete floor had been swept clean. There was a framed poster of a charging elephant on one wall and a desk and chair near the doorway. A grubby black telephone, clipboard and pen had been provided. A notice requested that visitors 'Dial 9 for Site Office'.

'We could ring and say we have a delivery,' said Martine.

Ben was staring at the elephant poster. 'Too risky for too little reward. I'm not confident I could make myself sound like a fifty-year-old Namibian truck driver on the phone. Martine, don't you think it's a bit odd that they've decided to decorate this dusty old warehouse?'

Martine sat down on the chair and began flicking through the pages on the clipboard. The previous day there had been deliveries of bread, milk, fertilizer and twenty vials of medicine. Marine recognized the name of it, but couldn't for the life of her remember what it was for. 'Perhaps they were trying to be welcoming.'

'Or conceal something.' Ben pushed the poster aside. Behind it was a green lever. 'Hey Martine, look at this. It has fresh oil on it, as if it's regularly in use. I wonder what it does?'

He tugged at it.

'No!' cried Martine, but it was too late. Before Ben could react, a trapdoor had dropped open beneath his feet. Ben dropped with it. Martine had a fleeting glimpse of his startled face as he twisted away down a chute, then the mechanism purred and the trapdoor snapped shut again.

Twice before in her life Martine had felt a terror so extreme that it was as if she'd been turned into a block of ice. Once was on the night of the fire, and the second time was when she fell into a shark-infested ocean. Now she felt it again.

This could not be happening. She could not have just watched her best friend vanish. She could not be left alone with no food, water, money, passport or transport in the middle of the Namib desert.

This could not be happening – but, her fevered brain told her, it was.

She was faced with two choices. Either she walked back to the Welcome Centre, waited for it to open and attempted to call the police, who might arrest her for entering the country illegally and refuse to listen to her pleas for assistance.

Or she could pull the lever and follow Ben into a void from which they might never emerge.

She knew which was the smarter choice. She also knew that it would take her a minimum of forty-five minutes to run back to the Welcome Centre when she was already weak from hunger and thirst. By then, her best friend, whom she now realized she loved as much as she did Jemmy, her grandmother, Grace, Tendai and Khan, might have been consumed by whatever it was that waited at the bottom of the chute.

What *did* wait there? Martine had visions of an underground stream packed with piranhas or a bottomless shaft that went to the molten centre of the earth. But even those fates would be preferable to ending up in the hands of Reuben James and Callum.

So there was the wise decision, or the decision she could make because Ben was her best friend and there was nothing she wouldn't do for him. For Martine, there was no contest. She gathered up some pale stones and made another white giraffe, which she laid on the ground behind the warehouse. By some miracle, Gift might stumble across it.

The sky was streaked with pinks and greys and oranges as Martine returned to the stifling shed and pulled the lever. The mechanism gave a small sigh, as if resigning itself to dispatching yet another victim. Her stomach lurched in fear.

The trapdoor snapped open and she was swallowed.

24

Martine had never understood the appeal of rollercoasters. It was beyond her why anyone would want their stomach left behind while their body plummeted like a human cannonball and their heart threatened to burst from their chest. Unfortunately, that's the exact sensation she was experiencing now.

Teeth gritted, she hurtled down a silver chute, flailing helplessly around the corners. Time passed in dentist minutes, the way it did when she was having a filling and the dentist was leaning on her jaw with his drill and talking about his beach holiday with his family while the nurse sprayed water up her nose. She'd have preferred time to go in giraffe minutes. When she was out in the game reserve with Jemmy, whole nights went in the blink of an eye.

Martine popped from the tube like a cork from a bottle and hit the ground hard. It was a relief to find it was cushioned. A soft landing area had been installed to prevent fragile deliveries from being damaged. And if there was one thing Martine was feeling it was fragile.

She dusted herself off and stood up. She was in a neon-lit room, empty apart from a hotel housekeeping trolley, a sink and a row of white coats on pegs. There was a door but no windows. An iron-runged ladder rose to meet a hatch in the ceiling overhead. She was trying to decide which exit Ben might have taken when she heard footsteps approaching the door. At the same time, a hand clamped over her mouth.

'Martine, whatever you do, don't scream,' Ben whispered in her ear. 'I'll wedge something under the door to keep it closed. Go up the ladder.'

Martine recovered from her fright and rushed to do as he asked. A key scraped in the lock. Ben had wedged a broom handle under it, but it was already splintering as he shinned up the ladder and clambered out into the morning sunshine.

Two gardeners were trimming the maze not fifty feet away from them. Fortunately, they were talking and didn't hear anything above the buzz of the hedge trimmers. Martine and Ben had a split second to take in the vivid beauty of the oasis – the brilliant beds of flowers; the cool blue fountain and the soaring, creeper-hung forest rising up a slope towards the white dome; the hotel nestled among its branches like a human version of a community weaverbird nest – and then they were diving into the maze.

Once again, they seemed to have got away with it. They ran along the dewy green passages, backtracking whenever they came to a dead-end. They wanted to get as far away from the gardeners as they could before pausing to come up with a plan. The hedges, thick as castle walls, muffled nearly all noise apart from the birdsong, which was as continuous and cheerful as ever.

'You know what's really peculiar,' whispered Ben, 'I haven't seen a single bird since we got here. Yet they're chirping and whistling so loudly it's as if we've walked into an aviary.'

'Maybe they're hidden in the jungle,' said Martine, but goosebumps rose on her arms. There was something creepy about Moon Valley. It was too impossibly perfect.

She wondered where the okapi was. Thinking about him reminded her of Jemmy and her chest began to ache again. How many days, or weeks, would it be till she saw him again? *Would* she ever see him again?

Ben squeezed through a narrow gap between the hedges and stopped so abruptly Martine ran into him. In the square centre of the maze was a table spread with a starched white cloth and laid with shining silverware and white china plates. On it was a breakfast feast of fruit, apricot juice, water, a selection of cheeses and jams, and a basket of bakery goods. The basket was upended and its contents – fat, buttery croissants, chocolate chip and banana nut muffins, and health breads – were strewn across the tablecloth.

The okapi, which had its front hooves on the table, was gleefully nibbling a muffin and didn't notice them at first. When it did, it bounded away guiltily, leaving a trail of crumbs in its path.

There was only one chair and a single place laid.

'Are you thinking what I'm thinking?' said Ben.

Martine grinned. 'Well, my first thought was, this has to be Reuben James's breakfast. My second is, now it's ours!'

'Martine, you're a mind reader.' Ben reached for a roll and spread it thickly with butter and strawberry jam. He poured himself some apricot juice.

Martine drank two glasses of water and devoured a chocolate chip muffin and a croissant dripping with butter and honey. She said: 'You do know that our lives will not be worth living if we get caught?'

'Mmmhmm,' Ben mumbled through a mouthful of roll. His eyes were laughing.

Over the relentless singing of the birds came the unmistakable tinkle of cups, saucers and teaspoons on a tray. Martine and Ben bolted through the gap in the maze just as a waiter stepped into the square and let out a curse. He set down his tray with a crash. 'You wicked okapi!' he cried. 'Wait until I get my hands on you. Tonight you will be okapi curry. I will serve you up with rice and mango chutney!'

'Okapi curry?' mouthed Martine, horrified.

'If we don't get out of here, we'll be in the same pot,' Ben mouthed back. 'Follow me.'

Earlier he'd spotted a red thread running along the bottom of some sections of the hedge, which appeared to show the way out. They were stealing along a cool green passage, feeling like mice about to be devoured by a cat, when Ben tripped over a wire. Instantly the birdsong ceased. An unnatural silence descended on the valley.

'Oh. My. God,' whispered Martine. 'It's a recording. There *are* no birds in Moon Valley. I guess it is haunted after all.'

The sudden shutting off of the birdsong CD told the waiter that all was not well in the volcano and that something bigger than the okapi might be to blame for the ruined breakfast. He yelled for the gardeners. They came pounding into the maze, shouting and wielding sticks.

Martine and Ben clung to one another in panic. There was no escape route. Men were coming at them from both directions. They were trapped. The game was up.

From across the desert came the wail of an ambulance siren. It was approaching at speed. All sounds of pursuit ceased. The siren grew louder and louder until it was right inside Moon Valley, where it petered out with a squawk.

Ben peered through a hole in the hedge. 'Martine, you have to see this.'

Martine crouched beside him. The ambulance men were carrying a stretcher up the forest paths to the white dome. A door opened and two men in white coats lifted out a bloodied figure, plainly unconscious. The paramedics laid him on the stretcher, checked his pulse, and then whisked him back down the hill.

The gardeners, the waiter and the men in white coats gathered around the ambulance, watching with anxious faces as the paramedics attempted to stabilize the injured man.

'Ben, this is our chance,' said Martine.

Crouching low, they sprinted from the maze to the hatch. In the storage room below, Ben put on a white coat and used the sink to wash the volcanic dust off his face and hands at the sink. Martine was about to do the same, but he stopped her.

'I might be able to pass as a worker but I don't think a girl will. *But*,' he added hastily as Martine opened her mouth to protest, 'I have a solution.'

He slid back the curtain on the trolley, removed a pile of towels, and shoved them out of sight beneath the sink. It was a tight squeeze, but Martine managed to wedge herself in.

The hatch opened and a man in a white coat slid down the ladder like a fireman down a pole. He was bald and wearing milk bottle glasses. His hands were large and hairy. Ben closed the trolley curtain calmly.

'Who are you?' the man demanded. 'Why are you wearing a white coat? Those are only for pod workers.'

'I'm the new cleaner, sir,' said Ben. 'I apologize if I'm in the wrong clothes. I was still waiting for my instructions when I received an urgent call to mop up . . . to remove some *blood*.' He whispered the last word.

The man grimaced. 'Good thing it's less than twenty-four hours till they're gone. Any longer and we'd have a dead body on our hands. If you want my opinion, the old man is losing control. He's the real deal, but he's not a magician.'

Ben filled the bucket with soap and water and whipped it into foam with a mop. 'Losing control?'

'Of the elephants,' the man said impatiently. 'What else? They've been cooped up so long they're on the verge of rampaging.'

25

'The *elephants?*' Martine said, pulling aside her trolley curtain and trying to wriggle into a more comfortable position. Her left foot had gone to sleep. After the pod worker had helpfully typed in the keypad security code and held the door open for Ben, he'd rushed on ahead, leaving them to negotiate a long tunnel with solar lighting. 'That means there's more than two and there could be a whole herd. I guess we've found your Bermuda Triangle, only it's a white dome in an extinct volcano with fake birdsong.'

'Shh,' said Ben, closing her curtain firmly. 'I'm not sure this is a good idea. It would make more sense for us to try to get out of Moon Valley and get help. We don't want to end up like the man on the stretcher.'

'Of course it's not a good idea,' retorted Martine. 'It's a terrible idea. But we've come this far. We can't turn back now. The elephants need us.'

The explosion they'd heard in the desert sounded again; only down here it was an express train roar, booming down the corridor. It didn't last long and when it was over they heard a discordant hammering. Then that, too, ceased.

For all her brave words, Martine was cold with fear. She and Ben had travelled thousands of miles and risked everything to try to uncover the truth about Angel's story and investigate Reuben James's business dealings. Faced with learning the answers, she realized they might be more than she could bear.

She focused on Jemmy: 'I will get back to him, I will get back to him, I will get back to him,' she told herself over and over, like a mantra.

The trolley halted. She heard Ben take a deep breath. 'We're here,' he said. 'Ready?'

Martine wriggled her toes in an effort to restore sensation to her foot. 'Ready.'

Once, many years ago, Martine's mum and dad had taken her to a gallery in London. The spirit-lifting paintings by Turner, Van Gogh and other Old Masters had made such an impression on her that she'd briefly entertained the idea of becoming an artist, but one picture had depressed her – a vision of hell by Hieronymus Bosch. The artist's name had stuck in her head because she couldn't understand what sort of parents would name their child Hieronymus.

Peering through a slit in the compartment curtain, she was reminded of it. It wasn't that it actually looked like hell. Far from it. Two-thirds of the vast dome had been transformed into the most remarkable indoor environment any desert elephant could have wished for. Whole dunes had been transported intact, and in between there were acacia trees, a small baobab hung with cream of tartar pods (an elephant treat), and a muddy pond for them to swim in. There was even an elephant play area, with coloured balls, sticks and bells. The roof of the dome had been painted sky blue and had wisps of cloud on it and a few painted birds.

It wasn't the fake desert that caused Martine such anguish; it was the elephants. There were nineteen of them. All were shackled but they were in very different states of being. Some were swaying listlessly, eyes half-closed, as if they were lost in a world of their own. One was aggressively destroying an acacia tree, another was feeling every inch of the walls of the dome with her trunk in the vain hope of finding a way out. The rest were just shuffling back and forth in their shackles, variously bored, depressed or agitated.

As Martine gazed out on the diabolical scene, a pair of white double doors opened in the far wall. She caught a glimpse of a laboratory behind, with rows of test tubes and blinking machines. There was a horrible rattling and a steel cage was wheeled out by two white-coated workers. Inside was an elephant. One of the workers pulled a lever and the elephant burst out, was caught short by her shackles, and fell to her knees.

A gaunt man with fine features and caramel-coloured skin rushed from the shadows and ran to her side. He was the only person not in a white coat and his loose trousers and shirt were thin and worn. He stroked the elephant's wrinkled grey-brown face and tried to soothe her. When a lab worker tried to approach, he sent him away with an angry gesture. Gently, he urged the elephant to her feet.

'Gift's father,' Martine breathed.

'We've got to get out of here and get help,' whispered Ben. 'I'm not sure what's going on here, but we're in way over our heads.'

'Animal experimentation, that's what's going on,' Martine said furiously. It took all her self-restraint not to leap out of the trolley. 'If we don't find a way to stop it, that's what Reuben James will be doing to Jemmy – experimenting on him. And Gift's father, the so-called elephant whisperer, is involved.'

'You don't know that.'

'What else would he be doing in this hideous place?

It's not *him* that's being kept prisoner and tortured in the lab, is it?'

'Just because he isn't in handcuffs, doesn't mean he's not a prisoner,' Ben pointed out.

'Oi, you! What are you looking at?' A short, stocky pod worker was striding across the dome. 'Where's your ID? What are you doing here?'

'Leave him alone, Nipper,' called the bald man. 'It's his first day on the job. Hey, kid, what's your name?'

'Ben.'

'All righty, Ben, get your mop and head on over to the lab.'

'Yes, sir!' called Ben. Under his breath he said: 'This is about to get very complicated.' He pushed the trolley forward.

Martine risked another glance through the curtain. Gift's father was leading the traumatized elephant to the muddy pool. Her stride was uncertain and her eyes were locked on Gift's dad, as if he were a lighthouse in a storm.

Martine realized with a shock that the second part of Grace's prophecy had just come to pass. The circle – the Moon Valley volcano, that is – *had* led to the elephants. Now all that remained was the last part. 'The elephants will lead you to the truth,' Grace had promised. '*Your* truth.'

One of the elephants trumpeted. The sound ricocheted around the dome and blasted Martine's eardrums. The ailing elephant had collapsed again, only this time she wasn't getting up. Gift's father was cradling her head. All around the dome, elephants were straining at their shackles and flapping their ears or tossing their tusks, desperate to go to the aid of their fallen friend.

'Ben, we have to do something,' said Martine, forgetting to keep her voice down. Patience was not one of her virtues.

'Martine, if we run back down the tunnel, we might still be able to get out of here, expose this whole operation, and save all the elephants. If we stay here, we might not save any. We might not even—'

Martine hopped out of the trolley, staggering a little on her cramped, bloodless limbs. 'Save ourselves? Is that what you were going to say. Well, right now all I care about is saving her. What's going on here is like something out of the Dark Ages. We can't just walk away.'

Ben glanced in the direction of the fallen elephant. The bald man and two other pod workers were preoccupied with the unfolding crisis. Another man had retreated to the safety of the laboratory. However, Nipper was staring at the intruders with intense interest. He took a cellphone from his pocket.

'Ben, go without me,' urged Martine. 'Find Gift or call the police and come back for me.'

'Not a chance. We came into this together and we're going to stay together. But I think one of the workers has just called security. We'll have to move fast.'

Martine had the advantage of surprise. By the time Nipper had alerted the other pod workers that a thin, pale girl with flying brown hair and green eyes was racing across the dome, she was almost upon them.

She slowed to a walk. She didn't underestimate what she was about to do. Her gift was her most precious secret. She'd first discovered she could heal animals purely by accident, on a class trip. Afterwards, the children who'd witnessed her revival of an Egyptian goose had chased her through a forest, screaming 'Witch! Witch! Witch!'

Since then she'd been very careful to hide her gift from everyone but Grace and Ben, and even with them she played it down. Now she was about to attempt a healing in front of an audience. Nipper tried to grab her but the bald man stopped him.

'Wait. Let's see what she's going to do.'

Nipper folded his muscled arms across his chest and a smug smile came over his swarthy face. Ben, who was hovering anxiously nearby, noticed that his gaze kept shifting to the door.

Gift's father was still cradling the elephant's head. He lifted weary, hurt-filled eyes when Martine knelt down.

'Do you mind if I try to help her, Joseph?' Martine asked. He started when she said his name but nodded dumbly. The elephant's thick lashes lay flat against her rough grey-brown cheek. Her whole body trembled. When Martine touched her tenderly, a tear rolled down her face.

Unzipping her survival kit, Martine took out the bottle labelled Love Potion No.9. Grace had explained to her that it was the plant equivalent of adrenalin, only to be given in extreme emergencies when the heart was failing. But some sixth sense told Martine that the elephant's heart was failing not because she was having a cardiac arrest, but because it had been broken. Her freedom and family had been stolen from her. She had nothing left to live for.

Martine returned the bottle to the pouch without opening it. She would have to trust in her gift alone. She laid her hands on the elephant's heart. 'What do you call her?' she asked Joseph.

'Ruby,' the elephant whisperer told her. 'I call her Ruby.'

Martine barely heard him. Already the gawking faces were swirling away from her and her hands were so hot her blood was virtually boiling in her veins. Most times when she healed an animal Martine had dreamlike visions of warriors with spears and great herds of animals and men in animal masks. Today she saw Sawubona.

She was standing by the waterhole in front of her grandmother's house. Jemmy was at her right shoulder and Angel at her left, and the savannah was surface-lit with a golden light, the way it was when a storm threatened. Martine had a strong feeling the animals were trying to tell her something. She put a hand on Angel's trunk and the elephant's unspoken words came to her as clearly as if they'd been written on her soul with indelible ink: 'Bring me my sister. Bring me my sister.'

'Where is your sister? Where do I find her?' asked Martine, but Angel's words were lost in the wind.

Martine pressed her face to Jemmy's silver muzzle. She could feel its silky softness against her cheek. 'I love you. Come home soon,' he told her in his wordless, musical way.

She was in the midst of saying, 'I love you too,' when applause cut short her trance. She came round in a daze to find that Ruby was on her feet. She was swaying, but the light had returned to her mournful brown eyes. With the tip of her trunk she caressed Martine's cheek in an elephant kiss. Moved beyond words, Martine kissed her back.

She stood up, suddenly self-conscious. She was afraid to look behind her; afraid to think what might happen next.

Joseph was speaking, his voice was barely audible. 'Not much surprises me these days, miss, but you have truly amazed me. I wonder if I am dreaming, but I fear I will wake soon enough in this nightmare without end. How did you know my name?'

'Hey, how did you do that?' interrupted the bald man. 'We need some of that medicine you gave her. That's some kind of a miracle cure. Who are you, anyway? Reuben's niece?'

A heavy hand slammed down on Martine's shoulder and Nipper wrenched her round, almost knocking the bald man over.

Before her, looking rather more tired than the last time she'd seen him but wearing the same sardonic, confident smile, was Reuben James.

26

'So, Martine,' said Reuben James, 'we meet again.'

Without waiting for her to reply, he went on: 'I must say these are not quite the circumstances in which I imagined our paths next crossing, but it's always a pleasure to meet a worthy adversary.'

Martine wriggled out of Nipper's grasp, and glared at her arch enemy. 'The feeling's not mutual, I assure you.'

He laughed at that. Incensed, Martine said: 'I suppose you think it's funny that an elephant almost died just then because she's so traumatized by your experiments. It's one thing stealing Sawubona out from under us, but

I didn't think even you could stoop so low as to masquerade as a caring conservationist when you're nothing but an animal torturer.'

That brought another smile to his lips. 'Torture? Is that what you think we're doing here? Martine, you have me all wrong. We're doing the complete opposite. These elephants undergo the occasional blood test and go the odd day without food or water so we can study their endurance levels, but their sacrifice is nothing compared to the rewards that will be reaped by future generations of elephants. And though they may not understand it, many of these particular elephants owe their lives to me. Out in the desert, they might already have been killed by poachers, or have died of hunger and thirst.'

He paused as one of the pod workers came up with Ben, his arm twisted behind his back. Reuben James frowned at the man. 'Matheus, what are you thinking? Release him at once. He's only a boy.'

Ben rushed to Martine's side, rubbing his arm to get the blood flowing. Martine put a protective hand on his shoulder and glared at Reuben James. 'Ruby doesn't owe her life to you,' she snapped. 'She almost lost it because of you. And I suppose Angel was caged and experimented on until she was broken and bleeding too. That's why you sent her to Sawubona. That's why you lied about her coming from a zoo which had shut down.'

Reuben James looked mystified until she said the last part. 'You're talking about the elephant I sent to Sawubona? Angel? Is that what you call her? Yes, well, that was very unfortunate. It happened in the early stages of our development, when we were still learning the ropes as it were. She was our test-case and we didn't yet have this custom-built facility. I'd hired Lurk – you remember my chauffeur? – to supervise the early experiments. Let's just say he was over-zealous and that particular elephant, Angel, was impossible to handle. But regardless of what you might think of me, I can't abide cruelty to animals. Lurk was severely reprimanded and transferred to another position. We ceased all experiments until about a year ago when the dome was completed and the Moon Valley oasis was well on its way.'

He jerked his chin in Joseph's direction. 'That's when we brought in the elephant whisperer.'

'Brought him in?' scoffed Martine. 'Kidnapped him, you mean.'

'Martine, why do you persist in seeing me as a villain? Do you see handcuffs? He can leave at any time. He chooses to be here with his beloved elephants, don't you, Joseph?'

Joseph nodded quickly and busied himself giving a bucket of food to Ruby.

'What about your son?' Martine burst out before she could stop herself. 'Don't you care about him?' The elephant whisperer flinched as if she'd hit him, but he didn't look round.

Reuben James's eyes narrowed. 'How do you know about his son?'

Martine said quickly: 'One of the guides at the Stone

Age etchings told us that the elephant whisperer had gone missing. He mentioned a son.'

Reuben James wasn't convinced, though he didn't argue. 'There is a boy, but he's in his late teens now. I've been like a second father to him. That's the agreement we have, Joseph and I. Joseph takes care of the elephants and I take care of Gift. I doubt he has a bad word to say about me.'

He fixed Martine with a brooding look. 'Lurk said he saw you in the hotel shop. I didn't believe him.'

'Why Sawubona?' asked Ben. 'Why not have Angel sent to a sanctuary in Namibia? Why go to the trouble and expense of sending her to another country?'

Rebuen James returned his gaze coolly. 'To leave her here would have been to risk derailing the Ark Project . . . ' He swept an arm across the dome.

'This, by the way, is the Ark Project. We didn't want it shut down when it had hardly begun. As you've rightly pointed out, I have a reputation as a conservationist. If a heavily pregnant elephant with the extensive injuries of Angel had turned up at a sanctuary in Namibia, people would have started asking questions. I'd met your grandfather at a wildlife conference and was impressed by his dedication to animals. I thought that if anyone could save her it was Henry. Logistically it was a bit of a challenge to get her to South Africa but we managed in the end.'

'Hasn't that worked out well for you?' Martine said sarcastically. 'Now you have Angel *and* our game reserve. What a coincidence.'

'Not a coincidence, just smart business, Martine. I did your grandfather a good turn and, by passing away without repaying the debt, he unintentionally returned the favour. As it turns out, Sawubona is the perfect location for the South African branch of the Ark Project.'

'But why?' cried Martine. 'Why *our* home? There are a million game reserves where you could perform your awful experiments. Are there diamonds in ours or something?'

Reuben James sighed. 'Martine, you disappoint me. I thought you'd have it figured out by now. The Ark Project has nothing to do with diamonds or gold or platinum for that matter. It's about something much bigger than that.'

'Global warming,' Ben put in quietly. 'It's about global warming.'

'Not bad,' drawled Reuben James. 'Not bad at all.'

'You've lost me,' said Martine.

'All right, forget about Sawubona for a moment . . .' Ben explained.

As if, thought Martine.

'Remember the Bushman legend the rock seller told us about? The one where God granted their dream of great wealth by turning all of Namibia's lakes and rivers into diamonds?'

'But that's just a fable.'

'Yes, but think about it. In a desert country, what could be more valuable than diamonds, gold and platinum put together?'

'*Water?*' cried Martine. 'That's what this is all about – water?'

She stared around her and a lightbulb finally went off in her head. 'That's what you're doing at Moon Valley, isn't it? You're planning to divert the spring that's provided the people and animals of Damaraland with one of their only sources of water for thousands of years, so that you alone can control it. And you've built it in an extinct volcano which local people believe is haunted and stay well away from, in order to do it undetected.

'I suppose the oasis provides extra insurance. It's so beautiful that it would never occur to anyone that, behind the scenes, a devious plot is unfolding.'

Reuben James's eyes gleamed with excitement. He seemed to have forgotten their bizarre circumstances or the fact that Martine and Ben were, in effect, trespassers, and was talking to them as if they were interested in buying a stake in his company.

'In the future, as pollution spreads, global warming kicks in, and the heating of the earth's surface leads to an increase in droughts and other extreme weather, more wars will be fought over water than have been fought over oil or religion throughout history,' he told them. 'The people who control the water supplies will control the earth.'

'So at the end of the day it's about money and power and not about conserving animals or water at all,' Martine said.

Reuben James's mouth twitched. 'It is possible to do both.'

'Is water the reason you want Sawubona so much?' asked Ben. 'Because there's a lake in the game reserve?'

Reuben James regarded him with suspicion, as if it had occurred to him for the first time that he might be telling them too much. 'Among other things,' he answered vaguely.

He glanced at his watch and gestured to the stocky man. 'Nipper, do me a favour and take Martine and Ben to the hotel. They're probably not hungry, given that they've already partaken of my breakfast in the maze, but if they are see that they're given lunch and one of our best rooms for the night.'

'Thanks,' said Martine, 'but we need to be getting back. My grandmother will be worried.'

Reuben James chuckled. 'I doubt very much that your grandmother knows where you are. Indeed, I'm rather keen to know how you got here myself, but we'll save that story for another day.'

'You're keeping us prisoner?'

'Don't be absurd. You're free to leave Moon Valley any time. Any time, that is, after Christmas Eve, three days from now. You see, that's when Sawubona becomes mine. And I'd hate anything to happen that might interfere with the smooth transfer of the title deeds.'

27

'If we're free to go, why don't we just walk out of Moon Valley and call the wildlife authorities or Grace and Tendai?' asked Martine.

There was a pause while Ben swallowed a mouthful of steak and chips. To annoy Reuben James, they'd ordered the most expensive items on the room service menu shortly after being shown to a suite on the top floor of the hotel. Their view was spectacular. The front of the room was all glass and they could see right across the oasis to the crystal fountain, sharply-cut green maze and the wildflowers that lay at the foot of the tropical forest. The mountainous walls of volcanic rock which ringed the crater and kept the world at bay were silhouetted against the sky.

Martine's first action had been to take a steaming hot bubble bath, and now she was lying pink-faced on one of the beds, swaddled in a gown so vast and fluffy it was like wearing a cloud. Their filthy clothes had been whisked away to the laundry.

'Don't you see that's exactly what he wants us to do?' said Ben, who was wearing a red and blue striped robe several sizes too large for him. 'He can't kidnap us because that's a serious offence and could ruin his chances of taking Sawubona. But if we walk out of here on our own, before it suits him, there's nothing to stop him calling the police and having us charged with breaking and entering, trespassing, and elephant assault . . . '

'*Assault?*' cried Martine. 'I was trying to help Ruby. His pod workers were the ones who assaulted her.'

'I know that and you know that but it's our word against his. And frankly I don't think the police are going to be all that happy to find we're in Namibia with no passports and no guardians. After they're done with us, they'll probably charge Gwyn Thomas and my mum and dad with child neglect. The thing is, I don't believe Reuben James has any intention of harming us. He only wants us out of the way until Sawubona is safely in his hands.'

Martine sat up. 'I've just remembered something. When we were in the storage unit this morning I saw an entry on the delivery sheet for twenty vials of medicine.

I couldn't remember what it was for at the time, but now I do. It's an animal tranquilizer.'

Ben put down his knife and fork. 'That bald man, Tony, he said that it was just as well it was only twenty-four hours until the elephants were gone, because they'd been cooped up so long they were ready to go on a rampage. If the hotel is due to open soon, it makes sense that Reuben James would want them gone. I bet you he's planning to ship them out to Sawubona tomorrow.'

'*Sawubona*?' Martine pulled the robe more tightly around her. 'Ben, we have to stop them. But how?'

'Well, right now what we really need to do is sleep. We're going to be no use to elephants or anyone else if we're half-dead with tiredness.'

Martine wanted to disagree, but her brain was foggy with exhaustion and the words wouldn't come. 'Okay,' she said weakly, flopping back onto the bed.

As the afternoon sun boiled down on Moon Valley, not a single bird sang.

Martine was awoken by a keycard clicking in the lock. Ben stirred at the same time and she heard him reach for the torch they'd left on the floor between them. He didn't turn it on, but Martine could sense him lying there in the twilight darkness, poised to fight or flee.

The door opened briefly and a figure slipped into the

room. Ben flicked the torch on. The intruder was the elephant whisperer. He blinked as the beam seared his pupils.

Martine's fear gave way to fury. 'What do you think you're doing, Joseph? You nearly gave me a heart attack.' But she softened once she saw that he was more frightened than she was.

'Forgive me for disturbing you, and for frightening you,' he said. 'I had to find a way to speak to you both alone. It has taken me up until now to find the key for your door. I beg you, please give me news of my son if you know anything at all. Although you denied it to Mr James, I had the feeling that you'd met Gift or seen him.'

Martine tried to harden her heart. 'What do you care? According to Reuben James, you're here of your own free will. He says he has a deal with you to look after Gift if you look after the elephants. Obviously it doesn't matter to you that your son doesn't know whether you're dead or alive.'

Joseph hung his head. 'You are correct. I have had the choice to walk out of here at any time and be reunited with my son. And in the beginning Mr James would often offer to take me to him, provided, of course, that I never spoke of this place. He is not a wicked man. He genuinely believes in the Ark Project and the good that can come out of it. It is not him I am afraid of.'

'Then who?' asked Ben.

Joseph lowered his voice. 'His business partner, Callum. It's he who convinced Mr James they should divert the stream in order to control all the water in

Damaraland. Mr James was very much against it but now he has agreed. I think Callum might have some kind of hold over him – perhaps to do with money. If they are allowed to succeed with this plan tomorrow, devastation will follow.'

'I don't understand,' said Martine. 'You claim to love elephants, but you are helping these men with their sick experiments. You claim to love your son and say you're free to go, yet you are still here.'

The elephant whisperer sank onto a chair and put his head in his hands. 'Do you know the expression, "If you make your bed, you must lie on it"? A long time ago, I made a terrible decision. I'm afraid I have to live with the consequences.'

'Everyone makes mistakes,' Ben told him.

Joseph looked up. 'Not like this. My elephants are family to me. They are like my brothers and sisters and uncles. Do you know what it's like to watch them die slowly in their hearts because the freedom of the desert winds has been taken from them; because they are confined? Elephants lose their minds in such a situation. They become so desperate to be free of captivity that they have been known to take their own lives. I thought I could help them endure this period with patience, play and love but I was wrong.'

'You care for the elephants more than you care for your own son,' accused Martine.

Joseph paled. 'That is not true and besides, it is not a competition. I love them all. Please don't judge me until you know the facts.'

'We've been searching for the facts ever since we came to Namibia,' Martine said a little sarcastically. 'We'd love to know what they are.'

A shudder went through Joseph. 'One year ago, I had a row with my son. I had noticed some changes in him since he started attending school in Windhoek and I felt they were not good ones. He was cocky. Cheeky. He had this notion to become a famous news photographer. To tell you the truth, I could not admit to him that I could no longer afford to pay for him to go to school, let alone college. I told him to get his head out of the clouds. He accused me of trying to take away his dream and destroy his future. He ran out of the house, threatening never to return.

'During the long night I searched for him, I had much time to think. I realized that I was a stubborn old fool, stuck in my ways, and that the world was changing. I saw that I was a fortunate man to have a son with a dream to become a photographer when so many of my friends have sons who are bone idle and wanted nothing more than to hang about the town, stealing and drinking and causing trouble. I vowed to do whatever it took to find the money to help him achieve his goals.'

Martine and Ben were riveted. They sat side by side in their gowns and listened to the gentle man.

'Go on,' Martine encouraged.

'Towards morning I was passing Moon Valley when Reuben James came by in his car. I have known him for many years and when he asked me what was wrong, I told him. After swearing me to secrecy, he brought me to

Moon Valley and showed me the dome, which had just been completed. He told me of his ambition to create a super-race of animals, ones which would survive global warming. He believed that this could be done by studying the desert elephants.

'He offered me more money than I had earned in my whole career to manage, train and take care of the elephants and, when I hesitated, he doubled it.'

'But the money came with a price attached?' guessed Ben.

Joseph nodded. 'The Ark Project was top secret, which meant that if I wanted to be part of it I had to make a decision there and then. I could not even go home for one hour to explain everything to my son. I had to agree to cut off all contact with my former life for a period of twelve months. In return, Reuben said he would educate Gift and care for him as if he was his own son. He promised to do everything in his power to help him achieve his dream.'

'So you signed on the dotted line,' said Martine.

'I signed. The gates of Moon Valley closed and my life ended, all in the same moment.'

Outside the hotel room, night had fallen. Martine listened for the crickets and frogs that made African nights so musical, but the crater was eerily still.

Ben made them coffee and they sat at the dining table

drinking it. Joseph's story had made Martine worry again about Gift and why he'd never returned to the Welcome Centre. There was a catch in her voice as she said: 'If it's any consolation, Reuben James has at least honoured his promise about Gift.'

Over the next half hour, she and Ben told Joseph every detail of the days they'd spent with Gift, starting with him rescuing them in the red dunes of Sossusvlei and ending with him dropping them off at the Stone Age etchings in Damaraland. Neither of them said anything about Gift failing to reappear and their concerns that something might have happened to him. Rather, they put the blame on themselves, saying they'd wandered off and got lost in the desert.

Seldom had Martine seen a man so transformed by a piece of news. It was as if they'd given Joseph a tonic. He looked twenty years younger.

'The way my son helped you makes me proud,' he said. 'And this photography career you say he has and the home he has built, these are the best things a father could hear. Knowing that my boy has become a man and, not only that, a gentleman, these words are like the sunshine to me.'

He stood up. 'I am already in your debt and we don't have much time, but I wonder if I can be permitted to ask you one more question.'

'Go ahead,' said Ben with a smile.

'I heard you talking to Mr James about the elephant which was tortured and tormented by Lurk. You said she was living at Sawubona? Sawubona is your home in South Africa?'

'It is,' said Martine. 'It's a game reserve near Storm Crossing. My grandfather and our game warden, Tendai, took Angel in and made her well again. She's happy now, I think, but she always seems lonely.'

She decided not to mention that, barring a miracle, in three days' time Sawubona would be taken over by Reuben James and Angel would belong to him. So, agonizingly, would the white giraffe.

'That is good to hear. They had sent her away a long time before I was brought to this place, but as soon as the other workers described her I knew they were talking of one of my favourite elephants – one I knew for over thirty years. I was heartbroken, imagining the worst. My comfort here has been the companionship of her sister.'

Martine stared at him as if he'd grown wings. 'Her *sister*!'

Joseph nodded. 'Ruby, the elephant you healed today. She is the twin sister of your Angel.'

He stood up to leave.

Ben stood up at the same time. 'I'm confused, Joseph. You signed up to be at Moon Valley for twelve months. That means you must be due to go home to Gift any day now?'

The elephant whisperer looked down. 'I have reached the end of my contract, yes, but there is a problem.'

'I don't suppose it has anything to do with Callum?' said Martine.

Joseph reacted as if she'd poked him with a burning stick. 'Please, Miss Martine, keep your voice down. These walls have ears. A few months ago, Callum warned me that if I walked away from the Ark Project, I must do so knowing that one day – it could be tomorrow or in ten years – Gift would meet with an accident. I hope it is his idea of a joke, but I am afraid to test him. If it is a choice between my life and my son's, I will choose to save Gift's, even if it means he must grow up without a father.'

There was a knock at the door. They almost jumped out of their skins.

'What if that's him?' Joseph fretted. 'He must not find me here. He'll think I've been telling you secrets.'

'Hide in the closet,' said Martine. 'Don't worry. Whatever happens, we'll protect you.'

The knock came again, louder this time.

Ben bounced up and went to the door. 'Can I help you?' he mumbled in a polite but sleepy voice.

'Housekeeping.'

He opened up cautiously, scared it might be a trap. A smiling maid handed him a parcel. It was their ragged clothes, washed and ironed.

'Good evening,' she said. 'I am here with your laundry and a message from Reuben James. He sent me to ask if you would like some dinner.'

28

They were ready to go before first light. They'd done all they could to persuade Joseph to come with them, but he wouldn't leave his elephants. If his elephant family was going to be moved he wanted to be with them. And he refused to do anything that might endanger his son.

After making Martine and Ben promise that they wouldn't reveal his location to a living soul, he gave them an elephant hair bracelet and said: 'If you see Gift, find some way to put this in his possessions so that he will come across it one day and know that I am alive and I love him.'

'No,' said Martine. 'You're going to give it to him yourself.'

Despite that, the elephant whisperer had agreed to tell them the code that opened the main gate, and the time the guards took their morning tea. He confessed that he'd memorized everything because he'd dreamed so often of escape, or of sneaking out to see Gift.

Outside, the morning air was bracingly cold and the wooden walkways were slippery with dew. Martine rubbed her arms to try to generate some warmth as they crept through the still, quiet forest. She'd never realized that a world without birdsong could be so spooky or lonely or empty. She didn't blame the local people for not wanting to come here.

The sky was mauve above the black ring of volcanic rock as they neared the main gate. The guards were still there, but at 5.15 on the dot they disappeared into their guardhouse for tea, as Joseph had promised.

'This seems too easy. I keep expecting something to go wrong,' Martine whispered as Ben typed the code into the keypad next to the gate.

'It *should* be easy,' he said. 'We're not supposed to be prisoners, remember.'

The gate clicked open. Standing on the other side, poised to ring the bell, were Lurk and Callum.

Lurk's eyes bulged. He lifted a finger and pointed. 'Maxine!'

Callum stepped through the gate just as Reuben James ran up and the security men emerged from the guardhouse with crumbs on their faces, stammering apologies and excuses.

'What are you up to now, Reuben?' Callum said. 'Thought you'd give the local school kids a guided tour at the crack of dawn, did you?'

His black eyes flickered over Martine like a lizard's tongue. Up close, his chilly smile, blue-black crow's feather hair and thick black brows gave him the appearance of a movie hit-man. Martine had never met anyone she could truly have described as evil-looking before, but this man fitted the bill.

'Martine and Ben, meet my business partner, Callum,' said Reuben James, rattled but doing his best not to show it. 'Lurk, you already know. Callum, you're a bit earlier than expected, but it's not a problem. I'll wake the chef and organize you some breakfast.'

Martine noticed that he didn't answer Callum's question. Callum must have noticed it too because his gaze slid over to Martine, then Ben, and then back to Martine again.

He said silkily: 'Have we met before?'

'I tole you she was not Anna,' Lurk said, glaring at Martine over Callum's shoulder. 'I tole you she was the one who made the elephant to chase me.'

Reuben James said: 'Shut up, Lurk. Of course you haven't met her, Callum. She and her friend are not from Namibia. Don't worry, they're just leaving.'

Callum continued to scrutinize Martine. 'You're the

girl from the game reserve in South Africa, aren't you? I've seen a newspaper photo of you and your white giraffe. For some reason, that rings alarm bells for me. I'm wondering what you might be doing at Moon Valley, which is a top secret project. Could someone enlighten me?'

'I was showing them around the hotel and they know not to tell anyone about it,' said Reuben James. 'They're good kids and they've done nothing wrong, Callum. Come on, Martine and Ben, I'll take you home.'

Callum smiled his evil smile. 'What's the hurry, Reuben? Surely Martine and Ben would like some breakfast, too. Maybe they'd also like to know what you have planned for their game reserve in South Africa?'

Reuben James froze. 'What are you playing at, Callum?'

Callum put an arm around the other man's shoulders. 'I'm wondering the same thing about you, my friend. Why don't we take a little walk to the pod and see what's going on there? Oh, and Reuben, I wouldn't bother trying to persuade the guards to have me removed from Moon Valley. Like Lurk, they're all in my pay, and, as the old saying goes, the piper calls the tune.'

A hush came over the dome when the door crashed open. The pod workers, who were stuffing elephant toys into boxes and dismantling laboratory equipment, halted where they were like freeze-framed figures in a film. Anything moveable had been cleared away, including the elephants, who were assembled in their shackles on the far side of the dome. Joseph was struggling to get them in order. As soon as he had them quieted, he stopped what he was doing and turned round.

'Is it spring cleaning day or are you and your workers going somewhere, Reuben?' asked Callum. He nodded to the men in white coats. 'Gentlemen, would you leave us?' They scuttled out without a word.

It was cold in the dome but Martine noticed diamonds of sweat had broken out on Reuben James's forehead. He cleared his throat. 'Callum, I told you that we were preparing to move the elephants to Sawubona today.'

'You don't have the right to do that,' cried Martine. 'It's *our* game reserve and my grandmother is in England right now making sure that you never get your hands on it.'

Callum raised his eyebrows. '*Your* game reserve. Not for much longer, I'm afraid. You know the old Bible story about the Great Flood and Noah saving the animals by taking them two by two onto his Ark. Well, Reuben plans to breed global warming-resistant animals on *our* game reserve using the genes of species like the desert elephants and Oryx who can live on a fraction of the food and water of ordinary wildlife. Hence the name: the *Ark* Project.'

'Nothing wrong with preparing animals for the

future,' Reuben James said defensively. 'I'm doing my best to learn how to save them. It's conservation.'

Martine felt a chill go through her. 'That depends on how you go about it.'

Callum laughed. 'Isn't it obvious? You conduct experiments with the most unique and rare animals, animals with special powers, animals such as the white giraffe.'

'No!' cried Martine.

'It won't be like that, Callum,' Reuben James said furiously.

'It will when I take over Sawubona. Or maybe I'll just auction the animals off to the highest bidder. The white giraffe alone should fetch a cool million. You haven't forgotten, have you, Reuben, how much you are in my debt. If you don't start remembering who's boss around here, there'll come a day when everything you own will be mine.'

Reuben James curled his lip. 'I'm finished with this, Callum. I want nothing more to do with you and your spy.' He glared pointedly at Lurk. 'I convinced myself that by diverting the stream, we'd be doing more good for the people and animals of Damarland than bad. Now I realize that you poison everything you touch. That you care nothing for anyone but yourself. I'll have my lawyer contact yours to draw up some repayment plan with the money. Come, Martine and Ben, let's go. I'm sorry you had to see this.'

Startled at this turn of events, Martine and Ben moved to follow him, but Lurk and Nipper barred their way.

'I don't think so,' said Callum.

Reuben James gave a harsh laugh. 'How are you planning to stop us? Are you going to kill us?'

On the other side of the dome, Martine saw Joseph go rigid. She tried to catch his eye, but he turned away and began fussing over Ruby.

Callum flashed his business partner a smile. 'You've been reading too much fiction, my friend. Of course I'm not going to kill you. Not only would that would be bad for my reputation as a businessman, it's messy and unnecessary. I mean, we have a whole desert on our doorstep. Terrible things, deserts. Even the most experienced travellers could run out of petrol in the middle of nowhere on the very day that they've forgotten their water bottles. They could easily perish from heatstroke. It could be years before their bones are found. Elephant whisperers and small children can run into the same sort of trouble. It's a shame but these things happen.

'Oh, and don't worry about the elephants. They're very valuable dead or alive. I'll take very good care of them.'

'You monster,' said Reuben James, his voice barely audible. Lurk and the two guards closed in on him.

'Right, Nipper,' Callum said. 'Time to get on with the business of the day. Are you ready with the dynamite?'

Nipper saluted.

'In some ways it's a relief that you'll be out of the picture, Reuben,' Callum said. 'It means a bigger piece of the pie for me. In a few minutes' time, we're going to blast the final wall that holds back the spring and then we will control all the water in Damaraland. Next I'll move on to a project in the red dunes of Sossusvlei and do the same there, and pretty soon I'll own all the water in Namibia. I'll be able to charge what I like for it. It'll be a license to print money.'

A shrill whistle cut short his speech. Everyone turned to look at Joseph in surprise. His right arm was raised. He dropped it and the elephants cast off their shackles and charged, many of them trumpeting along the way. It was like some centuries-old army tearing into battle, blowing their bugles.

Martine grabbed hold of Ben, convinced they were about to be trampled to death, but the first elephant to reach them was Ruby. She encircled them both with her trunk and stood over them protectively.

Elsewhere in the dome it was pure chaos. There were swinging tusks and yelling men everywhere. Lurk was tossed about like an elephant football, and Callum Murphy, Reuben James and the guards disappeared inside an elephant scrum.

Joseph hurried over to Martine. 'Go now,' he said. 'Nobody will stop you.'

'Come with us,' pleaded Ben.

Joseph smiled. 'I'll be right behind you. First, I must take care of my elephants. For twelve long months, they have taken care of me.'

They tore through the door and down the hill to the main gate. Ben typed in the code. 'Forty-eight hours,' he said to Martine. 'We have forty-eight hours to save Sawubona.'

The gate clicked open and they stepped, dazed, into the morning. Ringed around the construction side were a dozen police cars, some with rifles trained out of the windows. Before they could react, the rifles lowered. The door of one of the cars opened and out jumped their friend. He was positively beaming.

Ben grinned. 'We're in luck. Gift's brought the cavalry.'

'About time too,' said Martine. 'Hey, Ben, look.'

A line of elephants was streaming down the hill with Joseph at its head, but something even more incredible had caught Martine's attention. A weaver bird had settled on the roof of the guardhouse and was trilling its heart out.

29

They flew back to South Africa first class next morning, courtesy of the Namibian government, who had agreed to 'turn a blind eye' to their lack of passports.

'It's the least we could do,' a government official told Ben and Martine as a delegation bearing treats such as Black Forest gateaux and Nara melons saw them off at the airport in Windhoek. 'If these men had been allowed to carry out their fiendish plan, our most precious resource might have been destroyed, bringing ruin and devastation to vast areas of our country.'

The environment minister had been so overjoyed that

twenty rare desert elephants, thought to be dead, had been saved that he'd offered Martine and Ben a free holiday in Namibia with their families as a thank-you. They'd asked if they could have Ruby instead. He was bewildered by their request until Joseph explained that Ruby was related to their own desert elephant, Angel, at which point he agreed at once. Unlike Martine and Ben, Ruby was going to be travelling to Sawubona by road, and would be reunited with her twin on Christmas Day.

For Martine and Ben, landing amid the crowds and buzz of Cape Town airport was a shock to the system after the space and silence of the desert. The first thing they saw was a newsstand. Gift's striking photographs of Reuben James in handcuffs and Callum and Lurk being lifted into an ambulance on stretchers, were prominently displayed on several front pages. The *Cape Times* also carried his picture of his father Joseph leading the elephants to safety.

Martine bought a couple of papers with her remaining change and tucked them into her bag to read later. She smiled at the thought that Gift was already well on his way to achieving his dream of becoming a news photographer – an achievement made all the more special because he could now share it with his dad. There hadn't been many dry eyes after their reunion. They'd promised to visit Martine and Ben at Sawubona in the New Year. Martine hadn't been able to find the words to tell them that she and Ben might not be on the game reserve by then. Following Reuben James's arrest, the future of Sawubona was more uncertain than ever.

Tendai was waiting in the arrivals hall to greet them. He shook hands formally with Ben and swept Martine off her feet, his booming laughter attracting stares.

'There's nothing left of you, little one,' he scolded. 'Grace is going to have something to say about that. What have you been eating for the past week?'

'Oh, Nara melons and Hoodia cacti mainly,' said Martine as they walked out to the car park. 'Plus a few croissants. How is Grace?'

Tendai rolled his eyes. 'That impossible woman! After you and Ben went missing, I wanted to call the police, but she admitted that she'd read the bones and told you to go as far as you needed to in order to pluck out the thorn that was hurting you. I told her she had finally lost her mind. I was so angry I didn't speak to her for a week. I have had sleepless nights thinking of the many ways your grandmother would punish me for allowing you out of my sight.'

He opened the jeep door and Martine and Ben climbed in.

'I'm sorry for worrying you, Tendai,' said Martine, 'but you know, Grace was right about everything. The circle did lead us to the elephants.'

Tendai started the engine. 'She always is.'

'My grandmother?' Martine said, plucking up the courage to ask the question she'd been dreading hearing the answer to. 'Has she called from England? Does she know we were missing?'

'She doesn't, because after you went my aunt Grace persuaded the wife of one of the guards, a hotel receptionist, to record an answer machine message saying there was a fault on the line.' He held up a palm. 'I want you to know that I had no part in this.'

Martine tried to keep a straight face. 'I'm sure you didn't.'

'As a result, your poor grandmother has not been able to reach the house at all. Grace picked up the phone for the first time this morning, after we heard you were coming back. Your grandmother was on a payphone. All she had time to say was that she is flying into Cape Town tomorrow morning, on Christmas Eve, and that she has good news.'

They saved their story till they got back to Sawubona, and even then it had to wait because, although Martine paused to thank Grace and be smothered in the *sangoma*'s warm embrace, she could not wait another minute to see Jemmy.

The white giraffe and Angel were standing by the game park gate, almost as if they'd known she was coming. The elephant retreated shyly when Martine walked up. Her gaze was fixed on the road and Martine wondered if she'd sensed, or heard, that her twin was on her way. Gift had told her elephants could communicate across distances as far as ten kilometres, using low frequency calls that could be heard, or felt and interpreted by their trunks and sensitive feet, but it was a stretch to believe they could communicate between countries.

Still, they were supremely evolved beings – far smarter than people, in Martine's opinion – so anything was possible.

'Ruby will be here in two days' time,' she said to Angel. 'You'll be together on Christmas Day.' Under her breath she added: 'I only hope that I'm here too.'

The white giraffe put his head down and she threw her arms around his neck and pressed her face to his silken silver muzzle, as she'd longed to do so often during her desert ordeal. 'I'm so sorry I left you, Jemmy. If it was up to me I wouldn't be away from you for a minute, not even to go to school, but you can't believe the messes grown-ups get themselves into, or the trouble they cause. And Ben and I keep getting caught in the middle.'

She kissed him. 'If it's any consolation, thinking about you kept me strong. When you told me you loved me, that's what got me through.'

She didn't add: 'And that's what's going to get us through the next twenty-four hours until we know whether or not we've done enough to save Sawubona.'

Grace and Tendai eventually got to hear the elephants' tale – for that, Martine and Ben were agreed, was what it was – over coffee and chocolate cake.

They told the story jointly, with lots of interruptions. Martine started by describing how they'd stowed away on Reuben James's plane and had been stranded in the desert.

Tendai was aghast. 'What were the two of you

thinking? *Anything* could have happened to you. When your grandmother gets back from England, Martine, she will fire me for sure. No wonder I am a nervous wreck.'

'Tendai, you have nerves like a girl,' Grace told him rudely. 'If you cain't stand the heat, get out of my kitchen. Now go on, honey. How did ya find the circle?'

Martine continued, explaining how they'd ended up at Moon Valley and about Gift's dramatic reappearance. It turned out that the text he'd received about his camera lens had been a hoax. When he reached Hoodia Haven, Lurk had tricked him into a storage cellar and locked him up for the night as revenge for the gift shop humiliation.

'If it wasn't for the white giraffe, I don't know if we'd have found you,' Gift had told them. 'It would never have occurred to me that you'd been mad enough or brave enough to walk miles across the desert in the dead of night, sneak into a heavily secured extinct volcano and start causing havoc.'

In the kitchen at Sawubona, Tendai spooned condensed milk into his tea. He'd pulled himself together since being told off by his aunt, but his hand still shook. 'So the elephant whisperer saved you by getting the elephants to stampede?'

'Joseph blew the whistle that started it, but the elephants came up with the plan to pretend they were still shackled on their own,' Martine told him. 'Tendai, you can't believe how sensitive and intelligent and incredible they are. Their hearts break when they are separated from their loved ones or trapped in captivity.

When Ruby collapsed, I think they decided that they'd had enough. They were so desperate for freedom they were prepared to die rather than be tormented any longer.'

Ben said: 'Well, they definitely got their own back. The paramedic I talked to told me that Callum was going to be in hospital for at least three months and one of the detectives said he was pretty sure the courts would lock the man up and throw away the key. The ambulance guy also told me that Lurk would be spending a lot of time in the hospital before he went to jail as well. Apparently he has a string of previous convictions for burglary, assault and other crimes.'

'Do you think it was him who broke into your grandmother's office?' Tendai asked, shocked.

'The Namibian police thought it was highly likely,' answered Martine. 'He was Reuben James's chauffeur, but he was paid by Callum to spy on his boss. Their guess is that when Reuben began getting cold feet about the Ark Project, Callum sent Lurk to try to find some documents that would help them steal Sawubona from under him if necessary.'

'What are your feelings about Reuben James now?' Tendai wanted to know. 'Did you change your mind about him after he turned against Callum and stood up for you?'

It was a question Martine and Ben found difficult to answer. Was Reuben James as corrupt as his business partner? Or was he a well-intentioned man who'd genuinely wanted to save animals and water but had been blackmailed into doing the wrong thing? In return for not going to jail, he'd promised to sell all his Namibian hotels and, after the debts were cleared, donate half the profits to global warming and elephant charities. He was also going to set up a trust fund for Gift, in an attempt to make up for the time the boy had spent without his father.

'I guess we'll know if he's nice or nasty tomorrow when we find out whether he's still planning to take our home,' said Martine. 'Oh, I hope so much that my grandmother's good news is about the game reserve. Keeping Sawubona and Jemmy and Khan would be the best Christmas present I could ever wish for.'

After the meal, Ben went out with Tendai to check on the game reserve and Martine helped Grace do the dishes. Standing at the sink, up to her elbows in warm soapy suds, Martine found that the whole Namibian adventure had already taken on a dreamlike quality.

'You're very quiet, chile,' said Grace. 'Was I right to tell ya to go as far as you needed to go to find truth?'

Martine dried her hands and put an arm around the *sangoma*'s ample waist. 'Yes, you did the right thing. I'm proud if Ben and I played some part in freeing the elephants, but . . .'

'But what?'

'It's nothing really.'

'It ain't nothin' if it make you feel blue. It ain't nothin' if the thorn is still in your heart.'

'It's just . . .'

'Go on.'

'Well, it's just that when you told me that the elephants would lead me to the truth, I thought you meant that I'd find out the truth behind my gift. I suppose I'm a bit sad that I'm no wiser.'

Grace smiled. 'The four leaves led you to the circle, didn't they? And the circle, the volcano, led you to the elephants, right?'

'Right.'

'Where did the elephants lead you?'

Martine thought about it for a second. 'The elephants led me back here. They led me . . . they led me to Sawubona.'

She took a step back. 'What are you saying, Grace? That the truth is here? You know it, don't you? You know my story.'

Grace pulled out a chair and sat down. Her face gave nothing away. 'I know a little.'

Through the kitchen window, Martine saw Jemmy. He was still at the gate; still waiting for her. At the sight of the white giraffe, the frustration that had been building in her for months suddenly bubbled up and spilled over. It was driving her mad that she'd been given a gift and yet she didn't really know what it was for, or why she'd been given it in the first place. It was almost cruel.

'Why would the ancestors choose *me*?' she said emotionally to Grace. 'It doesn't make any sense and in some ways it feels wrong. Although I was born at Sawubona, I grew up in England so I'm more British than South African. Plus I'm a white girl and dead ordinary. Why didn't they choose an African child – someone special like Gift, for example?'

'The ancestors didn't choose you. You chose yourself.'

Martine sat down slowly. 'What do you mean?'

'I mean, chile, that the gift is not to do with skin colour or place of birth. It ain't nothin' to do with ordinary or extraordinary. It's to do with love.'

Grace took a sip of tea. 'Take your elephant whisperer friend. You tell me he were snatched by an elephant during a raid, and that he was found a couple a months later, living happy as can be with the herd. A million other boys, they woulda been crushed by these same elephants. But Joseph, he had a pure love in his heart for these elephants and they knew he spoke their language.'

Martine felt tears spring into her eyes. That's how she'd felt the moment she encountered Jemmy. She'd known then that he was her soul mate and that she'd go to the ends of the earth, as she'd done in the past few weeks, to love him and keep him safe. It was agony not knowing if she and Ben had done enough.

'Same with you, chile,' Grace went on. 'Every generation has its healers – some for people, some for animals. A thousand eleven-year-old children coulda looked out their window one stormy night, as you did, and seen the white giraffe. Most woulda been excited and a few mighta been bold enough to go into the game reserve, like you, ta take a closer look. But only one of those children would have cared enough, been patient enough and loved enough to tame the white giraffe.

'The forefathers, the ancestors, they predicted that a

white giraffe would be born on this here piece of land; that it would be orphaned and rescued by an elephant and find sanctuary in the Secret Valley. They saw that only the unconditional love of a chile could heal this creature and that, in turn, the white giraffe would give something back – a power to heal other animals.'

'But they didn't know it would be me,' said Martine softly.

'No, they didn't know it would be you.' Grace put a hand on her shoulder. 'But I did, chile. I did.'

Martine's heart was pounding as if she'd run a marathon. Outside, she could hear the peaceful crooning of doves. She wondered if they'd sound so content if Reuben James took over Sawubona, or whether he'd have speakers dotted around the garden again, booming out birdsong.

She covered Grace's brown hand with her pale one. 'Thank you for telling me what you know about my gift. It helps. I've been feeling guilty about it. I've been thinking, 'Why me? I've done nothing to deserve this.' But now that I know it's about love, I'm not so scared of it. I feel lighter somehow, as if a burden has lifted. Maybe there's something in that saying about how the truth can set you free.'

'Sure is,' said Grace heartily. 'Sure is.'

'Grace, I've faced quite a lot of challenges in the year I've been at Sawubona, haven't I?'

'Sure have, honey. And you've come out of them stronger.'

Martine smiled. 'Does that mean I now have the eyes

and the experience to read the meaning behind the paintings in the Memory Room?'

The *sangoma* gave her a squeeze. 'Why don't ya go there and find out.'

'Really? Can I go tonight? Grace, do you think it would be okay if I showed Ben the Secret Valley? We've shared so much together.'

'Of course. Like I tol' you. He's part of your story.'

30

The thing Ben couldn't get over was how smooth and rhythmic Jemmy's stride was. 'It's like riding a flying carpet!' he told Martine as they galloped across the moonlit savannah, past a pride of watchful lions and a herd of skittish springbok.

Martine was in her element because she'd never had the chance to share the experience of racing the white giraffe with anyone (she and Grace had proceeded across the game reserve at a sloth-like pace), and never thought she would. Her grandmother wouldn't have approved, but the way Martine saw it, riding Jemmy across Sawubona by the light of a full moon, with Ben accompanying her for added protection, was a lot safer than stowing away on planes, or being stranded in foreign deserts with megalomaniacs and marauding elephants.

When they reached the barren clearing and the twisted tree that guarded the Secret Valley, Ben was incredulous. 'I've passed this place a hundred times with Tendai, and would never have guessed there was anything here. It's always seemed so desolate.'

'Shut your eyes and hold on tight,' ordered Martine. She gripped hard with her calves and grabbed a fistful of silver mane. Jemmy's quarters bunched and then they were crashing through the thorny creeper and the invisible space between the shelves of rock behind.

'It would be great if my mum and dad don't return from their cruise to find me in full traction in a hospital bed,' Ben said, clinging white-knuckled to Martine as the white giraffe came to a snorting, shuddering halt. 'Am I allowed to open my eyes yet? What is this place anyway? It has a wonderful perfume.'

'That's from the orchids. Ben, do you trust me?'

'I'd trust you with my life.'

'Then keep your eyes closed a while longer. Down, Jemmy, there's a good boy.'

The white giraffe's knees buckled and he sank to the ground. Martine helped Ben to dismount. She took his hand and led him along the twisting tunnel, keeping hopeful watch for Khan, up the mossy steps, through the bat antechamber and into the Memory Room.

'All right,' she said. 'You can look now.'

Ben opened his eyes and stared, dazzled by the paintings. Their ancient hues were so fiery and vivid they seemed to dance across the rock walls.

Martine giggled at her friend's incredulous expression.

'Martine, this is the most magical place I've ever been to. It's like your own private art gallery.'

Martine sat down on the cool stone bench. 'That's how I always feel. It's my favourite place on earth and I can't believe we're here. There were so many times in the desert when I didn't think we'd make it.'

Ben sat down beside her. 'Same here. But this place makes everything worth it. Hey, what's that? It looks a bit like an elephant footprint.'

Martine stared. He was pointing at the patch that she had asked Grace about, the splotch she'd considered a mistake. Looking at it from a distance, she saw that it was indeed an elephant footprint. She noticed something else too. It occupied a single, hexagonal cell in a faintly drawn honeycomb structure. All of the other cells were empty, apart from one, which contained a series of miniature symbols. Martine couldn't begin to think how to interpret them.

Out in the antechamber, the bats started squeaking wildly. Through the cave entrance, they could see a black whirlwind of them. Ben leapt to his feet. 'Could someone be coming?'

'Only Khan,' said Martine, but when the leopard didn't appear unease began to gnaw at her. 'Nobody else knows about this place except Grace and I.'

Ben settled down again, but she could tell that he was jumpy. To get his attention she said: 'I've got an idea.'

Ben groaned. 'Whenever you have an idea, it seems to involve illegal activities and sabre-toothed wild animals.'

'No, this is easy. All we have to do is lie on our backs in different parts of the cave and look at the ceiling.'

'What's the catch?'

Martine gave him a playful shove. 'There is none, silly. It's an experiment, that's all.'

They lay on their backs on the cold stone, gazing up at the roof of the cave.

'Well, this is fun,' said Ben. 'Can we do it again some time?'

Martine couldn't help giggling. 'Tell me what you see.'

'I see a lot of rock.' He wriggled to another section of the cave. 'Oh, and there's more rock. Hold on, I think I can see . . . yes, it's definitely rock!'

He was moving once again when Martine let out a yelp of excitement. 'Ben, come over here. The roof of the cave. Can you see? It's shaped like a hexagon.'

Two minutes later, they were in the labyrinth of tunnels Grace had led Martine through on the night they'd found the elephant tusks. As they walked, Ben left a trail of crumbs from the rusks they'd brought to snack on, so they could find their way out again. 'Like Hansel and Gretel in the fairytale,' he said with a laugh.

They soon found that Martine's theory was correct. Through some quirk of geology, every cave was hexagon-shaped. Some were more lopsided than others, but basically the Secret Valley was a giant honeycomb. If the Memory Room was, as Martine suspected, the cave indicated by the elephant's footprint, then the cave with the symbols would be the one furthest from the valley entrance.

Deeper and deeper they went under the mountain, their torch beams piercing the darkness. The structure of the walls around them deteriorated as they went. Soon the slightest brush of the wall produced a trickle of granite powder, and the evidence of rock falls became more frequent. Each new cave was dustier and more cobweb strewn than the last.

Once, Martine thought she heard footsteps. The hairs stood up on the back of her neck. 'Do you think there are ghosts in here?'

'Probably,' Ben said, 'but it's more likely we're hearing bats or *dassies*. I reckon we should turn back. If the tunnel collapses, we'll be buried alive.'

'Please, Ben, we only have one cave to go.'

Knowing how much it meant to her, he relented. 'One more cave and then we're going back even if I have to carry you.'

The air was stale and musty and laden with dust. It was like breathing in old cobwebs. The roof of the tunnel was not much higher than their heads. Part of Martine wanted to run away screaming, but something stronger than her seemed to be pulling her forward, almost dragging her.

At last the cave was before them. It was the smallest so far and the most damaged. Pyramids of broken rock were heaped about the floor. Spiders scuttled from webs as thick as net curtains.

'There's nothing here,' Martine said in disappointment. 'If there were symbols or paintings here once, they've long since faded. Let's go.'

'Hold on a second.' Ben shone the torch at the cave roof. 'Do you notice something? It's not hexagonal.'

Martine was more concerned with the trickle of dirt falling from a hole above her. Was it her imagination or was it getting faster? 'Ben, I think we should get out of here. The roof looks as if it's about to come down on our heads.'

'All right, but give me one second. I want to look at something.' He moved towards the far wall. There was a blood-curdling roar and Khan sprang from the shadows. His massive paws thudded into Ben's chest, throwing the boy to the ground.

'Khan!' screamed Martine. 'No!'

There was a crack like a rifle shot and a slab of rock fell from the ceiling, landing where Ben had been standing a moment before. Rocks rained down as the roof of the cave began to crumble.

Martine ran to Ben's side and they crouched on the floor with Khan, covering their heads with their arms as shale showered down on them. There was nowhere to run. One side of the cave was breaking away. It seemed certain that they'd be entombed with the spiders and bats. All Martine could think about was Jemmy and how much she wished she'd had a chance to say goodbye to him.

Gradually, the rockslide slowed. The dust it left behind clogged their lungs and coated their mouths. Coughing, Martine picked up the torch and climbed shakily to her feet. Dirt cascaded from her clothes and hair. She rubbed her eyes, trying to clear the grit from them.

Behind the fallen wall was another cave. Khan walked forward and Martine followed. Ben hung back, watching as Martine and the leopard stopped and gazed about them. He could see that the walls of the cave were covered in faded paintings, strewn with spiderwebs, but something told him that Martine could see far more. He turned away, not wanting to intrude.

Only time and experience will give you the eyes to understand them, Grace had told Martine about the cave paintings. And now, finally, she did. Her life's journey, unfolded before her, just as Grace had always predicted it would.

She squatted down with her arm around the leopard, and saw her destiny unfold in the faded sketches as clearly as if she was watching a movie. Every image involved animals – jungle gorillas fleeing poachers, tigers caught in snares, polar bears on melting ice caps or whales escaping the ships of hunters. And in every scene a boy and girl were helping them.

There was a low rumble. Khan snarled. He nipped at Martine's ankle. A thunderous roar blasted her eardrums and then the rest of the roof gave way.

'Run!' yelled Ben. He grabbed Martine's hand and the two of them flew into the tunnel. The leopard raced past them. Martine and Ben tore after him, trusting he knew the way. The crumbs were no use to them now.

The noise was deafening. The tunnel collapsed behind them as they ran, throwing forward stinging shards of rock and a steam-train plume of dust. Martine was starting to despair of ever getting out alive when the starry sky that lit the mountainside exit came into view. Coughing and choking, she stumbled into the open air. She sank to the ground and gulped in oxygen. The leopard came over to her and licked her face with a tongue like sandpaper.

'Thanks, Khan,' Martine said, half laughing, half sobbing. 'You saved our lives.'

Ben put a cautious hand out to stroke the leopard. 'He saved mine twice.'

Dawn was breaking when they reached the bottom of the mountain, where Jemmy was waiting, pacing up and down in a state of agitation. He'd heard the terrifying roar of the collapsing catacomb and had been almost out of his mind with fear because he couldn't get to Martine. They were amused to see that a friend had come to comfort him.

'Looks like you have a ride home, Ben,' Martine said, her tongue firmly in her cheek.

'Oh, no,' protested Ben. 'You're not getting me up there. The last time I saw that elephant, she was hurtling after Lurk and trying to trample him to death.'

'That was out of character,' said Martine with a grin. 'You'll be fine. Angel by name, Angel by nature.'

31

G wyn Thomas arrived home on the morning of
Christmas Eve. By then, Ben and Martine were
showered, scrubbed and in their best jeans and shirts,
which wasn't saying much but it impressed the returning
traveller. She was so thrilled to see them that she forgot,
for once, to be reserved. She threw her arms around
them and was quite overcome.

'I'm so thankful to be back at Sawubona, a herd
of stampeding elephants couldn't drag me away,' she
said. Martine had to restrain herself from adding:
'You'd be surprised what a herd of stampeding elephants
can do.'

They led her into the kitchen, where the table was spread with one of Grace's finest brunches – a meal of sliced paw paw and mango, Jungle Oats, farm eggs, wild mushrooms, roasted tomatoes and great slabs of homemade seed bread. Martine marvelled that Grace had managed to find the time get to the local farm store with everything else that had been going on.

'What a welcome,' said Gwyn Thomas, visibly moved. 'And what a picture of domestic bliss. When I couldn't get through on the phone, I was imagining all kinds of mayhem going on at Sawubona. I was worried sick that the two of you,' – she nodded toward Ben and Martine – 'were getting into all sorts of trouble in an attempt to save our home and animals. Obviously my sleepless nights were for nothing. You've looked after the game reserve and each other beautifully.'

Martine realized she was holding her breath. 'The deadline for us to move out of Sawubona is midnight tonight, but you told Grace when you called that you had some good news. Please tell me that I'm not going to be taken away from Jemmy. Please tell me that everything is going to be okay.'

Her grandmother smiled. 'Everything *is* going to be okay, but it's taken some doing. You wouldn't believe what I've been through. At times I've felt like a character in a thriller.'

Grace handed her a glass of fresh orange juice and took her place at the table. She winked at Ben and Martine. 'Why don't ya tell us all about it, honey?' she said.

Gwyn Thomas had been getting nowhere fast in England until she learned that the solicitor who'd drawn up the will produced by Reuben James had been sacked from Cutter & Buck, and was facing fraud charges.

'He was on bail, pending trial, and was quite aggressive with me,' she explained, 'but I soon had him remembering his manners.'

Martine smiled to herself at the thought of this hardened fraudster being reduced to quivering jelly by her grandmother.

'After a series of quite extraordinarily creative lies and excuses, he admitted that Henry had been to see him at Cutter & Buck the summer before he died and had paid back all the money he owed Reuben James. That very morning, however, this solicitor had overheard Mr James saying that he would do anything to get his hands on Sawubona. He saw an opportunity to make a fast buck. Unknown to my dear husband, he placed a new copy of the will beneath the paper which acknowledged receipt of the money. Henry signed it without knowing that he was in fact signing away the game reserve.'

'What a devious, treacherous man this solicitor is,' said Tendai, appalled.

'That was my opinion. His plan was to extract money from Reuben James for helping him to get Sawubona. He claims that Reuben wanted nothing to do with it at first and even threatened to get him sacked, but that as his debts mounted and he became obsessed with some animal project he had planned for the game reserve, his business partner pressured him to go along with it.'

She smiled. 'The good news I have to share with you is that Reuben James, in an apparent attack of remorse, contacted my solicitor yesterday and said he is withdrawing any claim to the game reserve. Our home is safe and so are our animals and the jobs of our staff.'

They all cheered and clinked mugs. It was the best Christmas present any of them could wish for.

'What about the key?' asked Martine. 'Did you ever find out what it was for?'

'Quite by chance I did,' said Gwyn Thomas. 'I went to visit your old Hampshire neighbours, the Morrisons, and Mrs Morrison reminded me that she'd written to me not long after the fire to say that Veronica had given her a suitcase for safe keeping and did I want her to send it. I had so many other things to think about at the time that it went clean out of my mind.'

'What was in the suitcase?' Ben said curiously.

'Documents mainly. Research on global warming, elephants, and something called the Ark Project. I always believed that Veronica wrote about nothing but sponge cakes and sofa upholstery, but it turns out that Henry had told her the story about our elephant, Angel, who came to us from some dreadful Namibian zoo, and she was looking into it before she died. I passed all her files over to a detective at Scotland Yard.'

She paused to spread gooseberry jam on her toast. 'I didn't think anything would come of it, but right before I boarded the plane for Cape Town, he called my cellphone. He said something about Mr James being arrested in Namibia for abducting elephants and trying to start a water war. It was most peculiar. I think I must have misheard. I'm sure everything will be revealed in the coming weeks.'

She heaved a contented sigh. 'It makes you realize how fortunate we are to be free of people like that now.'

It was after eleven when Ben and Martine stole downstairs and out into the darkness. Martine blew her silent whistle and the white giraffe came trotting over to the game park gate. She hadn't wanted to upset her grandmother on her first day back by asking if she could go for a Christmas Eve night ride on Jemmy, but she'd thought of the perfect compromise: Jemmy could come into the garden.

It wouldn't please Sampson who tended the lawn and flowers, but it would keep her and Ben out of the jaws of any passing lions or snakes. After the week they'd just had, that had to be a positive thing.

Jemmy had no complaints about being led into Gwyn Thomas's neatly tended yard, especially since Martine and Ben lay down on the grass beneath the delicious honeysuckle tree. He wrapped his long tongue around the bell-like flowers and savoured their nectar and the company of his human friends.

Martine felt the same joy at being close to her beloved white giraffe, who'd now be hers for years to come and not at the mercy of people who wanted to experiment on him or sell him to the highest bidder. And she was glad, as always, to be with her best friend. A lot of the healing and happiness she'd experienced this year was directly down to Ben's kindness, loyalty and unwavering courage. It was comforting to know that their destiny was interwoven.

'What are you thinking?' asked Ben, propping himself up on one elbow. His tousled black hair fell across his face. A year ago, when Martine met him, he'd been the runt of Caracal School, as thin and small as she was, but since then he'd shot up and his muscles had filled out. He was, thought Martine, quite handsome.

'I'm thinking about how far we've come. On New Year's Eve I'll be twelve years old, and soon after that we'll be starting high school.'

'High School! That's a scary thought,' said Ben. 'But it's exciting too. It'll be a new chapter with new adventures. Martine, do you really believe our destiny is going to be the one you saw in the cave pictures? That we'll be going around the world saving whales and polar bears and other endangered animals? That's quite a responsibility.'

'It is,' agreed Martine, 'but we can do anything if we face it together.'

Ben smiled at her. 'I wouldn't want it any other way.'

They lay there in silence for a while, listening to the sounds of Sawubona's night creatures and breathing in the sweet fragrance of the frangipani and mango trees. Above them, the white giraffe was outlined like a silver statue against the night sky, his head quite literally in the stars.

Ben checked his watch. 'Hey, Martine, it's one minute past midnight. It's Christmas morning! We made it. Against all the odds, we made it.'

Martine laughed. She jumped up and gave the white giraffe a Christmas kiss and he lowered his head to nuzzle her back. 'Yes, we did, but Jemmy, we couldn't have done it without you.'

AUTHOR'S NOTE

One of my clearest childhood memories is going to a farm close to ours in Africa to see fifty baby elephants. They'd been orphaned in a cull and were on their way to zoos across the world. I'm not a fan of zoos and wasn't then, and I'm dead set against culling – the practice of killing elephants "for their own good" if there are too many in a particular area. But, though I feared for the future of the babies, I was entranced by them. I sat on the corral fence and watched them tussle and play and rush around their enclosure on ungainly legs, little trunks swinging, and thought they were beyond adorable.

Over the years I've been fortunate enough to have many opportunities to be around elephants. I've rubbed their rough, prickly hides, cooed over their long eyelashes, watched them wallow joyously in muddy waterholes, ridden them and been charged by them in safari vehicles. But like Martine in *The Elephant's Tale*, I'd never really given much thought to the intelligence and astonishing natural gifts of elephants until I discovered how their acute hearing means they are able to pick up communications from other elephants from as far as ten kilometers away. Or that their family bonds are so strong that youngsters orphaned by culls wake up screaming with nightmares. Then I remembered the babies I'd seen on that farm and felt devastated.

On a more positive note, while I was writing *The Elephant's Tale* I was able to spend months researching elephant behaviour. What I learned convinced me that we have to do everything in our power to save these magnificent creatures, with their intricate and loving communities. We can't do that unless, like Martine, we learn to understand them.

Another part of my research was travelling to Namibia, the setting for this story. It is one of the most breathtakingly beautiful countries in Africa, but its existence depends on a limited source of rainfall, which is increasingly being affected by global warming. Other desert regions, such as the Australian Outback are in the same position. My own father, a farmer in the Southern African country of Zimbabwe, often tells me of the catastrophic changes in climate that he has witnessed in his lifetime. We're now using the resources of 1.4 earths. When those resources are gone, there'll be none left.

The best part about writing the *White Giraffe* series has been living with characters whose mission is not only to heal and save animals but to make their lives better. There are nearly 6.8 billion people on earth. Imagine if every one of us did one small thing to help wildlife or the environment, the earth would soon begin to recover and we'd all benefit by having a more beautiful planet to enjoy.

The wonderful thing about the world now is that it has become a much smaller place. We're all connected. Don't ever feel that you're too far away to make a difference. The smallest action, whether it's stopping to be kind to a dog or cat on your way to school, or not dropping litter, or perhaps doing a school project on the endangered species of Africa, makes a difference, although you might not realize it at the time.

With that in mind, Orion Children's Books and I have joined forces with the international wildlife charity, the Born Free Foundation, to create the Last Leopard Fund (www.lastleopardfund.com). The mission of the fund is to rescue, protect and rehabilitate endangered animals, with a special emphasis on leopards. Our long term aim is to open a Born Free sanctuary dedicated to saving endangered species in Southern Africa.

We'd love you to get involved. Hold sponsored events at your school or in your local community. Have an Animal Day at your school, where everyone donates a small amount to dress up as their favourite animal.

In the meantime, follow your dreams, follow your heart, and consider conservation.

Lauren St John,
London 2009
www.laurenstjohn.com

ACKNOWLEDGMENTS

I've loved writing this series but it would not have been possible without the faith and wisdom of my Orion editor, Fiona Kennedy, my agent, Catherine Clarke, and my Dial editor, Liz Waniewski. One of the best things about writing the books has been having David Dean bring them to life with his stunning illustrations. I'm immensely grateful to Jane Hughes for finding him and to everyone else at Orion for their support, hard work and passionate commitment to children's publishing, especially Alexandra Nicholas, Helen Speedy, Sally Wray, Kate Christer, Jessica Killingley, Pandora White, Victoria Nicholl and Lisa Milton.

A special thank you to Ruth Wilson for doing me the huge honour of reading the audio books of *The White Giraffe* and *Dolphin Song*. Andjoa Andoh also did a fantastic job on the unabridged audio books. Last but definitely not least, thanks to Kellie Santin, for being there through thick and thin, to my mum for her elephant research, to my dad for the Matopos road trip and my sister, Lisa, for the Namibian adventure. Can't wait for the next one!

If you've enjoyed *The White Giraffe* series you'll also love Lauren St John's Laura Marlin Mysteries.

Dead Man's Cove

'What I want,' Laura declared, 'is to have a life packed with excitement like some of the characters in my books.'

Orphaned Laura is sent to live with her uncle in Cornwall, convinced that a life of adventure is hers at last. But everywhere she turns she's confronted with mysteries. Is Tariq, the shopkeeper's silent son, a friend or an enemy? Why does her uncle seem intent on erasing his own past? And why is everyone so afraid of Dead Man's Cove?

Kidnap in the Caribbean

'We've brought you here to teach you a lesson you'll never forget, Laura Marlin…'

Laura Marlin has no idea that her dream holiday to the Caribbean might cost her and everyone she loves their lives.

But almost as soon as they board the luxury cruise ship mysteries begin to pile up and sinister events spiral out of control.

When her uncle disappears, Laura, her best friend Tariq, and beloved husky Skye must play a deadly game with their enemies. Thousands of miles from home, face to face with pirates, a volcano and hungry sharks, their best hope of survival is the advice of a fictional detective and the help of disaster-prone Jimmy Gannet!

Kentucky Thriller

'Don't believe anything you see or trust anyone you meet, Laura Marlin...'

When Laura and Tariq help to rescue a stolen racehorse, their reward is a holiday on a beautiful American farm. Little do they know that this will be their most hazardous adventure yet.

Sinister forces are at work on Fleet Farm, mysteries pile up, suspects abound and old enemies are dead set on revenge.

The stage is set for a showdown at the famous Kentucky Derby, Laura faces a race against time to unravel a clever and cunning plot. Can she trust her own eyes?